OPERATION NANNY

BY
PAULA GRAVES

MILLS & BOON

First Published in Great Britain 2017
By Mills & Boon, an imprint of HarperCollins*Publishers*
1 London Bridge Street, London, SE1 9GF

© 2017 Paula Graves

ISBN: 978-0-263-92875-4

46-0417

Our policy is to use papers that are natural, renewable and recyclable products and made from wood grown in sustainable forests. The logging and manufacturing processes conform to the legal environmental regulations of the country of origin.

Printed and bound in Spain
by CPI, Barcelona

Paula Graves, an Alabama native, wrote her first book at the age of six. A voracious reader, Paula loves books that pair tantalizing mystery with compelling romance. When she's not reading or writing, she works as a creative director for a Birmingham advertising agency and spends time with her family and friends. Paula invites readers to visit her website, www.paulagraves.com.

For my nieces, Sarah, Kathryn, Melissa and Ashlee, and my nephew, Nathan. Most of you aren't old enough to read my books, but maybe you'll look them up in a few years, see this dedication and smile.

Chapter One

The blue pickup truck was in her rearview mirror again. It had been there, off and on, since shortly after she'd crossed the Potomac into Maryland. Of course, many vehicles—not just the pickup—had shared the road into Frederick with her, many of them staying behind her for miles at a time before turning off.

Maybe that was the problem, Lacey thought. The pickup had never turned off.

A soft whine from the backseat drew her attention away from the rearview mirror. She dared the quickest glance at the child seat belted in behind the passenger seat, reassuring herself that Katie was just being fussy. Her niece's bright gray eyes stared back at Lacey, reminding her so much of Marianne that she had to suck in her breath against a sharp stab of grief.

"Almost there, sweet pea," she said as brightly as she could manage. They were only a few minutes out of Frederick now, and early for the appointment for once.

She glanced in the rearview mirror. She couldn't see the pickup anymore.

Frowning, she looked forward, her gaze drawn to the green directional sign coming up fast on her right, informing her of an upcoming exit. It was a couple of exits before the one she'd planned to take, but the prickling skin on the back of her neck made the decision for her.

She moved to the exit lane as quickly as she could and took the off-ramp. As she came to a stop at the bottom of the off-ramp, she spotted the blue pickup driving past her, continuing on the highway.

Blowing out a pent-up breath, she couldn't hold back a soft bubble of laughter. Talk about jumping at shadows.

"Firsty," Katie announced from her car seat.

"I know you're thirsty, sweetie. As soon as we get to the employment office, I'll get your apple juice for you, okay?" Lacey wasn't sure how much her niece really understood at the age of two, but the little girl subsided into silence for the remainder of the slightly longer drive into Frederick.

Elite Employment Agency occupied a tall, narrow redbrick building near the end of a block of old restored row homes in the downtown area. To Lacey's chagrin, there were no parking slots available on the street, but a small sign in front of the office indicated there was more parking available in the alley behind the building.

Lacey tamped down a creeping sense of alarm and followed the sign until she reached a narrow alley flanked on either side by what looked like large, sprawling garages. At the time some of these homes had been built, she realized, these garages might have been stables for carriage horses. They'd obviously been updated once automobiles became ubiquitous, but there was a quaint feeling here among the garages, as if she could pull open one of the doors and find herself immersed in the remains of the town's rich history.

But as she parked in the small gravel lot behind the

employment agency, some of the alley's charm faded, for she found herself hemmed in between two large garages on either side and also behind her, where garages for the buildings on the next street closed the alley in like a narrow gorge.

Sunlight struggled to penetrate the steel-gray winter sky overhead, reminding Lacey that snow was expected later in the week. She hoped the interview with the prospective nanny would go quickly and well. The sooner she could get a nanny hired and settled into the old farmhouse, the better.

"Firsty?" Katie ventured from the backseat as Lacey turned off the car.

"Just a second, baby." She reached across the seat for the diaper bag, praying she'd remembered to pack the apple juice. And extra diapers.

With relief, she found the cup of apple juice and snapped off the drinking-spout cover. "Here, sweetie."

Katie grabbed the cup and upended it, drinking with greedy sucking sounds. Lacey took advantage of her niece's preoccupation to gather up the bag and her purse. She checked twice to make sure she had the car keys before she got out and walked around to the trunk to retrieve Katie's stroller.

The crunch of gravel was the only warning she got. It was just enough for her to reach into the trunk before a pair of arms wrapped around her and started dragging her away from the car.

She fought to stay with the car, wrapping her fingers around the first thing they found—the cold metallic bite of a tire iron. As the arms around her tightened like a vise, she twisted to one side and swung the tire iron downward. It wasn't a solid hit, but the iron connected with her captor's leg, and she heard a loud bark of pain and a stream of profanities in her ear.

The arms around her loosened, just a bit, but it was enough for her to jerk out of his grasp. Her first instinct was to run as far and as fast as she could, but the sound of Katie's cries, muffled by the car windows, stopped her cold.

She swung around to face her captor, wielding the tire iron in front of her like a club. But whatever small bravado she could muster faltered as she saw the barrel of a large black pistol aimed straight for her heart. All of the earlier ambient noises of the day—the rustle of wind in the winter-bare trees, the hum of nearby traffic—were swallowed by the thunderous throb of her pulse in her ears. Her entire focus centered on the dark, black hole of the pistol's barrel and the masked man who wielded it.

"Hey!" A man's voice broke through the swoosh of blood in her ears, and the pistol barrel swung quickly away from her, aimed at the newcomer.

Jerking out of her frozen trance, she swung at the man as hard as she could, hitting his shoulder and sending him stumbling toward the alley. The pistol went flying under a nearby car as the man caught himself against its trunk. He pushed upright again, staring at Lacey for a moment, then at something down the alley.

"Stop!" The voice that had broken through her paralysis belonged to a tall, broad-shouldered man in a neat charcoal suit who was running toward the man in the mask. He was still several yards away but gaining ground.

The masked man bolted down the alley, moving fast for someone his size. The man in the suit tried to pick up speed, but his dress shoes slipped and slid across the slick surface of the alley, and the man who'd pulled the gun on Lacey outdistanced him easily. There was a green van waiting halfway down the alley. The man in the mask jumped into the passenger seat and the car sped down the alley, took a turn and drove quickly out of sight.

Lacey opened the back door of her car and unbuckled her sobbing niece from the car seat, pulling her close and murmuring soft words of comfort to her as the man in the suit returned to where she stood, giving her a look of apology.

"Are you okay?" he asked, stopping short as she backpedaled away from him. "You're not hurt, are you?"

She tucked Katie closer, keeping a wary eye on the newcomer. Just because he'd tried to come to her rescue didn't mean he was anyone she could trust. Especially not now.

"I'm fine."

He reached into his pocket slowly and withdrew a cell phone. He waggled it toward her as if to reassure her that it wasn't any sort of weapon. "I'll call the police."

She looked behind her, where the back door of the building posed an almost irresistible temptation. She didn't want to deal with the cops. She'd had her fill of the police in the past few weeks since her sister's death. She knew they were just doing their job. Intrusive questions and suspicious minds came with the territory. Her own line of work shared some of those pitfalls; the people she interviewed were often emotionally distraught or shattered by the events they'd witnessed.

But knowing those facts didn't make it easy to be on the other side of the interrogation. Especially when what was left of your sister and brother-in-law had just been zipped into body bags and carted off to the morgue.

"I don't remember anything about him," she murmured, feeling sick. Katie sniffled against her shoulder, but at least her wails had subsided.

"Not much to remember," her rescuer said gently. "Did you see where his weapon went?"

"Yes," she said quickly. "Under that car." She nodded toward the late-model Buick parked next to hers. "But don't try to retrieve it. He might have left trace evidence."

"I know." He punched numbers into the phone as he crouched beside the Buick and looked under the chassis. "A woman was just accosted by an armed man in the alley behind Elite Employment Agency on Sixth. No, nobody's injured. The man lost possession of his weapon. I'm looking at it right now."

Lacey's knees began to shake, and she had to lean against the side of her car. Katie began to feel like deadweight in her arms, and, to her horror, she felt herself losing her grip on the little girl.

"Whoa, now." The man rose quickly to his feet and caught Katie as she started to slide out of Lacey's arms. "I've got her."

Lacey waited for Katie's wails to start, but to her surprise, the little girl just stared up with bright, curious eyes at the man in the suit. Bracing herself against the side of the car, Lacey held out her arms. "I'm all right. I can take her back now."

He ignored her outstretched arms and opened the passenger door of her car. Nodding toward the seat, he said, "Why don't you sit down right there, and then I'll give this cutie back to you."

It was a good idea, so she sat sideways, her feet still on the pavement. The man handed Katie back to her, and the little girl wriggled around until she was facing the stranger.

Katie was smitten, Lacey realized with some surprise, glancing up at the man, who was still making funny faces at Katie. Now that she wasn't drowning in adrenaline, Lacey could see why. Their rescuer was a good-looking man, with a mobile face that seemed made for smiling. His exertions had mussed his short, sandy-brown hair, revealing a tendency to curl.

His gaze shifted away from Katie and settled on Lacey, warmth shining in his hazel-green eyes. Sympathy tinged his voice when he spoke. "Feeling a little less shaky?"

"Yes, thanks." The moan of sirens in the distance seeped through the sound of traffic noise. "That must be the cops."

"Must be." The man smiled faintly. "I'm Jim Mercer."

"I'm Lacey Miles."

His smile spread. "I know. I've seen you on TV."

"Oh." She still felt strange when people recognized her, even though she had just finished her third year on air with the news network. "I haven't thanked you. I don't know what I'd have done if you hadn't shown up and chased that creep away."

He glanced at the tire iron she'd dropped by the car. "Probably brained the guy," he said wryly.

She laughed, even though nothing about the past few minutes was funny.

The sirens grew louder, and the flash of blue and cherry lights lit the gloom of the alley. A second later, a white-and-blue Frederick Police Department cruiser pulled up behind Lacey's car.

The next half hour proved to be almost as stressful as the attempted ambush, as Lacey had to answer dozens of questions, first from the responding officers, then from the detective who arrived a few minutes later. Because of the cold, the detectives took them inside the employment-agency building to ask questions, but the warmer temperatures didn't do much to improve Katie's mood. She cried every time Lacey tried to put her in the stroller, so Lacey ended up answering the detective's questions while bouncing a fretful Katie on her knee.

"He was wearing a mask," Lacey answered for what felt like the tenth time. "I didn't see his hair or his eyes. He was pointing a gun at me. I just saw the gun."

At the other end of the conference-room table, Jim Mercer was answering questions posed by another detective, who looked bored and sleepy. Jim glanced her way once, his eyes soft with concern. A warm sensation spread through her chest in response, catching her off guard.

He's a stranger, and you are in no position to feel anything for a stranger, she reminded herself. *Trust no one.*

Detective Braun finally closed his notebook and held out a business card. "We'll see if we can get anything off the weapon. But even if we can track it with the serial number, it's possible it was stolen. However, you can call me if you remember anything else, and I'll be in touch if we're able to track anything down on your assailant. It's just—"

"I understand." She took the card. "I know there's not much to go on."

"You might want to call a friend to drive back to Virginia with you," he suggested. "So you're not out there alone."

She nodded even though she knew there was nobody she could call. Her work had been the center of her life for the past ten years, to the point that it consumed her life almost entirely. The low pay and bad hours paying her dues on the local level, then the big move to the occasional national gig and, finally, a regular investigative slot on a national network—all those steps up the career ladder had taken a big toll on the rest of her life.

She'd always thought there would be time later, time to rebuild friendships and family ties that had suffered during her upward climb.

Now Katie was all she had left, and she had absolutely no idea how to be a mother to her sister's child.

"Do you think it could be connected to the bombing?" she asked Braun as he started toward the conference-room door.

He stopped and looked at her. "It's possible. But this attack seems pretty random."

"Someone set a bomb in my car. My sister and her husband were killed because they borrowed it. Maybe you remember that bombing—Marianne and Toby Harper? Ring any bells? And now, two weeks later, I'm accosted at gunpoint. I'm not sure I'd call that random."

Braun looked both sympathetic and frustrated. "I don't know what to tell you, ma'am. You may be right. It may be connected. I plan to make a call to the DC police and compare notes with the lead detective in the bombing case. Maybe we can come up with a more solid connection."

As he left the room, Lacey tucked Katie closer,

breathing in the warm scent of powder and baby sham-
poo. *Meanwhile*, she thought, *Katie and I are sitting
ducks.*

"AND YOU'RE SURE you didn't make out anything about
the license plates?" Detective Marty Ridge stifled a
yawn.

"No," Jim answered, trying not to let his impatience
show. If he'd seen a license plate, he'd have described it
in detail. But the plate on the green Chevy van had been
obscured with mud. Probably on purpose. He couldn't
even be sure whether they were Maryland or Virginia
plates.

"Well, we'll have to hope the weapon gives us something to go on," Ridge said in a tone that suggested Jim's
testimony was going to be no help at all.

Jim stifled a grimace of annoyance and glanced
down the table at Lacey Miles and her niece. The little
girl was fussing despite her aunt's attempt to soothe her.
From the expression on Lacey's face, she didn't know
how to comfort the child, which made him wonder just
how much she knew about taking care of a baby.

"Call if you think of anything else." Rising, Ridge
handed Jim his card, but from the look on his face, it
was something he did out of habit rather than any real
hope that Jim could add anything to the investigation.

After Ridge left, Jim walked to where Lacey sat.
Katie looked up at him and her pout turned into a smile.
Something inside him melted as the little girl held out
her arms to him.

"No, Katie. Mr. Mercer has to go now." The smile
Lacey flashed in his direction was halfhearted at best.

"Actually, I have an appointment here. A job interview."

"Oh." Lacey's sandy brows lifted slightly as she looked him up and down. He quelled the urge to squirm a little at her scrutiny, even though her gaze seemed as sharp as that of any drill sergeant he'd ever faced during an inspection. "Well, good luck."

"Thanks." He left the room, his steps faltering briefly when Katie began to cry. As he closed the door behind him, he heard Lacey's soft murmurs of comfort, and he wondered if the little girl would be appeased.

At the front office, he gave his name to the receptionist, apologizing for being late and explaining the situation.

"You're lucky," the woman said with a friendly smile. "Your appointment is late, too."

He glanced back toward the conference room, where he'd left Lacey Miles and her little niece. "I know."

THE EMPLOYMENT OFFICE MANAGER was a tall, sharp-eyed brunette with the bone structure of a model named Ellen Taylor. She wore a sleek blue suit that fit her angular body to perfection, and her voice was inflectionless and polished. "I'm so sorry for your ordeal, Ms. Miles." She spared a brief smile for Katie, but she was clearly not someone who had much experience with small children.

Join the club, Lacey thought. "I hate that I've kept the prospective nanny waiting."

"It's not a problem," Ellen assured her. "Are you ready?"

Lacey glanced at her own rumpled suit and Katie's tear-streaked face. She sighed. So much for a good first impression. "Sure."

"Good. Before we start, how do you want to handle this? Do you want me to sit in or do you want to handle the interview yourself?"

If she thought Ellen Taylor knew anything about babies or nannies, she might have asked her to stay. But she might as well go into this interview the way she'd continue after she hired someone—clueless and needy.

Besides, she was a professional reporter. She'd interviewed presidents, prime ministers and kings, as well as rebels and terrorists. If she couldn't handle asking a prospective nanny a few pointed questions, what kind of reporter was she?

"Very well. I'll let you handle it, and then when you're done, you can tell me whether you want to interview any other prospects." Ellen left the room in a faint cloud of Chanel No. 5.

"Oh, wait—" Lacey began, but the door had already clicked shut behind the woman. "Damn it."

She'd forgotten to ask for a résumé beforehand. She'd planned her early arrival so she could do a quick read through the potential nanny's employment history so she could ask intelligent questions. No reporter liked to go into an interview blind.

"Oh well," she murmured against Katie's cheek. "Guess we'll find out soon enough if we've found our own Mary Poppins."

There was a quiet knock on the conference-room door.

"Come in," Lacey said, taking a deep breath to calm her sudden rattle of nerves and pasting a smile on her face.

The door opened and Jim Mercer entered, a faint smile on his face. "Hello, again."

"Oh. It's you." Her smile faded. "Did you forget something?"

"Actually, no." He smiled at Katie, who reached out for him again. "Hey there, sweetie."

Lacey tugged her niece closer. "I hate to seem rude, considering how you came to our rescue, but I don't really have time to talk. I'm about to conduct a job interview."

Jim pulled out the chair across from her and sat. "I know. I'm the one you're interviewing."

Chapter Two

Lacey Miles stared at Jim a moment, her only reaction a slight narrowing of her eyes. Otherwise, she maintained a pretty impressive poker face. "I see."

When she said nothing more, he asked, "Is that a problem? Ms. Taylor said you had specified that you had no issues with hiring a male caretaker."

"I don't," she said bluntly in a tone that suggested just the opposite.

"You seem as if you've been blindsided."

Her lips curved in a faint, perfunctory smile. "I guess I have been, in a way. I didn't have a chance to look over your credentials or even get your name. I just wasn't expecting a man."

"Oh."

"I'm in a hurry to make a hire, you see," she added quickly, as if she realized what she'd just admitted made her sound ill prepared. "I haven't had much luck since I sent my request to Ellen. In fact, you're the first person who's even applied for the job."

He was pretty sure he knew why. The story about the car bomb that had been meant for her—the one that had killed her sister and brother-in-law instead—had made the national news. There weren't a lot of wannabe nannies willing to walk into a situation like that.

"Anyway, best-laid plans and all that." Lacey breathed a soft sigh. "So tell me about yourself."

"I'm thirty-four years old. I spent a decade in the Marine Corps, and then over the next four years, I went to college and earned a degree in early-childhood education."

"Really? First a Marine, now a nanny?" That piece of information seemed to pique her interest.

"I'd eventually like to run my own day-care center," he said, wondering if she'd believe it.

"What sort of experience with child care do you have?"

"I raised my younger siblings from the age of fifteen. My father was a police officer who died in the line of duty, and my mother had to go back to work. I had three younger siblings, ages two through eleven. I was their full-time caregiver until my mother remarried shortly after I turned eighteen. At that time, I joined the Marine Corps."

"That's your most recent child-care experience?"

"After college, I worked a couple of years as a nanny for a family in Kentucky." He slid his résumé across the table to her. "Their contact information is on my résumé."

She set Katie on the floor and picked up the paper. After a few minutes silently reading what was written there, she put the paper down and looked up at him, her gray eyes narrowed. "Assuming your references check out, how quickly can you start work?"

"As soon as you hire me."

"What about the family you were working for? You don't need to give them any notice?"

"No. Mrs. Beckett decided she was missing too much of her children's lives by working in an office, so she took a job that enables her to work from home. So I'm back in the job market."

"I see."

She fell silent again, her gaze wandering back to the résumé, as if she might find something new written in the words on the page. What was she looking for? Jim wondered. A reason to hire him?

Or a reason not to?

A tug on his pants leg drew his attention. Katie stood at his knee, her gray eyes gazing up at him with curiosity. When she saw him looking, her little face spread into a big grin.

"Hey there, Katiebug."

At the sound of his voice, she lifted her arms.

"May I?" He looked at Lacey for permission to pick up the child.

"Sure."

He picked up Katie and set her on his knee. She grew instantly intrigued by his blue-striped tie, her fingers playing with the fabric. He couldn't hold back a smile, which she returned with a giggle.

She was at a very cute age, just a shade past two. Pretty steady on her feet, starting to build her vocabulary, curious about everything that crossed her path— she had probably already started becoming a handful before her parents suddenly and tragically disappeared from her life, leaving her in the care of her aunt.

Her aunt, who was a single woman with a high-powered, very public career. Earlier, he'd wondered just how much Lacey Miles knew about taking care of a small child. He was becoming more and more certain she was clueless. No wonder she was desperate to hire a nanny.

"Katie likes you," she said. "A point in your favor."

"Ms. Taylor said you needed a live-in nanny. Does that mean you'll be going back to work soon?"

Lacey's sandy brow notched upward. "What makes you think I haven't been working?"

"I haven't seen you on air. I guess I shouldn't have assumed you weren't working behind the scenes." It wouldn't do for her to realize just how much he already knew about her. She was already on edge as it was, and the attack this afternoon had only made things worse for her.

It had been a brazen attack, during daylight and out in the open. Although, if he hadn't happened to be walking down that alley when he had, it might have been very easy for her attacker to kill her outright or carry her and the child away in the van that had been waiting for him.

The big question was why. Why had someone gone after her today? Why had someone set a bomb under her car a couple of weeks ago?

Just how much danger were she and her niece really in?

"I guess you know why I have custody of my niece now. I'm all she has. Both sets of grandparents are dead, and Toby didn't have any brothers or sisters."

He nodded. "I'm very sorry about your sister and your brother-in-law."

"They were killed in my car." She spoke as if she had to force the words from her lips. She was clearly dealing with some pretty hefty guilt about her sister's death. And he gave her points for being honest about the threat hanging over her head, too, even though it might be enough to scare a prospective nanny away in a heartbeat.

"If you're trying to tell me there might be a little danger involved in this job, I'd already gathered that much before I ever agreed to apply for the job."

Her sharp gaze met his. "And yet, here you are. Even after you had to chase away another attack on us just today."

"I did mention I was a Marine, didn't I?"

For the first time since they'd met, a genuine smile touched the edges of Lacey's lips. "You did."

"Danger doesn't impress me the way it might someone else."

"I'm not asking you to be a bodyguard," she said sharply. "I don't need a security detail. I think that would probably make things worse, not better."

He wasn't sure why she felt that way, but he didn't want to start asking questions that would make her even more reluctant to hire him. "I'm just saying, I'm not afraid to work for you. If you think I'll suit your needs."

She gave him another long, sharp-eyed look. "You'd have to live with Katie and me at my late sister's farmhouse in Cherry Grove, Virginia. It's a small town about a forty-minute drive from here in Frederick. The house isn't completely renovated, but enough has been done for it to be a comfortable place to live." Her voice faded for a moment, and what was left of her faint smile disappeared completely, swallowed by a look of hard grief. "Marianne and Toby were hoping to have it finished by this summer, but they ran out of time."

Jim felt a dart of sympathy. "Were they living there when they died?"

Lacey shook her head. "No. Why?"

"I was just wondering why you choose to live there instead of in DC. I thought maybe it was to make things easier for Katie. Not wanting to take her away from the home she knows—"

"No, that's not it. Just the opposite, actually. See, I was keeping Katie at my apartment when... That night. Marianne and Toby were celebrating their wedding anniversary. New Year's Eve." Lacey's lip trembled briefly before she brought her emotions under control. "I don't want her watching my front door, waiting for them to come back and get her."

He looked over at Katie, who'd slid off his lap and wandered over to play with a stuffed cat hanging by a red ribbon from the push bar of her stroller. He felt a rush of sadness for the child, and also for her tough but grieving aunt. Neither of them had expected to be where they were, the only family either of them had left.

Both of them in danger they couldn't predict or easily prevent.

"I want the job if you want to hire me," he said flatly, meeting Lacey's gaze. "I think I can help you. And I need the work."

She didn't say anything for a long moment, and he began to worry that she was going to turn him down. It wouldn't be a complete disaster if she did so, he knew. There were other ways to accomplish what he wanted to do.

But it would be so much easier if she'd just give him the nanny job.

She rose slowly, still looking at him through cautious

gray eyes. "I'll call your references today and see what they say. I'll be in touch, one way or the other. May I contact you directly?"

He rose, too. "My number is on the résumé."

She continued to look at him for a long, silent moment, as if trying to assess his character in that lengthy gaze. Finally, she extended her hand. "It was good to meet you, Mr. Mercer."

"Jim," he reminded her, taking her hand firmly in his.

She withdrew her hand. "Thank you again for your help this afternoon."

"I'm glad I was there. I'm sorry I wasn't able to catch the guy before he got away."

"Two against one isn't good odds. Even for a Marine."

He waited for her to gather up Katie and settle her in the stroller, noting the way her hands shook slightly when Katie started to whine at being confined again.

She needed his help. A lot. And not just with Katie.

He was counting on that fact.

IN NO BIG hurry to return to the isolation of the Cherry Grove farmhouse, Lacey detoured southeast to Arlington, calling Detective Bolling with the Arlington County Police Department Homicide/Robbery Unit. As lead investigator into the car bomb that had killed Marianne and Toby, he was certain to be interested in what had happened to her in Frederick earlier that day.

He met her in a small café a few blocks from her apartment, smiling at Katie as they sat. "How's she doing?"

Lacey shrugged. "Hard to know. She's not a big talker yet."

Bolling gave her a look of sympathy before he went into business mode. He listened intently as she told him about the ambush in Frederick, copying the name of the Frederick detective who'd given her his card. "I'll give him a call. You sure you and the little one are okay?"

"Someone came to our rescue. Chased the guy away. There were two of them, did I mention that? The one who pulled the gun on me got into a van waiting for him down the alley from the employment agency."

Bolling frowned at that. "Sounds premeditated. Having a getaway vehicle in place."

"That's what I thought, too. I think they wanted to abduct me, Detective Bolling. Otherwise, why didn't he just shoot me right there?"

Bolling's brow furrowed as he considered that possibility. "That's a departure from a car bomb."

"Do you think the situations could be unrelated?"

"Maybe. But it doesn't seem likely, does it?" Bolling's frown deepened. "What were you doing at an employment agency in Frederick, anyway?"

"Hiring a nanny."

Bolling looked at Katie. "Does that mean you're going back to work?"

Why did everyone assume hiring a nanny equaled returning to her job at the network? What did they think—that all women just naturally knew how to care for a two-year-old when one was dropped in their laps?

Immediately, she felt guilty for the flash of irritation. Most women probably did have at least some clue how to care for a small child. Even those who weren't in the position financially and professionally to take a sabbatical from work.

"No, I'm not going back to work yet. But I don't

have a lot of experience caring for a child." She stirred her glass of ginger ale with a long red straw, not meeting Bolling's gaze. She didn't want to know what he thought of that admission. Pity or disapproval would be equally unwelcome.

"Did you find a suitable candidate?"

"Maybe."

"If you'd like, we could run a background check before you hire her."

"Not necessary," she assured him. She was as capable as the police to run a background check on Jim Mercer. Maybe more so, since her network connections gave her access to information even the police couldn't get their hands on. Not without a warrant, anyway. "But I'd like to stay in the loop if you hear anything from the Frederick police about my assailant. I didn't get the feeling Detective Braun was interested in keeping me updated."

"I will tell you if anything important comes out of the investigation," Bolling promised. "You sure you don't want something to eat? My treat."

"No, but thanks." What she wanted, she realized with despair, was to go to her place in Virginia Square, sleep in her own bed and wake up to find everything that had happened in the past couple of weeks was nothing but a bad dream.

But that wasn't going to happen. Marianne was gone. She wasn't coming back. And Lacey couldn't shake the feeling that there might be worse yet to come.

"Have you given any more consideration to hiring private security?" Bolling asked.

"I've considered it. But I'm trying to stay off the press's radar, at least for now. Hiring security guards would just draw more attention to me." She lowered her voice to a whisper after looking around to see if anyone was listening. "Especially in Cherry Grove."

"You're afraid that instead of covering the story, you'll suddenly be the story?"

She nodded. "Katie has enough to deal with as it is. I don't want her little face plastered all over cable news for the next few weeks."

"You have enough to deal with, too. I get it." Bolling put a ten on the table between them and stood up. "Come on. I'll walk you to your car."

The temperature had dropped by several degrees while they were in the café, Lacey noted. The snow predicted for the end of the week might come sooner than expected. She'd have to make sure they were stocked with plenty of firewood in case the power to the farmhouse went out in the storm.

"Is this vehicle registered in your name?" Bolling asked as he helped her settle Katie in her car seat.

"No," she answered. "It belonged to Toby and Marianne, so I guess it belongs to Katie and me now. I might as well use it until I can get another vehicle."

"Just be careful, Lacey. Okay? I know it's possible what happened to you today was random, but..."

But it wasn't likely. She knew that already.

"I'll be in touch," she promised.

Meanwhile, she had some background checking to do.

JIM HADN'T FIGURED on hearing from Lacey Miles for a few days. He knew she'd already talked to the references he'd provided on his résumé, but he was pretty sure she wouldn't have stopped there. He'd been watching her reporting for a few years now. He knew she was smart, prepared, resourceful and very, very thorough.

So it was with some surprise that he heard her voice on the phone shortly after lunchtime the day after the interview. "Mr. Mercer? This is Lacey Miles."

He put down the Glock he was cleaning and sat up straighter. "Ms. Miles. How's Katie? How are you, for that matter? Recovered from the attack?"

She didn't answer for a moment, as if his questions caught her off guard. "We're fine," she said after a couple of beats of silence. "Just fine. I'm calling about the job you interviewed for yesterday."

"Yes. Have you made a decision?"

"I have," she said, her voice a little stronger. "I'd like to hire you to care for my niece. Were you serious when you said you could go to work immediately?"

"Yes, I was."

"Then could you be here by four this afternoon? I have somewhere I need to go this evening. Somewhere I can't take Katie."

He frowned, not liking the sound of that. "You're not going out alone, are you?"

"I beg your pardon?"

Damn it. You're a nanny, not a Marine. Remember that. She's your boss, not someone you're protecting. "I'm sorry. You're right. I have no right to ask you such a question. I just— After the bombing and what happened to you yesterday…forget I asked. Yes, I can be there by dinnertime. I just need the address."

"Do you know how to get to Cherry Grove? East of Lovettsville, near the Potomac. There's a big fountain in the center of town. Shaped like a cherry." She couldn't quite keep a hint of laughter out of her voice.

"Trust me, you can't miss it. If you'll stop at the gas station across the street from the fountain, just ask for the old Peabody farm. They'll tell you how to get here."

"Got it," he said. "I'll pack a bag and be there by four. Will that work?"

"Yes. Thank you. We'll give this a try and see how it goes." She hung up before he could say anything else.

He punched in a phone number and waited. He got an answer on the second ring. "It's Mercer."

"Any news?"

"Yeah. I'm headed to Cherry Grove. This evening. She's going out and needs me to watch Katie. Says we'll give this a try and see if it works out."

"It'll work out," the voice on the other end of the line said firmly. "You'll make it work out."

"Understood." He hung up the phone, picked up his Glock and started cleaning the weapon again.

Chapter Three

"What do you say, sweet pea?"

Katie gazed back at Lacey, her gray eyes bright with curiosity, as if she was trying to make sense of the question.

Lacey ruffled the baby's blond curls and laughed self-consciously. "It's okay, sweetie. If Aunt Lacey doesn't know whether she's done the right thing, she doesn't expect you to know."

"Wacey," Katie said solemnly.

Lacey picked her up and gave her a hug. Apparently not in the mood for a snuggle, Katie wriggled in her grasp, and Lacey set her down on the floor again with a sigh. "You sure know how to make a girl feel better about her mothering skills, Katie."

Katie flashed a lopsided grin and toddled off to the window, where she'd left her favorite stuffed cat sitting on the windowsill.

Lacey looked around the small front parlor, feeling entirely overwhelmed. When she'd decided to move herself and Katie out here to Nowheresville, Virginia, she hadn't realized just how little of the farmhouse had been renovated. Half the sprawling old Folk Victorian house was still trapped in limbo, somewhere between demolition and reconstruction, and she had no idea how or when she'd be able to finish the work.

The contractor she'd hired to assess the status of the renovation had assured her that the foundation had been made sound, the roof was new and there were no safety hazards to worry about, although there had been some question about the safety of an underground tunnel the contractor had discovered in the basement, which was the only remaining part of the antebellum home that had burned to the ground a few years before the farmhouse had been built on its foundation.

But most of the upstairs rooms had yet to be repaired and painted. There was a whole bathroom in the master suite that had been completely gutted. And the sprawling kitchen at the back of the house was only halfway finished, though most of the remaining work was cosmetic rather than functional.

Poor Jim Mercer didn't have any idea what kind of mess he was about to walk into.

Her cell phone rang, a jarring note in the bucolic peace of the isolated farm. She checked the display and grimaced when she saw the name. "Hi, Royce."

"I heard you're hiring a nanny."

"Where'd you hear that?" she asked, wondering which employee of Elite Employment Agency had let that information slip to the wrong person.

"Oh, around. You know."

Maybe it had been Jim Mercer himself who'd spilled the news. Maybe he'd decided to do a little background checking on her, as well. She couldn't really blame him if he had, she realized. He had a right to know just what sort of mess he was walking into if he took the job. "You called to find out whether or not I'm hiring a nanny?"

"No," Royce said in a tone of long-suffering forbearance. "I called to find out whether your decision to hire a nanny meant you were coming back to work."

"Not yet. You said I could take a few months. Have you changed your mind?"

"If I said I had, would you come back to work?"

"No," she answered flatly. "I need this time off, Royce. If you can't give it to me, I'll turn in my notice. Then when I'm ready to return to work, I'll give one of the other networks a call."

"No," Royce said quickly. "I said you could have the sabbatical. I'm not going to renege."

"I really do appreciate your understanding."

"I hear the cops still don't know who set the bomb or why. Do you think it had something to do with that piece you were doing on al Adar?"

"I don't know," she admitted. Not long before the car bomb that had killed Marianne and Toby, Lacey had spent several months in Kaziristan, a Central Asian republic fighting for its very existence. A terrorist group known as al Adar had risen from the ashes earlier in the year, after several years of near dormancy, taking advantage of an economic downturn in the nascent democracy to stir up trouble and violence. Her exposé on the troubling rise of the terrorist group had just been nominated for a Murrow Award for investigative reporting.

But al Adar hadn't yet made a name for themselves outside of Kaziristan. They hadn't really started exporting terrorism on a regular basis, despite a few aborted attempts a few years back.

Or had they?

"I want to hire security for you and your niece."

"Royce, we've talked about this. If I make a big

deal out of what happened, the press will do the same. They'll start publicizing where I am now, something that only a few people know about at the moment. Since I'd like to keep it that way, no—I'm not going to hire a bunch of bodyguards that'll start tongues wagging all over the East Coast."

"You're a target, Lacey."

"I've taken a sabbatical. I'm not reporting on al Adar or anyone else. Maybe that'll be enough to appease whoever it was who came after me." She wasn't sure she believed it, but the last thing she wanted right now was to live under the watchful eyes of a bunch of muscle-bound security contractors who'd try to watch her every move and keep her from doing what needed to be done.

Regardless of who had set the bomb under her car, she was the one who felt responsible for her sister's death.

She had to be the one who figured out who hated her enough to kill her. And stop him before he could take another shot at killing her.

"Do you really think it'll be enough to appease someone who wants you dead?" Royce asked.

"I don't know. But it's better than living in a cage until the cops finally figure out who set the bomb."

Royce was silent for a long moment before he spoke in a hushed tone. "Tell me you're not thinking about tracking down this killer yourself."

She didn't respond.

"Damn it, Lacey. You're a reporter. You're not a cop."

"I tracked down the head of al Adar when the US government thought the man was dead."

"Different situation. You weren't his target, for one thing."

There was a knock on the front door. "I have to go, Royce. I'll call you later."

She hung up the phone and walked to the front door, sneaking a peek through the security lens. Jim Mercer stood on the other side of the door, dressed in a brown leather bomber jacket, his hair ruffled by the cold wind moaning in the eaves outside.

She unlocked the door and opened it. "You're early."

His eyebrows lifted slightly. "Is that a problem?"

"No, of course not. I just mean, you're not late." She forced a smile, acutely aware that the past two weeks had done a number on her social skills. "Come in. I'll show you your room and you can get settled before I have to leave." She closed the door behind him, careful to lock the dead bolt.

He stopped in the middle of the foyer and looked around. "This place is great. How old is it?"

"I think it was built in the eighteen nineties. Something like that. It was updated in the sixties or seventies, I think, but Marianne and Toby were planning to renovate the place with its history in mind. You know, try to match the styles of the Folk Victorian era even while they updated the plumbing and electrical." She led him into the large family room. "They did take down a couple of walls to make this place more open concept, but the hardwood floors are all original, and so are the window trim and the crown molding."

"It's beautiful," he said.

Katie turned at the sound of his voice, staring at him with a look of sheer delight. "Hey!"

Jim grinned back at her. "Hey there, Katiebug!"

She ran toward him, her chubby legs churning, and tugged on his jeans until he put down his duffel bag and picked her up. She patted his cheeks and again said, "Hey."

"She's usually so shy," Lacey murmured, not sure her niece's crush on her new nanny was such a good idea. What if Jim didn't work out? What if another person disappeared from Katie's life?

But what could she do? She needed help with her niece, someone to take care of the little girl while she continued her investigation into her sister's death. Better that it be someone Katie liked than someone she didn't, right?

Jim tucked Katie into the crook of one arm and picked up the duffel bag with the other. "Kids like me," he said with a shrug, nodding for her to continue the tour of the house.

She took him through the kitchen to the narrow hallway that led to the first-floor master bedroom. She had been staying there because it was close to the nursery, although for the past two weeks, Katie had been sleeping in the bed with Lacey.

She thought it might be better for her to move to one of the other bedrooms downstairs and let Jim have the bedroom suite. Katie could move to the nursery next door, and he'd still be close enough to go to her in the night.

"This is your room," she told him as she opened the door and led him inside.

He looked around the large room, his brow furrowed. "This is a nice room."

"It's technically the master suite, but it's next door to the nursery, so..."

He nodded, understanding. "You'll be upstairs?"

"No, the upstairs hasn't really been renovated yet.

There are a couple of other bedrooms on the first floor. I'll take one of those."

"Of course. Whatever you want to do." He turned to look at her. "How are you doing? After the ambush, I mean."

"I'm fine," she said with a firmness she didn't quite feel. Despite her determination to show no fear, the most recent attack had rattled her nerves almost as much as the car bombing had, despite the fact that neither she nor Katie had been hurt. Maybe because it had come out of the blue, in a place she hadn't expected to face danger. She had almost convinced herself that the bombing had been a onetime act of violent rage. A venting of hate and anger, perhaps, emptying a twisted soul of the unspeakable darkness inside him.

Much easier to deal with the idea of a psychotic outburst than to contemplate the idea that someone had deliberately set out to kill her in cold blood, driven not by emotion but rational if diabolical intent.

Jim set the duffel bag on the floor by the bed, bouncing Katie lightly in the crook of his arm. "I'll unpack after you get back home," he said, turning to look at Lacey. "Any idea how long you'll be out? So I know whether to start calling around to find you if you don't show up on time."

She couldn't decide if she found his words irritating or endearing. As she'd told Royce Myerson, she didn't want a bodyguard. She didn't want her movements tracked or to be trapped inside this farmhouse, afraid to stick her head out the door for fear of having it lopped off.

At the same time, she couldn't deny a sense of relief that she now had someone around who cared whether or not she came back home safely. Someone to call in the cavalry if things somehow went wrong.

"I should be home by eleven at the latest."

"If Katie and I need you, we can reach you by phone?"

"If it's an emergency."

"Listen, I know you're not looking for a bodyguard, and I don't imagine you care to tell a virtual stranger where you're going and who you're seeing, so I'm not going to ask you to tell me that." Katie had started wriggling in his arms, so Jim set her on the floor, not missing a beat. "But could you leave that information somewhere here in the house so that I can find it if you don't get back on time and I can't reach you?"

She narrowed her eyes. "You mean so the cops will have somewhere to start looking when you call it in?"

His brow furrowed. "Well, I hadn't planned to put it quite that bluntly."

She smiled. "It's a smart idea. I'll leave the address where I'll be on the message board in the kitchen. Will that work?"

"That works." He returned her smile, and she felt an unexpected twisting sensation in the center of her chest. Damn, he was awfully cute when he smiled. She didn't need to start thinking about him as a tall, attractive man instead of her niece's nanny. Definitely needed to nip that in the bud.

"There are some jars of peas and carrots in the cabinet," she told him, leading him back to the kitchen. "And some creamed chicken in the fridge. She likes her food lukewarm. Not hot, not cold."

And she liked to throw her food around and make a mess, which Jim would find out soon enough.

"She's still eating food from jars?" he asked, sounding surprised.

"Marianne used to cook, and I think Katie was eating some regular table food, but I'm not quite that domestic," she admitted, guilt tugging at her chest. "I guess I'm going to have to buy a cookbook or something."

"I can cook," he said. "I don't mind."

"I don't expect you to be a housekeeper and chef, as well as a nanny."

"I like to cook. I like to eat. You'll be buying the groceries, so it's not like you'll be taking advantage." He crouched as Katie toddled up to him, smiling at the little girl. "We'll see if we can find the fixings to make a chicken potpie tonight. How does that sound, Katiebug?"

"Pie," she said in a tone of approval.

Damn it, Lacey thought. Great body, adorable dimples—and he cooked?

Even Mary Poppins couldn't touch that.

"Should I save you a plate? Or will you be eating out?"

"I was planning on grabbing something while I was out, but you're making this potpie sound tempting."

He slanted a smiling look at her. "Don't get too excited. We're talking about canned vegetables and crumbled-cracker topping here."

She really needed to get out of here before he tempted her to change her plans and stay. "Save me a plate. If I don't eat it tonight, I'll eat it tomorrow."

She grabbed her purse from one of the hooks in the small mudroom off the kitchen. "Don't start calling the police and hospitals until after ten," she said, keeping her tone light, even though she knew her safety wasn't really a laughing matter.

But she couldn't afford to live in fear. She had to find a killer before he struck again. She had to do it for Marianne and Toby. For her orphaned niece.

For herself.

Outside, night had fallen completely, and the first grains of sleet peppered her windshield as she started Marianne's Chevrolet Impala. With Katie still small enough to fit easily into a car seat buckled to the sedan's backseat, Marianne and Toby hadn't yet seen the need to upgrade to an SUV or minivan. But it wouldn't be long before Lacey would have to start thinking about getting a more family friendly vehicle.

Stopping at the end of the long driveway, Lacey rubbed her temples, where the first signs of a headache were beginning to throb. How was she supposed to be Katie's mother? Katie had had a good mother. A great mother. A mother Lacey didn't have a hope of emulating. Marianne had been a natural. Chock-full of maternal instincts and glowing with the joy of motherhood.

And now she was gone, and all Katie had left were memories that would fade with time and an aunt who had no idea how to be a mother.

"Stop," she said aloud, gripping the steering wheel tightly in her clenched fists. "You'll learn what you need to know. You'll do your best."

And you'll start with finding the son of a bitch who killed Marianne and Toby.

A call had come early that morning from Ken Calvert, a source in the State Department, an analyst in the department's South and Central Asia division. She'd dealt with Calvert several times following up on the stateside elements of her investigative report on the re-juvenation of al Adar. Calvert claimed to have new information about a possible domestic al Adar connection, but he didn't feel comfortable telling her about it over the phone. He wanted to meet her at the Vietnam Veterans Memorial at seven.

Maybe she was crazy to go out there alone. But she needed to know if it was possible that al Adar had put out a hit on her here in the United States. At least the Vietnam Veterans Memorial was a public place. It might not draw hordes of tourists on a snowy night in January, but Lacey had never been to the sleek reflective memorial wall when there weren't plenty of visitors around. She should be safe enough.

She went east on River Road, heading for the highway that would take her into the capital. It was an hour's drive from Cherry Grove to DC. She hoped Ken Calvert really had come across something useful for her. She didn't look forward to driving home in the snow.

For the first third of the drive, traffic was moderate and, at times, light. But the closer she got to DC, the heavier it got. Headlights gleamed in her rearview mirror like long strands of Christmas lights stretching out along the highway behind her.

Any one of those vehicles could be carrying the man who had attacked her in Frederick, she thought. Or whoever had set the bomb in her car.

The thought that she might be sharing the road with a killer made her stomach tighten. She forced herself to take deep breaths past the sudden constriction in her chest.

Stay focused, she told herself. *Keep your eyes on the goal.*

It was a relief when she reached the outskirts of Dulles, Virginia, and the relentless darkness of the highway gave way to well-lit civilization. The endless stream of lights behind her became vehicles she could recognize—eighteen-wheeler trucks, expensive sports cars, sturdy SUVs and the occasional pickup truck.

Including a familiar-looking blue pickup just a few cars behind her.

Her heart skipping a beat, she checked her rearview mirror again to be certain.

It was the same truck she'd seen following her on the highway into Frederick yesterday.

She didn't like using her cell phone when she was driving. But she found herself reaching for the phone anyway. She shoved it into the dashboard holder and pulled up the farmhouse number on her contacts list. The phone rang twice before Jim Mercer answered, his deep voice instantly reassuring. "Hello?"

"Jim, it's Lacey Miles." She glanced at her mirror and saw the blue pickup keeping pace with her, staying a couple of vehicles back. Swallowing her fear, she forced the words past her lips. "I think I'm being followed."

Chapter Four

The fear in Lacey's voice caught Jim by surprise. She normally seemed so composed and competent that her shivery words made his chest tighten with alarm. "Tell me what's happening. What makes you think you're being followed?"

"The other day, before I got to the employment agency, I thought I saw a blue pickup truck following me. I left the highway early, and it passed on by, so I didn't think about it again. But the same truck is behind me right now."

"Are you sure it's the same truck?"

There was a brief pause. "I think it is." Her voice took on a sheepish tone. "I guess I'm not sure. It's dark out. Maybe I'm wrong about the color. I'm sorry. I'm probably overreacting."

"Where are you?"

"I just passed the exit to Dulles."

Dulles? She was nearly to DC. "I don't suppose you could cancel whatever you had going on tonight and come back here?"

There was a long pause on the other end of the line, and Jim realized the question was entirely inappropriate coming from a nanny she'd just hired that day on a probationary basis.

"I'm sure I'm overreacting," she repeated. "I shouldn't have called." She hung up without saying anything further.

Jim pressed his head against the wall, feeling stupid. He had to remember why she'd hired him. She was expecting him to take care of Katie, not protect her from whoever was trying to kill her. He couldn't come across as overprotective of her.

Katie looked up at him from her seat on the floor, where she was playing with brightly colored letter blocks. "Wacey?" she asked.

"Yeah, that was your aunt Lacey," he answered, settling himself on the floor in front of Katie, trying to decide what to do next. If he called Lacey back, she'd be suspicious. But what if that blue pickup really was following her? And why was she going to DC in the first place? A date? A meeting with the network?

Or had she been lured into a trap?

He bit back a curse, pulled his phone from his pocket and dialed Lacey's number.

She answered on the first ring. "What?" she asked, her voice tight. He couldn't tell if she was worried or impatient. Maybe both.

"Look, I know you think you're overreacting, but at least stay on the phone with me until you get where you're going safely."

There was a long pause on the other end of the line. For a moment, he thought she'd hung up on him, but then she said, "The truck's still back there."

"Has it gotten any closer?"

"No. It hasn't turned off or fallen back, either."

"Wacey?" Katie queried, looking up at him with troubled gray eyes.

"Yes, Katiebug."

"Don't worry her," Lacey said quickly. "Kids can sense things."

"I know." He pasted a smile on his face until Katie's expression cleared and she went back to playing with her blocks. He spoke calmly into the phone. "I know you don't want to tell me where you're going—"

"I'm meeting someone at the Vietnam memorial."

He started to frown but froze his expression before Katie could pick up on his anxiety. "There's no parking near the memorial."

"I know. I'm going to park at my apartment in Arlington and take a cab into the city." She released a soft sigh. "I thought it would be safe. There are always tourists at the memorial. A wide-open public place."

"Maybe not in this weather. And you have to get there first."

"I know. I should have thought it through more." She sounded angry, but Jim knew it was self-directed. "I'm not used to being afraid of my shadow. I don't want to get used to it."

"Maybe you should call and reschedule whatever this meeting is."

"I can't. It might be something I need to know."

Jim lowered his voice, even though Katie didn't seem to be listening to him any longer. "About the bomb?"

"I don't know. Maybe about the bomb. I got a message from one of my State Department contacts. Said he had some information I could use. I didn't get the details, but I've dealt with this person before. He's been reliable."

Paula Graves 47

"Was meeting at the war memorial his idea or yours?"
"His."
"And you're sure you can trust this guy?"
"I'm not sure about anything right now," Lacey answered, her voice taut with frustration. "Sometimes I think my whole life has been turned upside down and I don't know where to go or whom to trust."

Anything he could say in answer to that lament would probably make her suspicious, he knew. So he fell silent a moment, waiting for her to speak.

Finally, she said, "I'm in Arlington now. I should be at my apartment in a couple of minutes."

"Is your parking place outside or in a garage?"

"Private garage. Lots of security. I should be okay until I leave the garage."

"You want me to hang up so you can call a cab?"

"No. I'm going to go up to my apartment. I need to grab a few things anyway. That's why I left an hour early. I can call the cab from my landline. Listen, I'm at the garage entrance. I always lose cell coverage in the garage, so I'm going to hang up. I'll call you back in five minutes, when I get to my apartment."

"Be careful," he said softly, smiling at Katie, who had looked up sharply at his words.

"Five minutes," she said and ended the call.

"Five minutes, Katiebug. We can handle waiting five minutes, can't we?"

Katie gazed back at him, her expression troubled.

He held out his hands, and she pushed to her feet and toddled into his arms. He hugged her close, breathing in the sweet baby smell of her, and settled his gaze on the mantel clock.

Five minutes.

THERE HAD BEEN a time when her apartment had been nothing short of a sanctuary. It was her home base, the place where the craziness of the world she traveled as part of her career couldn't touch her. Here, she was just Lacey Miles, sister and aunt. Good neighbor and, when she could find time to socialize, a halfway decent friend and girlfriend.

Until the night Marianne and Toby had died.

Just a couple of days ago, she remembered, she'd wanted nothing more desperately than to come home to this condo and try to recapture that sense of safety and calm. But as she walked through the apartment, listening to the silence enveloping her, she felt as if she'd walked into a strange world she'd never seen before.

Furniture she'd spent weeks shopping for looked alien to her, possessions that belonged to a different person from a different time. The vibrant abstract painting on the wall she'd found in a little art studio a few blocks away seemed lifeless, stripped of its beauty and meaning.

She pushed the thought aside and headed to her bedroom. When she'd moved into the farmhouse, it had been an impulsive choice. An attempt at escaping reality, if she was brutally honest with herself. The apartment was a vivid reminder of that night, of the phone call and the police visit that had shattered her life. She'd packed in haste, almost frantic to get out of this place, away from those memories. The farmhouse was a connection to her sister, but one without any memories to haunt her. She'd never even been there. Marianne and Toby had still been living in the city when the bombing happened. The farmhouse had still been a project, not a home.

Surveying the contents of her closet, she looked past the sleek, vividly colored dresses she wore on air. They had no place in her life at the moment. Pushing them to one side, she selected several sweaters and coats, the fleece-lined outerwear that she'd need, since the weather forecasters were predicting a snowy late winter. Rolling them up, she packed them in a medium-sized suitcase and set the bag by the front door so she wouldn't forget it.

She picked up the phone sitting on an antique cherry table by the door and called for a cab. A car would be there in ten minutes, the cab company promised. It would make her a few minutes late for her meeting with Ken Calvert, she realized, but it couldn't be helped. Meanwhile, it gave her time to pack the bag in her car for the trip home.

She was halfway down to the garage when she realized she hadn't called the nanny back.

Jim Mercer answered on the first ring, his voice tight with tension. "Is something wrong?"

"No," she said quickly, surprised by his tone.

"You were in the garage a long time. Longer than five minutes."

"I got busy. I packed a few things I'm going to need at the farm and I had to call a cab." She felt guilty, which was ridiculous. The man was her nanny, not her keeper. Why did she feel the need to explain herself to him? "I think you may be right. That truck was probably just headed to town like I was."

"I'd still feel better if you stayed on the phone until you reach the memorial."

"I'd feel better if you were concentrating on Katie."

"She's right here," Jim said. "We ate while we were

waiting for your call. Now she's half-asleep in her high chair."

"Did she make a mess with her food?"

"No more than the average two-year-old. I'll clean her up before I put her to bed."

Lacey felt a quiver of envy. Most of the time, she felt completely out of her element with Katie, but the one thing both of them enjoyed was that brief time between dinner and bedtime, when Katie was drowsy and at her sweetest. She loved bedtime stories, and Lacey loved telling them. They'd cuddle in the rocking chair in Katie's pretty yellow nursery while Lacey spun the familiar old tales of princesses and evil queens, wicked wolves and hapless pigs, evil old crones and two hungry children lost in the woods.

"Give her a kiss for me." She reached the elevator to the garage. "I'm about to lose my connection again. I'm heading to the garage to put my bag in the car so I don't forget it."

"I'll get Katie cleaned up and in bed while I'm waiting for your call back." Jim's voice was firm.

"I think we need to have a talk about who's the boss and who's the nanny," she muttered.

"You were attacked a couple of days ago, and now you think you're being followed by the same blue truck that followed you that day. On top of what happened to your sister—" Jim's voice cut off abruptly. "I'm sorry."

"You said the guy who attacked me drove off in a van."

"He was the passenger in the van. But when he attacked, he came from the opposite direction, right?"

"Yeah."

"Maybe he had the blue truck parked nearby."

As much as she wanted to talk herself into believing she was letting her imagination run away with her, Jim had a point. "Okay, okay. I'll call you back. All right? But I've got to go down to the parking garage now, or I'll miss my cab." She hung up the phone and shoved it into her pocket.

A woman exited the elevator when it opened. She looked up in surprise at Lacey, her expression shifting in the now-familiar pattern of recognition, dismay and pity. The woman smiled warily at Lacey as they passed each other, and for a moment Lacey feared her neighbor was going to express some sort of awkwardly worded sympathy, but the elevator door closed before either of them could speak, and she relaxed back against the wall of the lift, glad to have dodged another in a long line of uncomfortable moments.

Nobody knew how to express condolences for Lacey's bereavement. Lacey herself would have been at a loss for the right words. How do you say *I'm sorry your sister was murdered in your place* without making everything a whole lot worse?

She stashed her suitcase in the trunk of her sister's Impala and took the elevator back to the lobby to wait for the cab to arrive. As promised, she dialed her home number. Jim answered immediately, his voice slightly muffled by a soft swishing sound Lacey couldn't quite make out. "Thanks for calling me back. I know you think I'm overstepping my bounds."

Surprised by his apology, she bit back a smile. "I know you're just concerned for my safety."

"But you're a smart, resourceful woman who's made her way through war zones. I know you know how to take care of yourself." A touch of humor tinted his voice. "I mean, I saw you with that tire iron the other day."

She released a huff of laughter, some of her tension dispelling. "Still, it doesn't hurt to have someone out there watching your back, right? Even if it's over the phone."

"When's the cab supposed to arrive?"

She glanced at her watch. "Should be anytime now. How's Katie?"

"I got about three pages into *Goodnight Moon* before she fell asleep. I'm just washing up from dinner now."

That explained the swishing sound. It was the water running in the sink. "You know, we have a dishwasher."

"I know. But when I'm worried, I like to keep my hands busy."

"I thought you knew you didn't have to worry about me." She looked up as lights flashed across the lobby glass. Probably her cab arriving.

"Knowing you can take care of yourself is not the same thing as not worrying about your safety," he murmured in a low, raspy tone that sent a ripple of animal awareness darting up her spine. It had been a while since anyone outside of Marianne had really worried about her safety, she realized. Her bosses at the network wouldn't have been happy for her to be killed on assignment, of course, but she knew it was more about liability and the loss of a company asset than about her as a person.

Maybe Jim's concern for her was more about not wanting to lose his new job almost as soon as he'd gotten started. But something in his voice suggested his worry for her was more personal than pragmatic.

And while her head said there was something not

quite right about his instant preoccupation with the danger she was in, she couldn't quell the sense of relief she felt knowing there was someone who cared if she lived or died, whatever his motivation might be.

The lights she'd seen moved closer, and she reached to open the lobby door as they slowed in front of the building.

Until she realized the lights belonged to a familiar blue pickup truck.

She froze, her breath caught in her throat.

She must have made some sort of noise, for Jim's voice rose on the other end of the line. "What's happening?"

"The blue pickup truck is in front of my building," she answered, slowly retreating from the door until her back flattened against the wall.

"Is it stopping?"

The pickup slowed almost to a halt, then began to move again, moving out of sight. Lacey released a soft hiss of breath. "No. It almost did, then it drove on."

"Lacey, you can't go meet your friend out there tonight. You need to get in your car and come home." Jim's tone rang with authority, reminding her that he'd spent a lot of years in the Marine Corps. She could almost picture him in fatigues, his hair cut high and tight, his voice barking instructions in the same "don't mess with me" tone he was using now. "Call him and cancel."

She wanted to argue, but he was right. Whatever Ken Calvert wanted to tell her could wait for another night. "Okay. I'll call him right now. I'll call you back when I'm on the road."

She hung up and dialed the cab company first, canceling the cab. "I have an account," she told the dispatcher when he balked at canceling the cab when it was nearly to her apartment. "Bill me for it."

Then she phoned Ken Calvert on her way back to the elevators. After four rings, his voice mail picked up.

"Ken, it's Lacey. I can't make it tonight. Call me tomorrow and we'll reschedule." She hung up the phone and entered the elevator, trying to calm her rattling nerves.

The walk from the elevator to the Impala was a nightmare, as she found herself spooked by the normal noises of cooling engines and the muted traffic sounds from outside the garage. She didn't start to relax until she was safely back on the road out of town.

Settling her phone in the hands-free cradle, she called Jim. "I'm on my way home."

"Stay on the line," he said.

"I'm feeling like an idiot right about now," she admitted. "Jumping at shadows."

"You're being safe," he corrected her firmly. "It's not like the danger isn't real, right?"

"Can we talk about something else?" she asked, trying to control a sudden case of the shivers. She turned the heat up to high, wishing she'd donned one of the heavy coats she'd packed before she got behind the wheel of the car.

"Sure. I could read to you. After all, I know where to find a copy of *Goodnight Moon*."

"That'll put me to sleep." She didn't know if it was the blast of heat coming from the vents or Jim Mercer's warm, comforting voice doing the job, but the shivers had already begun to subside. In their place, a creeping lethargy was starting to take hold, making her limbs feel heavy. "Don't you have any salty tales from your time in the military? Tell me one."

He told her several, with the seductive cadence and natural delivery of a born storyteller. Katie was going to love him, Lacey thought. Her little niece was a sucker for a well-told story.

The drive home seemed to pass in no time, unmarred by any further sightings of the blue pickup. As she drove through the tiny town of Cherry Grove, the snow that had been threatening all day finally started to fall, first in a mixture with tiny pebbles of sleet, then as fat, wet clumps as she turned into the long driveway to the farmhouse. "I'm here," she said into the phone.

"I know. See you in a minute." Jim hung up the phone.

The outside lights were on, casting brightness across the gravel drive. The front door opened as she walked around to the Impala's trunk to retrieve her suitcase. By the time she hauled it out, Jim Mercer stood beside her, tall and broad shouldered, a wall of heat in the frigid night air.

He took the suitcase from her numb fingers. "You okay?" he asked.

"I'm fine," she answered, almost believing it.

He followed her inside, waiting next to her while she engaged the dead bolt on the front door. "I heated up the potpie. I thought you might be hungry."

She was, she realized. "Starving."

He set the suitcase on the floor in the living room and led her into the kitchen, where a warm, savory aroma set her stomach rumbling. "It's not much," he warned. "Canned vegetables, canned chicken and canned cream-of-mushroom soup."

"Beats ramen." She shot him a quick grin as he

waved her into one of the seats at the kitchen table and retrieved a plate of casserole from the microwave. It was warm and surprisingly tasty for something straight out of a can. "Not bad."

"I'm glad you're home safe," Jim said. The warmth in his voice and the intense focus of his gaze sent a ripple of pleasure skating along her spine. She quelled the sensation with ruthless determination.

He was Katie's nanny. Nothing more.

"Why don't you try to relax?" he suggested when she started to carry her empty plate to the dishwasher. "I'll clean up."

"That's not your job, you know—" The ring of her cell phone interrupted. With a grimace, she checked the number, frowning at the display. It had a DC area code, but there was no name attached. She briefly considered letting it go to voice mail before curiosity made her pick up. "Hello?"

"Lacey Miles?" the voice on the other end asked. It was a male voice, deep and no-nonsense.

"This is Lacey," she answered, troubled by something she heard in the man's voice.

"This is Detective Miller with the Metropolitan Police Department. Did you place a phone call to a Ken Calvert earlier this evening, telling him you couldn't meet him?"

She tightened her grip on the phone and dropped into the chair she'd just vacated. Jim paused on his way to the sink, turning to give her a worried look. "How did you know that?" she asked Detective Miller.

There was a brief pause on the other end of the line. "We found the message on Mr. Calvert's phone. I regret to inform you that Mr. Calvert died earlier tonight."

Chapter Five

Lacey's face had gone pale, and her gray eyes flicked up to meet Jim's. Whatever she'd just heard over the phone had been a gut punch. "What happened?"

Jim eased quietly away from the sink and sat in the chair across the table from her, trying to guess the other end of the phone conversation by reading Lacey's expression. But she had recovered quickly from the shock of whatever she'd just been told over the phone and now sat composed and quiet, only a faint flicker of emotion in her eyes betraying her inner turmoil.

"I see," she said a moment later. "Of course. You want to see me tonight?"

Jim glanced at the clock on the wall over the table. It was eight-thirty. If someone was planning to meet with Lacey this late in the evening, something pretty significant must have happened.

But what?

"I'll be here," Lacey said finally before she ended the call and set her cell phone on the table in front of her, looking at it for a moment as if it was a dangerous beast she expected to strike.

"Are you okay?" Jim asked.

She looked up at him. "The man I was supposed to meet tonight was murdered."

Jim's gut tightened. "My God."

"He was found at a parking deck on Virginia Avenue, near the memorial, shortly after seven." She passed a hand over her eyes. "The police didn't give me any details, really. But a detective wants to talk to me tonight. Since I was the last person to call Ken on his cell phone."

"I'm sorry about your friend."

She shook her head as if to ward off his sympathy. "It wasn't like we were close. He was a source for some stories I did in the past."

"He had a new tip or something? Is that why he wanted to meet you tonight?" Jim tried not to sound too eager for her answer.

"Something like that," she answered vaguely, sounding distracted.

"Can I do anything to help you?"

She shook her head. "I don't know that I'm going to be able to add anything of use to the police. Ken was pretty vague about what he wanted to tell me."

And she was being pretty vague herself, Jim thought. It was too soon in their relationship for her to share anything personal. He'd helped her escape an ambush, which was probably why she'd hired him so quickly, but her gratitude went only so far.

He wasn't here to uncover all her secrets, he reminded himself. But his curiosity gnawed at him like a ravenous beast.

"You don't have to stick around for this," she said suddenly, pushing to her feet. "You can go read or watch TV or something. Go on. I'll be fine."

"I don't mind keeping you company if you don't mind," he said. "And if the cops start to suspect you of murder, I'm your best alibi, since I was on the phone with you for most of your drive time."

She slanted a look at him, a smile hovering near her lips. "You may have a point."

He followed her into the parlor, where she sat in an oversize armchair, tucking her legs under her. He took the chair opposite and tried to look relaxed, despite the adrenaline coursing through his body.

"Do you think the blue pickup truck has any connection to the murder?" he asked.

She frowned. "I guess it depends on when the murder happened. I saw the truck in Arlington around six-thirty."

"Mr. Pickup Truck may have an accomplice."

She gave him a narrow-eyed look. "For a nanny, you're sounding a lot like a cop."

"Too much true-crime TV, I guess," he said with an easy smile. "And the whole Marine Corps thing."

"Right." Her expression seemed to relax, and Jim breathed a quiet sigh of relief. He was going to have to be careful with this one. She was far too observant. Part and parcel of her career as a reporter, he supposed.

They sat in silence for several long moments, the clock inexorably ticking away the time as they waited for the police detective's arrival. Finally Jim had all the silence he could stand. He pushed away from the table and rose. "I could use a cup of coffee. You?"

"Please."

He found the coffee in the cabinet over the coffee-maker and set a pot brewing. He took two mugs from a cabinet nearby and turned to look at her. "How do you like yours?"

"Creamy and sweet," she admitted with an almost sheepish smile.

"Nothing wrong with that," he said.

"It's hardly in keeping with my hard-boiled reporter reputation." She played her fingers around the edges of her phone. "Not much about my life now is in keeping with that, I suppose."

"Nothing wrong with that, either."

She crossed to where he stood, turning to lean against the counter next to him. "How did you do it? How did you transform yourself from Marine to nanny so easily?"

"Who said it was easy?"

"You're so good with Katie. It was almost instant. I've tried so hard to connect with her and sometimes I think she just barely tolerates me."

"Maybe you're trying too hard." He turned his head to look at her, and he was struck hard by the cool beauty of her. Cool, composed and untouchable, like porcelain under ice.

But there was a flicker of fire in those cool gray eyes that intrigued him, far more than he should have allowed, and it occurred to him that he had more to worry about than just Lacey Miles discovering his true purpose for being here.

"I don't know how to be a mother. My own mother died when I was ten, and Marianne only a couple of years older. I had never been one to play with dolls, the way Marianne had. She took to it so naturally, and to me it's such a mystery."

Against his better judgment, he reached out and

touched her arm, almost surprised at its warmth. He'd been thinking of her as cool and untouchable, but she was neither.

"I wish you could teach me what to do," she said softly, turning toward him. He couldn't stop himself from facing her as well, closing the distance between them to scant inches.

A fierce tug of attraction roared through him, drawing him closer to her. Alarm bells clanged in his brain, but he found himself ignoring them.

Her eyes widened, but she didn't draw away, and he knew he was seconds away from a dreadful mistake. But he was damned if he knew how to stop himself from making it.

Rattling bangs on the front door made Lacey jump, and she turned toward the front of the house.

"Let me get it," Jim offered when she took a step forward.

"No," she said. "I'm sure it's Detective Miller. I'm perfectly capable of answering my own door."

He didn't argue, but he stayed in step with her, wishing he'd thought to wear his Glock. It was too far away if their late-night visitor proved to be a danger to Lacey.

The man at the door had cop written in every line and crease of his face, in the misshapen flatness of a once-broken nose and the cool suspicion gleaming in his dark brown eyes.

"Ms. Miles? I'm Detective Gerald Miller of the Metropolitan Police Department." He showed them his credentials. "May I come in?" Though his words were polite, his gravelly voice betrayed his assertive intentions.

He'd come in one way or another, no matter how Lacey answered.

"Of course." Lacey stepped back to allow him to enter and locked the door behind him. "Detective Miller, this is Jim Mercer. He's my niece's caregiver."

Miller's gaze coolly assessed him. "You're a nanny, eh?"

Jim didn't smile. "I am."

Miller's eyebrows notched upward, but he said nothing and turned back to Lacey. "I'd like to speak to you in private."

The last thing Jim wanted to do was leave Lacey alone with the detective, even though he didn't doubt that the man was exactly who he said he was. He'd seen his share of corruption among policemen and others in positions of legal authority. The badge was no promise of honor.

But Jim was in no position to make demands. He would be close should anything happen. He'd have to hope that was good enough.

"I LEFT THE message for Ken and drove back home." Lacey leveled her gaze on Detective Miller, waiting for his reaction to her story. He had listened without interrupting, which had surprised her. No doubt he'd have more than enough questions now to make up for the silence.

"What was it about the blue truck that worried you, Ms. Miles?"

"The fact that it had appeared to be following me. Not just this evening but also yesterday, just before I was ambushed in Frederick."

He nodded, but she didn't think it was any sort of

confirmation of her words. "You spoke to which detective on the Frederick force?"

She had to think a moment to remember. Though only a day had passed since the ambush at the employment agency, it seemed almost a lifetime ago.

"Detective Braun," she answered. "I don't remember his first name, but he gave me his card. I think it's in my purse." She started to get up, but Detective Miller waved her back to the sofa.

"The last name should be enough," he said. "Did you tell him about the blue truck?"

"I didn't," she admitted. "At the time, it slipped my mind. I could write it off as a bit of paranoia on my part. You can imagine I've been jumping at shadows these days."

"I certainly can," Miller said in a tone that suggested he thought she might be jumping at shadows even now. Or did his tone suggest something else altogether? Perhaps he suspected she was using the tale of the mysterious blue truck to construct an alibi for herself.

Her heart sank. "I never spoke to Ken after his call this morning. When I called him this evening, I got his voice mail."

"We believe he was probably already dead by the time you called this evening."

"Do you consider me a suspect, Detective? Should I call my lawyer?"

"You're not under arrest. I haven't read you your Miranda rights."

"I'm not stupid, Detective."

"Is there anyone who can vouch for your story?"

She glanced toward the back of the house, where she could see Jim Mercer sitting at the kitchen table.

He looked up at her, his gaze intense.

"Jim Mercer can," she said, suddenly glad she'd made the decision to hire him.

"SHE STAYED ON the phone with me for the duration of the drive home. And she was on the phone with me for about a half hour before that, except for twice when she was in the parking garage of her apartment building. Apparently there's a cellular dead zone there."

"So she told you," Detective Miller said.

"Yes. I would think it would be simple enough to check her phone to see what cell towers the call pinged off."

Miller gave him a look of jaded amusement. "You'd think that, would you? You're a police officer, are you?"

"Fan of crime TV," Jim answered, letting his own jaded amusement show. "Look, Detective, I know you have a job to do. But I was on the phone with Ms. Miles tonight. I know she was worried about the truck following her. It was enough to make her cancel her meeting, the one she'd driven for an hour into town to make. I don't think she had time to do anything to Mr. Calvert, especially since I was on the phone with her for most of that time."

"It takes only a second to shoot a man."

"That's how he died? Gunshot?"

Miller's lips pressed into a tight line, as if he was annoyed with himself for having let that bit of information slip from his tongue. "I will check her phone records, as you so kindly suggested. And I believe I may ask a few questions about you as well, Mr. Mercer."

Jim kept his expression composed, but inside his chest, his heart jumped with alarm. His background had held up well enough to the employment agency's scrutiny, but if the police—or Lacey Miles herself, for that matter, with her access to a wide array of information-gathering resources—dug a little deeper into his background, they might find out that he was anything but a simple nanny.

Lacey came back into the front parlor, her posture straight and her expression cool and forbidding. "I believe we've both told you everything we know about the events of this evening, Detective. It's late, and I have a small niece who gets up very early in the morning. If you have any more questions, feel free to call tomorrow, but it's time to call it a night."

Miller's lips curved in the faintest of grim smiles. "I've heard you're a formidable woman, Ms. Miles. I've certainly seen your grit in action on my television screen. Your reputation was honestly earned, I believe."

She gave an almost regal nod, as if accepting his words as a compliment and nothing short of what she was due.

Damn, Jim thought. Formidable, indeed.

Lacey walked Detective Miller to the door and locked it behind him when he left. With a deep breath, she turned to look at Jim. Her earlier composure had slipped, and he saw worry lines creasing her forehead.

"Do you think there's a connection?" she asked.

He crossed to where she stood, shoving his hands into the pockets of his jeans to keep from reaching out to touch her. "Between what happened to Ken Calvert tonight and what happened to you in Frederick the other day?"

"And what happened to Marianne and Toby."

"I don't know," he answered honestly. "What do you think?"

"I don't know, either." She moved away from the door, edging past him. He followed her into the kitchen, where she picked up a dishrag and began to clean the table. "I think that's what scares me. I don't know what any of this is about. If I did, maybe I could figure out what to do next."

He took the rag from her hand, surprised to feel her fingers tremble beneath his. She looked up at him, her eyes solemn and vulnerable.

The temptation to put his arms around her and hold her close to him was intense. He resisted it, but the effort left him feeling shaken. "I get the feeling you're not the type of woman who'd sit back and do nothing."

Her shoulders squared, and the vulnerability in her gaze hardened to steely resolve. "No, I'm not."

"Well, you don't have to do anything tonight," he said firmly, nodding toward the door to her bedroom. "Try to get some sleep. Maybe everything will make more sense in the morning."

"Maybe." She stepped away from him, and the warmth of her body fled, replaced by a wintry chill. He watched until she closed the bedroom door behind her, then sank onto one of the kitchen chairs.

He fished his cell phone from his pocket and dialed a number.

A voice answered after a single ring. "Roy's Auto Repair."

Jim answered with the code phrase. "I'm calling about my red Dodge Charger."

"What's the latest?" Alexander Quinn asked.

"Everything's gone straight to hell," Jim answered.

Chapter Six

The snow had ended before midnight, leaving a crusty dusting over the winter-dead grass. But the streets were clear, and the temperatures had risen above freezing by midmorning, leading Jim to suggest a trip into town to stock up on groceries.

"You know I didn't hire you to cook," Lacey protested mildly, more for the sake of appearances than for any real objection to his taking over some of the household duties. It would certainly free up more of her time to get to the truth about the recent attempts on her life. Besides, she had all the cooking skills of the average male college student, which meant she could manage a decent omelet and a pot of ramen, but not much else.

"I don't mind," he said. "What do you say, Katiebug? Want to go into town with me?"

"Go!" she answered with a grin, holding up her arms to him.

He picked her up and settled her on one hip, flashing a smile at Lacey that made her insides twist with inconvenient pleasure. "We'll be back in an hour or so. You can reimburse me for what we spend, okay?"

"Sure," she said, dragging her gaze away from his friendly smile.

"Anything you'd like me to pick up for you? Got a sweet tooth or an addiction to chips?"

She shook her head. "I'm not a picky eater. If it's edible, I'm fine."

"Okay. By the way, is there a spare car seat for Katie? I should put one in my car so we don't have to keep swapping back and forth."

"Yeah, there's one in the hall closet. I'll get it for you." She found the extra seat and took it back to the parlor. Jim was helping Katie into her coat and boots with enviable ease. "She's a lot more cooperative with you than she is with me."

"I have a way with the ladies," he joked, smiling up at her.

She couldn't argue with that, she thought wryly. "You want me to put the car seat in your car while you finish getting Katie ready?"

"That would be great." He fished his car keys from his pocket and handed them to her.

She grabbed her coat from the rack by the door and headed outside with the seat.

Jim drove a black Jeep Cherokee that looked to be a few years old. It looked neat and well cared for and had a leather and faint citrus scent. So besides being good-looking, a competent cook and great with kids, he was also tidy.

How the hell was this man still single?

The car seat fastened easily in the middle row of seats. She gave the seat a tug to be sure it was secure, then walked slowly up the flagstone walk to the front porch, where Jim and Katie had just emerged through the front door.

He took the keys from her, his warm fingers sliding over hers. She ground her teeth and allowed herself only a brief glance at him. "Be careful."

"I will," he promised.

"Call if you're going to be more than a couple of hours, okay?" she added. "So I won't worry."

"Of course." He touched her arm lightly. "Katie and I will be fine. But you should lock all the doors and windows until we get back, okay? So *I* won't worry."

"Will do." She eased past him, taking care not to let their bodies touch, and entered the warm house. She turned in the doorway, watching until Jim's SUV had reached the road at the end of the driveway. He made the turn toward town and she closed the door, pressing her forehead against the thick, weathered wood.

What was wrong with her? She hadn't had this kind of reaction to a man in years. Probably not since college.

It was embarrassing, really. She was a grown woman, near the top of her chosen field. She'd won awards and accolades for her hard-hitting journalism, earned the praise of world leaders and average citizens alike.

If anyone should be feeling flutters and shakes, it should be the nanny, not her, damn it.

She needed to get her mind on what was important. She needed to put those world-renowned journalistic skills to work on figuring out who was trying to kill her and why.

The second floor of the farmhouse still needed work, but one of the first things Lacey had done when she'd moved in with Katie was to clear out a small corner bedroom to use as her office. Morning sunshine flooded the room with both warmth and light, making it an ideal spot for her work.

Maybe, eventually, she would use it as her home office for her journalism work, but that wasn't how she was currently using it. Instead, it had become a sort of situation room, to use a political term. Here, she'd compiled every potential lead she'd been able to come up with in the days and now weeks following the car bombing.

If she'd ever made an enemy, his or her name was up on the big whiteboard she'd purchased and set up against one of the four walls. Her laptop and a Wi-Fi signal booster sat on an old desk she'd commandeered from the attic. It had been slightly rickety when she'd found it, but an old boyfriend of hers had been the handy sort, and she'd been interested enough in his woodworking hobby to learn a few things about furniture repair. She'd shored up the table enough that now it was as sturdy as the small desk she'd used whenever she worked from the news station.

She paused at the desk only long enough to check her email, which was different from the work account she used on her phone. Deleting the spam messages, she found only a couple of new emails. Both were from friends at the station, asking how she was doing.

She'd answer them later.

Moving to the whiteboard, she looked at the options she'd listed. There were eleven names, but most of those she could probably eliminate as people with grievances too petty to generate the sort of homicidal rage that would drive a person to set a car bomb.

She didn't kid herself that the bomb itself would eliminate anybody on her list. The internet was full of sites explaining how to build an improvised explosive device, how to place it at the most advantageous place in the car to create maximum destruction and even the variety of ways to trigger the detonation.

Detective Bolling of the Arlington County Police hadn't shared the details of the bomb with her, but she had seen the gruesome aftermath of detonated IEDs during her time in the Middle East and Central Asia to be able to imagine the last seconds of her sister's life.

She forced those images to the back of her mind with ruthless ferocity and focused on the names on the whiteboard. After a few moments of consideration, she erased eight of the names, leaving the three potential enemies who best fit the profile of a homicide bomber.

Top of the list, based purely on their past methods of murder, was the rebel group al Adar. At the time of their inception during Kaziristan's move toward democracy, they'd claimed to have a religious impetus for their protests, stirring up anxiety and unrest among the country's conservative religious communities and throwing up roadblocks to the government's efforts at liberalization.

But after the group had taken the US and British embassies under siege nearly a decade ago, the group had transformed into a political entity that sought power and, along with it, control over the lucrative oil and natural gas resources of Kaziristan.

In concert with US, British and other Western allies, the democratic government of Kaziristan had solidified their position in the country, and al Adar had for a while been relegated to the sidelines.

But there had been rumblings over the past year or so that al Adar was trying to rebuild itself by taking a page from the playbook of ISIS, the Islamic State in Syria, and expanding their activities to other countries. There had been al Adar operatives discovered in Europe and Africa, and an email Lacey had received shortly before Marianne's death had come from an old, trusted informant in Kaziristan, who claimed that there were also al Adar sleeper cells in South and Central America, as well.

Could al Adar have already made its way into the United States?

Stupid question, she thought, using her dry-erase marker to draw a line under the words *al Adar* on the whiteboard. The United States would always be a target of any group wanting to make a name for itself.

She had meticulous files saved outlining al Adar's power structure, operational tactics and purported goals. She would open those files and give them another read, see if she could find anything she'd missed that might give her greater insight into just what that group was capable of doing.

If al Adar was, indeed, involved, she had no doubt she'd be one of their primary targets for retribution, given the hours of news time she'd devoted to their operations over the years.

Unfortunately, al Adar was just one of the possible threats to her, based on her reporting.

Walking back to the whiteboard with a sigh, she moved on to the second possibility.

SMALL TOWNS WERE the same all over, Jim thought. Friendly on the outside, suspicious on the inside, at least until you'd proved yourself. The scrutiny had begun at the grocery store and continued when he'd stopped at the coffee shop on Main Street to grab a coffee for himself and apple juice for Katie.

The tall, broad-shouldered woman covering the front counter smiled at Katie. "Well, hello there, Miss Katie. Your usual this morning?" Her smile flickered down a notch when her brown eyes met Jim's. "Don't tell me you're the new nanny."

"Guilty as charged," he said, flashing her an easy smile. The badge on her blouse read Charlotte.

"Mind if I ask what Katie's usual is, Charlotte?"

"Apple juice," the woman responded, her smile still wary. "Can I get you something, as well?"

"Hot, strong coffee. One creamer, one sugar."

"For here or to go?"

"Sadly, to go. I have to get the groceries back before all the frozen food thaws." He added a touch of flirtation to his voice. "But I'll make sure I have time to sit a spell next time."

Charlotte's smile warmed up several degrees as she poured his coffee in a to-go cup. "You're a Southern boy, aren't you? We don't get near enough of those this far north in the state. I grew up in Roanoke, myself. I do so miss a good Southern drawl."

"I'm from High Point, North Carolina," he said, which wasn't the exact truth. High Point was just the closest town to the tiny mountain hamlet where he'd been born and raised.

Cooley Cove, North Carolina, wasn't on anybody's map.

"I have cousins down that way," Charlotte said, handing him the coffee and reaching into the cooler beneath the counter to retrieve a bottle of apple juice for Katie. "You got a sippy cup or something? I can pour it straight in for you."

Definitely warming up to him, he thought with a

hidden smile. "That would be great. Thank you." He reached into the diaper bag slung over his shoulder and retrieved a clean cup with a sipper lid. As Charlotte poured half the bottle of apple juice into the cup, he took the opportunity to scan the small coffee shop, taking in the layout, as well as the handful of customers sitting at the tables and window booths around the room.

Five people. Two men, both over the age of sixty, and three women. Two mothers with children, who gave him curious looks, and an older woman sitting by herself in a corner booth, reading a novel.

No sign of a threat, and his Marine's sixth sense didn't raise his hackles.

"You enjoying working for Ms. Miles?" Charlotte asked as she handed the cup to Katie, who began drinking with greedy slurps.

"She's a nice lady," he answered carefully.

"A bit of a celebrity around here," she added. "Big-time reporter like her. Lots of people are curious."

Something about the tone of her voice pinged his radar. "People asking questions about her?"

She seemed to sense his sudden shift in intensity. "Oh, nothing bad. Just curious folks. It's not every day someone you see on TV moves into your little town, you know."

She was holding something back. Jim could tell. He lowered his voice conspiratorially. "I know *I'm* a little starstruck myself when she walks into the room."

Charlotte gave a soft chuckle. "She's a pretty thing— now, that's the honest truth. I suppose that's going to bring out the curiosity in some folks. That and…"

"The accident," he finished for her.

Charlotte's expression darkened. "That wasn't an

accident. It was murder. Such a nice young couple, so looking forward to making their lives here. For such a thing to happen…" She shook her head. "What's this world coming to?"

"I guess you've probably had to drive off nosy reporters with a fire hose."

His dry comment was enough to make Charlotte smile a little. "Not quite, but there have been a few strangers coming through acting a little too curious about the Harpers and Ms. Miles for my liking."

"Anybody in particular? In case I need to watch out for them."

"Well, there was a fellow came through a couple of days ago, a stranger. Didn't bother with any hellos or how-do-you-dos, just got right to the point. He wanted to know more about what happened to the Harpers. He was asking if they had any enemies around here."

Pushy question, Jim thought, for some random passerby. "Could it have been a policeman?"

"I don't think so," Charlotte said with a shake of her head. "He'd have identified himself as such, wouldn't he?"

Almost certainly, Jim thought. The bluntness of the stranger's questions sounded more like an inept private investigator or maybe a young and hungry reporter, someone who didn't realize that a little schmoozing went a long way toward getting the information wanted. "Did you get his name?"

"He introduced himself as Mark, but he didn't give me a last name."

"Can I ask you to do something for me, Charlotte?" He reached into his pocket and pulled out a small business card. On one side was his name and cell-phone number. "If you see that man around here again, will you give me a call? I think Ms. Miles would like to know if someone's snooping around, trying to poke into her personal grief, you know?"

Charlotte took the card, giving Jim a solemn nod. "I'll do that. You bet I will. It's not right for people to come here trying to add to her problems. I'll definitely give you a call."

He gave her arm a light squeeze, then pulled a ten-dollar bill from the pocket of the diaper bag and laid it on the counter in front of her. "Thanks for the drinks and the conversation. I'm sure I'll be seeing you around."

He settled Katie in her car seat with her cup of apple juice and took a moment to look around him. Cherry Grove Diner was smack-dab in the middle of the town's small downtown district. Besides the diner, there were a couple of antiques stores situated across the street from each other, a small boutique that seemed to cater to teenagers and a small green park across the street from the tiny town hall.

It would be hard for a stranger to pass through town without people noticing, he thought. That was a plus.

But the farm where Lacey and Katie lived wasn't close to town. There was no police department in tiny Cherry Grove, only the county sheriff's department a couple of towns over. If trouble struck, he might be the only protection Lacey and her little niece had.

He climbed into the driver's seat of the Jeep, unease prickling the skin at the back of his neck. It would be all too easy for someone determined to do harm to ac-complish his goals.

Picking up his phone, he called Lacey's cell-phone number.

She answered on the second ring. "Everything okay?" she asked, sounding tense.

"Fine. We're on our way home."

"Okay. Great."

"Do you have a security system?"

There was a brief pause on the other end of the line. "No. I've been considering putting one in."

"I think you should," he said. "If you need a suggestion, I know a company that can put together a system to your exact requirements."

She sounded bemused. "Is that a service you've had need of before?"

"My previous employers used the same company for their security system," he answered. It wasn't a lie, though he left out the fact that his employer had, in fact, worked for Campbell Cove Security and had installed the system himself.

"I appreciate the suggestion," she said in a tone that suggested she didn't appreciate his interference at all. "But I have contacts of my own if I decide I need a security system."

"Of course," he said, making sure his tone of voice portrayed a contrition he didn't feel. "See you soon."

He ended the call and shoved the phone into his pocket with a soft growl. The woman was being stubborn and hardheaded, determined to maintain her independence to the detriment of her own safety, and her niece's safety, as well.

Well, that was just too damn bad. Jim had come to Cherry Grove on a mission of his own, and he wasn't about to let Lacey Miles and her bloody contrarian streak get in his way.

Chapter Seven

After nearly a week of forecasts threatening heavy snowfall, the winter storm finally arrived, blustering into Cherry Grove midday on a gray Sunday and dumping nearly a foot of snow by the next morning.

For Lacey, the snowfall was nothing but an annoyance. There was too much snow for safe driving, and the county snowplows wouldn't make it out this far before the snow melted off. Jim offered to drive her into town in his four-wheel-drive Jeep if she needed anything, but the truth was, she didn't. She just didn't like feeling trapped.

Katie, on the other hand, seemed utterly delighted with the thick blanket of snow outside the farmhouse windows. Jim bundled her up and took her to the backyard, where they proceeded to construct a lopsided snowman with twigs for arms and coals from the barbecue on the back deck for eyes and mouth. Lacey dug a half-wilted carrot from the refrigerator's crisper for their use as a nose, and by the time they'd added Jim's baseball cap and Lacey's woolen scarf, the snowman looked almost respectable.

"Not a fan of the cold white stuff?" Jim asked as he settled on the back porch step next to her, his sharp gaze following Katie as she happily trudged through the snow.

"When you spend a winter in the mountains of Kaziristan…"

"Or Afghanistan," he added.

She turned her head to look at him. He was still watching Katie, but grim lines creased his face. "You did a tour of Afghanistan?"

"And Iraq."

"You spent a decade in the Marine Corps. Why did you decide not to re-up?"

He gave a shrug. "It wasn't the life I wanted anymore."

"And caring for children was?"

He looked at her, his gaze serious. "I enjoy it. I have a lot of experience with kids. I'm good at it."

She gave a slow nod. "Katie certainly responds well to you."

"Katie's easy. She's eager to make connections."

And yet, Lacey had yet to make a real connection with her niece. Katie always seemed tentative with her, as if she wasn't quite sure what she should do when Lacey was trying to interact with her.

"I could use some of your talent with kids," she murmured.

"Mind if I offer some advice?" He asked the question as if he expected her to say yes, she did mind.

She gave a wave of her gloved hand. "Offer away."

"Sometimes, the best communication is a hug. Or a touch." He looked at the little girl plunging through the snow with peals of delighted laughter. "Katie likes hugs. She likes to give them, too."

"To everyone but me."

"It's not about you, Lacey. You think you're doing something wrong, but to Katie, that nervousness and fear translates to her thinking she's the one who's doing something wrong. She wants to please you. The other day, when we went to the store in town, she talked about you constantly."

Lacey frowned, not sure she believed him. "She did?"

"Relax with her. Every interaction isn't a matter of grave importance. Let yourself enjoy her. You do like children, don't you?"

"I guess. I haven't really been around kids that much. Not in happy circumstances, anyway," she added, remembering some of the nightmarish scenes she'd witnessed during her time as a reporter in Central Asia. Being a child in a war zone was a deadly risk. The little ones were often the ones who suffered the most from man's depravity.

"Why don't you go play with Katie now?" Jim suggested. "In the meantime, I'll fix us some nice hot soup for lunch."

He stood and held his hand out to her. She took it, letting him pull her to her feet. As he started up the porch steps, she walked out into the snowy backyard to catch up with Katie.

The little girl looked up at her, a worried expression on her face. Lacey remembered Jim's advice and grinned down at her niece. "How's the snow, sweet pea? Cold enough for ya?"

Katie grinned up at her. "C-c-c-cold!" she agreed, reaching up one snow-packed mitten to Lacey.

Lacey dusted the snow off Katie's mitten and took her niece's small hand, nodding toward the snowman.

"We need to give Mr. Snowman a name, don't you think? How about Marvin?"

"Mahbin?" Katie laughed. "Mahbin!"

"Marvin, it is." Lacey reached her hands down to her niece.

Katie practically threw herself into Lacey's arms, hugging her tightly when Lacey tugged her close.

A flood of emotion poured into Lacey, threatening to swamp her. She blinked back a swell of tears and buried her face in Katie's damp curls, wishing like hell that Marianne and Toby were still here for them both.

"She spends a lot of time upstairs," Jim said into the phone, using his free hand to spoon chicken and vegetable soup into three bowls to cool. "She keeps the door to one of the rooms upstairs locked, so I think that's probably where she goes. I haven't tried asking her about it, though."

"Probably best you don't." Alexander Quinn's tone was firm. "You're not there to poke into her business."

"I know." He lowered the heat on the stove, glancing toward the door to the mudroom. "But I can't shake the feeling that she's conducting her own investigation into her sister's murder."

"Can't blame her for that, can you?"

"No, but if she's going to be taking risks that way, it's going to make my job a whole lot more difficult."

"That's why you're paid the big bucks," Quinn said with a hint of humor in his voice.

The sound of footsteps in the mudroom off the kitchen gave Jim a moment's warning. "Gotta go." He ended the call and shoved his phone into his pocket, looking up with a smile as Lacey entered, Katie on her hip. Their noses and cheeks were red with cold, and Jim hurried them to the kitchen table. "You ladies look frozen."

Lacey set Katie in her high chair. "I think we're even colder than Marvin out there."

"Mahbin!" Katie echoed with a toothy grin.

"We named the snowman." Lacey pulled out the chair next to Katie's. "Please tell me that delicious soup I'm smelling is ready to serve."

"It is." Jim checked to be sure the soup wasn't too hot to eat, then set the bowls on the table in front of them. "I also toasted some French bread with butter to go with it. Would you like a slice?"

"My waistline says I shouldn't. But I think I will anyway." Lacey's wry grin transformed her normally solemn expression, shaving years off her age. Makeup-free, with cheeks reddened by the cold, she seemed barely out of her teens, though he knew from his research that she was thirty-two years old, only a couple of years younger than he was.

He set a slice of warm, butter-slathered French bread on a napkin beside her soup bowl. "How about you, Katiebug?"

"Thpoon?" she asked.

He retrieved three spoons from a nearby drawer and passed them around, giving Katie the small one. Katie took it and dipped it into the soup, on the verge of making a mess.

"How about I help you with that?" Lacey suggested, taking the spoon from Katie's fist.

"I know it's messier, but maybe you should let her feed herself," Jim suggested.

Lacey paused with the spoon halfway to Katie's

mouth and looked at him. "You think she's ready for that?"

Katie's mouth opened and closed like a hungry little bird, much to Jim's amusement. He quelled a laugh. "She's the right age to start learning how to use a spoon."

Lacey slowly put the spoon in Katie's bowl of soup. "Did you learn that sort of thing in college? What age they start feeding themselves? I feel so useless sometimes. Is there a book I should be reading?"

She looked so lost it drove all humor from Jim's mood. "You and Katie have been thrown together without any warning and, yeah, I could suggest a book or two, but honestly? Most of what you need to know you're only going to learn by trial and error."

Her eyes were bright with unshed tears when they met his gaze. "More error than anything else, I'm afraid."

"You had a good day with her today, didn't you? Out there with Marvin the Snowman?"

"Mahbin," Katie said around a spoonful of soup.

Lacey chuckled. "Yeah, we did."

"So, let's call that one a victory. Give yourself a pat on the back."

The look Lacey flashed in his direction was surprisingly full of vulnerability, and he realized just how over her head she felt in the role of instant mother.

He might have had other motives for taking this job as Katie's nanny, but he could also take some time out of his other activities to help Lacey learn to relax and enjoy taking care of her niece. He had been thrust into instant parenthood years ago, adopting the role of father to his younger siblings after his own father's death. It had been terrifying, learning how to parent by doing it because he'd had no other choice.

Katie had stopped eating and was now lazily drawing circles in what was left of the soup, big yawns and droopy eyelids signaling her need for an afternoon nap. "Katie, would you like me to read you a book?" he asked, unfastening her stained bib.

She nodded, reaching up for him.

"I'll clean up." Lacey watched them with a bemused smile.

After extracting Katie from the high chair, he took her into the bathroom for a quick washup, then carried her into her bedroom. She was still sleeping in a crib, though she was getting close to the age where she could handle sleeping in her own bed.

He settled in the rocking chair next to the crib, Katie on his lap, and looked through the reading choices. "What'll it be, Katiebug? Moons, brown bears or dirty dogs?"

"Doggy!"

Her enthusiasm suggested there might be a canine or two in Lacey's future. He wondered if she liked dogs.

He wouldn't mind having a dog or two. Especially if a gray-eyed heartbreaker was determined to have one.

He tucked Katie closer, picked up the book and started reading.

THE LOW RUMBLE of Jim's voice carried down the hall, soothing Lacey's nerves as she tucked her feet up under her on the sofa and checked her phone for messages. She had several texts from some of her friends in town, but most of them were quick check-ins she could deal with later.

There was a series of messages from her boss at the station, most trying to track down files and information that she could have found in a heartbeat if she were there. She texted back the answers and set the phone on the table beside her, leaning her head back against the sofa cushions and letting her eyes drift shut.

Had she been wrong to take the sabbatical from work? She had instant access to so much information at the office, plus plenty of face time with the handful of people who'd been with her in the war zones, both the literal ones across the globe and the figurative ones in the capital. They could help her work through her not quite coherent thoughts on the threats she faced.

Here at the farmhouse, all she had was a sleepy two-year-old and a nanny. Granted, the nanny was a former Marine, but was that enough to make him a decent sounding board?

What she needed to do was stop thinking. Just for a little while. All the stress she was putting on herself, on top of the natural stress of losing her sister and brother-in-law and gaining sole custody of her niece within the span of a few explosive seconds, was going to make her sick or crazy or both.

Shifting until she was lying on the sofa with her head on one of the sofa's throw pillows, she tried not to think of anything at all. But memories of her morning in the snow with Katie intruded, and they were so happy and carefree that she didn't fight them.

The air out here was so crisp and clean, a benefit of country living she'd never really considered before. She had never expected to feel the pull of the land itself, but it was starting to speak to her the way it had obviously spoken to Marianne and Toby when they'd decided to make Cherry Grove their home. The snow-covered fields stretched toward the mountains to the west, as pretty as a Christmas card.

Katie's peals of laughter had drawn her attention away from the distant beauty, focusing Lacey's attention on the pink-cheeked, laughing child.

She had no idea how much Katie understood about the loss of her parents, but Lacey was determined to make sure she always remembered them with love and peace.

Which meant she needed to forget her last sight of her sister, a wretched glimpse of charred body parts being gathered into a zippered body bag.

She tried to push that memory away, to let her drowsy thoughts drift back to the pristine memories of Katie and the snowman, but the dark night prevailed, an image streaked with blue and cherry lights from the vehicles of the first responders that cast the twisted metal remains of her car in stark relief.

No one could have survived that blast, but she had held on to hope until the final, stark image of the body bags. The police had tried to turn her away, but she had been determined to be there, to find out the truth.

The image remained so vivid in her mind it brought tears stinging to the backs of her eyes. The smell of charred flesh had lingered in her nose for days, long past the time it should have. It was a memory, not an odor. She knew that rationally, but even now, lying on her sofa, the smell memory filled her nose and invaded her lungs, making her feel as if she were suffocating.

She was in the moment again. Standing on the damp sidewalk a few yards from the incident scene. Crime scene, she corrected mentally, although she had clung to the idea of a terrible accident long past the time it should have been clear that what had happened to Marianne and Toby had been intentional. She was still thinking accident, still hoping maybe the police were wrong, that maybe in the explosion something had happened to the license plate that had made them read the plate number wrong.

But they hadn't been mistaken. And the desperate hope that the explosion had been a terrible accident had lingered only as long as it took for a crime-scene investigator to find the evidence of a detonator.

Surrounded by busy people trying to pull together the pieces of a deadly puzzle that had clearly been meant for Lacey herself, she'd felt separated from them, outside of time and space, as if she were floating somewhere near the scene like a wraith. Dead inside, yet still lingering in the world of the living.

She found that she remembered every detail of the scene, of the night itself, of the people moving about and the vehicles driving past the scene, heads twisted toward the destruction because nobody was incurious enough to drive past without looking.

She saw a limousine roll past, moving at a stately pace, but the black-tinted windows hid the occupants from view. Some senator, maybe. Or a high-ranking official in the Pentagon or at State. For a second, perhaps in need of a distraction, she thought about trying to read the license plate so she could later identify just which DC bigwig had slowed to get a better look at the evidence of her loss.

But what would that accomplish? The senator hadn't set the bomb that killed her sister. Nor had a general or a diplomat.

The only person responsible was Lacey herself. She had been the target. She'd pissed off someone or uncovered something that had earned her a death sentence.

A death sentence that Marianne and Toby had paid instead.

Lacey tried to drag herself out of what she now knew was a nightmare. All she had to do was wake up.

Just wake up.

She felt herself coming back to reality, but just as the dark dream started to disintegrate, she saw another vehicle drive slowly past the bomb scene.

A familiar blue pickup truck.

Lacey sat up with a jerk, her heart racing and her head pounding.

"Lacey?" Jim's voice was closer than she expected. She turned her head and found him crouched next to the fireplace, lighting kindling under the logs. He put down the lighter and rose to his feet, crossing quickly to her side. "Are you okay?"

"Just a dream," she said hoarsely.

"Looked like a nightmare."

She threaded her fingers through her hair, pushing it back from her face. Now that the dream had receded, her heart rate was approaching normal, and the throbbing behind her eyes had eased to a mild ache. "I was dreaming about the bombing."

He sat on the coffee table in front of her. "That's a nightmare, all right."

"I went to the scene not long after it happened. One of my reporter friends had learned from a cop that the license plate on the car was registered to me and had given me a call. Until I showed up at the scene, the police were going on the premise that I was one of the people inside the car."

Jim put his hand over hers, his touch gentle and un-demanding. "I'm sorry. That must have been terrible for you, to see the wreckage."

"I saw a blue pickup truck that night," she said bluntly.

He leaned back slightly, dropping his hand away from hers. "You remember that?"

"Not until the dream."

He frowned, and she could see the skepticism in his eyes. "I'm not sure you can rely on what comes to you in a nightmare."

"It was real. I saw it. That night, the pickup drove by slowly, just like all the other rubberneckers. He wanted to see what had happened." Her voice dipped lower. "Maybe he wanted to see his handiwork."

"You don't even know it's a man," Jim pointed out reasonably. "And there are a lot of blue pickups out there—"

"It was the same truck. I'm sure it was. And do you know what that means?"

He shook his head slightly, but she saw the realization dawn in his expression.

"The police were filming the scene that night. Three-hundred-and-sixty degrees, to take in everything. I think maybe they had the thought that the bomber would want to see the fruits of his handiwork."

"So if the blue pickup was there..."

"It'll be on film," she finished for him, pushing to her feet. She looked down at him with a grim smile. "Maybe they were able to get the license plate. And if they did, I'm going to nail that son of a bitch to the wall."

Chapter Eight

It had taken Lacey most of the afternoon to get through to the detective leading the bombing task force, primarily because he and the other members of the team had been at a meeting in the White House, where the president's chief of staff had told them the investigation was moving too slowly. This information Lacey had learned not from the police but from her colleagues in the White House press corps. By the time she finally got through to Detective Bolling, it was close to six in the evening, and he sounded frazzled and surly.

"Do you have any idea how much footage you're talking about?" he asked Lacey when she asked about the blue pickup. "We took note of the vehicles that passed the scene and someone on the task force is going through license plates to see if there's anyone who matches our database of bomb makers. But that kind of thing takes a lot of time, and it's not the priority of our investigation, as you can imagine."

"So let me do it," Lacey said. "I can look at the footage and find the truck I'm talking about."

"If it was even there," Bolling muttered.

"It was there."

"Ms. Miles, you had a dream about the crime scene,

and your mind probably conflated your more recent experiences with what you experienced that night—"

"Even if that's so, what would it hurt for me to look at the footage?"

"For one thing, it's police evidence, and we don't normally allow the press to view our evidence."

"I'm not the press. I'm the victim's sister. And I'm also apparently the real target of the bombing, even if it was my sister who was killed." Lacey looked up from her seat on the sofa to find Jim watching her from the kitchen entryway, his gaze warm with concern. An answering warmth flooded her body, and she forced herself to look away, not comfortable with how increasingly dependent on him she was becoming.

It would be bad enough if she was just relying on him for help with Katie, but the truth was, she was starting to need him just to keep herself from burrowing away from the world and obsessing on her sister's death.

"Look," Bolling said finally, his weary sigh a soft roar of wind over the phone. "This is what I can do. I'll talk to the head of the task force. If she agrees, I'll get someone to make me a copy of the footage, and I'll let you take a look. But it could be a couple of days."

"Can you ask today? And get someone to do the dubbing overnight?" she pressed. She glanced at Jim and saw his eyebrows lift at her insistent tone.

"That's asking a lot." Bolling sounded frustrated.

"I know it is. But the sooner I take a look, the sooner we'll know if this is a viable lead or not, right? If it is, you've got a new avenue of investigation. And if it isn't, you've eliminated said avenue of investigation."

And maybe she could discount all the blue-pickup sightings as a sign of her own paranoia.

"Fine. If Agent Montoya agrees, I can get someone on the night shift to dub the video and get you a set of DVDs."

"I can drive into town tomorrow to pick them up," she offered quickly, before he changed his mind.

When he spoke, his voice held a note of caution. "Ms. Miles, I don't even know if I'll get the go-ahead."

"Well, if you do…"

There was a brief pause before he said, "Well, I was planning to talk to some of your sister's neighbors tomorrow anyway. Just to rule out the possibility that she and your brother-in-law were the targets rather than you."

"They weren't," she said firmly.

"Nevertheless, questions have to be asked. I'll be in Cherry Grove in the morning. If I get the go-ahead, I'll give you a call and maybe I can meet you somewhere in town to hand over the DVDs."

"I'll buy you lunch for your trouble," she suggested, feeling a little guilty for pushing the detective so ruthlessly now that she'd accomplished her goal. "There's a good diner in town. Southern home cooking."

"You're just trying to make up for being such a pain in my backside, aren't you?" Bolling sounded amused. "I'll let you know."

"Thank you, Detective," she said sincerely. "I know it's asking a lot."

"Well, maybe it won't hurt to have fresh, motivated eyes on the evidence." Bolling's tone was grudging, but she could tell he was starting to see the benefit of her suggestion.

They said their goodbyes and she laid her phone on the side table. "If he can get the head of the task force to agree, I might get the DVDs as early as tomorrow before lunch," she said to Jim, who was still standing in the doorway, watching her with that disconcerting gaze of his. She could almost feel it moving over her like a caress, which was a ridiculous notion, especially for someone as levelheaded as she was.

She prided herself on her rationality. Girlish crushes, especially on someone who was her employee, were not part of her repertoire.

"You want Katie and me to come with you?" Jim asked in a low rumble that made her shiver.

She squared her shoulders and shook her head. "It's just a drive into Cherry Grove. I'll call when I get there and call when I'm leaving, Mom."

His lips curved in a sheepish grin. "One of the pitfalls of being a nanny. Feeling the urgent need to take care of everybody, not just your charge."

"Sounds like something a Marine might say," she pointed out, allowing herself to smile.

"That, too," he agreed with a grin that made her insides twist with pleasure. "Katie should be up from her nap soon. I thought maybe we could do something fun for dinner. I bought some wieners and the fixings for s'mores. Hot dogs, marshmallows, chocolate and graham crackers—sounds nutritious to me."

She supposed she should be appalled by a dinner of junk food, but the thought of hot dogs and s'mores had her mouth watering. Katie had eaten healthy food for breakfast and lunch—why not do something a little decadent for dinner?

"Do we have any cabbage? I could make slaw so we don't go completely veggie-free," she suggested.

He flashed her that dangerous grin again. "I think

I can come up with what you need." He headed into the kitchen and started gathering the makings of their dinner.

Lacey felt a disconcerting pull toward the kitchen, as if Jim were a magnet and she were steel. She pushed against that sensation, heading down the hall to Katie's room.

She was awake, drowsy eyes open and following the bird mobile over her crib. Marianne had confided in Lacey that she was dreading the day Katie outgrew her crib. "It'll be like she's not a baby anymore, and I'm not sure I'm ready for that," she'd told Lacey just a few days before the accident.

Toby, on the other hand, was happy to see his baby girl grow to the next phase of her development. "I feel like the baby years are all mommy time," he'd told Lacey with a rueful smile when Marianne was out of the room with Katie. "I'm looking forward to a little more daddy time."

Tears stung Lacey's eyes as Katie's gaze turned to meet hers and her niece's Cupid's-bow lips curved in a smile. She stood up in the crib and stretched her arms out. "Wacey."

Lacey lifted her out of the crib and hugged her tight, fighting to keep the angry tears from falling.

Now there'd be no more mommy or daddy time for Marianne and Toby, and it just wasn't right. Their deaths demanded justice.

Or maybe vengeance. Lacey wasn't sure which she wanted more.

DINNER HAD BEEN...STRANGE, Jim thought the next morning as he watched Lacey's car move slowly down the driveway. Katie had loved the adventure, watching with wide eyes and open mouth as Jim cooked first the wieners, then the marshmallows, over the fire in the parlor. But while Lacey had been all smiles and laughter, Jim had sensed that the show of gaiety was just that— a show. She was hiding her real feelings behind the smiles, and he got the sense what she was really feeling was bleak anger.

She had gotten a call from Detective Bolling shortly after breakfast. The bombing task force had called an unexpected meeting for early in the afternoon, which meant he had to be in Cherry Grove much earlier than he'd planned. Lunch wasn't a possibility, but he could grab a coffee midmorning and pass over the DVDs of the crime-scene videos.

It was a smaller window of time than Jim had hoped for, and it coincided with Katie's active time, but opportunities to snoop were few and far between. He wanted to know what Lacey was hiding behind the locked door on the second floor, and this was his best chance to find out.

He had never been one to let television be a babysitter, but at least PBS was educational, and Katie loved the morning block of programs.

He settled her in her favorite chair, gave her a sippy cup of apple juice and headed upstairs to the locked room, lock-pick tools tucked in the pocket of his jeans.

The doorknob lock was an easy pick, but at some point in the recent past, someone had put a dead bolt on the door, as well. Jim assumed it had been Lacey, since he doubted Toby and Marianne would have had any reason to do so.

But even the more complex lock proved to be no obstacle, and within a few minutes he entered the mysterious room.

There wasn't much there, he saw in a quick sweep of the room, but what was there was...illuminating. A table, obviously acting as a desk, was occupied by Lacey's laptop computer, with paper files stacked neatly beside it. On the wall opposite the windows, she'd hung a whiteboard now filled with her neat writing.

This was Lacey's situation room, he thought. But there was no task force working out of this space. Just Lacey alone.

Pulling his phone from his pocket, he crossed to the whiteboard and started taking photos. He did the same with the files on the table, though a couple attempts to guess her laptop's password proved fruitless. He closed the laptop and looked around, feeling both queasy at his invasion of her privacy and deeply curious about what the whiteboard revealed.

There were three columns, separated by vertically drawn lines, with titles at the top.

Al Adar. Whittier Family. J.T. Swain.

Jim knew all about al Adar. He'd done a tour of duty in Kaziristan at the height of their power there. They were vicious and deadly. But their power in Kaziristan had been waning for years, and he had to admit that for the past few years, since he'd left the Marine Corps, he hadn't exactly been focusing on the life he'd left behind.

If anything, he'd been hiding from it all.

He couldn't afford that anymore, he thought grimly. Not if al Adar was behind the bombing that had killed Katie's parents. He'd call Quinn and see just what information Campbell Cove Security had on the Kaziri terrorist group.

He'd heard of the Whittier family, as well. Everybody in America knew who Justin and Carson Whittier were. Handsome, charismatic and highly accomplished, the Whittiers were this generation's answer to the Kennedys. Their father and uncles had been highly successful stockbrokers who'd played the market with skill and ruthlessness during the volatile dot-com bubble. The sons were equally successful investing their money, and by the time they both ran for Congress from neighboring districts in Connecticut, they were multimillionaires in their own rights.

They were media darlings and, in the case of the unmarried younger brother, Carson, constant fodder for the tabloids. He was still in the "looking for his soul mate" phase of life, he liked to say. In the meantime, he was sampling all the fish in the sea.

With a Marine's inbred distrust of politicians, Jim had learned his life was far less stressful if he paid more attention to the things in his life he could control and less to the Machiavellian exploits of the political class, so he wasn't quite sure why the Whittiers would be on Lacey's list of suspects. There had been whispers of scandal that haunted any public figure, of course, but the Whittier brothers had managed to navigate those murky waters without getting any lasting mud on them.

Was it possible that Lacey knew something about them that, for legal reasons, she hadn't been able to report?

He didn't even recognize the last name—J.T. Swain. The name Swain sounded vaguely familiar, but he couldn't place it. Maybe he'd call Quinn and ask. If there was anybody who knew where all the bodies were buried, it was his boss at Campbell Cove Security.

With a glance at his watch, he saw he'd been in the room for under ten minutes, all the time he was willing to leave Katie on her own, even with the toddler gates blocking her exit from the small entertainment parlor.

He engaged the doorknob lock as he left the room, then took care with his lock-pick tools to relock the dead bolt without leaving any obvious pry marks. He disengaged the portable gates and settled on the sofa behind Katie, smiling back at her when she managed to drag her attention from the television screen long enough to flash him an adorable grin.

She was a real heartbreaker, he thought, acutely aware of the tug of affection he felt every time he looked at her. After playing father to his younger siblings, he had been determined never to have children of his own. They were too much responsibility. Too fragile for him to dare to love. His own brother and sisters he'd loved because they were his family, but the more they'd come to depend on him for everything they needed, the more aware he'd become of just how easily one or more of them could be snatched away from him.

This job as Katie's nanny was never supposed to be a long-term situation. He was supposed to come here, assess the situation, provide Lacey Miles with the protection she had refused to hire for herself, and once the police found out who had killed her sister and brother-in-law, he'd be out of here, showing up for duty back in Kentucky at Campbell Cove Academy, where he'd be teaching combat tactics for civilians and law enforcement to advanced students at the school.

He needed to put some emotional distance between himself and Katie and Lacey. It would be all too easy to let himself get so tangled up with them and the danger they were in that he wouldn't be able to easily find his way out.

Rubbing his forehead, where the first twinges of a tension headache were forming, he pulled out his phone and called Alexander Quinn. He quickly ran down Lacey's list of prime suspects. "I get why al Adar is on the list," he said quietly, keeping an eye on Katie to make sure she wasn't paying attention, "but what do you know about the Whittiers or this J.T. Swain?"

"The Whittiers—I'm not sure. I'd have to poke around, call in a few favors and see if I could separate fiction from fact. But I know someone who could put you in touch with someone who knows a whole hell of a lot about J.T. Swain."

"Who is he?"

"He was a backwoods drug kingpin. Part of a family of redneck thugs headed by Jasper Swain before he was arrested and died in prison. J.T. was his nephew, the son of Swain's sister Opal. His real name is Jamie Butler, but his mother convinced him to take the Swain name instead. Maybe she thought it would put him in a better position to take over the whole family business."

"A real stage mom, huh?"

"She was a piece of work. Even her son must have thought so, since he killed her before he disappeared."

"Disappeared?"

"Law enforcement has been looking for Swain for nearly five years now. He shot Opal and disappeared into the woods. Nobody's admitted to seeing him since, although there's folks in that part of Alabama who might be inclined to see him as a folk hero." Quinn sounded disgruntled. "He's a bad guy. And he had bomb-making experience."

"Ah."

"I'll call her bosses at the network, see why she might see him as a threat to her specifically. I suppose she might have done an investigative report on his story. It's a pretty tantalizing mystery."

The sound of vehicle tires crunching up the gravel driveway drew Jim's attention. He crossed to the front window in time to see Lacey's car take the turn into the side parking area. "She's back. I'll email you the photos of her suspect list later. See if you can make anything out of them."

He turned to Katie. "Your aunt Lacey is home. Why don't you come give her a hug?"

Katie toddled over to Jim, lifting her arms to be picked up. He lifted her and pasted a smile on his face, wondering if he looked as guilty as he was starting to feel.

When he'd agreed to take this job, it had seemed a worthy cause, even if he'd have to engage in a little deception. Lacey Miles was an independent, strong-willed woman who'd just lost her sister in a bombing that the police believed had been meant for her. Her bosses had wanted to supply full-time security to her, but she'd resisted, insisting that all a security entourage would accomplish was drawing more attention to her and putting her in even more danger.

The suits at the network had disagreed. So they'd called Alexander Quinn at Campbell Cove Security, who'd apparently done some work for one of the top bosses. Quinn had made a call to Jim, who had just applied for the instructor job at the company's civilian-and-law-enforcement training academy a couple of days earlier.

"I'll admit, I wasn't sure how your experience as a child caregiver was ever going to come into play in your job," Quinn had said with a grim laugh. "But it turns out, it's the answer to a knotty problem."

Lacey Miles was in need of both security, which she refused to consider, and child care, which she was desperate to obtain. Jim Mercer was the perfect person to provide her with both.

He just had to make sure she never knew that being a nanny was only half his job.

But the problem with that was, he had to lie to her to keep her in the dark. And it was becoming harder and harder to justify those lies to himself.

Chapter Nine

Lacey felt completely drained, even though her meeting with Detective Bolling had lasted only a few minutes, as he had to be back on the road to DC for his task-force meeting that afternoon.

It hadn't been her blink-and-you'll-miss it meeting with Bolling that had left her feeling so wrung out, however. She'd made the mistake of sticking one of the DVDs he'd handed over into the backseat DVD player in Marianne's car, too impatient to wait for Katie's nap-time to start looking for the blue pickup truck.

What a stupid, stupid mistake. She hadn't made it five minutes into the video before she'd felt the urge to throw up. She'd thought her own memory of the night was painfully unfiltered, but the camera's objectivity was brutal. It captured everything, all the images she'd been spared seeing that night.

"Are you okay?" Jim asked, concern warm in his eyes when she refused his offer of a turkey sandwich for lunch.

She couldn't bear the kindness of his gaze, so she looked at Katie instead, her heart aching as she thought about what her niece had lost. At least she hadn't been there, too. At least she had a chance at the life the car bomb had stolen from her parents.

"I made the mistake of trying to watch one of the DVDs in the car," she said bluntly. "I wasn't prepared."

"I don't know how you can prepare for something like that."

She let herself look at him then, just a brief bump of gazes. "No."

"Do you think you'll want to eat later?"

She shook her head, unsure she would ever want to eat again. "I should push through these disks."

"Let me put Katie down for her nap and I'll help."

"That's not necessary."

"I'm not as close to it as you are. And I've seen worse, believe me."

She was too drained to argue. He was probably right—his objectivity would be a benefit. And if he was there watching with her, maybe she could be stronger and more objective about the videos, too.

While he coaxed Katie from her high chair, Lacey walked down the hall to the small room her brother-in-law had turned into an office. She put the set of DVDs on the desk and headed back up the hall to Katie's bedroom.

Jim had settled her in the crib and stood beside her, giving her golden curls a brush. He looked up at Lacey with a smile.

"Mind if I join you?" she asked.

"Of course not."

"Wead?" Katie asked, looking up at Jim.

"You want to read to her this time?" Jim asked Lacey.

After watching the video, she realized, the thing she needed most in the world was to cuddle Katie and remember that not everything she loved had been lost that night. Giving Jim a grateful smile, she settled in the rocking chair with Katie and picked up the book lying on the bedside table. *"Mrs. Moon's Lullaby,"* she said aloud, peering at the cover. She'd never read this one before.

"We bought it at a shop in town the other day," Jim told her. "Katie loves it."

Lacey flipped the page and started reading about Mrs. Moon telling bedtime stories to the stars. It was a charming graphic poem and Jim was right—Katie loved it. By the end, Katie was yawning her way through the final lines, then babbled softly about the pirates, snow-flakes and penguins all featured in Mrs. Moon's tales until she fell asleep.

Jim had waited at the door for Lacey, his expression sympathetic. "Feeling any better?" he asked quietly as he closed the door behind her and followed her down the hall to the office.

"Yes, actually." She sat at the desk in front of the large monitor of an all-in-one computer that had be-longed to Toby and motioned for Jim to pull up a nearby chair. "Now I'm just going to have to suck it up and watch these things. Were you serious about helping me?"

"Absolutely." He sat beside her. "If you want, I can grab my laptop and look through these for a blue pickup truck while you see if anything in the videos catches your attention."

"That's asking a lot of you," she said, starting to re-gret asking him to help. "It's not pretty."

He put his hand over hers, his palm warm and slightly rough against hers. Working hands, she thought, sur-prised. She hadn't expected a nanny's hands to be so calloused.

She felt a little sexist, assuming he'd be soft. If she'd learned anything from the time she'd spent caring for Katie since her parents' deaths, it was that child care was hard. It was rewarding but difficult. And to choose to do the job as a vocation surely required strength, stamina and a willingness to get your hands dirty.

In no hurry to get to the videos again, she let her gaze slide up his body. The Marine Corps training still showed, from his sinewy, muscular arms to the sharp gaze that met hers when her roving eyes finally reached his face.

He was still holding her hand, she realized, in no hurry to let go.

"You don't have to do this today." His voice was gentle, and his fingers flexed over hers. "Take a day. Get it out of your head and start fresh."

She started to move her hand out from under his, but somehow, she ended up turning her palm upward to grip his hand. "I need to get this over with. Putting it off won't make it any easier. It might just make it worse."

He ran his thumb lightly across the inside of her wrist. It was a gentle, almost thoughtless caress, but the touch detonated a string of tiny explosions along her nervous system.

She was attracted to him. It was wrong on so many levels, and nothing she could ever let herself think of pursuing, but she couldn't deny it anymore.

He was handsome. He was strong and kind. And he smelled delicious, a heady blend of crisp soap and pure, masculine musk.

He was watching her with a gaze that surely missed nothing, including her helpless attraction to him, but he didn't move closer, didn't press the advantage. Even

though he could have. Even though she'd have probably rewarded the daring with a helpless response of
her own.

She made herself pull away, squaring her shoulders
against her own weakness. "Katie won't sleep that long.
Let's get as much done as we can."

"Okay. Let me grab my laptop."

The room seemed bigger and colder when he left,
an uncomfortable reminder of how large a presence he
was becoming in her life.

It was the last thing she'd planned for, nothing she'd
hoped for. It was a complication in a life already bur-
dened by a heavy load of complexity.

What the hell was she supposed to do with these unexpected feelings about Jim Mercer?"

He came back into the room, filling the space he'd
left before. Overfilling it, consuming all the air until
Lacey felt as if she couldn't draw a full breath. "Where
do you want to start?"

Struggling against the undertow of attraction, she
pulled out a disk and put it in the computer's DVD
drive. "I've watched the first thirty minutes of this one.
I think it's probably a good idea to get to the part after
the traffic starts slowing down for people to rubber-
neck the crime scene. That's when I remember the truck
showing up."

For the next hour, Lacey steeled herself against the
images and sounds of the police video of her sister's
scene of death, trying hard not to give in and watch
through her fingers as if she were a frightened child.
But it was wrenching and difficult, every bit as difficult as it had been when she'd first stuck the DVD into
the SUV's backseat player.

"There you are," Jim murmured.

Lacey paused the video she'd been watching and rolled the desk chair closer to where he sat. Sure enough, she spotted her own dark red trench coat on the left side of the video frame. She was pacing near the crime-scene tape, her cell phone to her ear. When her relentless pacing turned her video self to face the camera, Lacey saw a pale oval looking back at her, shock and strain lining her features.

Sympathy rolled off Jim in waves, swamping her. She couldn't allow herself to meet his eyes or she'd be lost.

"Look for a limousine," she murmured, keeping her gaze glued to the laptop screen. "The pickup truck comes shortly after that."

This was a different angle from the one in her dream, she realized as she spotted the limousine she'd dreamed about come into view. "That's it," she said."

Jim paused the video. "Can you make out the license-plate number?"

She peered at the screen, but she couldn't make out the number. "It's not a governmental plate," she said aloud. "I thought it would be."

"Is that a *W*?" He pointed to the blurry first letter of the plate. "And those could be two *T*s together, couldn't they?"

Sudden excitement fluttered in her chest. Could the limousine belong to one of the Whittier brothers? They were both spending a lot of time in the capital these days, building their networks as they ran for two open seats in western Connecticut.

"Does that say Whittier?" Jim asked.

Something about his tone struck her as odd, but she

was too excited by the prospect of a lead to give it any further thought. She'd gotten so focused on the blue pickup truck that the possibility of a different clue hadn't even crossed her mind.

If the limousine belonged to one of the Whittier brothers, it might mean that she was on the right track. Even though nobody, not even the most vehement of the Whittiers' detractors, had suggested either of the brothers or their family might be involved in anything as criminal as murder, Lacey hadn't been able to shake the feeling that the family's ruthless pursuit of public office—and the power that came with it—might have no upper limits. The brothers might be all charisma and smiles, but their father and uncles hadn't made their fortunes following all the rules. Attaining the sort of wealth and position the Whittier family had amassed over the past half century hadn't happened without some brutal methods.

Were the brothers or their political handlers just as willing to get blood on their hands?

"You were right," Jim said, his voice breaking into her thoughts. She saw he'd let the video run a few moments longer and had paused it on the image of a blue pickup truck. "There's the truck."

She leaned closer. "It's the same truck I saw the day I went to Frederick," she said after closer study. "See the dent on the front panel on the driver's side? I didn't remember that, exactly, but I think that's why I've felt so certain it was the same truck each time."

"It's a Toyota Tacoma. Looks as if it's had a bit of wear and tear, so I'd say it's probably a few years old."

"I'll call Detective Bolling." Lacey reached for the phone.

As she dialed Bolling's number, Jim ran the video ahead a few frames, leaning toward the screen to peer at the images. "I can't make out any numbers on the license plate. It looks as if there's mud splattered across the plate, obscuring the numbers."

"Intentional?" she asked as she waited for Bolling to answer.

"Hard to say."

"Bolling," came the detective's voice in her ear.

"Detective Bolling, it's Lacey Miles." She told him what she'd found and included the time stamps on the video. "Was anyone recording license-plate numbers at the scene?"

"Not specifically, but I can have the original video enhanced at the times you mentioned to see if we can clear anything up." Bolling's voice dipped a half octave with sympathy. "I know watching that footage can't be easy for you."

"It's not," she admitted. "But I think it's worth doing in the long run."

"Don't push yourself too far," Bolling warned. "Remember, we have a whole task force of people looking into the bombing."

"What about the Whittiers? Have you had any dealings with them?"

Bolling was silent for a long moment. "Obviously, even if I were looking into any allegations about any of the Whittier family, I couldn't discuss it with anyone outside the investigation without departmental sanction."

Which meant they were suspicious that the Whittiers might be involved in something at the very least shady, but they were under strong pressure to keep it under wraps—and maybe even sit on the investigation completely.

"I understand," she said. "Thanks for listening. You'll let me know if you find out anything about the blue truck?"

"We'll check it out and I'll get back to you one way or the other." Bolling sounded relieved that Lacey didn't seem inclined to push him further on the question of the Whittier brothers.

He clearly didn't know her very well.

After she hung up, she turned to look at Jim. "I think the DC police may be suspicious of the Whittier brothers."

"What do you think they're involved with?"

"Insider trading at the very least, although I wasn't able to come up with proof of it. But their stock-market investments seemed to have thrived while other people were losing their life savings during the stock-market crash several years ago. It's as if everything they touch turns to gold."

"Well, that eventually came back to haunt old King Midas, didn't it?"

"It did," she said with a smile. The expression felt strange on her face, as if her skin was about to crack from the unfamiliar strain.

He moved closer to her, one hand lifting hesitantly to her face. When she didn't pull away, he brought his other hand up to cradle her jaw between his palms. "Tell me what you want to do now."

She stared up at him, surprised by the question itself, and the intensity of his gaze as he asked it. Nobody had asked her that question since Marianne and Toby had died, she realized. Not her employers, not Marianne and Toby's attorney, not the social worker who'd helped her get custody of Katie, not even her sister's friends who'd shown up for the funeral. They'd told her what was going to happen, how things should go, what she should do and what she shouldn't.

But nobody had once asked her what it was that she wanted to do.

"I want to find out who did this heinous thing," she answered bluntly. "I want to make them pay. I want them in jail or dead and posing no more danger to me or Katie. That's what I want."

His lips curved in a whisper of a smile. "Then let's make that happen."

For a long moment, he gazed down at her, his expression a promise she wanted to grasp with both hands and hold on to for dear life. She hadn't realized how much she'd needed someone to listen to her, to believe she could find justice for Marianne and Toby, instead of telling her to keep her head down and let the professionals do the job for her.

She was a professional, damn it. She might not be trained in law-enforcement procedures, but she knew about ferreting out hidden truths in desperately dangerous places. She had an advantage the police didn't. *She* was the intended victim, and she knew herself and her history better than anyone else in the world.

His gaze shifted, drifting down to her lips. Heat flooded her body, head to toe, as she let her own gaze dip to his mouth. She imagined his lips moving over hers, teasing her with whisper-soft kisses, coaxing a response she knew she wouldn't be able to resist.

She waited for him to realize just what sort of tense heat was building between them. Surely he would move away, murmur some soft excuse or maybe make a little joke to snap the tension.

But he moved closer instead, his breath hot on her lips. She told herself to be the one to back away, to act with good sense, to make the tension-breaking joke.

Instead, she stepped closer, closing the heated space between them, lifting to her toes as he threaded his fingers through the hair at the back of her head and tugged her into his arms.

He brushed his lips against hers, the faintest of caresses that left her aching for more. He teased her with another soft kiss, a little nip at her bottom lip with his mouth that promised amazing things.

She curled her fingers into the hard steel of his shoulder muscles and pulled him closer, needing to feel the slide of his body against hers. He wrapped one long arm around her waist, guiding her closer as he took her mouth in a long, thorough kiss.

She was drowning in him, in his kiss, in the way his hard body moved with sensual intent against hers. She felt something press hard into her buttocks and realized he'd edged her back against the desk.

The desk where her dead brother-in-law's computer held a disk detailing his gruesome death, along with her sister's.

Cold rushed in, as if someone had opened a floodgate to let in a torrent of icy water. She stiffened against Jim's body, and he let her go, taking a step back from her.

She gazed at him, pushing one shaky hand through her hair. She tried to think of something to say, maybe that awkward joke she'd been planning before they'd acted on the fierce heat roiling between them.

But she could come up with nothing.

"Not the right time, huh?" Jim managed a smile that looked as uncertain as she felt.

"No."

"I should check on Katie. She should be waking up from her nap soon."

Lacey nodded, afraid to move for fear her wobbly knees would betray her. "Okay. I'll take these disks up to my office and finish watching there, so Katie doesn't see or hear anything…" She let her words trail off, pain throbbing in her throat.

"Okay." Jim started to leave, but he stopped and turned back to face her. "I should probably apologize for what just happened and promise never to let it happen again. But I'm not sure I'd mean it."

She didn't know what to say in response. She could hardly disagree, because she didn't feel very sorry about it herself. Nor could she promise she'd never give in to her desires again.

His lips curving slightly at the corners, he left the room, taking all the air with him.

Lacey gripped the edge of the desk until her trembling limbs could hold her, then she grabbed the disks, including the one in the computer, and headed upstairs to the locked room on the second floor.

She wasn't sure which images were going to haunt her more, the merciless videos of the aftermath of the car bomb or the gentle, tender way Jim had soothed away some of the pain with his tempting kisses.

She stopped at the locked door, looking down at the disks she held in her hand. She'd seen terrible things in her life, in her career as a reporter. Aftermaths of deaths just as brutal as the ones that had claimed her sister and brother-in-law.

She could handle this. For Katie's sake, for Marianne's and Toby's, she *would* handle it. The truth about what had really happened that night, and at whose hands it had come to pass, might be there in those videos, waiting for the right person to see the right thing and make the right connection.

She would be that person. She had to.

Jim had told her she could do it. He'd made her believe it.

Pulling her key from her pocket, she inserted it into the dead-bolt lock and gave it a turn. It seemed to stick for a second before the lock disengaged. She then inserted a thin piece of metal into the small hole in the doorknob to disengage the knob's lock, feeling a little silly as she did so. If the dead bolt wasn't enough to keep someone from getting into the room, the doorknob lock certainly wouldn't.

Closing the door behind her, she stood still a moment in front of the doorway, taking in the whiteboard and the words printed across its surface.

Nothing seemed out of place, but she had a strange feeling that something in the room was different.

She walked slowly to the desk, where her laptop sat closed on its dented, well-worn surface. Setting the DVDs next to the computer, she lifted the lid of the laptop and looked at the screen. It was the same lock screen as usual. Nothing different.

Except…

It was a faint scent she could smell over the general mustiness of the room, she realized. Crisp soap. Heady musk. Clean and masculine.

It smelled like Jim.

Chapter Ten

Katie was restless and fussy after her nap, refusing the peanut-butter crackers Jim offered her and throwing her sliced carrot pieces onto the floor with her cup of milk. He gave up on trying to coax her to eat, recognizing her mood for what it was—a child's uncanny ability to sense tension in the adults around her.

Instead, he took her back into the parlor and sat in the old rocking chair with her on his lap, humming an old Marine Corps marching cadence under his breath until she'd stopped fussing and settled down for a cuddle.

He had worse luck trying to calm his own restless nerves. What the hell had he been thinking, kissing Lacey that way? He had been behaving like a teenage boy who didn't have a clue how to control his raging hormones. She was his boss, for Pete's sake!

And he was supposed to be protecting her and Katie, not trying to charm his way into Lacey's bed. He was damn fortunate she hadn't fired him on the spot.

She wanted you, too, a rebellious voice whispered in his ear.

Maybe so, but she, at least, had been wise enough to get her desires under control and put a stop to what was happening.

Between his growing guilt about his own lies of omission, Lacey's ongoing grief and anxiety, and whatever emotions and desires had fueled their make-out session in the office a little while earlier, there were a whole lot of conflicted vibes for poor Katie to pick up on these days. Maybe he should try to get her out of the house for a while. They could play in the park in Cherry Grove for an hour or so, then maybe grab takeout at the diner to bring home for dinner.

Lacey came down the stairs, pausing at the landing to look at him cuddling Katie, one golden eyebrow lifted. "I thought she just got up from her nap?"

"We're just de-stressing," he said lightly. "In fact, I was thinking I could take her into town, to the park. There are some swings there, and places for her to run and play. What do you say? I could grab us something to eat for dinner when we're done."

The look of relief on Lacey's face made his gut clench. Clearly, she was happy to get rid of him for a while. Was she working up to firing him altogether?

"That's a good idea. I need to do a little research, and I can probably get more done by myself. Be sure to bundle her up—it's cold out there."

"Will do," he said with a smile that made his face feel as if it were about to crack.

The day had warmed enough for the remaining patches of snow to melt, but the higher temperatures would be long gone by dark. If the local weather forecasters were right, they'd see more snow before the end of the week. Jim liked a good snowball fight as much as the next kid from western North Carolina, but snowfall made his job protecting Lacey and Katie a little harder, especially if it managed to knock out the power.

He took the opportunity to call Alexander Quinn from the car, catching him up on what he'd learned while watching the crime-scene video with Lacey, leaving out the part about the kiss, of course.

"The insider-trading allegations are probably true," Quinn said bluntly. "But I'm guessing there's no way to prove it, and the Whittiers know it."

"So you don't think they're likely suspects."

"Well, they're not obvious suspects. Let's put it that way."

"Most of the tabloid trash about them may or may not be true, but surely none of it is enough to inspire murder."

"No, but I've just gotten my hands on a raw copy of footage from a report Lacey Miles was working on a couple of months ago."

"Was working on?"

"My sources say that the Whittiers sicced their lawyers on the network and the report got nixed."

"With no respect to whether the report was true or not?"

"Apparently the Whittiers weren't the only people applying pressure. I'll upload the video to the company cloud storage and email you the link. It'll give you a better idea why Ms. Miles considers the Whittiers as possible suspects."

Jim glanced in the rearview mirror. Katie was quiet in her car seat, her gaze directed out the window. Jim was using his Bluetooth headset to keep her from hearing Quinn's side of the conversation, but she'd proved sensitive to tension, and right now, Jim's car was chock-full of volatile emotions.

"Any chatter from al Adar around the time of the bombing?" he asked Quinn.

"No, but al Adar has learned from the mistakes of their terrorist predecessors. There was very little communication between known cells at all around the time of the bombing. Which may mean everything or nothing. We just don't know yet."

Jim thought about the third suspect he'd seen on Lacey's whiteboard. "And what about J.T. Swain?"

"I've arranged a meeting between you and a couple of people who should be able to answer a lot of your questions about Swain. They're going to be up in Washington on business later in the week. I'll text you their number so you can set up the meeting. Their names are Ben and Isabel Scanlon. Ben knew J.T. Swain when they were boys, and he also spent almost a year undercover among the Swain clan, trying to bring down their criminal enterprise from the inside."

"And lived to tell?"

"Well, he had some help from his partner in the FBI. Who happens to be his wife now."

"Okay. I'll give them a call."

"You sound…strange."

Jim grimaced. Of course a man like Quinn would pick up on even the tiniest hint of turmoil in his voice. "It's just proving hard to keep secrets, you know?"

"You mean your real reason for taking the nanny job."

"Yeah."

"Is she suspicious?"

"I don't think so." He thought about the way Lacey had been behaving when she came back downstairs from the locked room. He had assumed her slight reserve had been about the kiss they'd shared earlier, but what if he was wrong? What if she'd somehow figured out that he'd been in her room earlier that morning?

He'd taken care to leave everything as he'd found it, and he was pretty sure she wouldn't have been able to find a single piece of paper out of place. But even the most seasoned of operatives could make a mistake, and Jim was pretty new to the job.

Had she found something in the room that had given away his earlier presence? Was that why she was so eager to get him out of the house?

"Jim?"

"I'm here," he said quickly. "I'm nearly at the park, so I'll have to talk to you later."

"Okay. Keep me apprised of everything you find out." Quinn's words sounded a lot like a warning.

"Will do." Jim hung up the phone and parked in one of the slots at the edge of the green park, just a few yards away from the swings. He eased Katie from her car seat and held her hand as they walked down the gravel walkway to the swings.

"Wings!" Katie exclaimed, raising a joyous face to Jim. "Wings?"

"Yes, ma'am. We're going to play on the swings."

Katie tugged her hand away as they reached the swings, stopping in front of the one swing on the set that was made for toddlers, complete with a high-backed bucket seat. She lifted her arms to him and he put her in the seat and gave it a push.

"Wing!" Katie exclaimed, wriggling insistently. He took it as a plea to let her swing higher.

He gave her a little sturdier push, and the swing flew a little higher, making Katie laugh with delight.

Jim tried to relax, tried to push away the cares of his world and just enjoy this sweet, magic moment when he'd made a little girl laugh with simple joy.

He would find a way to protect Katie and her mercurial, fascinating aunt. Whatever it took.

SHE HAD CHASED violent warlords up the mountains of Kaziristan to obtain an interview. She had braved the icy disdain of the Connecticut neighbors while trying to gain access to Justin and Carson Whittier in hopes of getting their side of the scandalous rumors swirling around their family. She'd faced down the barely leashed violence of the ragtag remains of what had once been a brutal family of drug dealers and gunrunners.

So why was it so hard to open the door to the room she'd given Jim to use and find out what he was hiding?

She tried his door handle. It gave easily, the door creaking partially open. Lacey pressed her forehead against the door frame, debating her next move. His door wasn't locked. He wasn't trying to keep anyone out.

Surely that meant he didn't have anything to hide.

Just go in there and take a look around. You're an investigative reporter. Investigate.

She gave the door a push. It swung all the way inward, bumping lightly against the doorstop attached to the baseboard of the bedroom wall.

Inside, she found a neatly made bed—military neat, she thought. No clutter on the bedside table, just a small alarm clock next to the lamp.

She opened the top drawer of the nightstand. Drugstore-brand lip balm. A nearly full pack of breath mints.

A slightly dog-eared paperback novel with a cover and title that screamed action thriller.

Nothing unexpected. Until she opened the next drawer down. Inside was a large black box that nearly filled the whole drawer. She didn't need to open it to know what it was.

A handgun case.

It was locked, of course. A former Marine wouldn't leave his firearm unsecured.

She didn't find any ammunition in the night-stand drawers. But she came across several boxes of .40-caliber rounds in the middle drawer of the dresser at the foot of his bed.

Sinking onto the edge of the bed, she stared at the boxes of ammo and tried to think clearly. He was a former Marine, so of course he'd probably have a personal weapon. Probably had a concealed-carry license, as well.

But he was here as a nanny, not as a Marine. What was he thinking, bringing a weapon into her home without letting her know? It was easily grounds for dismissal, and she doubted he'd bother to argue.

And then what? She'd have to find another nanny. She'd lose days, maybe weeks, of investigation trying to settle her domestic affairs.

Maybe he had a good explanation. Maybe she should wait until he got home to hear what he had to say.

Maybe she didn't want to believe the man who'd kissed her with such sweet passion just a couple of hours ago could be playing on her emotions for his own purposes.

She heard the sound of a car door closing outside, followed by Katie's happy, excited chattering. Her first instinct was to jump up and leave Jim's room to avoid being caught snooping, but she made herself sit still. She left the dresser drawer open, revealing the spoils of her investigation.

"Lacey?" Jim's voice carried from the front parlor.

"In here," she answered, waiting for him to reach her.

He stopped in the open doorway, his hand still curled around Katie's. His gaze moved to the open dresser drawer, then flicked back to meet hers.

What she saw there made her heart sink. He didn't look offended or outraged by her snooping.

He looked guilty as hell.

She leaned forward, pushing his dresser drawer shut, and pasted on a bright smile for her niece. "Did you have fun at the park, sweet pea?"

"Wings!" Katie responded with a look of rapturous delight lighting up her face.

"She likes to swing," Jim said.

"Yes. I know." Lacey picked up her niece and edged past Jim into the hallway. "Let's get you out of this coat, baby."

Safely alone with Katie in the nursery, she locked the bedroom door behind her and helped the little girl out of the thick jacket and pants in which Jim had dressed her for their trip to the park, concentrating on keeping her mind free of any thoughts about Jim Mercer or what she planned to do next.

Katie was the priority. She had to be. Lacey was all the family her niece had left in the world, and she took that reality seriously. Which meant that she couldn't take chances with her own safety or Katie's.

Was Jim a threat to their safety? If she'd seen anything but guilt on his face, she might believe otherwise.

A few minutes later, there was a light knock on the door. "Lacey?"

She pressed her lips into a thin line, her treacherous mind going directly to those electric moments a few hours earlier when Jim had kissed her in Toby's office. And she'd let him, without putting up any sort of resistance.

"Not now," she said.

"You're just going to spend the rest of the night in there with Katie?" he asked. "She hasn't had dinner yet. Or a bath."

"Go the hell away, Jim."

Katie looked up at her, a look of confusion on her sweet face. Lacey picked her up, cuddling her close.

"It's okay, baby," she soothed, carrying Katie to the rocking chair next to the crib. "Everything is going to be okay."

As Katie settled down, Lacey forced her scattered thoughts into some semblance of order. Should she call the police? On what grounds? Because a former Marine who probably had all his paperwork in perfect order had brought a firearm into her house without telling her?

She wasn't some wilting flower who couldn't deal with robust self-defense. She knew how to handle a weapon herself, though she had decided not to carry a weapon of her own. She had no problem with law-abiding citizens exercising their second-amendment rights.

But Jim had kept something from her. More than just the presence of a pistol in her home, if the look of regret and guilt in his expression was anything to go by.

Just what was it that he was really hiding?

"Jim?" Katie queried softly a few moments later.

"We'll go see Jim in just a minute," Lacey promised, meaning it. If she really wanted to know what Jim was hiding, she wasn't going to find out by hiding in Katie's room.

She gave her niece a quick diaper change, soothing the worried look on the little girl's face with a few kisses and a quick raspberry blown against her belly, which made Katie giggle madly.

Jim was in the kitchen when she and Katie entered, standing at the sink looking out the window at the backyard, where the last pitiful remains of Marvin the Snowman was giving up the ghost.

He turned at the sound of Lacey's footsteps. "I'm sorry."

"Katie might be ready for that snack now," Lacey suggested, setting the girl down on the floor.

Katie toddled over to Jim and held her arms up. He glanced at Lacey, as if asking for permission.

Lacey gave a slight nod, her heart aching at the pure delighted affection she saw in her niece's face when Jim swung her up in his arms.

"Want to try those peanut-butter crackers again, Katiebug?"

"Mmm," Katie said with a grin.

Jim put her in the high chair and went to the cabinet to retrieve the box of crackers and the jar of peanut butter.

Lacey crossed to his side. "Why did you take this job?"

He paused in the middle of opening the jar of peanut butter. "Because I was hired to do so."

Lacey glanced at Katie and lowered her voice. "By whom?"

"By a company called Campbell Cove Security. I

was already being interviewed for a position as an instructor at the company's civilian-and-law-enforcement academy when the company received a request for a security expert who could double as a nanny."

"So they sent you?"

He nodded and finished opening the jar of peanut butter. He took a butter knife and started to spread the peanut butter over the first of a small stack of crackers.

"Do you even have experience as a nanny?"

"That part of my background is entirely true," he answered quietly. "After my father's unexpected death, I raised my younger siblings while my mother worked. After I left the Marine Corps, after college, I really did work as a child caregiver for a Kentucky couple before I was contacted by Campbell Cove Security."

"Who hired Campbell Cove Security to protect me?"

He glanced at her but didn't answer.

"I know nothing about that security company," she pressed on. "I very much doubt your boss there would send you as a double agent on his or her own initiative. So who hired you?"

Jim put together the last of the peanut-butter crackers and released a faint sigh. "Your network."

Of course. She'd said no to their offer of security, so her bosses had taken it upon themselves to give her security anyway.

"I don't think they should have been deceptive about it," he added.

"That's rich, coming from you."

He looked as if he wanted to argue, but he kept his cool, turning to face her. He lowered his voice to a near whisper, his gaze slanting toward Katie. "You're in danger. So is Katie. I can help you both."

She lowered her voice, as well. "So, after your deceptive manner of getting inside my house, I'm supposed to continue paying you to take care of my niece and allow you to moonlight as our bodyguard? Is that what you're suggesting?"

He gave her a level look. "Pretty much, yeah."

Clamping her mouth shut, she turned away from him and grabbed a clean sippy cup from the cabinet nearby. She filled it with milk from the refrigerator and turned back to face Jim. "I'm not stupid, you know. I didn't make the choice to refuse security lightly. I'm trying to keep a low profile here in Cherry Grove. If I were suddenly followed around town by an entourage of armed men, that would draw far more attention to me and my niece than I want."

"And those security guards might impede your investigation into your sister's murder."

She met his gaze. "You *did* pick the lock on my situation room."

His lips curved slightly at the corners before he brought his expression back under control. "You didn't make it nearly as easy to figure out what you were up to as I did. All you had to do was open my door and snoop around my bedroom, while I had to pull out the lock-pick tools to get to your secrets."

"A locked door is an invitation to enter and look around?"

"So, apparently, is an unlocked one."

It was her turn to fight the urge to smile. Damn him.

"I'm going to let you continue your job here," she said quietly as she fit the lid on the sippy cup. "Both of them. I'm even willing to consider allowing you to assist me in my investigation, on the condition that you don't tell your boss or my boss anything else about the investigation."

"My boss has access to information that might help us."

"I gave you my condition."

He didn't look happy, but he nodded. "Okay."

She handed the crackers and the cup of milk to Katie, who began consuming both with crumb-flinging eagerness. Turning back to Jim, she leveled her gaze with his. "There's one more thing."

His brow furrowed. "What?"

"If you think I'm ever going to trust you again on a personal level, you can forget it. From now on, there's nothing but business between us."

Chapter Eleven

"So, you know by now that I'm concentrating on three possible assailants," Lacey said the next morning as they sat side by side—but carefully not touching—on the steps of the farmhouse's back porch while they watched Katie run around chasing squirrels that had ventured out that chilly morning to pick up walnuts that had fallen from the two large trees growing in the backyard.

"Yup. The Whittiers, al Adar and J.T. Swain."

"I assume by now you've familiarized yourself with all three?" The dry tone of her voice made him writhe inwardly. She would not be quick to forgive him for his lies of omission. If she ever did.

No matter. He deserved her mistrust.

"I was already familiar with al Adar. I've caught up, mostly, on the other two."

"There may be a few things you don't know about the Whittier brothers."

"Maybe not." He'd risked using the house internet connection to watch the video Alexander Quinn had uploaded to Campbell Cove Security's cloud storage. A far less careworn Lacey Miles had delved into the details of a Whittier Enterprises real-estate-development deal that was supposed to benefit hundreds of lower-to-middle-class residents of the Bronx. "I know you suspect the Whittiers' real-estate-development company changed the plans for a housing development near the Bronx in order to facilitate the cover-up of a mysterious death."

Lacey stared at him. "How the hell could you know that?"

"Because I saw the raw footage of the report you had planned to do."

Lacey looked away, turning her cool profile to him. Silence extended between them until he was ready to speak just to break the tension. But she spoke first. "Your company was able to get their hands on that footage? It must be better connected than I realized."

"I think maybe you're right."

Katie lost interest in chasing the elusive squirrels and came running over to the porch, launching herself into Jim's arms. He settled her on his knees, where she beamed at Lacey. "Snowman," she said firmly.

"I'm afraid Marvin's almost melted away," Lacey said with an exaggerated frown.

"Make snowman!" Katie insisted. "Mahbin."

Lacey glanced at Jim. He shot her a sympathetic look and shrugged one shoulder.

"Make Mahbin!" Katie demanded.

"We'll have to wait for it to snow again, sweetie." Lacey reached over to zip up Katie's jacket just as Jim moved his hands to do the same thing, and her fingers brushed his, setting off sparks. He wasn't sure if the sensation was the real result of static or just his body's electric reaction to her touch.

He wasn't sure it mattered.

Lacey dropped her hand quickly, flicking a swift

glance Jim's way before she settled her gaze on Katie. "I bet you're hungry, aren't you, baby?"

Distracted by the demands of her stomach, Katie nodded.

"I'll get her settled in her high chair if you'll heat up some chicken-noodle soup for her," Lacey said, reaching out to take Katie from his arms.

Katie didn't fuss when Lacey took her inside, though she did shoot Jim a questioning look, as if she didn't understand why he wasn't the one carrying her through the mudroom door.

While Lacey helped Katie shed her snowsuit, Jim heated leftover chicken-noodle soup and poured it into one of Katie's favorite bowls. He set it in front of her and took a step back, pretending to watch Katie dig into the soup while he secretly took every chance he could get to look at Lacey.

To say she was still angry with him was an understatement. But at least they were talking. It was a start.

"How much of the footage was your company able to get their hands on?" Lacey asked a few minutes later when she joined him near the refrigerator. She pulled apple juice from the refrigerator and poured a cup for Katie.

"I think maybe all of it."

She slanted a quick look at him before she handed Katie the drink and sat in the chair to her right.

Jim took a seat across from Lacey. "I can show you."

She shook her head. "I've seen it, remember. I'm the one who put it together."

"Why didn't the network let you air it?"

"Because the Whittiers threatened to take the whole

network down if we did. It went all the way up to the network suits, who capitulated."

"I thought the press was supposed to be the ones who spoke truth to power and all that."

"I can't prove this, but I think someone in the Whittier clan applied a little leverage to someone pretty damned high up in the network."

Jim frowned. "You mean blackmail?"

"That's exactly what I mean." Lacey grabbed a paper towel from the roll hanging on the wall and crossed to Katie to mop up the soupy mess the little girl was making. "I can't think of any other reason the network would have put a stop to my report."

"Any idea who? Or what?"

She shook her head. "I may be an investigative reporter, but I learned a long time ago that indulging in behind-the-scenes gossip is a great way to lose your job. I've always steered clear of that sort of thing, and all my coworkers know it. They don't even bother to whisper anything anymore."

"But it's a case now, isn't it? You could approach it as if it's something you're investigating, not gossip."

"I have to work with those people. I can't start digging around in their personal lives and pasts just because I'm sort of suspicious about why my investigation was shut down. If they're being blackmailed, it's probably about something in their lives I don't want or need to know about. I'll find another way to get to the truth about the Whittiers. Whatever it is. And when I do, not even the network is going to be able to stop me from revealing it."

Which explained why the Whittiers might want to put her out of action for good, Jim thought. "Okay. So let's change gears. J.T. Swain. What if I told you I could get you a meeting with someone who probably knows more about Swain and his history than anyone else in the world?"

She gave him a skeptical look. "The person who knows the most about Swain is a former FBI agent who knew him as a kid and also went undercover with Swain's organization for a while. Ben Scanlon. But, believe me, I tried to talk to Scanlon and his wife, who's the next best expert on Swain, when I was doing my investigation into his disappearance. Neither of them would talk to me."

"They'll talk to you now. I already have a meeting set up."

She stared at him, disbelieving. "I spent months trying to get an interview with them. How did you manage it?"

"My boss at Campbell Cove Security has a knack for making the impossible happen."

"When will they meet me? And where?"

"Us," Jim corrected. "They'll meet us."

The scowl that creased Lacey's forehead was impressive, but Jim waited for her to figure out the reality: if she wanted to talk to the Scanlons, she was going to have to accept Jim as a partner in the investigation.

Her lips finally pressed into a thin line. "Fine. When and where?"

"They're going to be in the area later this week. I'm supposed to call and set it up."

"The sooner, the better," she said firmly.

"Yeah, I figured that."

Now finished with her soup, Katie had turned the bowl upside down and was using her spoon to bang on the bottom of the bowl. Jim gently extricated her make-shift drum from her hands, earning a scowl nearly as intimidating as her aunt's.

"I'll call as soon as I get Katiebug cleaned up and settled for her nap."

Lacey stood. "Go make the call. I'll take care of Katie."

"You sure?"

She nodded. "Go. The sooner the better, remember."

Jim deposited the bowl in the sink for a rinse, then pulled out his cell phone and retreated to the front parlor to make his call. He reached Ben Scanlon on the first ring.

"I've been expecting your call." Scanlon's voice was deep, his words edged with a twang that reminded Jim of a gunnery sergeant he'd known in the Marine Corps, a Texan through and through. "Isabel and I will be in Washington for a seminar on domestic terrorism this weekend, but we thought we'd drive rather than fly. Make a road trip out of it. We'll be overnighting in Strasburg on Wednesday. I've been taking a look at the map—we could take a detour on our way into DC and meet up with you in Leesburg Thursday around noon."

"Leesburg on Thursday at noon. We'll be there."

There was a brief pause. "Who's we?"

"I want to bring Lacey Miles with me."

"She's a reporter." Scanlon said the word as if it was a pejorative.

"She's a woman whose sister was murdered in her place," Jim said with more heat than he'd intended. "Her life is still in danger, and she wants to know if there's any way J.T. Swain could be behind it."

"I can tell you now, I don't think he is."

"I think Lacey will want to get all the facts and make that decision for herself." Jim looked up to find Lacey standing in the doorway to the parlor, her clothes a little rumpled and her hair flying wildly. Katie wasn't with her, so she must have been successful putting her niece down for a nap.

She gazed back at him, questions flickering in her cool gray eyes.

"Okay. Thursday at noon in Leesburg. I'll text you the place when we pick it out." Scanlon's voice deepened a notch. "I'm not looking to end up on the network news here, Mercer. The Swain family may not be running Halloran County anymore, but there are enough of them left to make life dangerous for us. We're trying to stay off their radar as much as we can."

"Understood. This isn't about a news story."

"Good. I'll text you soon."

Jim hung up and looked at Lacey, who'd moved to the armchair across from where he sat. "Thursday in Leesburg at noon."

She gave a brief nod. "We'll have to take Katie along."

"Of course."

There was a brief softening of her eyes before her cool reserve returned. He quelled his disappointment. He'd earned her distrust, and if he wanted the tension between them to ease again, he'd have to be patient. He knew with time he could prove to her that he was serious about keeping her and Katie safe.

But there was no chance in hell she'd ever risk letting him get close to her again. And now that the reality of that fact began to sink in, Jim was starting to realize just how much he wanted to find out how far their mutual attraction could take them.

LEESBURG ANIMAL PARK was a surprising choice of venue for a meeting, but by the time Katie had petted goats and lambs and worn herself out playing with other toddlers in the play area, she fell asleep in Jim's arms halfway through her picnic lunch, leaving Lacey, Jim and the Scanlons to talk in peace.

"I wish we could've brought Delia with us," Isabel Scanlon commented, her tea-brown eyes softening as she looked at Katie sleeping in Jim's lap. "She just turned three last fall. But the seminar is all work, and she'll be a lot happier home with her cousins."

"I appreciate your agreeing to talk to me." Lacey pushed aside the half-eaten remains of her lunch and met Ben Scanlon's gaze. His smoky-blue eyes were sharp but kind, and she felt the last of her tension seeping away. "I'm not going to use anything you tell me in a news report. This is purely for me. I need to know if J.T. Swain could have been involved in the bombing that killed my sister. In revenge for my report that dredged up his story. I know public reaction to my report put Swain back onto the active investigations list for several law-enforcement agencies. Would he want revenge for that? Enough to try to kill me?"

Ben and Isabel Scanlon looked at each other. In that brief meeting of gazes, they seemed to hold an entire conversation before Ben said, "He's capable of setting a car bomb. But I've spent the past few years watching for any sign that he's back in business, and I've come across nothing. I think he's holed up somewhere in the mountains, living off the land and bothering nobody."

"You think he's retired." Jim sounded skeptical.

"He killed his mother because she turned him into a monster," Ben said quietly, sadness tinting his voice. "When we were kids, we were best friends. Jamie was a good kid from a bad family. But his mother thought he was growing up soft. She blamed his father, who was an outsider, for turning her son into a normal human being."

As Ben's voice faltered, Isabel reached out and covered his hand with hers. He seemed to draw strength from her touch, his shoulders squaring and his chin lifting.

"J.T. Swain's real name is Jamie Butler. He didn't take the name Swain until he was older. His mother, Opal, had nothing but contempt for her husband, so she had Jamie's name legally changed to her own maiden name."

"She wanted her son to be part of the family business?" Jim guessed.

"So much so that, when Jamie and I were eight years old, Opal took him out in her truck, gave him a loaded gun and goaded him into shooting the sheriff of Halloran County. To prove he was a true Swain."

Lacey frowned. "You mean Bennett Allen was killed by a child?"

"Yes. I saw it happen."

"But…" Lacey felt ill as realization dawned. In her research into J.T. Swain and the Swain family, the story of Bennett Allen's murder had been a showcase of just how depraved the Swain family could be. Allen had been murdered in the driveway of his own home, in front of his young son. "You're Bennett Allen's son?"

"Yes. After my father's death, my mother remarried, and my stepfather adopted me. Changed my last name. There were times over the years when I almost believed my father's murder had been nothing but a bad dream. That my mother and stepfather had moved us all to Texas for job opportunities, not so that the Swains couldn't find me and make sure I never remembered what I saw that night."

"How did you end up undercover among the Swains?" Jim asked. He was lightly stroking Katie's hair. She looked so right in Jim's arms, as if being there was the most natural thing on earth for her. Lacey felt a hard ache forming in the center of her chest as she contemplated how difficult it would be to separate her niece from Jim when the time came for him to move on to a different job.

Hadn't he thought about the consequences of his lies? Hadn't he realized that Katie might grow so attached to him that he would hurt her by walking away?

Jim's gaze connected with hers, his eyes darkening as he seemed to read her thoughts. He looked at Katie, his expression pained.

"Several years ago, I was nearly killed in an explosion. In fact, most people believed I did die, from my parents to almost everyone I worked with in the FBI." Scanlon glanced at his wife. "That includes my FBI partner."

"That would be me." Isabel's voice was a soft rasp.

"Isabel had been working on a serial-bomber investigation, and the explosion that nearly killed me was meant for her."

Isabel reached across the picnic table and touched Lacey's arm. "I know what it's like to see someone else take a hit meant for you."

Lacey blinked back tears. "I'm glad for you that Ben survived."

"I didn't know he had for a long time." Isabel reached for her husband's hand, twining her fingers with his. "I felt so guilty and alone."

"When I survived mostly uninjured, the special agent in charge of our team and I agreed it was a perfect opportunity to go undercover in the Swain enclave. I posed as a disgruntled wounded veteran living on disability and looking for some way to make fast, easy money." He looked at Isabel. "Not only did I get a chance to do something active to keep Isabel safe, but I was able to finally remember the truth of what happened the night my father died."

"I don't know how all of this somehow convinces you that J.T. Swain has retired from bomb making," Jim said.

"Like I said, I've been keeping my ear to the ground. And if he's been out there building bombs, he's doing it in the middle of nowhere, with nobody to impress. And that's just not how the Swains do anything."

"What kind of bomb killed your sister?" Isabel asked.

"Honestly, I don't know. The police are keeping some things to themselves on this investigation."

Isabel nodded impatiently. "Do you at least know what kind of detonator was used?"

"Yes, but they don't want this getting out."

"It won't," Ben said firmly.

"The bomb was detonated by a tilt fuse combined with a timer. The timer set the tilt fuse, which then detonated the bomb at the depression of the accelerator."

Ben and Isabel exchanged glances. "Any idea of the explosive material used in the bomb?"

"I'm not sure," Lacey admitted. "That's one of the things the police have held back even from me. But, based on the damage to the car, it seemed to be a small charge directed up into the front seat of the car. It was meant to kill anyone in the passenger-carrying part of the car."

"Any loaded shrapnel?" Isabel asked.

Lacey closed her eyes, wishing she hadn't eaten lunch. Even though Katie was asleep, she lowered her voice. "Ball bearings and sheet-metal screws."

"It's not Swain," Ben and Isabel said in unison.

"How can you know?" Jim asked.

"Needles and nails," Isabel answered. "It's a Swain signature. All their bombs included needles and nails as shrapnel."

"I can't see Jamie setting a bomb without them," Ben agreed.

Lacey leaned closer. "How certain are you about that?"

"Pretty positive. Needles and nails were a matter of pride. It was how the Swains made bombs. To make one without that signature would be like a painter signing someone else's name to his masterpiece."

"That happened, sometimes," Jim murmured.

"Nothing in life is a sure thing," Isabel answered. "But I think Ben is right. There would be needles and nails in that bomb, mixed in with the screws and ball bearings."

"So I guess he goes to the bottom of my suspect list." Lacey tried to quell an overwhelming sense of disappointment. Of the three main suspects she'd settled on, she'd hoped that Swain might be the one who'd killed Marianne and Toby. He was one man, not rich, not particularly powerful, and now that his family members were either in jail or scattered to the winds, he didn't have many allies. Even if he had never been caught, a threat from J.T. Swain would be easier to anticipate and contain.

She felt Jim's fingertips brush her arm, the touch light and tentative. She looked up to find him watching her, his expression concerned.

She moved her arm away from his hand and looked at the Scanlons as she rose to her feet. She extended her hand to Ben. "I appreciate your time. It was generous of you to come out of your way to talk to me."

Ben rose as well and shook her hand. "I wish we could have helped."

By the time they parted company with the Scanlons in the parking lot, the weather conditions were starting to deteriorate, the threat of snow that had followed them into Leesburg finally becoming a reality. Snow fell lightly at first, then in thickening clumps that deteriorated visibility and forced Lacey to slow the Impala to a near crawl only a few miles west of Leesburg.

"Should we stop for a while to see if it slows down?" Jim peered through the windshield at the wall of white flakes. He didn't look worried, exactly, only hypervigilant. Thinking like a bodyguard, she realized.

"I'll feel safer at home than parked out here on the road. It'll be a lot warmer there, too."

The farther they got from Leesburg, the lighter the traffic, which should have made Lacey feel safer. But there was something about the blanket of snow fog that made her feel oddly exposed. The hair on the back of her neck rose, her skin prickling.

Beside her, Jim leaned forward, as if it could help

him see farther into the white void only a few yards ahead. They were moving as slowly as Lacey dared, though she didn't want to be going so slowly that a car moving up through the snowfall behind her couldn't stop in time when the driver spotted her taillights.

"This is creepy, isn't it?" she asked. "Like we're all alone in this void."

"We're not alone," Jim growled, turning in his seat to look through the back window.

Lacey checked her rearview mirror. There, emerging through the thick white snow fog behind them, was the now familiar front grille of a blue Toyota Tacoma pickup truck.

Chapter Twelve

"Where the hell did that thing come from?" Lacey's voice rose as she dragged her gaze from the mirror to watch the road ahead. She'd pressed the accelerator on instinct, Jim realized as the Impala picked up speed.

Trying to get away from their pursuer.

He looked behind them, hoping that the truck had dropped back once it spotted the vehicle ahead of it. But it remained close enough that he could almost see past the misting snow and the rapid swish-swish of the truck's windshield wipers.

At first, he didn't quite believe what his eyes were telling him. But after a couple of seconds, the truth sank in. The driver of the blue Tacoma was wearing a ski mask.

Jim slipped his phone from his pocket and dialed Quinn. No point in calling the Virginia State Police. So far, the blue truck's biggest offense was tailgating in a snowstorm. Even if the state police were to respond, by the time they could arrive, whatever the blue pickup had planned would have happened.

He'd carried his Glock on this trip, holstered it inside his jacket. At the moment, the heft of the weapon pressed cold and hard against his rib cage, reminding him that he had options.

Impatiently, he went through the code-phrase rigmarole, then tersely told Quinn what was happening.

"Are you driving?" Quinn asked.

Jim glanced at Lacey, who gripped the steering wheel in two white hands. "No."

"Ms. Miles?"

"Yes."

"Does she have any evasive-driving skills?"

"Do you know anything about evasive driving?" Jim asked Lacey.

"I took a course before I went to Kaziristan a few years ago, but I never had to test what I learned, since I had a driver." She sent another worried glance toward the rearview mirror. "Is that driver wearing a ski mask?"

"Yes."

Lacey made a sound of distress low in her throat. "What should I do?"

"Keep driving," Jim said urgently. "Pick up some speed, but keep your eye on the road ahead." He spoke into the phone again. "So far the truck driver is just keeping pace. Hasn't made a move yet."

"Then just keep moving. Don't go too fast—speed kills," Quinn warned. "I'll see if I can get someone to meet you for an escort."

Jim didn't ask how Quinn would accomplish such a thing. He had come to realize there were few things that his boss couldn't make happen. "I'll be in touch," he told Quinn, then hung up and turned around to look through the back window, half hoping the truck had fallen back.

But, if anything, the front grille of the truck was

closer than it had been, bearing down on the back of the Impala like a monster seeking to devour the vehicle and its occupants.

He shifted his gaze to the car seat where Katie still slept, oblivious to the danger that had suddenly engulfed her world in the span of a few heartbeats. A rush of protective affection swamped him, making his head spin for a dizzying moment before his vision cleared and determination steeled his spine.

Katie and Lacey were his to protect, no matter what they or anyone else thought about the matter. If he had to die to protect them, so be it.

Movement in the back window drew his gaze away from Katie's soft face. The truck was pulling up beside the car, its driver's-side front panel aiming for the Impala's rear-side panel.

"PIT maneuver!" Jim shouted, turning to brace himself for the collision.

The truck hit the Impala's right back panel, sending the bulky sport-utility vehicle into a dizzying spin that sent Jim slamming against the passenger door. He kept his head clear of the window, despite the violent jerk of the Impala's rotation.

The car hit a snowy patch and slid across the road toward the ditch on the other side. Lacey steered into the skid and the vehicle came to a stop short of the ditch.

The blue truck had driven past them, disappearing into the white void.

For a long moment, there was nothing but the rumble of the Impala's engine and the hard swish of the windshield wipers. Then a frightened wail rose from the backseat, making Jim's heart skip a beat.

He twisted in his seat until he could see Katie. She

was still strapped in her car seat, her eyes crinkled at the corners as she cried.

"It's okay, Katiebug." He searched her visually for any sign of injury. She looked okay, just shaken by the sudden jerks and spins caused by the light impact. "You're okay."

"Are you sure she's okay?" Lacey's voice was a soft rasp beside him.

He turned to look at her. She looked stunned and scared, but he didn't see any sign of an injury on her, either. "She's fine. How about you?"

She lifted her hand to her head. "I hit my head on the window when we took the impact, but it was just a bump. Otherwise, I'm fine. I need to get the car off the road before we get hit."

Jim peered down the road, wondering if the blue truck was waiting just out of sight ahead of them. "Good idea."

Lacey put the car in gear, parked it on the shoulder and engaged the hazard lights. Like Jim, she peered through the whiteout ahead of them. "Do you think he's still up there?"

"Maybe. Now's the time to call the police." He dialed 911 and told the dispatcher what had happened. "We're on VA-9 West. I think we just passed the Loudoun County Animal Shelter a few miles back."

"Is the vehicle that ran you off the road still visible?" the dispatcher asked.

"No, but he could be nearby. The visibility here is bad due to the snow."

"Stay put," the dispatcher said bluntly. "I've got a cruiser headed your way. Anybody injured? You need medical response?"

"No, we're okay," Jim assured her. Even Katie had stopped crying, save for a few soft sniffles now and then.

"I should get her out of the seat, shouldn't I?" Lacey asked, sounding almost helpless as she looked back at her scared niece.

"No, leave her there. We're off the road, but that doesn't mean we're safe. We all need to stay buckled in and alert." He didn't add that they also needed to keep their eyes peeled for the truck that had run them off the road. He didn't think Lacey needed the reminder.

"Was he trying to make us crash?" she asked a few minutes later as the snow started to fall faster than the windshield wipers could brush the flakes away. "Was that the point? If so, why hasn't he come back for us?"

"I don't know," Jim admitted. "Maybe he was surprised you weren't alone."

"Then why didn't he just drive on without bothering us?"

"Maybe it was too tempting a target to resist." Jim reached across the space between them to cover her hand where it gripped the steering wheel. "The police are on the way. We're all safe."

"Do you have your weapon?" she asked quietly, not pulling her hand away from his grasp.

"Yes."

Her jaw muscle tightened into a knot. "Good."

Moments later, swirling blue lights bled through the snowy void, and a Ford Taurus police interceptor marked with the Virginia State Police insignia loomed into view. The cruiser pulled up behind the Impala on the shoulder and a large black man in a tall black campaign hat and dark blue jacket over a gray uniform stepped from the driver's-side door, approaching the car carefully.

He took their information, including their driver's licenses for routine checks, before he returned to the car and bent to talk to Lacey through the lowered window. "If you think your vehicle can still drive, and you're up for it, I'll escort you to your residence to make sure nothing else happens to disturb your drive."

Jim gave the state policeman a look that didn't quite hide his surprise. "A personal escort home?"

The policeman met his quizzical look with a grim expression. "We don't like it when people get murdered in our state. We're all real sorry for your loss, Ms. Miles. We'd like to make sure you don't suffer any more, so I'll be escorting you home myself."

Jim exchanged a look with Lacey, who smiled at the policeman with genuine gratitude. "Thank you."

The drive home still took longer than it normally would have, since the snow showed little sign of letting up, but eventually, they turned onto the long driveway to the farmhouse without further incident. To Jim's surprise, the state policeman followed them up the drive, parking behind them when they pulled the Impala into the gravel area next to the house.

"I thought I'd take a look around inside, just to be sure nobody's been there while you were gone," said the policeman, whose name badge identified him as Epps. "If you'd like, you can wait out here until I'm done."

"No, we'll come in with you," Lacey said before Jim could insist on the same thing. Epps had been nothing but helpful, but Jim wasn't about to outsource his job of protecting Lacey and Katie to the policeman, however nice and helpful he might be.

Epps looked around the first floor, quickly reassuring himself that there were no signs of forced entry. "Mind if I take a look upstairs?"

"Jim will show you," Lacey said, cuddling Katie close. The little girl was eyeing the big policeman with a combination of wary shyness and curiosity, but she was showing signs of overstimulation, which in Katie led to tantrums. "I'll settle Katie down to finish her nap."

Jim left them reluctantly and joined Epps on the stairs. The policeman sidled a look Jim's way when he encountered the locked door.

"Ms. Miles's office. She's working from home these days, and since her reports can often deal in proprietary information..."

"Right," Epps said, not sounding convinced by Jim's explanation but apparently deciding it was none of his business. "I don't know that it'll help much for you to give your statements on what happened if you didn't get the license plate of the truck that hit you, but I'll be happy to file a report, in case we can track down the vehicle."

"Good idea," Jim agreed, and when they returned to the first floor, he and Lacey took turns telling Epps what they could remember about the vehicle that had tried to run them off the road.

"Ski mask?" Epps's dark eyebrows rose when Jim described what he'd seen.

"I know it sounds strange."

"I reckon *strange* is a relative thing when someone's already set a car bomb to take you out." Epps finished taking the report and got Jim to sign his statement. "We'll be in touch."

Jim locked the door behind Epps and headed down

the hall to Katie's room, where he found Lacey rocking her niece slowly in the rocking chair next to the crib. Katie was asleep, but Lacey showed no signs of letting the little girl go.

"It wasn't the same truck, was it?" she asked as Jim leaned against the door frame.

"I don't think so," he admitted. "It didn't hit me until I was telling Epps about the PIT maneuver. The blue truck we saw in the bomb-scene video had that dent in the driver's-side front panel. The truck that hit us this afternoon didn't."

"Probably does now," Lacey murmured, bleak humor in her voice. "I'm not sure what it means that it was a different truck. Any thoughts?"

"Maybe he bought a new truck."

"Same as the old truck?"

Jim shook his head. "Not likely, is it?"

"Maybe it's a different person," Lacey suggested. "But someone who wants us to think it's the same blue truck that's been following me."

Jim pulled the tufted ottoman that matched the rocker closer to where Lacey sat. His legs were far too long for the small footrest, but he perched there as well as he could and settled his gaze on Lacey and the sleeping child, his heart pounding a little harder at the memory of how close he'd come to losing them both that day.

"What would be the point of making us think it's the other truck?" he asked softly, unable to keep from reaching out to touch the velvet curve of Katie's cheek.

"I'm not sure," Lacey admitted. "Maybe to lead us off track? Misdirection of some sort?"

Jim dropped his hand away from Katie's face. "Focus

us in one direction so we don't see trouble coming from another one?"

"Maybe." Lacey's fingers followed the path Jim's had traced along Katie's plump cheek. "There's a more pertinent question, though."

He watched the slow glide of her fingers over Katie's skin, wishing she would reach across the space between them and touch him with that same tenderness.

Not that tenderness was all he wanted from her. Not by a long shot.

But he'd ruined his chances for more. It was time he learned to accept that fact.

"What question?" he asked when Lacey didn't immediately continue.

"I haven't told many people about the truck," she said quietly. "You know, of course, but I don't think you'd do anything to put Katie—or me—in danger."

"God, no."

"Your boss, but the same applies. They'd have no reason to put us in danger that way."

"Which leaves whom?"

"Detective Bolling at the Arlington County Police Department, and Detective Miller with the DC Metro Police. I told both of them about the truck. But nobody else."

"What about the cop in Frederick? You told me you saw the blue truck following you that day. Did you mention it to that detective?"

"No, I didn't. I'm sure I didn't, because I remember thinking later that day that I should have mentioned it, but I didn't."

"So you think our copycat truck driver was a cop?"

"Or someone one of those cops told about it."

Jim frowned, not liking the implications. Protecting

Lacey and Katie was hard enough with the cops on his side. But if one of them was working with the enemy...

"This seems like something the Whittiers would pull," Lacey said bluntly. "Maybe the point is to scare me, keep me so tangled up in the threats against me that I'm not poking my nose into their business."

"It's certainly not the sort of thing al Adar would bother with," Jim agreed. "But compared to a car bomb, what that truck did today is pretty mild."

"If he'd succeeded in driving us completely off the road, it could have been much worse. We could have been killed."

"I don't mean that what he did to us wasn't dangerous. Of course it was. But it wasn't a sure thing, the way that bomb was." He frowned, his mind racing through the possibilities. "If you really think about it, everything that's happened since the bombing has been weak in comparison. The mugging in Frederick. The truck following you all over DC."

"Ken Calvert was murdered," Lacey pointed out. "That's not exactly a downgrade."

"If his death was connected to what's been happening to you," Jim said. "We don't know that it was anything more than a mugging gone tragically wrong."

"It would be a hell of a coincidence."

"But coincidences do happen."

Lacey rose from the rocking chair, forcing Jim to rise as well and pull the ottoman out of her way. She carried Katie to the crib and gently laid her on the mattress, stroking Katie's hair when she stirred until the little girl drifted back to sleep. Putting her finger to her lips, she motioned for Jim to lead the way out of the nursery.

They ended up in the kitchen, facing each other

across the table. Outside, artificial twilight had fallen with the snow, reflecting their images back at them in the windowpanes.

"Maybe we've been going about this all wrong," Lacey said, resting her chin on her palm as she gazed wearily across the table at Jim.

"How's that?"

"We've assumed it's just one person after me. But I had three suspects."

"One of which we're pretty sure we eliminated today after talking to the Scanlons."

"But that still leaves two parties with a reason to want me out of the way." Lacey rose and crossed to the counter, coming to a stop in front of the coffeemaker. After a brief hesitation, she opened a cabinet, pulled out filters and a can of dark roast, and set about brewing a fresh pot of coffee.

Jim watched her going through the motions, realizing that she was one of those people who thought best when she was in action. He could almost see the wheels turning in her brain, moving in concert with her busy hands.

"I think whoever was driving the original blue truck, the one that showed up at the scene of the car bomb and later followed me to Frederick and then DC, has one agenda. The person in the truck today had another one." She finished filling the coffeemaker with water and turned to face him, looking as if she'd lost her train of thought when she finished her task of putting on a pot of coffee to brew.

"I agree," he said, rising to join her at the counter. "You hungry? I could use a snack."

"I'll get it," she said quickly, already heading for the refrigerator. "Cheese and fruit?"

"Perfect." He opened the cabinet and pulled out a couple of mugs for their coffee. "I've been thinking about the suspects on your list, and the ones who make the most sense, in terms of having access to police information and the means by which to produce a nearly identical truck, have to be the Whittiers."

She had gathered a bunch of grapes, a small bag of cherries and a couple of navel oranges from the refrigerator and deposited them on the counter by the sink. "They'd definitely have the means to come up with a blue pickup," she agreed as she started washing the fruit. "But that also suggests maybe they're not the ones who arranged for the bomb in my car, doesn't it?"

"Because of the de-escalation of attacks?"

"Exactly. The first strike was a deadly car bomb that would have killed me had I been driving that night." Her hands faltered as she pulled a clean cloth from a nearby drawer and laid the freshly washed fruit on the cloth to dry. "But the things that happened after that seem more like attempts to scare me rather than kill me. Like the mugger that day in Frederick. He could have shot me rather than tried to grab me. I had thought maybe he wanted to get me alone and start asking me questions, and maybe he did. But even that could have been meant to scare me."

"Maybe the blue truck that followed you that day really did have nothing to do with the mugger."

She retrieved a block of Havarti cheese from the crisper, carried it to the counter and started slicing. "Maybe not." She put down her knife suddenly, turning to look at him. "But if the guy in the blue truck set the bomb that killed Marianne and Toby, why hasn't he made another real attempt on my life?"

Chapter Thirteen

"How did you get these?" Lacey looked with skepticism at the pair of Quik-Trak train tickets Jim had set on the kitchen table at breakfast the next morning.

"Quinn had someone drop them by last night. You were already asleep."

She frowned. "Why does he think we should go to Connecticut? What will it accomplish?"

Jim sat beside Katie's high chair, retrieving a piece of orange that had escaped the baby's sticky grasp and landed on the table. "If nothing else, it'll change the paradigm."

"What does that even mean?" Lacey picked up the tickets and read the details. "Jim, this train leaves before seven tomorrow morning."

"I know. We need to start packing."

She felt rebellion rising in her chest. This was happening too fast and was completely out of her control. A man named Alexander Quinn had decided a trip to Connecticut to meet with the elusive Whittier brothers was in order, and suddenly she was holding two tickets on the train from Union Station to the station in Stamford, Connecticut, which was the closest town to the coastal Whittier family compound. "I need to think about this, Jim."

"I know I've just thrown this at you without any notice, but I think Quinn is right. We're sitting ducks out here, waiting for things to happen to us." He reached across the table and put his hand over hers. She felt a warm shock, as if he'd touched a live wire to her skin. Her fingers tingled in response, even though she knew the electric sensation was all in her head. "That's not the way I like to live my life. I don't think that's the way you like to live yours, either."

She wanted to argue with him, but on that subject, at least, he was right. She was a risk taker, an envelope pusher. She made things happen rather than waiting for things to happen to her.

"How are we supposed to convince the Whittiers to talk to us?"

"Quinn said he was working on that."

"So we go there without any plan?"

"It's better than sitting here twiddling our thumbs."

"What about Katie?" She forced herself to pull her hand from his warm, gentle grasp. She was letting herself get too close to him again, letting herself feel more than she wanted to, more than was safe.

"Remember the family I worked for, the Becketts? They've agreed to come out here to the farm for a couple of days to take care of Katie. They have a six-year-old daughter named Samantha, who will love spending a couple of days with Katie."

"I don't know these people."

"But I do." He leaned closer to her, capturing her gaze. "I would never do anything to put Katie in danger. I know you don't trust me anymore, and maybe you never will again. But you have to know at least that much about me. Don't you?"

His gaze ensnared her, blazing with the truth. He might have lied to her about who he really was and why he was there at the farmhouse with her and Katie, but she believed with every fiber of her being that he would take a bullet for her or Katie. "I know you'd never do anything to hurt her," she admitted softly.

"Cade Beckett is a retired Navy SEAL with more awards and commendations than you could fit on the wall of your office upstairs. His wife, Julie, was an FBI agent before she decided she was missing too much of her daughter's life and decided to take a consulting job with the Kentucky Bureau of Investigation so she could stay home with Samantha."

"They're willing to drop everything for a couple of days to babysit Katie?"

"Cade works for Campbell Cove Security. Coming here to stay with Katie is sort of his job. Julie works from home via computer, which she can do just as easily from here, as long as the Wi-Fi holds up. And she homeschools Samantha."

She looked at him through narrowed eyes, wondering if she was being played a little bit. "You have this all figured out."

"It wasn't my idea. That was all Quinn. But the more I think about it, the better I like it. I'm not sure it's good for Katie to be stuck out here with only us for companionship. Having Samantha around to play with her for a couple of days could be a good thing for Katie, as well."

"And meanwhile, we're standing at the gates of the Whittier compound yelling *Here we are, come get us*?"

"That's not exactly how I'd put it," Jim protested.

"But it's pretty close to how it will be, isn't it?" she asked, automatically picking up a napkin to wipe the orange juice from Katie's fingers before the little girl started to rub her drooping eyes. Funny, she realized, how she'd somehow transitioned from hapless aunt to practiced mother figure without even noticing it had happened.

She wasn't Katie's mother. She'd never be that, not really. She'd always make sure her niece knew all about Marianne and Toby, thought of them as her parents and never forgot she was their daughter.

But, for all intents and purposes, Lacey was truly Katie's parent now, and it had happened without her realizing it.

The urge to cry was suddenly overwhelming. She rose quickly to her feet and crossed to the window over the sink, gazing out at the snowy backyard as she fought against the tears beating at the backs of her eyes.

Behind her, she could hear the sounds of Jim taking charge of Katie, extracting her from the high chair and wiping up the remains of her breakfast of oatmeal and orange slices. When she brought her emotions back under control, she turned to watch him finish wiping orange juice from Katie's sticky hands with a wet cloth and lower the little girl to the floor.

"I'm going to take her outside to make another snowman," Jim said quietly, clearly pretending he hadn't noticed Lacey's struggle with her emotions. "I left the phone number for the Becketts on the table in the parlor in case you didn't keep my résumé. You may want to give them a call and talk to them yourself before you decide what to do."

"Thank you."

He gave a shrug as if to say it was no problem and herded Katie out of the kitchen.

She found the number Jim left for her and made the call. She had spoken to Cade Beckett when she'd called to check Jim's references, but this time, it was a woman who answered the phone. In the background, Lacey could hear a little girl laughing.

"Mrs. Beckett? This is Lacey Miles. Jim Mercer works for me as a nanny." Among other things.

"Oh, yes! He said you'd be calling." Julie Beckett's voice was low and warm, with just a hint of the Midwest in her accent. "He's told you about what Alexander Quinn proposed?"

"He did, but I'm not sure why you and your husband agreed."

"Because Jim told us about your situation. I'm sorry for your loss."

Unexpected tears pricked Lacey's eyes. Julie Beckett sounded genuinely sympathetic. "Thank you."

"Quinn told us you and Jim need to go out of town for a couple of days to investigate a lead, and you need someone to watch your niece."

"Yes. Katie's two. She can be a handful, and I don't want to put her in any more dangerous situations."

"I understand completely." Julie's voice softened as if she could sense Lacey's sudden vulnerability through the phone line. "I can give you references. For my FBI work, anyway."

"What field office?"

"Louisville for the past five years. I spent my rookie years at a variety of field offices and resident agencies."

Lacey knew an agent in the Louisville field office.

She'd give him a call later this morning. "When do you plan to get here?"

"It's about a seven-hour drive, so we were hoping to get on the road early today. Do we need to bring air beds? Samantha loves camping, so it wouldn't be a big deal if we need to rough it a little."

"It's a huge house with six bedrooms. I'll air out a couple of rooms for you." Was she really agreeing to having strangers come into her house and stay with her niece?

Yes, a treacherous little voice answered, *because they're Jim's friends and he trusts them.*

"I'm looking forward to meeting you. I'm a big fan of your reporting, and Jim speaks so highly of you."

"He speaks well of you, too. We'll have rooms ready for you when you arrive. I'll go shopping, too, so you'll have plenty of food in the pantry. Any food allergies I should know about?"

"No, we'll eat anything!" Julie laughed.

They worked through a few logistics before they hung up, and, despite her earlier misgivings, Lacey had begun to agree with Jim that having the Becketts come to the farm to watch Katie just might be a good idea.

BY THE TIME Cade and Julie Beckett arrived with their daughter, Samantha, Lacey and Jim had managed to wash and dry fresh linens for the guest bedrooms, and Jim had made a trip into town to pick up groceries.

Jim was looking forward to seeing the Becketts again, especially Samantha. He'd received a few letters and cards from her and the Becketts since he'd left their employ, but it wasn't the same as seeing them every day. He'd jumped in when their previous nanny quit to get married, and he'd begun to feel as if he was part of the family. While he'd understood Julie's decision to work from home so she could be with Samantha, he hadn't been happy about looking for a new job.

"When I left the Marine Corps," he confessed to Lacey over lunch, "I was at loose ends. I had joined up thinking it was a life about as far from my crazy, close-knit family as I could get, and at that time in my life, I guess, that was the escape I'd needed. But after a few years, I knew that I wouldn't be happy doing that kind of work. I missed being part of a family. My own brother and sisters are all grown up, and while we see each other on holidays, it's not the same."

"You thought working with children would help you recapture that feeling?" Lacey observed him over the rim of her coffee cup, her gray eyes sharp, making him feel as if she were trying to read the emotions behind his words. It was a disconcerting sensation but also a strangely welcome one. Her curiosity suggested she wanted to know what made him tick.

Maybe that was a good sign. If she cared what he thought, maybe she could eventually forgive his lies of omission.

"I thought it might. It didn't really fill in all the gaps in my life, but it did make me realize that what I'd been running from when I joined the Marine Corps was the life I really want. A home. Wife and kids and maybe a dog in the backyard or a cat or two."

Lacey's lips curved in the first genuine smile he'd seen from her in what seemed like days. "Domestic bliss?"

"More like the knowledge that there's somewhere in the world you belong, no matter how far you roam."

A suspicious brightness glittered in her eyes, and

she blinked a couple of times as if to keep tears from forming. Her gaze settled on her niece's face. "Katie is that for me now. You know?"

Katie looked up at Lacey and grinned around her bite of cheese sandwich, making Lacey laugh.

"I know," he said, reaching across the table to cover her hand with his. She didn't pull away. Progress. "Julie and Cade will take good care of her. They're both trained to handle dangerous situations. She couldn't be in better hands. And she'll love playing with Samantha."

"Mantha!" Katie repeated with another big grin. Jim and Lacey had prepared her for the arrival of their visitors, and she was almost as excited to see the Becketts as Jim was.

The phone rang as she and Jim were cleaning up the kitchen after lunch. It was Detective Miller of the DC Metro Police. "I thought you'd want to know, we've made an arrest in the Ken Calvert murder case."

Lacey gripped the phone more tightly, looking across the kitchen at Jim. "Who killed him?"

"His ex-wife. She confessed an hour ago to hiring someone to shoot him. They were tangled up in a custody battle over their two kids, and it looks like the ex–Mrs. Calvert decided killing him was easier than coming to some sort of agreement."

"My God. How awful."

"Yeah, ain't love grand?" Miller's flat tone suggested he'd seen too many senseless murders in the course of his police career. "Thought you'd want to know."

"Thanks for calling." She hung up and turned to Jim. "It looks like Ken Calvert's murder really was a coincidence. His ex-wife hired someone to kill him. She just confessed."

"My dad used to say, always look at the spouse first." Jim folded the dish towel he'd used to wipe the table and laid it on the counter. "Well, at least it's one loose end tied up."

"Yeah, but poor Ken. And those poor kids." Lacey looked at Katie, who was sitting in the corner of the kitchen, trying to get the top off her empty sippy cup. "The death of a parent is never fair to the kids."

"Yeah," Jim said with a sigh. "I know."

"But I still don't know what Ken was going to tell me." She sighed. "What if it was important?"

Jim put his hand on her shoulder, leveling his gaze with her. "Then we'll find out another way."

The Becketts arrived a little after three that afternoon, rumpled from the long drive but smiling as soon as they saw Jim in the open doorway. After a round of hugs, Jim introduced them to Lacey and Katie.

Julie was a tall, slim woman with a shoulder-length bob of shiny dark hair and eyes the color of black coffee. She spoke with a soft Midwest accent and was quick with a smile. Her husband, Cade, was tall, fit and quiet, with sharp blue eyes beneath a rusty buzz cut that made him look as if he was fresh out of boot camp.

As expected, Samantha and Katie took to each other immediately, heading outside with Cade to play in the snow that lingered in the yard from the snowfall the day before.

Julie stayed behind, happily accepting a cup of hot chocolate at the kitchen table. "Anything new happen while we were on the road?"

"No, just handling all the last-minute details." Jim glanced at Lacey. She met his gaze calmly enough, but he could see thoughts sparking behind her eyes. This must be what she looked like when she sniffed out a hot new story, he thought. Part excited, part anxious and part pure, gritty nerve.

"There's a guy I know in Stamford," Julie said in a casual tone that Jim knew was anything but casual. "His name is Mickey Grimes, and he used to be in the Bureau. He left the FBI a few years ago, but if there's anybody in Connecticut who can get you a meeting with one of the Whittier brothers, it's Mickey."

Lacey apparently picked up the undertones in Julie's words. "He left the FBI...of his own volition?"

"He was encouraged to retire early." Julie shrugged one shoulder. "He's not squeaky clean, but he's also not a monster. He's been working security for Justin Whittier for the past couple of years. He's loyal to Whittier, but his loyalty doesn't extend to condoning murder."

"Are you sure?"

"Yes." Julie took a long sip of her hot chocolate, as if she was carefully considering her next words. "I know you think that the Whittiers are being treated as untouchables, but the FBI was investigating them both at the time I left the Bureau. There are details I'm not at liberty to share with you, but I can tell you this much. Of the two brothers, Carson is the wild card. Justin has secrets, but they're personal, not criminal. And from a few things Mickey let drop the last time I talked to him, I think Justin may be getting a little tired of being lumped in with his brother's misadventures."

"So if Mickey could get us a face-to-face meeting with Justin Whittier..." Jim began.

"He might be willing to tell you whether or not the threats against you are coming from his family. Just to get it off his chest." Julie set her cup down on the table in front of her. "I'd better go see what my crew is up to," she said with a smile that belied the seriousness of the previous conversation. She gave Jim's shoulder an affectionate pat and headed out to retrieve her coat from the mudroom.

"I like her," Lacey said bluntly.

"I knew you would." Jim gathered up the empty hot-chocolate cups and put them in the dishwasher. "She was a real go-getter in the FBI. Driven to succeed. Reminds me of you."

"That's how you see me?" Lacey gave him a thoughtful look. "A go-getter, driven to succeed?"

"Isn't that what you are?" He leaned his hips against the kitchen counter, folded his arms over his chest and met her gaze. "It's not a bad thing."

"Julie left that life behind to be with her daughter."

"She did."

"Nobody at my office expects me to do that for Katie, you know." She stood and crossed to the window over the sink, close enough that Jim could feel the warmth of her body wafting over him. She gazed out at the backyard, where the Becketts and Katie were finishing up a small lopsided snowman. It had taken nearly all of the two-inch snowfall in the yard to build, but Katie wouldn't be denied. "They're surprised I haven't already returned to work, if you want to know the truth. I can hear it in their voices when I call in for my messages. They're confused and worried that I haven't met their expectations."

"Do you think you're ready to go back?"

She shook her head. "I thought I'd be climbing the walls here by the end of the first week, but it's turned out to be much more comfortable than I'd anticipated. I've had my own investigation into the car bombing to keep me occupied, of course. I suppose that might be part of the reason I haven't been as restless as I thought I'd be. But I don't miss the hustle and bustle of the newsroom, and I really thought I would."

"I don't miss the Marine Corps the way I thought I would, either. Change is constant, and it doesn't have to be a bad thing."

Lacey gave him another thoughtful look, then turned back to the window, her gaze following Katie as the little girl ran ecstatic circles around the off-kilter snowman.

THE TRAIN ARRIVED in Stamford on time, shortly before noon. On the busy concourse, a stocky man with thinning black hair stood with a sign that read "Jim Mercer."

Lacey pointed out the man to Jim as they grabbed their overnight cases. "That must be Mickey Grimes." At Jim's request, Julie Beckett had called Grimes to set up a meeting with him once they arrived in Stamford. Instead, Grimes had insisted on meeting their train.

"Do you think we're crazy to trust him?"

"I'm not sure I'd call this trust," Jim murmured, draping the canvas strap of his overnight bag over his shoulder. "But Grimes has access to the Whittiers. We need that access."

Grimes flashed a friendly smile when he spotted their approach. But Lacey perceived a certain wariness there as well, as if he realized he was walking a thin edge between honest work and illegal activity. When they were close enough, he spoke in a quiet tone. "Justin Whittier is waiting in his limousine. He wants to speak to you. But I have to search you for weapons and wires before he'll talk to you. He's arranged for a room where we can conduct the search."

"That's out of the question." Jim's tone was tight with fury.

Lacey put a hand on his arm. "I'm willing to meet that requirement."

Jim looked at her, frustration seething in his hazel-green eyes. Whatever he saw in her expression seemed to calm his anger, for he simply nodded.

The room Grimes took them to looked to be little more than a closet a few dozen yards down the concourse from where they'd exited the train. Grimes entered first, took a quick look around as if to ensure that they were alone, then nodded for them to follow.

Inside, the room was crowded and smelled of antiseptic. Bottles on a shelf at the back of the room suggested it might be a place where the train station stored cleaning supplies.

"Either of you armed?"

"No," Jim answered.

"Lift your shirts."

Lacey did so without hesitation. She had gone through more humiliating searches during her reporting career, conducted by men who were far less businesslike about the process.

Jim grimaced as he showed Grimes he wasn't wearing a wire. "Does Justin Whittier require this sort of degradation from everyone he talks to?"

Grimes didn't answer. "Let's go.

They followed him out of the station to a long black limousine parked in what should have been a no-parking zone. But if the security personnel at the Amtrak station had noticed, they showed no sign of trying to move the vehicle along. There was a driver standing outside the passenger compartment doors, apparently awaiting their arrival.

"You can leave your bags here. Jaffe will watch them for you," Grimes said as they reached the vehicle.

Reluctantly, Lacey set her bag on the curb in front of the driver. Jim did the same as Grimes opened the car door and waved them into the limo.

Jim went first, pausing for a moment, blocking the door. After a moment, he continued into the car, turning to give Lacey a warning look.

"In," Grimes said firmly when she considered making a run for it.

Reluctantly, she stepped into the limousine and sat next to Jim, who was staring at the occupants of the bench seat opposite them. Lacey found herself face-to-face with Justin Whittier and another man she'd never seen before. But what arrested her attention about the stranger was the bruise on his cheek that matched almost perfectly the bruise on her own cheek where she'd hit the window of the SUV when the blue truck had tried to run them off the road.

"Ms. Miles, a pleasure to finally meet you," Justin Whittier said smoothly. He had a cultured, easy tone, nearly accent-free, and if he found anything worrisome about this impromptu meeting, he hid it well.

"I think we both know this has nothing to do with pleasure," she said flatly. Beside her, Jim's body felt tightly sprung, as if he was just waiting to jump into action. She hoped that wouldn't be necessary.

"Perhaps not. Nevertheless, I want to make an apology on behalf of my brother, Carson. I believe he may have been involved in the accident you had a couple of days ago."

Chapter Fourteen

Justin Whittier looked sincerely apologetic, but Jim knew better than to take anyone, especially a politician, at face value.

"Can you be more specific about your brother's involvement in the accident?" he asked, his voice taut with rising anger. Who the hell did this man think he was, pulling a stunt like this? Did he think the show of power and wealth would impress him or Lacey in the slightest?

Maybe he was used to getting what he wanted just by waving a few bills or favors in people's faces. It had gotten him this far, apparently.

"Carson's involvement was, I'd like to assure you, entirely inadvertent. I'd like to apologize for my brother's judgment in employees, for one thing." Whittier looked at the man sitting beside him. "Morris? Would you like to tell Ms. Miles what you did?"

The man named Morris slanted a furious look at Whittier before he schooled his features—though not without visible effort—into a look of regret. "Mr. Whittier asked me to find a way to discourage you from continuing your investigation into his congressional run," Morris said in a meek tone that Jim was pretty sure he'd never used before. His accent was pure Brooklyn, and his bulky build suggested he might have been hired more for his muscle than any particular talent.

Lacey nodded toward his bruise. "You drove the Toyota Tacoma that ran us off the road the other day."

Morris's only answer was a grudging nod.

"Morris has, of course, been released from my brother's employ, and we will be happy to pay for any repairs to your vehicle and other costs incurred, with the understanding that our name must never be connected to the payment."

"There's no need. I can't be bought," Lacey said flatly. "In lieu of the payment, I'd like a truthful answer to one question—who told Mr. Morris to drive a blue Toyota Tacoma to run me off the road?"

Whittier looked honestly puzzled, and for once, Jim was inclined to believe him. He looked at Morris, who turned his gaze to Mickey Grimes.

"I'm afraid that might be my doing," Grimes said ruefully. "See, I have a friend in the Arlington County police department, and he told me about the video of one of the Whittier limos passing by the crime scene the night of the car bombing."

"Forgive me," Whittier interrupted. "I should have said this earlier. I am truly sorry for your loss. I lost a younger brother when I was in my teens, and it was a devastating blow. I can sympathize with your grief."

"Thank you," Lacey said, her voice tight with impatience. She turned to look at Grimes. "You were saying about the limousine?"

"My friend in Arlington wondered if I could tell him why one of the Whittiers was in the area that night, and I explained that Mr. Carson had a meeting with some donors nearby that evening. He accepted my answer and told me it was a formality. It seems the police were a little more interested in a blue Toyota Tacoma that was also in the area and was believed to be following you around since the bombing."

"And you shared this information with Morris?" Jim asked through gritted teeth.

"Well, Mr. Carson, actually, but Morris was there."

"I thought it would distract you, send you looking in another direction rather than bothering Mr. Carson and Mr. Justin all the time," Morris growled, looking less and less apologetic by the minute.

"Please accept my apology on behalf of my brother and his former employee," Whittier said. "You could have been badly hurt by his idiotic stunt, and I'm deeply grateful that you seem to have incurred no lasting damage."

Lacey was silent a moment, but Jim could feel the vibration of her anger sending tremors through her slim body. She finally spoke, in a voice rattling with rage. "My two-year-old niece was in that vehicle, Mr. Whittier. She could have easily been hurt or even killed. What your brother's employee did, no doubt with your brother's approval, could have resulted in first-degree murder. Do you understand that? Do you even care?"

"I assure you, my brother knew nothing of Morris's plans. Morris will not receive any further payment from anyone in my family, nor will he receive any sort of recommendation for future employment, and if asked, we will certainly inform potential employers of his reckless lack of judgment."

"What about the attack in Frederick?" Lacey asked.

Jim looked at her, surprised. She was looking at Morris, her gaze narrowed. He held her gaze, anger in his eyes, but he said nothing.

"What attack in Frederick?" Justin Whittier seemed genuinely surprised.

"Your brother's associate here—"

"Ex-associate," Whittier corrected.

"Whoever. He's the man who attacked me in Frederick."

Jim stared at her, wondering if she was bluffing. But she looked utterly confident in what she was saying.

"You see, he may have been wearing a mask, but when I hit him with the tire iron from my trunk, he let fly a stream of invective that would have made a long-shoreman blush. He had a rather distinctive voice. With a Brooklyn accent."

Whittier shot a black look at Morris before he looked back at Lacey with an expression so bland Jim almost thought he'd imagined the previous anger he'd seen in the man's face.

"I'm sure you must be mistaken. Is that the only evidence you can supply of Morris's alleged involvement in an attack on you?"

Lacey's lips pressed into a thin line that Jim knew meant she was pissed, but she merely nodded.

"Well, you can see the dilemma, then. Despite our conversation here today, there is no evidence that Morris was involved in the attack on you in Frederick, or that he caused your unfortunate accident. My brother and I have no knowledge of the whereabouts or even the existence of the blue Tacoma in question. You can see the difficulty in pursuing legal charges against Morris, since I'm certain that Morris will not be so willing to tell the police what he told you today."

Morris muttered a profane agreement.

"My hands are tied, legally at least. This is the best reparation I can offer you, and I do so at some risk, considering your career as a journalist. I am hoping that you understand the need for discretion, as you have no evidence to back up anything you might want to share about this situation."

"She has me as a witness," Jim said bluntly.

Justin Whittier turned his cool blue gaze to Jim. "Yes. Ms. Miles's recently employed nanny." He spoke the last word with a touch of pure disdain, which did nothing to cool the anger rising in Jim's chest.

"And a decorated Marine Corps sergeant with connections to a lot of people in high places," he snapped, leveling his gaze with Whittier's.

For a second, Whittier's placid facade slipped, revealing a look of alarm and, quick on its heels, anger. But he quickly brought his expression back under control. "What exactly do you propose?"

"Mutual assured destruction. Of a sort." Jim leaned a little closer to Whittier, using his size and his gritty anger as a weapon of intimidation.

Next to Lacey, Grimes started to move toward the escalating confrontation, but Lacey grabbed his arm, holding him in place. She nodded at Jim to continue.

"We have the information we need about what happened on that snowy road in Virginia. And the added information about what happened in Frederick. If any further threat arises from your family or their employees, we will not hesitate to tell the police everything we know, including your attempt to bribe us into silence."

"That was *not* a bribe attempt," Justin protested.

Jim ignored him. "In exchange for your promise that

no harm or trouble will come Ms. Miles's way from your family and associates, we will not share this information with the authorities."

"What about Ms. Miles's investigation into my family's affairs?"

Jim shrugged. "I am not authorized to make any promises to that end."

"I am a reporter," Lacey said flatly. "If you or your family makes news, I am obligated to report it and to do so thoroughly and without prejudice. I will make no promises that would impede me from doing so."

Justin looked at her through narrowed eyes as if considering her words carefully. Finally, his expression cleared, and he nodded. "Fair enough. It is my hope that Carson has learned his lesson about his choices for employees." His voice grew steely. "If not, he is on his own."

"Are we done here?" Jim asked, looking not at Justin Whittier but at Mickey Grimes.

Stone-faced, Grimes nodded. He opened the door of the limousine and stepped out, allowing them to disembark, as well. He gave a polite nod to the driver, who opened the driver's door and slid in behind the steering wheel. Grimes stepped back into the limousine, gave Jim and Lacey a parting salute, and closed the door just as the limousine pulled away from the curb.

Jim looked down at the luggage at his feet and blew out a long breath. "Well, that was deeply dissatisfying."

Lacey lifted her bag, swinging the strap over her shoulder. "I don't know. It answered a lot of questions and kept us from chasing those particular wild geese." She nodded toward the concourse. "We could exchange our tickets for tomorrow's train for one this afternoon.

Cancel our hotel reservations and be back in Cherry Grove by dinnertime."

"We could," he agreed. "Or we could find a nice restaurant here in town, get some lunch and maybe use this baby-free time to revise and rework your suspect list."

She looked at him through narrowed eyes, as if weighing her options with care. Finally, the furrows that creased her brow disappeared, and she smiled. "It might be nice to be able to brainstorm this investigation without having to stop every few minutes to tend to a toddler." Immediately she looked guilty. "God, that sounded terrible. I adore Katie, you know I do."

He put his hands on her shoulders, bending toward her. "I do know. But you're right. It's nice to have a break from being a parent. And it's good for Katie, too, to be interacting with people outside her immediate family. So don't feel guilty. Take advantage of the break to reconnect with who you are outside of Katie."

She cocked her head. "Did you get that out of some child-rearing self-help book?"

He grinned. "Maybe."

She let out a long sigh and smiled back. "There's supposed to be an amazing sushi place on Main Street. How do you feel about raw fish?"

"Not quite as adventurous as some of the things I ate in Afghanistan, but I'm game."

Lacey nodded toward the taxi stand a few yards down the concourse. "Then let's hail a cab, stash our bags at the hotel and go eat some sushi."

THE NEREID LIVED UP to the rave reviews a couple of Lacey's fellow reporters had given it. The sushi rolls were fresh and delicious, and the miso soup was as close to the homemade miso soup she'd consumed on her last trip to Japan as she'd tasted on this side of the globe.

The company wasn't bad, either. They'd been shown to a table near the restaurant's glass front, and the afternoon sunlight slanting through the windows bathed Jim's face in golden light that seemed to highlight just what an attractive man he was.

Pretending she didn't find him nearly irresistible was only making things worse for her, she knew. She'd drop her guard and then he'd say something or do something or, hell, just look at her a particular way and she'd be gut punched by just how tempting a man he really was.

But she couldn't trust him. She couldn't. He'd come into her life on the basis of a lie and hadn't told her the truth until it was clear he'd been found out. What kind of basis was that for any sort of honest, sustainable relationship?

And in what position was she these days to have any sort of relationship with any man? She was still grieving her sister, still trying to sort out the tatters of her life, trying to figure out how to be a mother to her orphaned niece. What man would want to be part of that upheaval?

Jim, a treacherous voice in her head whispered. *Jim would want to be part of that upheaval.*

"There's that little crease," Jim said, looking at her over a cup of hot tea. The delicate porcelain cup looked ridiculously out of place in his big hand, but he didn't seem to notice the incongruity.

"What crease?" she asked, trying not to remember how gentle those big, strong hands could be when he touched her.

"The one between your eyebrows. It means you're

worrying about something you can't figure out." He sat back in his chair, setting the cup on the table. "So, want to tell Uncle Jim what's bothering you?"

"Just this mess Katie and I are in," she lied. It should be what was bothering her instead of what she wanted to do about her ridiculous crush on Jim Mercer.

"Take an hour's break from all that. You're in lovely Stamford, Connecticut, with nothing pressing to do until seven tomorrow morning."

"What are you suggesting? That we take a drive down to Cove Island Park and take a bunch of selfies to send to our families and friends?"

"Interesting that Cove Island Park is where your mind went immediately. Ever been there?" he asked.

She shook her head. "No. Have you?"

"Yes, actually." His smile softened with the memory. "I was maybe four years into my Marine Corps career, and my little sister Jen was a junior at Yale. At the time, I was assigned to a ship that had docked in the New York Harbor during Fleet Week. Jen had just finished her final exams and was planning to join a friend the next week for a trip to London and Paris, so it was our only chance to see each other. A buddy of mine who had family in the Bronx talked them into letting me borrow a car to drive to Stamford so I could meet Jen halfway. She packed a picnic and we spent the day in Cove Island Park, catching up on each other's lives." He sighed, some of the softness in his expression fading into melancholy. "Kids. They don't call, they don't write…"

"Where is Jen now?"

"Happily married to a brilliant surgeon at Johns Hopkins. Which she also happens to be. She's the poster child for success." His smile of pride was downright incandescent. "She calls every week or two, just to rub it in."

Lacey laughed. "What about the others?"

"Richard is a graphic designer for an ad agency in Knoxville, Tennessee, where he attended college. Huge Tennessee fan, which is bearable only because his beloved Vols and my beloved Tar Heels are in two different football conferences." He smiled. "And Hallie just got her master's in genetics from Princeton and is about to start her doctoral classes at Harvard. Thank God for full scholarships, huh?"

"You come from a family of overachievers, apparently."

Jim grinned. "I do. They make me look like a total slacker. At least my mom thinks I'm brilliant and perfect."

Lacey smiled. "Sounds like maybe you are. Your brother and sisters got where they are because of you. You're the one who stepped in when they needed someone to be their parent, even though you were just a kid yourself. You gave them the love and support they needed to fly."

Jim laughed. "Don't build me up too high here. Mom was still there, even if she had to work a lot of long hours. And goodness knows I made a lot of mistakes."

"Everybody does, right? But you didn't quit on those kids. You stuck with them until they were ready to make it on their own." To her surprise, she felt tears prick her eyes. Maybe a few for Jim and the life he'd led, but also a few for herself. For her own upended life and the hard new changes she was learning to make.

Would Katie end up nearly as well as Jim's brother

and sisters had? She hoped so. She hoped she would give Katie the love and support Marianne and Toby would have if they'd lived.

Jim reached across the table and took her hand, twining his fingers with hers. She knew she should pull her hand away, but she just couldn't bring herself to do it. "Let's rent a car and drive down to Cove Island Park." His voice was pure, raw seduction.

Now. Now was the time to pull away and say no. It was a crazy idea, for one thing. Despite the bright afternoon sunlight, the day was frigidly cold. And the last thing she needed was more alone time with Jim Mercer. She just had to open her mouth and say no. Period. End of story.

But what came out when she opened her mouth was "Let's do it."

Jim's smile in response came complete with dimples and a wicked glint in his eyes that made her stomach clench with nervous anticipation. "You won't regret it."

But she knew she probably would.

THE DAY WAS much colder than the warm day in late May when Jim and his sister Jen had shared a picnic lunch and walked along the shoreline catching up on all the things they'd missed in each other's lives. But Jim and Lacey had brought warm coats and sturdy walking shoes, so they fared well enough in the waning warmth of the afternoon sun.

Halfway through their walk along the beach, Jim reached for Lacey's hand, expecting her to pull away from his touch. But she merely curled her fingers around his and edged a little closer, until he could feel her warmth cutting through the brisk wind blowing over the water.

She finally gave his hand a tug and came to a stop, turning to look up at him. He was tall enough to block the sunlight making her squint, but enough of the light bathed her face to give her the golden glow of a sea goddess rising from the depths.

That, he thought, was an embarrassingly romantic notion. But he couldn't quite regret it, or the way her hand in his made him feel happy and at peace, despite the turmoil of life around them.

"We need to head back if we're going to get any brainstorming done." Was that a hint of disappointment he heard in her voice?

"I know."

"I'm glad we came here, though." She lifted her face to the breeze, let it blow her hair behind her in glittering golden strands. "It feels sort of magical, you know?"

"I know." He couldn't stop himself from lifting one hand to her cheek, pressing his palm to her cool flesh, letting her hair twist around his fingertips.

"Like anything could happen." She had moved closer, her body scant inches from his. Her gaze wandered away from his to settle on his mouth. "Anything at all."

He lowered his mouth slowly, giving her a chance to pull back. But, instead of moving away, she closed the dwindling distance between them, her lips pressing soft and warm against his mouth.

Magical, he thought, silently echoing her words as he deepened the kiss, tasting the sweet tea and wasabi spice on her tongue. She wrapped her arms around his neck, pressing closer, as if seeking to become part of him the way he wanted to meld himself to her.

It was perfect. It was right. He felt as if all the missing pieces of himself had suddenly fallen into place and he was whole again, the way he hadn't been whole since his father's death. Was such a thing possible? Or was he letting his desire for her, his need to be closer to her, fool him into believing there was more to their connection than really existed.

They'd known each other for days, not months. Surely this sort of feeling took time to build, to grow, to strengthen into something lasting.

And yet, when she curled her fingers through his hair and held him in place while she answered him, kiss for kiss, he felt that nothing in the world could be more right, more lasting, more perfect for him than being with Lacey Miles every day for the rest of his life.

He pulled away first, overwhelmed by the emotions galloping through him, emotions he didn't trust and couldn't reconcile to the reality of his life. Or hers.

She gazed up at him, her expression slightly dazed and wholly recognizable, as if the emotions still beating at his heart like hammer blows were echoing inside her, as well.

"I think we should catch a train home tonight," she whispered.

He nodded. "You're right."

They walked back to the visitor parking lot slowly, not touching, maintaining enough distance that Jim couldn't even feel the heat of her body between him and the sea breeze. But he felt her regardless, felt the steady beat of her presence like a pulse inside his chest.

She was inside him, somehow, a part of him that he might never be able to excise.

He didn't know whether that thought thrilled him or terrified him.

Chapter Fifteen

It was after midnight by the time Jim drove the Jeep into the gravel parking area at the side yard of the farmhouse. The house was dark except for the light shining in the front parlor, golden and welcoming.

Cade and Julie Beckett were still awake, forewarned by a call from Lacey before she and Jim got on the train back to DC. "How'd the trip go?" Cade asked cautiously, as if well aware that their early return might be the result of either good news or bad.

"A mixed bag," Lacey answered, stifling a yawn. "We've eliminated the Whittiers as the car bombers, at least."

"But?" Julie probed.

"But they also provided explanations for a couple of the incidents I've experienced in the past few weeks."

"Which means there's still a threat to Lacey and Katie," Jim growled, "and we're no closer to knowing who's behind that threat than we were before we went to Connecticut."

Lacey barely resisted the impulse to reach out and take his clenched fist in her hand, to gently ease his tension with her touch. Things between them had escalated rapidly at Cove Island Park, not just physically but emotionally. And it was the emotional connection growing between them that scared her to death.

"Well, I have a new lead for you to follow. Maybe." Julie pulled out her phone and ran her finger across the screen as if searching for something. "While y'all were gone, I contacted a friend of mine, Lanny Copeland, who's a special agent with the Richmond field office. I had this vague memory of a BOLO he'd sent out a few months back about a group of young men from Kaziristan who'd disappeared suddenly right before their student visas expired."

"Sleeper cell?" Jim asked, his muscles twitching as if Julie's words had put him on high alert. Lacey felt her earlier sleepiness drop away as curiosity and a touch of alarm took its place.

"Well, they haven't been considered terrorism suspects, exactly. They all seemed like normal students, westernized and showing no signs of trouble or radicalization. It was really just the fact that they all dropped from the radar right before they were scheduled to return to Kaziristan that pinged Lanny's radar. Okay, here we go." She handed her phone carefully to Lacey. "Does anything in that photo look familiar to you?"

The photo on Julie's phone was a shot of the front of a low-rent apartment complex. The angle was close up on two adjacent apartment doors, numbered 314 and 315, and the paved parking lot in front of the apartments. In the parking slot in front of the apartments were two vehicles, a black panel van that looked to be twenty years old and a later-model blue truck.

A ripple of recognition skated up Lacey's spine. "That's the truck."

"Ever since y'all told me about that truck, it's been

nagging at my brain. It seemed so familiar, but I couldn't quite place it, until suddenly I remembered that BOLO for those students and their vehicles. Fortunately, I'd saved the photo to my phone. So I took a look. Sure enough, it fits what you described. Blue Toyota Tacoma, later model, with a dent in the left front panel."

Jim edged closer, looking at the photo over Lacey's shoulder. He felt warm and solid beside her, his nearness easing some of the nervous tension roiling inside her. "Should I call Quinn?" he asked Lacey.

"Already done," Cade said bluntly. He glanced at Lacey. "Sorry if that was presumptuous."

"No, I think the more hands on deck, the better." Kaziri nationals gone missing just before their visas expired could very well mean al Adar was placing sleeper cells in the United States, just as law enforcement had begun to fear.

"He's calling in support from the DC area, but it will probably be morning before anyone can get here." Cade shot them an apologetic look.

"There's one more thing," Julie said, directing her words to Lacey. Her expression held sympathy, but the emotion Lacey saw in the other woman's eyes was darker, angrier. "I called Lanny to tell him about the truck. I explained why I'd thought about it, and he told me something that the FBI hadn't been sharing with other agencies yet. It seems that when the students went missing, something else went missing, as well."

"What's that?"

"Two dozen boxes of screws and ball bearings from the hardware store where one of them worked."

Lacey's knees wobbled. "Oh."

Jim put his arm around her and pulled up one of the

chairs across from the sofa. Lacey sat, clenching her hands together as a cold chill ran through her.

"Around the same time, there was an incident at a construction site in southern Maryland. A fire started in a storage area for explosives used to clear large boulders out of road-construction sites. There was a storm that night, and nobody could be sure that one of the lightning strikes in the area hadn't hit the storage site, but of course the FBI had to investigate. The security guard in charge of patrolling the site sustained a concussion, possibly from flying debris from the blast. He doesn't remember anything, including a lightning strike or anything else."

"So it was ruled an accident?"

"Actually, it was ruled inconclusive evidence of a man-made event, but the FBI hasn't ruled out the possibility of human involvement. You see, when the explosives storage hut went up in flames, the resulting blast wasn't quite as large as experts might have expected, leading them to wonder if there might have been substantially less explosive material in the hut than reported."

"Meaning it might have been stolen before the fire destroyed the evidence," Jim said. "Do you know what explosives were stored there?"

"Semtex," Julie answered. She looked at Lacey. "Is that what was used in the explosion that killed your sister?"

"I don't know. The police haven't released that information to the public."

"There aren't that many explosives that would be used in a car bomb, and Semtex is relatively easy to obtain. It just makes sense."

"The car bomb was also packed with ball bearings and sheet-metal screws," Lacey added.

"Which could also be found at a construction site," Jim said.

"That's a hell of a lot of coincidences," Cade muttered.

"Listen, we're not going to solve the mystery of the missing Kaziri students or the purloined explosives tonight," Jim said, his hand warm and firm on Lacey's shoulder. "Let's try to get some sleep and pick this up again in the morning, okay?"

"We think Julie should take Samantha and Katie back to Kentucky with her in the morning." Cade looked at Lacey. "The girls don't need to be here if there's trouble on the way."

"Maybe Lacey should go with them," Jim suggested.

"No way," Lacey said with a shake of her head. "I'm their target, not Katie and not Julie or Samantha. They'd go after us on the way to Kentucky."

"As much as I hate to duck out just when the action starts, I think Lacey's right. It's safest for the girls if she stays here with y'all. By morning, hopefully Quinn will have people here to shore up the security."

"Let's all get to bed, then," Jim said, giving Lacey's shoulder a squeeze. "Tomorrow will be a long day, no doubt."

While Cade and Julie headed down the hall to the guest bedroom, Lacey joined Jim as he went from window to window, door to door, to make sure the place was locked down tightly for the night. When Jim turned out the light in the parlor, plunging the house into darkness, the world outside the window seemed unnaturally bright as the blanket of snow shed an artificial glow across the darkened landscape.

"One good thing," she murmured. "It won't be easy to sneak up on us in all that snow."

"Famous last words." Jim's statement was a grim rumble in the darkness.

THE PHONE RANG just as Jim was starting to release all the tension of the long day and settle into a light doze. The trill shocked him awake, and it took a second to realize what he'd heard.

The number on the display was unfamiliar, and Jim almost hit the ignore button, but the fact that it was a local number gave him pause. He swept his finger across the phone and answered. "Jim Mercer."

"I know it's late," the woman's voice on the other end of the call said without preamble. "I wouldn't have called you except you told me to let you know if anything strange happened."

He tried to place the voice, which sounded familiar. "Who is this?"

"Oh, I'm sorry. It's Charlotte. From the diner in town? I'm the one who told you about that fellow poking around and you gave me your card with your phone number."

"Right." He sat up in his bed, rubbing his fingers through his hair as he tried to wake up. "Has something happened?"

"I'm not sure." She sounded nervous now, as if she'd made the call on impulse and was now second-guessing the decision. "It's probably nothing. You know how small towns can be—everything strange must be a conspiracy. I shouldn't have bothered you so late."

"Charlotte," he said patiently, "tell me why you called."

"Well, now that I think of it, it's silly. And I wouldn't have even seen it if I hadn't gotten up to check and make sure I turned off the oven downstairs in the shop."

"What did you see?"

"It was just odd, you see. We're a little town, and we don't get a lot of traffic coming through the area at this time of night. But while I was down in the shop, I saw four trucks drive by, one after the other, almost like a convoy, you know? It was odd enough that I went outside and watched them go, and one by one, they all took the turn down the road toward the farm. You sure don't get much through traffic, so I thought—"

Her voice cut off suddenly. Jim looked down at his phone and saw that there was no cell signal.

What the hell?

He pulled a pair of jeans out of his dresser drawer and pulled them on, sleep fleeing, replaced by instant alarm. Four trucks heading toward the farm and now he'd lost cell service. Maybe a coincidence.

Maybe not.

He turned on his bedroom light, half expecting that it wouldn't come on. But light blazed brightly in the darkness, making him squint, and he allowed himself a brief moment of relief.

Pushing open the bedroom door, he listened to the familiar noises of the night. The hum of electricity from the refrigerator and the soft whisper of heated air blowing through the vents. The faint ticks and groans of an old house settling in for the night.

He didn't want to wake Lacey, but he needed to know if her cell phone was picking up a signal. To his relief, he saw a light glowing under the door. Tapping lightly on the door, he spoke in a half whisper. "Lacey? It's Jim."

There was a long moment of silence before she answered in just as hushed a tone, "Come in."

She was in bed but awake, dressed in a long-sleeved T-shirt. She was frowning at the phone in her hand. "All my bars disappeared."

He crossed to look at her phone. "Mine, too."

"That's weird, isn't it?" She looked up at him, her brow furrowed. "I thought I heard your phone ring earlier."

"It did." He told her about the call from Charlotte, who ran the diner in Cherry Grove. "It cut off in the middle of her call."

"It wouldn't take long for someone to drive out here from town, would it?" Lacey's gaze slanted toward the window across from her bed, which looked out on the side yard and the parking area.

Jim crossed to the window, staying just wide of the glass. He lifted one edge of the curtain and looked out. With the light on, it was hard to see anything outside even with the glow of the snow-covered land.

"Maybe you should…" Suddenly the light went out in the room. "Turn off the light," he continued.

"I didn't turn off the light," Lacey said, her voice closer than he expected. He turned his head toward her voice and found her standing beside him, her back pressed against the bedroom wall.

He edged the curtain away from the window again and peered outside. In the side parking area, his Jeep along with the Becketts' Ford Explorer were the only vehicles in sight.

But there was a lot of land surrounding the farm, some of it thick with trees and underbrush. It wouldn't be hard to hide four trucks from view of the road.

"Maybe the lightbulb blew." Lacey's voice was shaky.

Jim crossed to the door and looked out into the hallway. His room was dark as well, even though he'd left his light on.

"My clock is dead. The power is out." Lacey crept closer to him in the dark, her blond hair catching glints of light from the snow glow outside. "I don't suppose the weight of the snow finally snapped a branch and it hit a power line?"

"Nice thought," he answered grimly.

"We'd better tell Cade and Julie."

"Already on it." Cade's voice came from the hallway. He was using a flashlight application on his phone to shed light into the gloom. Julie was right behind him. Already dressed in jeans and a sweater, she had a Ruger tucked into a holster at her side and looked ready for action.

Jim kicked himself for leaving his own room without his Glock. "I'll be right back."

He returned with his Glock holstered at the back of his jeans. "You said you know how to shoot, right?" he asked Lacey.

"Yes, but I don't have a weapon."

"Cade brought an extra," he said with confidence, looking at his former employer with a grin. "Didn't you?"

"Of course." Cade left Lacey's bedroom, plunging it back into darkness.

Jim opened the flashlight app on his own phone and

turned it on. It illuminated the tense, worried expression on Lacey's face, and he couldn't stop himself from reaching out to touch her. "We're going to figure out what's going on and we're going to stop it."

"There are four of us and two children," Lacey said with quiet despair. "Maybe we're all armed, but what if they're out there right now, rigging this place to blow? What good will it do for us to go out with guns blazing?"

The truth was, if their communications were jammed and the power had been cut, it was already too late to get out of the house.

Lacey must have read Jim's expression in the light of the cell-phone app, for she released a soft groan of despair.

Cade returned with a second weapon. "Smith & Wesson SD40. Ten in the mag, one in the chamber. Can you handle it?"

She took the pistol, her expression ambivalent. On the train ride to Stamford earlier that day, she had confessed to Jim that while she had been pretty good with a gun, she'd never really enjoyed shooting. But if it came to having to fire a weapon in order to protect Katie, she'd do it without hesitation.

"I can handle it," she said, and Jim believed her.

"Julie and I will take the north and east windows. You take the south and west." Cade nodded toward the hallway. "Call out if you see anything."

"Should we go to the second floor?" Lacey asked as they headed toward the back of the house. "We might have a better line of sight."

"Good idea." Jim followed her to the narrow staircase at the back of the house that had once been the servants' stairway. Less ornate and grand than the staircase off the parlor, it felt rickety and old beneath his feet. But it held them all the way to the second floor.

"There's a good line of sight from my workroom toward the west," Lacey said as they entered the second-floor hallway. "I'll check there. This back bedroom here looks to the south."

Jim didn't like parting company with her, but they each had a job to do. He peeled off and entered the empty back bedroom, crossing to the curtainless window that looked out on the snowy backyard and the pastureland beyond.

Snow blanketed the area with white, and, while inside the backyard the snow was neither smooth nor pristine thanks to the snowman building earlier in the day, the field beyond was a featureless white void. If anyone had approached the house from that direction, he would see their footprints in the snow.

But that didn't mean there wasn't someone out there. From his vantage point at the window, he couldn't see past the eaves that covered the back porch.

He headed back into the hall to see if he could find a room that wasn't blocked by the eaves. But before he had taken more than a couple of steps, a call rang out from downstairs. It was Cade's voice, sharp with urgency. "Bogeys from the east. At least five."

"Bogeys to the north, as well," Julie called. "I count three on this side."

"Four from the west!" Lacey came out into the hall, her eyes wide with alarm. "I saw four men in white outside, barely visible against the snow."

"My view of the yard closest to the house was blocked by the porch eaves," Jim said, already pushing her toward the front stairs. "But I think we have to assume they're out there, as well."

Lacey stumbled as her foot hit the first stair, and Jim had to grab her to keep her from tumbling down the steps. She clung to him, her grip tight on his arms. In the low light, her gray eyes glittered with fear.

"We're trapped in here, aren't we?" she asked.

He nodded, unable to do anything but tell her the truth. "We are."

Chapter Sixteen

Lacey had been under fire in Afghanistan. She'd waded into the middle of a Baltimore riot to interview protestors. She'd even been caught in a hostage crisis in one of the most dangerous prisons in the world. She'd thought herself nearly bulletproof, and certainly strong enough emotionally and physically to hold her own.

But when she thought about Katie sleeping in her crib downstairs, innocent and unable to protect herself, Lacey knew a fear as profound as any she'd ever known.

When she reached the first floor and came face-to-face with Julie Beckett, she saw a reflection of her own fear in the other woman's eyes. "If they're setting explosives," Julie said urgently, "where is the safest place in this house?"

"Is there such a place if they're setting explosives?" Jim asked, his grip on Lacey's shoulder tightening.

"We have children in here that we have to get out!" Julie turned to her husband. "Cade, we have to get the kids out of here. Can we create a diversion to open up an avenue of escape?"

"No," Cade said, his gaze fixed on a point beyond where they stood. Lacey and the others followed his gaze and saw the flames licking at the wood porch outside the farmhouse. The smell of gasoline hit Lacey's nose around the same time.

"They're burning us out," Jim growled.

Already the air in the house was growing thick with smoke and fumes. Lacey didn't wait another second; she raced down the hallway to Katie's nursery and flung open the door.

Flames climbing the outer walls of the farmhouse cast a flickering glow across the dark room. Lacey reached into the crib and lifted her sleeping niece into her arms, trying to think past her terror to find some sort of solution to their dire problem.

Heat rises to the top. So upstairs was no answer. But maybe the basement would give them some measure of protection? The basement had been the original foundation of the antebellum house that had once stood where the farmhouse now sat, a stone-and-mortar home that would have been built to withstand fires.

But would the musty basement be protection enough if the house above them burned? Or would it prove another trap from which they couldn't escape?

Jim found her in the doorway of Katie's room. "Julie is getting Samantha. Cade's wetting towels for us to breathe through. There's a stone foundation on this house, isn't there?"

"Yes, but—"

"No buts. There's fire surrounding the house. No breaks in the flames. We looked." He touched Katie's face, then Lacey's. "This is our best hope. Let's do this."

Tugging Katie's sleepy body closer to her, she nodded and followed Jim down the hall to the basement stairs.

"SOMETHING JUST AIN'T RIGHT." Charlotte Brady hadn't been able to get back to sleep after her call to Jim Mercer. The call had cut off in the middle of her words, and when she'd tried to call him back, it had gone straight to voice mail.

"He probably didn't appreciate your calling him in the middle of the blasted night," her husband, George, grumbled into his pillow. "Sort of like I don't appreciate you keeping me awake blathering about it."

"There was something not right about those trucks, and all of a sudden, while I'm trying to tell that man about possible trouble coming his way, the call cuts off? Nope." She pushed herself into a sitting position in the bed and reached for the phone. "I'm calling Roy."

"He ain't gonna be any happier about being jerked out of bed in the middle of the night, either."

"Maybe not. But he knows I'm not one to make up stories." One benefit of having a brother who happened to be the county sheriff.

As George predicted, Roy hadn't been happy about being awakened at two in the morning. But he listened to what Charlotte had to say with interest. He might just be a small-town lawman, but he knew the troubles Lacey Miles had been through in the past few weeks.

He also knew his force might not be enough firepower to handle whatever might be happening out there at the farm. "I'll call in the state boys. We'll get people out there right away to see what's happening."

As she hung up the phone with her brother, Charlotte was beginning to have a sinking feeling that she'd left the call to her brother a little too late.

"WE'VE GOT A couple of 911 calls about a fire out at the old Peabody farm." Roy Dobbins hadn't gotten more than half his order out when the dispatcher interrupted him. "Neighbors in the area called it in, but it sounds like the house is fully involved already. I've sent two trucks out that way."

"Send every deputy available out there, too," Roy ordered, pulling on his uniform pants. Behind him, his wife was already rolling off the bed to head into the kitchen to put on a pot of coffee. "And call in the state police and surrounding counties. This may not just be an ordinary fire."

By the time he'd dressed, Addie had the coffee made. She poured a couple of steaming cups into a thermos and handed it to him on his way to the door. "Come home safe, you hear?"

He kissed her cheek and headed out into the bitter cold, tucking the collar of his uniform jacket more snugly around his neck. He got on the car radio as he turned the heater on high blast and located a deputy already approaching the scene of the fire. "The whole place is up in flames already," Deputy Breyer said loudly, having to compete with the roar of flames and the moan of sirens audible over the radio. "Lots of footprints in the snow around the house, but we couldn't get real close yet. The fire crew has just arrived."

"What about the occupants of the house?"

"No sign of anyone."

Roy's chest tightened with dread.

BOTH CHILDREN WERE CRYING, their soft sobs swallowed by the sounds of rushing flames and crumbling timbers coming from the house overhead. Cade had pushed wet towels into the gap between the heavy oak door and the stairs below, but the fire would soon take those pieces of kindling as surely as it was consuming the beams and floorboards upstairs.

The only light in the basement was the glow from Cade Beckett's cell-phone app, barely enough to see a foot or two in front of their faces. But Lacey was close enough to Jim for him to see the bleak despair in her face as she pressed a damp cloth over Katie's weeping face to keep out the smoke growing inexorably thicker in the small basement.

The howl of sirens outside was muted by the thick stone surrounding them, but Jim knew the fire crew would be looking for survivors. Maybe there was still a chance for rescue.

But not if the house fell in on them, and it sounded as if it was gearing up to do that.

"Is there any other way out of here? Some chink in the foundation where we could dig our way out?" he asked Lacey.

She swung her troubled gaze to his face. "What?"

"This is an old house. Maybe there's a part of this basement that was patched up recently. We might be able to dig a way out."

She stared at him for a moment, almost uncomprehendingly, before her eyes lit up from inside. "The tunnel."

Cade Beckett moved closer. "What tunnel?"

"When the workers were shoring up the foundation, they found an old tunnel. It's over there, behind that door. I don't know if it leads anywhere, but it's still there, because it's considered a historic artifact. The local historians believe the original house was part of the Underground Railroad. I remember Marianne and

Toby were excited to be living somewhere that had such an important role in history."

"And you're sure it hasn't been filled in?"

"No, like I said, it's considered a historical artifact. The builders had to make sure it was structurally sound for the house, and that was it. The historical society was planning to take a better look at the tunnel come spring."

"Let's try it," Julie said, already moving toward the door.

Cade caught her arm. "Wait a second."

"For what? For the house to fall down on top of us? Listen!" She waved toward the ceiling, where the roar of the fire was louder than before. "Let's go, for God's sake. Now!"

The door covering the entrance to the tunnel was made of stone, and it took both Cade and Jim working together to make it budge. They could only pull it open a couple of feet, but that was enough for them all to slip through the opening. "Close it behind us," Lacey urged. "It might stop the fire from entering the tunnel if the house collapses into the basement."

They had barely gotten the door pushed back into place when the ground beneath their feet shook and the sound of breaking timbers and rushing flames penetrated the solid wall of rock. But no sign of flames penetrated the closed door, and only the tiniest tendrils of smoke seeped into the tunnel and floated up to the curved stone ceiling.

Beside Jim, Lacey was trembling wildly as she clutched her crying niece to her chest. Jim wrapped his arms around them both, pressing a kiss against Lacey's forehead. "We're safe for now."

"Do you feel that?" Julie asked.

"What?"

"Cold air. Moving air." She nodded toward the dark mouth of the tunnel ahead. "I think there's air coming in from somewhere ahead. And if there is…"

"Then we may have a way out," Jim finished for her.

ALEXANDER QUINN HAD long ago learned to trust his instincts, even when they seemed to make no sense. It had saved him from a terrorist attack in Iraq in 2003, and from sniper fire in Yemen a few years later.

Tonight, despite the assurance from Cade Beckett that assistance could probably wait for morning, Quinn's instincts had told him he needed to get to Cherry Grove, Virginia, as quickly as he could. Which meant gassing up one of Campbell Cove Security's pair of helicopters with all hands on deck.

The chopper was a modified CH-53E Super Stallion, equipped to carry a combat-ready assault team. Quinn had called in his best men and women for this mission, aware that the quarry they were hunting would be armed and dangerous.

Luckily, so were his agents.

His pilot landed the Super Stallion in a flat field about a half mile north of the Cherry Grove farmhouse just a few minutes past two in the morning. To Quinn's dismay, the glow on the snowy horizon suggested they might be too late to help his imperiled agents.

But they had another mission, already approved by an in-air radio call to one of the top commanders in the Virginia State Police, who happened to be an old friend of Quinn's from his days in the CIA. Ethan Tolliver had been an FBI legat before he'd taken the job with the state police, and he and Quinn had shared many a drink and a tall tale at the US embassy in Turkey when they'd both been assigned there in the late nineties.

"I'll let all the locals know you're coming in hot," Tolliver had assured him after catching him up on all that had happened since their liftoff back in Kentucky. "We've got unknown targets out there, probably up to no good. You folks try to hunt them down, and we'll do all we can to get your people out of that house."

Quinn gave the glow on the horizon another grim look, then barked orders at his team. "They'll still be around here somewhere. Track them down. And bring them all in. Alive is better than dead." He checked the magazine of his Ruger. "We have some questions we need answered."

THOUGH IT FELT as if they had been walking forever, a glance at her watch told Lacey that it had been only a half hour or so, each step taking them closer and closer to the source of the icy air that seemed to permeate her bones until her teeth chattered uncontrollably.

Jim had taken Katie from her earlier, wrapping his big frame around the little girl to keep her warm. Before they'd headed into the basement, Jim had been clearheaded enough to grab coats for them all, while Julie did the same for her family, so even though they were all cold enough to shiver in the frigid tunnel, they weren't likely to reach full hypothermia before they reached the end of the tunnel.

But what then? She had no idea where the tunnel came out, if it came out at all. Would they have to dig their way through some sort of collapse at the end? Or would the tunnel open into the snowy woods, where they'd have no protection from the elements at all.

"I think I see it." Cade stretched his cell phone toward the darkened tunnel ahead, and Lacey saw it, too. A steep stairway built of stone, extending upward into a hole in the roof of the tunnel.

"Wait," Lacey said as the others started moving faster toward the stairs. "Just because the people who burned us out of the house probably didn't stick around after it started to collapse, that doesn't mean they're not still out there somewhere, waiting for final confirmation that we died in the fire."

"She's right." Jim shifted Katie in his arms, tugging her even closer to him. "If we're right about those people out there being some sort of al Adar sleeper cell sent to take out Lacey, they won't go away until they have some sort of evidence to show for their actions."

"They'll want confirmation that I'm dead," Lacey said flatly. "They're out there, waiting to see the bodies pulled from the ashes."

"Well, we can't stay down here and freeze to death," Julie protested, hugging Samantha closer. The little girl had stopped crying, but she still looked terrified. Lacey wished they had a way to deal with their reality without terrifying the little girls, but they didn't have the luxury for anything but blunt talk at this point.

"Jim and I can go out there and scout around," Cade suggested. "See if we spot anyone."

"What about your cell phone?" Lacey asked. "Are you getting a signal now?"

Cade peered at the display. "No. But the stone walls may be blocking it. I need to get outside and see if I get any bars."

"If they're hanging around, they may still be jamming cell signals," Julie warned.

"We have to take a chance." Jim turned to look at Lacey, his expression intense. "You and Julie keep the children down here. Cade and I will go out and see what we're up against."

She shook her head. "None of you would be out here if it weren't for me. I'm the one they want dead. I can't send you out there like cannon fodder while I hide down here in safety."

"Lacey—"

"Let her go," Julie said flatly. "It's her fight as much as it's any of yours. I'll keep the girls safe down here."

"No." Jim shook his head. "There's no reason for you to martyr yourself, Lacey. Katie needs you alive."

"She needs us both alive. Both of us. I can't just send you out there for me, don't you get that? If something happened to you because I stayed back here like a coward... I'm going. We're going to find a way to safety. And then we're coming back for the others. End of story." Lacey leaned forward and gave Katie's cold cheek a swift, fierce kiss, her heart feeling so full she feared it would explode.

Jim closed his eyes for a long moment, his expression pained. Then he kissed the top of Katie's blond curls and handed the little girl to Julie. "Take care of my Katiebug."

"Y'all be careful," Julie said, lifting her face for her husband's kiss. "I'll keep these rug rats safe and warm, I promise."

Jim went up the stairs first, pausing as his head breached the top. He swiveled his face slowly, twisting on the stairs until he could see all the way around.

He dipped his head back below the hole. "I don't see any movement, but we can't assume there's not someone out there."

"Just be careful when you go out, okay?" Lacey stood at the bottom of the stairs, waiting for her turn to go. Once she saw Jim's feet disappear through the hole, she started up behind him.

The stone steps were slick with moisture and age, making it hard to keep her footing. She had pulled on sneakers rather than boots when Jim woke her, not expecting to have to trek through the snowy woods. But it was better than being barefoot, she supposed.

Like Jim, she paused at the top of the exit and took a look around. The tunnel came out in thick woods that would have been thicker still with summer foliage. As it was, there were enough evergreen trees and bushes to make the woods around them seem nearly impenetrable. Snow here lay only in scabrous patches, the forest floor protected by the trees overhead from the worst of the snowfall.

On the downside, there were plenty of places for wrongdoers to lie in wait.

Jim caught her hand and helped her up the rest of the way, practically lifting her off her feet to set her on the ground beside him. He put his arm around her, lending her his warmth. His eyes never stopped moving, scanning the woods around them as they waited for Cade Beckett to finish climbing the stone stairs.

"Where do you think we are?" Cade asked when he pulled himself out of the tunnel mouth.

"I'm not sure," Lacey confessed. "I think we're still on farm property, since the historical society didn't tell Marianne and Toby that they shared the tunnel with anyone else. If so, we're probably in the woods on the southern edge of the property. The town is about a mile east of here. If you can figure out what direction east would be."

"Any cell signal?" Jim asked Cade.

"No," he answered with a frown. "Those signal jammers don't have that large a range…"

"Which means they're still close," Lacey said, hair rising on the back of her neck.

"Very close," Jim said in a strangled tone, his gaze fixed somewhere behind her.

Lacey turned and saw three figures dressed in arctic camouflage moving toward them at a wary pace. Each was armed with a hunting rifle, though none of them, Lacey noticed, seemed at ease with the weapons.

Burning people in their beds more your style, cowards?

Jim and Cade had their weapons up before Lacey could blink, but at best, it was a standoff. And since rifles were far more accurate at a distance, they weren't looking at a best-case scenario.

She pulled the borrowed SD40 from the holster at her side and aimed it at the slowly approaching figures.

Suddenly, the woods lit up as bright as daylight. The approaching men froze in confusion as the woods erupted with a dozen men, similarly clad in arctic camo, emerging from their hiding places with weapons raised.

"What the hell?" Lacey asked, staring as the newcomers surrounded the other three men, shouting orders in Kaziri to lay down their weapons.

"That," Cade Beckett said with a spreading smile, "is why it pays to have Alexander Quinn for a boss."

Chapter Seventeen

"That's the problem with recruiting westernized kids," Alexander Quinn said with a grim smile, turning away from the monitor showing the occupants of interview room four at the Virginia State Police barracks a county over from Cherry Grove. "They never can keep their traps shut."

"So, Ghal Rehani is the one who put a hit on Lacey?" Jim asked. "Because she insulted him on air by calling him a self-proclaimed warlord?"

"I think it was the 'self-proclaimed' part that pissed him off," Quinn said. "I just got a call from an old friend in the Federal Police. They picked up Rehani about an hour ago."

Jim was still shaking his head. "I don't want to be the one to tell Lacey her sister and brother-in-law were killed because some Osama bin Laden wannabe got his little feelings hurt."

"It would be nice, wouldn't it, if it took a lot more than a schoolyard put-down to push a man to murderous rage?" Quinn put his hand on Jim's shoulder. "You did a good job, Mercer. I think you're going to be a real asset at Campbell Cove Academy." He paused as he reached the door of the office. "That is, if you want to keep working with us."

"I have a lot of decisions to make," Jim said. It wasn't exactly an answer to Quinn's implied question, but it was as much as he could offer until he had a chance to talk to Lacey and find out what her plans were for her and Katie.

He found her in the barracks commander's office, curled up asleep on one end of a small sofa, with Katie napping in her arms. Grimy and rumpled, with soot staining her hair and dark circles of exhaustion under her eyes, she was a mess. But he'd never seen anything more beautiful than the steady rise and fall of her breathing, a potent reminder of what he almost lost tonight.

At his desk, the barracks commander, who'd introduced himself as Ethan Tolliver when the county sheriff had delivered Jim, Lacey, Katie and the Becketts to the state police division headquarters, looked up from the paperwork spread across his desk. He put one finger to his lips and waved Jim over to the chair in front of his desk.

"Long night," Tolliver said quietly.

"You have no idea."

"Where are you folks going to go now? You have a place to stay?"

Jim rubbed his gritty eyes. "My boss has reserved some rooms for us in a local hotel. We're good for now."

"Reckon you all lost about everything in the fire."

Jim looked at Lacey and Katie curled around each other in slumber. "Not everything."

Tolliver followed Jim's gaze. "No, not everything."

"Any idea when you're cutting us loose from here? I could use a shower and about a week of sleep."

"I'm signing the papers now. I'll deliver them up to the front desk myself, and then you'll be free to go, though I'd appreciate it if you stick around the area for a few more days until we finish up the investigation."

Jim's gaze trailed back to Lacey. "I'm not going anywhere."

A knock on the door made Lacey stir. She sat up, her sleepy gaze locking with Jim's. "Hey."

"Hey," he said with a smile.

At Tolliver's bidding, a young uniformed state police officer entered the room, sparing a quick glance at Jim and Lacey before he looked back at the division commander. "There's an FBI agent here to see you."

Tolliver sighed. "I'm from the government, and I'm here to help," he muttered as he headed out the door.

Jim didn't bother reminding him he was also part of the government. He supposed every layer of bureaucracy probably resented the layers above.

Lacey nuzzled Katie's curls and stifled a yawn. "What's happening?"

"The state police are about to spring us."

"Yay." She made a face. "Where do we go now?"

"Quinn got us some hotel rooms. I guess we go shower and try to catch up on a little sleep."

"What about the guys they captured?"

"Quinn thinks they got them all, based on the numbers we saw outside. We can't be sure how many were on the southern side of the house, since the eaves blocked my view, but we figure at most there were four on that side, and we saw twelve others. They picked up sixteen men, so that fits."

"Have any of them said anything yet?"

"One of them told everything he knows. His story's being checked out, of course, but it rings true."

Her brow furrowed. "Why did they target me? Was it the story I did on Tahir Mahmood, speculating that he wasn't dead?"

Jim shook his head. "It was a report you did a couple of months ago on the rise of strongmen in the Kaziri countryside, the ones who were aligning themselves with al Adar in hopes of improving their standing in their villages."

Her frown deepened. "Why on earth would someone target me for that?"

Damn, he didn't want to tell her what he'd learned. But better from him than from someone who didn't care about her and how much she'd lost. "You called Ghal Rehani a self-proclaimed warlord."

She stared at him for a moment, looking puzzled. Then, suddenly, the realization dawned, and her mouth dropped open. "Oh, my God. You cannot be serious."

"I know it sounds crazy…"

"It is crazy. He's crazy. He put a hit on me for that? Because, what? I hurt his little feelings?" She got up suddenly, jostling Katie, who began to cry. Shoving Katie into Jim's arms, Lacey hurried out of the office, slamming the door behind her.

Jim wanted to follow, but he knew she needed time to process the truth about her sister's death. A small man's outsize vanity had cost Lacey her sister and brother-in-law. It had stolen Katie's parents from her life. It had left the world a smaller, meaner place, and nothing Jim could say or do would change that reality.

He pressed soft kisses against Katie's cheek, murmuring words of comfort. Eventually, she curled her hands in the collar of his jacket and snuggled close as he rocked her from side to side.

LACEY STOOD OUTSIDE in the frigid predawn, gazing up at the stars overhead and wanting to scream at the universe. Her voice seemed trapped in her throat, tears beating frantically at the backs of her eyes but unable to escape and give her any sort of release.

The world was insane. The people inhabiting it were petty and cruel, venal and ridiculous. Deaths were meaningless and lives cut short for no good reason at all.

It wasn't fair. It wasn't right.

It was all her fault.

She heard the door behind her open and footsteps move toward her. She steeled herself for Jim's voice, but it was Julie Beckett who came to stand beside her. She lifted her face to the sky as well, gazing up at the stars.

"This world sucks," Julie said.

"Yeah, it does."

"Except when it doesn't." Julie looked away from the stars, focusing her gaze on Lacey. "It's so easy to get drawn into the evil and insanity we come across every day in this business. You as a reporter. Me as a cop, of sorts."

"I used to think I was making a difference, you know?" Lacey pushed her hair back from her face, feeling as if all the grief in the world was bottled up inside her. "I thought what I did mattered."

"It does. You tell the truth, however harsh and unwanted it may be. That matters a lot."

She shook her head. "A careless choice of words got my sister and brother-in-law killed."

"No." Julie caught Lacey's arm and pulled her around until they were face-to-face. Julie's eyes blazed with anger. "A stupid, evil man sent other stupid, evil men to kill you. That's what happened. I'm terribly sorry about your sister and brother-in-law. I am. But if you give in to that man's evil, if you accept the blame instead of putting it square where it belongs, who wins? Not you. Not Katie. Not Marianne or Toby. Ghal Rehani wins, because you've validated his world view. Don't do that, Lacey. Do not do that."

"She's right." Jim's voice rumbled from the darkness. He came out of the shadows near the door, his arms wrapped around Katie. "You can't give up. Not on any of it."

Lacey closed her burning eyes. "Are we free to go yet?"

"Yeah. Quinn's already given me the keys to our hotel room." He looked at Julie. "Somehow, our vehicles survived without damage. He's had them delivered to the visitor parking area here. Cade has the keys. He and Samantha will meet you there."

"Wait," Lacey said as Julie started toward visitor parking. "Can you guys take Katie with you? There's somewhere I want to go first, before I head for the hotel."

Jim frowned. "You're ready to drop, Lacey. You need a shower and sleep. Whatever it is you want to do, can't it wait?"

She shook her head. "I need you to take me somewhere. Please."

Whatever he saw in her face seemed to melt his opposition. He handed Katie to Julie. "Katiebug, Julie's going to take you to play with Samantha for a little while. Wouldn't you like that?"

Katie looked up at him with bleary eyes, but she gave only a token protest when Julie pulled her from Jim's arms. She quickly settled into a snuggle against Julie's shoulder.

Julie smiled at them. "I love them when they're this age. Makes me want to have another one."

Lacey watched until Julie disappeared around the corner of the building. Then she turned to look at Jim. "Thank you for doing this. I know you must be exhausted."

"We all are. But I'm never going to be able to sleep until I know you're safe at the hotel."

She touched his arm, her fingers trailing down across his before she dropped her hand to her side. "It might be easier if I drive."

He handed over the keys to the Jeep and followed her to the visitor parking lot. "Are you sure you're awake enough to drive?"

"Believe me, I won't be able to sleep at all until I do this."

THE CEMETERY WAS small and secluded, tucked away behind an old stone church about five miles from where the farmhouse had stood in Cherry Grove. Lacey parked the Jeep haphazardly just outside the ornate iron gate that guarded the graveyard's entrance.

Jim wasn't sure he should follow, but Lacey motioned for him to join her. She caught his hand as they stepped into the graveyard and picked their way among the engraved headstones.

The stone straight ahead was new, gleaming brightly

among the other weathered stones. Lacey's grip on Jim's hand tightened, and he locked his fingers with hers, offering her all the strength he had.

"I wanted to come here one day and tell her we found the people who killed her," Lacey murmured, her voice almost as hushed as the cemetery surrounding them. "I didn't think it would end this way. It was all so incredibly senseless."

"Most murders are," Jim said.

She looked up at him. "It's not fair."

"No. It's not."

"All Ken Calvert wanted was to see his kids more, and now he's dead. It's so stupid."

"It is," Jim agreed.

"I think he wanted to see me that night because he found out about Ghal Rehani's vendetta. Central Asia is his beat. He'd have wanted to give me a heads-up, even though it was probably considered classified information." She looked down at her sister's grave. "I wonder if he'd still be alive if he hadn't tried to meet me that night."

The moon had finally broken through the clouds just as it was ready to leave the sky and give way to morning, lending just enough light for Jim to see the tears welling in Lacey's eyes before they spilled in silver tracks down her cheeks.

A hard sob escaped her lips, followed by another. Then another. Jim reached for her, pulling her into the shelter of his arms, letting her spill her grief on his strong shoulders.

When she was spent, she melted into his embrace, her breathing slowly subsiding to normal. The cold began to seep through their clothing, and Jim gave her a gentle nudge. "We're going to freeze to death out here."

She nodded, rubbing her face against his damp shirt. "Can you drive back?"

"Of course."

They didn't talk on the way to the hotel. Lacey seemed completely drained, and Jim didn't know what to say to her that would make her feel any better. He just hoped it was enough to be there with her, ready if she needed him. He hoped when she found her feet again, she'd want him at her side.

He parked the Jeep in the hotel parking lot and cut the engine. "We're here."

She stirred, lifting her head from where it had rested against the window for most of the trip back. "Oh."

When she made no move to get out of the vehicle, he walked around the Jeep and opened the door for her, giving her his hand to help her out. She twined her fingers with his, huddling close as if for warmth while they checked in at the front desk. His room was next to Lacey's, he saw with relief. He didn't think he could bear being far from her tonight.

He wasn't sure he could bear it any night, ever again.

She unlocked her hotel door and pushed it open, revealing a clean, spacious room with two double beds. She shrugged off her jacket and tossed it on one bed, her nose wrinkling. "Definitely need a shower."

"You sure you'll be okay? You want me to find the Becketts and get Katie for you?"

She turned to look at him. "I'll be okay. Let Katie sleep."

Reluctantly, he backed out of the room, letting her close the door and shut him out. He trudged the few feet between their rooms and let himself into his own hotel room.

The hot shower felt like heaven, sluicing away the grime and soot from their ordeal. He could still smell the smoke and knew he probably would for a few days to come, but at least none of them had experienced any smoke-inhalation problems. The paramedics on the scene had checked them all, paying extra attention to the children. Everyone was fine.

Thank God for abolitionists, he thought, still protecting the pursued even now.

Somehow, Alexander Quinn had provided clean clothing that actually fit Jim's lean-muscled build. He pulled on a clean pair of boxer shorts and was contemplating whether to put on a T-shirt as well when there was a knock on the door. He crossed to open it, expecting to find his boss on the other side.

But it was Lacey who stood on the other side of the door.

She'd showered and dressed in a clean pair of shorts and a long-sleeved T-shirt. Her hair hung in damp strings around her shoulders and her face was scrubbed clean.

"I love you," she said.

He stood in stunned silence, certain he'd misunderstood.

"I don't expect you to say it back, or even feel the same way. It's okay if you don't. I just couldn't let any more time go by without saying it. There are so many things I wish I'd said to Marianne and Toby, things I won't get to say to them, not in this life. I didn't want to make the same mistake with you."

She turned as if to go, but he caught her hand, tugging her back around to face him. "I love you, too. And it's okay if you don't know what to do with that, or what to do with how you feel. I don't need any promises or plans right now. I just need you to know I feel the same way."

She closed the distance between them in one swift step, throwing her arms around his waist and burying her face in his chest. He held her close, pressing soft, fervent kisses in her damp hair. "I love you, Lacey. I love Katie, too. And whatever happens next, nothing is gonna change that. You hear me?"

When she lifted her face to his, she was smiling through her tears. "I hear you."

He slowly lowered his mouth to hers, giving her time to back away if she wanted. The timing was all wrong, but he couldn't hold back the way he felt about her, letting his lips and tongue convey the complexity of emotions, of love and desire and commitment all tangled into one heady elixir.

She kissed him back, and in every brush of her lips, every stroke of her tongue against his, he felt his love for her returned with equal intensity.

She finally pulled back, ending the kiss, and gazed up at him with the first hint of joy he'd ever seen in her eyes. "I'm going to sleep with you tonight, Jim Mercer. Just sleep." Her kiss-stung lips quirked. "Sorry about that part."

He took her hand and led her to the nearest bed, smiling up at her as he sat on the edge and took her hands. "I'm not. I'm not sorry at all."

Epilogue

Four months was long enough.

Lacey had been busy during that span of time, nego-
tiating a lighter schedule with the network and trying
to make her Arlington condo work for life with a two-
year-old. And there was Jim, of course, as constant in
her life now as he'd promised. He and Katie had healed
a lot of her wounds, the ones that had scarred her life
when her sister died and a few she hadn't even realized
she had, from a life lived constantly on the edge, looking for something she couldn't define.

She'd found it, finally, in the one place she'd never
thought to look—inside herself. In her absolute adora-
tion for her niece and her deepening, broadening love
for the man who'd showed her that true love wasn't some
unreachable, unknowable fairy tale but something constant and real, in good times and bad. They'd married a
couple of weeks ago, had run off to a cheesy little wedding chapel in the Smoky Mountains and tied the knot.
Jim's family had been there, as loving and welcoming as
Jim himself, and Katie had taken her job as flower girl
seriously, carpeting the wedding-chapel aisle with rose
petals so thickly that she ran out halfway up the aisle.

She was Mrs. Jim Mercer now. Lacey Miles-Mercer.

She liked it. A lot.

It had been Jim who'd convinced her it was time to go back to Cherry Grove. Whether the house was still there or not, the farm remained, and she needed to make some decisions about it.

"This place looks so different," she commented as they drove through the middle of Cherry Grove.

"And exactly the same," Jim said with a grin as they passed the diner and waved at Charlotte Brady, who was sweeping the sidewalk in front of the store.

Winter had passed and spring was in full flower, the trees thick with their new green foliage and flowers blooming in pots and hedges in front of every building along Main Street.

Lacey found her stomach clenching with nerves as they made the turn down the road to the farm. Here, too, was a world reborn, the grass in the pastureland green and lush. One day, Lacey remembered, Marianne and Toby had planned to buy some horses to graze the pastures. Maybe a milk cow and some goats and chickens to supplement their supply of food.

Everything looked familiar and strange at the same time, but the overwhelming sense that seeped its way into her consciousness was that she was coming home.

She had lived here only a short month, but it had become part of her in a way that caught her completely by surprise.

Wrapped up in pondering what that unexpected feeling meant, it took her longer than it should have to realize that the blackened, ravaged ruin she had been bracing herself to see was no longer there.

In its place stood the half-built frame of a new farmhouse, surrounded by a crew of construction workers hard at work rebuilding the structure that had so recently burned to the ground.

"What…what?" Lacey stared at the rising bones of the new house, then back at Jim. He smiled at her, his hazel-green eyes twinkling with mischievous joy.

"Surprise," he said.

"How… I haven't even cashed the insurance check yet."

"You were going to put that toward Katie's college fund, so I thought maybe I should find another way to rebuild the house."

"What other way?"

"You knew when I swept you into an elopement last month there were still a few things you hadn't yet learned about me. Well, one of them was that I recently sold a piece of land in North Carolina that I'd bought after my first year in the Marine Corps. Since I wasn't planning on going to college at that point, my mother gave me the savings she and my dad had put away for my schooling, and I bought land to build a house after I got out of the Marine Corps. It was sitting there, undeveloped, for a long time. Until a land developer decided he wanted it for a new subdivision he was planning." Jim grinned. "Paid a bloody fortune for it. More than five times what I paid for it."

"And you, what? Used your money to rebuild the farmhouse?"

"It was your sister's dream. It was supposed to be Katie's home. I know you have other plans now, other dreams, but I thought at least Katie could have a place that connected her to her parents. If you don't want to do anything with it, the farmland could be rented out, and we could just keep the house as a vacation spot or something."

She stared at him, her heart so full she could barely find her voice. "How do you do that?"

He touched her cheek. "Do what?"

"Know what I want before I even know I want it?"

He bent to kiss her, a long, sweet, promising kiss that made her head spin and her heart soar. "Because I love you."

In the car seat behind them, Katie was growing impatient. "Home!" she said in a loud, insistent voice.

Lacey gave Jim a last, sweet kiss and turned to look at the farmhouse rising from the ashes.

"That's right, baby," she said. "We're home."

* * * * *

"Thank you. I really don't know what I would've done—or where I'd be now—if you hadn't appeared."

He knew where she'd be about now—sitting under some hot light, probably tied up and getting interrogated by some very bad people. He would never allow that to happen to her.

He'd been too late to protect her friend, but not too late to protect Sophia. Now that he'd met the woman with the sad childhood and the hard shell, he'd do anything to keep her safe.

He'd never kept anything from his superiors before, but he just might want to conceal his crazy attraction for Sophia. They didn't need to know, even though he wouldn't let his emotions get the better of him.

That had happened only once.

LOCKED,
LOADED AND
SEALED

BY
CAROL ERICSON

First Published in Great Britain 2017
By Mills & Boon, an imprint of HarperCollins*Publishers*
1 London Bridge Street, London, SE1 9GF

© 2017 Carol Ericson

ISBN: 978-0-263-92875-4

46-0417

Our policy is to use papers that are natural, renewable and recyclable products and made from wood grown in sustainable forests. The logging and manufacturing processes conform to the legal environmental regulations of the country of origin.

Printed and bound in Spain
by CPI, Barcelona

Carol Ericson is a bestselling, award-winning author of more than forty books. She has an eerie fascination for true-crime stories, a love of film noir and a weakness for reality TV, all of which fuel her imagination to create her own tales of murder, mayhem and mystery. To find out more about Carol and her current projects, please visit her website at www.carolericson.com, "where romance flirts with danger."

For all the military wives who keep it together

Prologue

A possible target came into view and a bead of sweat
rolled down Austin Foley's face and dripped off his chin.
It wasn't the mission making him sweat, even though
technically the SEALs weren't supposed to be operating in Pakistan; it was the heat rising from his rooftop
hideaway, even in the dead of night. The corner of his
mouth lifted. He had full confidence in the mission—
he always did.

He adjusted his .300 Win Mag slightly to the left,
repositioning the target in his crosshairs. The man in
his sights had just slipped around the corner of a white-
washed building and stepped around a whirlwind of sand
in his path—and his path led to the Jeep parked in front
of Dr. Hamid Fazal's house.

"I have eyes on a suspected target. How's it looking,
Grayson?"

Chip Grayson, his spotter, sucked in a breath. "It's
that guy who just came around the corner, right?"

"That's our man, and he's heading for the Jeep and
Fazal's house. Is the doctor out yet?"

"Not yet. Do you see a weapon?"

"Nope, but I don't see his hands."

"Movement at the front door. Whaddya got, Foley? Do or die time?"

Austin let out a measured breath, the man in the crosshairs his whole world, the man's movements determining Austin's next step and the target's own fate. The suspect turned his head to the side once. Austin blinked. Another drop of sweat plopped to the gravel on the rooftop.

"Fazal's at the door, outside, weapons up."

"The rescue team can't see our guy yet, which means nobody has a clear shot."

"Except you."

"Got that right."

"Are you gonna take it?"

"Patience, my man. He could be a friend coming to say goodbye to Fazal."

"Except nobody's supposed to know he's leaving, especially not in the company of a navy SEAL team."

The man hunched forward suddenly and Austin's finger tightened on the trigger, the action an extension of his brain. The suspect couldn't have a gun. He wouldn't be ducking if he wanted to shoot.

The target pulled his hand from a pocket, clutching something dark and pear-shaped. Austin's jaw tensed as he recognized the object. The man reached for the grenade with his other hand.

Austin took the shot. "Got him."

The man jerked and fell, the grenade dropping from his hand and rolling away from his body.

Grayson got on the radio to the team now assisting Dr. Fazal into the Jeep. After acknowledging Grayson's communication, one of the SEALs broke away and approached the dead man on the street.

A movement on top of a building across the way caught Austin's attention. With his scope, he zeroed in on the sniper raising his rifle and aiming at the SEAL in the street.

Austin took him out…and the fight was on.

Chapter One

Sixteen months later

The soles of Sophia's sneakers squeaked on the slick cement floor of the parking structure. She hit the key fob and her trunk popped open. As she swung her bag into the car, it fell on its side, scattering the contents across the carpeted trunk.

She huffed out a breath and hunched over to collect her junk—a hastily wrapped leftover sandwich from lunch, a dog-eared paperback…and Dr. Fazal's files.

"Damn." She must've swept them up by mistake in her rush to leave the office. She checked the time on her cell phone clutched in her hand, and grimaced. She'd planned to leave work a little early so she could get ready for her date tonight, but Dr. Fazal had wanted her to look up something for him and one thing had led to another, which it usually did with Hamid, including a stop at the pharmacy on her way out. Now she had to return these files to him since he was burning the midnight oil and might need them.

She hadn't disappointed her mentor's faith in her yet and didn't plan on starting now. His belief in her these past months had been the highlight of her year—hell, the highlight of her sorry life.

She grabbed the folders, shoved the rest of the stuff back into the canvas bag and slammed the trunk shut. As she turned with the folders pressed to her chest, a car squealed around the corner from the parking level above hers.

She jumped back, coughing on the exhaust the old beater left in its wake. The car had sped past her and was already too far down the aisle for its driver to benefit from a choice hand gesture from her, so she just shook her head.

Grinning, she shoved that hand into the pocket of her sweater. Dr. Fazal had been helping her curb her temper, too. In fact, the doctor had been like the father she'd never had. So, she had no problem going back up to the office to return his files—even if it did make her late for her date.

She hadn't been having much luck with the guys from that internet dating site anyway, although she had high hopes for Tyler.

The elevator settled on her floor, and she stood to the side as the doors opened in case anyone was coming out, not that she expected people hanging around the office building at this late hour. Dr. Fazal stayed late most nights.

Due to the emptiness of the building, the elevator car sped upward without stopping once. Sophia got off on the fourth floor and almost tripped over Norm's bucket.

Two doors down from the elevator, Norm looked up from his mop. "Sorry, Sophia. I thought you just left."

"I left a while ago, but I had to make a stop at the pharmacy downstairs and then got all the way to my car before I realized I forgot something. I'm assuming Dr. Fazal is still here."

"I just got up to this floor. Heard someone on the stairs a little while ago, and thought it was you. Maybe it was the doc." He returned to his bucket and dredged the mop in the soapy water. "Make sure you walk where it's dry."

"I will." She jingled her office keys in her hand as she made a wide berth around the wet linoleum.

Maybe Dr. Fazal left early tonight, and since he didn't call her about the files, he hadn't missed them. He had seemed distracted all day, for a few days actually, so maybe he'd decided to call it quits.

She strode to the last office on the left, where Dr. Fazal had his orthopedic practice. Leaning into the door, she tried the handle first. He'd locked up since she left.

"Dr. Fazal?" She tapped on the heavy door. Then she inserted her key and pushed it open.

He'd turned off the lights in the reception area, but a glow beyond the front desk area gave her hope. "Hello? I'm back."

She ducked beside a table where someone had fanned out all the magazines from the rack and stacked them together. Ginny from the front desk usually straightened up the reception area on her way out of the office. Sophia dropped the magazines into different slots on the wall rack and opened the door that led to the offices in the back.

The quiet suddenly unnerved her. Hamid must've gone home. She stepped through the door and the toe of her shoe kicked something on the floor. She dropped her gaze and her eyebrows collided over her nose as she nudged the stapler with her foot. Licking her lips, she peered around the corner to the front desk area where Ginny ruled the roost during the day.

Her heart slammed against her chest as she jumped back from the chaos that marred Ginny's typically orderly work area. Someone had whipped open all the drawers, and the contents of those drawers had spilled over onto the floor. The overhead bins yawned open, discharging their contents in a humble-jumble mess.

The hair on the back of her neck quivered, and she twisted her head over her shoulder, almost giving herself whiplash. Were the thieves still here? If they were looking for drugs, they could've targeted a better office.

Swallowing hard, she took one step toward Dr. Fazal's office and the exam rooms and paused with her head cocked to one side. Silence greeted her. They'd either left already or had heard her come in and were lying in wait, ready to pounce.

Her gaze darted to the front door of the office, which had closed behind her. Her street sense told her the thieves had left the scene of the crime. Her street sense was also sending a shiver up her spine.

She crept down the short hallway, trailing her fingers along the wall. She poked her head into exam room one, her jaw hardening. The intruders had rifled through this room, too…and the next.

She continued her stealthy approach to Dr. Fazal's office. He'd be devastated by the violence perpetrated against his practice. He'd come here to get away from the violence of his homeland.

Holding her breath, she walked into his office. She released the breath with a sputter. Someone had ransacked the room. Papers were strewn all over, sofa cushions were pulled out and hastily stuffed back in place and the drawers of the credenza behind Dr. Fazal's big desk stood open and half-empty.

These people must be some stupid junkies to think they were going to find drugs in here—but then weren't all junkies stupid? A heavy smell in the air made her shudder and close her eyes. Reaching for the phone, she stepped around his desk.

She froze. Then she dropped to her knees beside Dr. Fazal crumpled on the carpet next to his chair.

"Dr. Fazal! Hamid!" She curled her arm under his neck to raise his head and blood soaked the sleeve of her sweater. Blood—her subconscious had recognized the smell. One side of Hamid's head had been blown away. She choked out a sob and her throat burned.

The smell of gunpowder permeated the air. Why hadn't she noticed it before? She sat back on her heels and another shock jolted her body—a gun lay next to Dr. Fazal's hand.

"No, no, no." She shook her head. He never would've taken his own life. Why would he mess up his office first?

She closed her eyes and dragged in a long breath. She didn't like the police, didn't trust the police, but right now she needed the police.

THE BOSTON PD COP, Officer Bailey, scratched his chin with the end of his pencil. "It looks like suicide, ma'am. There's gunpowder residue on the doctor's hand, the shot to the temple looks like it was done at close range."

"And the condition of the office?" Sophia brushed the hair out of her face with the back of her hand. "He ransacked his own office, ran back in here and shot himself because he couldn't find a pencil? That's ridiculous. And I already told the detective that his computer's missing."

"Had you noticed a change in his demeanor lately? Depressed?"

"He was…" She pressed her lips together. She didn't want to betray Dr. Fazal, but she didn't want to withhold any information that might help the investigation into his murder—because this *was* a murder. "He'd been agitated the past few days, distracted."

"Was anyone hanging around the office? Disgruntled patients? Problems with the wife?"

"Dr. Fazal was a widower. I already told the detectives."

"You have my card, Ms. Grant. The detectives on the case will have more questions for you later." He circled his finger around the reception area where he'd been questioning her. The coroner hadn't removed Dr. Fazal's body from the office yet. "We'll finish up here and barricade it as a crime scene. Are you expecting patients tomorrow?"

"It's Saturday. No. But I'll call Ginny Faraday, our receptionist, to let her know what happened. She can start calling our patients."

The cop tapped his notebook. "That's the name and number you gave me earlier?"

"That's right." She hugged the framed picture she'd taken off the floor next to Dr. Fazal's body.

Officer Bailey noticed the gesture and pointed to the picture. "What's that?"

She turned it around to face him. "I-it's a picture of Dr. Fazal congratulating me on an award I won last year."

"Was it in his office?"

"On the floor. He must've knocked it over when he fell." She pressed it to her chest again as one tear rolled down her cheek.

"Sorry for your loss, ma'am. You can take that with you."

Bailey asked her a few more questions, double-checked her contact info and asked her if she wanted an escort to her car.

"I do, thanks." The cops might think Dr. Fazal had committed suicide, but she knew his killers were on the loose out there somewhere.

Bailey called over another officer on the scene. "Nolan, can you walk Ms. Grant down to her car in the parking structure?"

"Absolutely. Lead the way."

Sophia took one last look at the office where she'd spent just about the happiest year of her life and sucked in her trembling bottom lip. Dr. Fazal hadn't killed himself. He wouldn't have left her like that—not like everyone else had.

When Officer Nolan touched her back, she jumped and then barreled out the office door. A detective was questioning Norm by the elevator.

Sophia stabbed the call button and then turned to Norm. "Did you tell the detective that you heard someone on the stairwell right before I came back, Norm?"

"I sure did, Sophia."

"They think it was suicide." She snorted. "No way. You should've seen the office."

"D-do you think that was the doc's killer on the stairs?" Norm's eyes bugged out.

The detective questioning Norm raised his eyebrows

at Officer Nolan. "I'd like to question the witness in private."

"Sure, sure." Nolan's face turned red up to his hairline and he prodded Sophia into the elevator when the doors opened.

When she got inside, she slumped against the wall, folding her arms over the framed picture. "I just wanted to make sure Norm told the detective about hearing someone on the stairwell. That could've been the killer."

"You're convinced Dr. Fazal didn't kill himself?"

"He wouldn't do that."

To me, the voice inside her head screamed. *He wouldn't do that to me.*

She lifted her shoulders and dropped them. "Besides, why would he search his own office like that?"

"Maybe he was looking for something, couldn't find it and decided to end it all. Did you know he kept a gun in his office?"

"Who said it was his gun? Maybe the killers shot him in the head and planted the gun in his hand."

"I guess we'll know more when the homicide detectives look into everything and we get the ballistics report and the autopsy."

The elevator reached level two of the parking garage and the doors opened on an empty aisle.

Sophia grabbed the officer's arm. "Wait a minute. When I was returning to the office, a car came careening around the corner, tires screeching and everything. Do you think it might be connected?"

"What kind of car? Did you get a look at the driver?"

"It was an old car, beat-up, midsize and dark. I didn't see who was driving, but can you tell the detective?"

"I'll tell him and you can tell him yourself when you

talk to him again. This lot is straight in-and-out, right? No attendant?"

"If you're a visitor, you take a ticket on your way in and pay at a machine before you leave. There should be some record around that time." She slipped the photo into her purse.

"I'll pass it on. This your car?"

It was the only car left in the aisle, maybe on the entire level.

"This is it. Thanks." She hit the key fob, and the officer waited until she got into the car. She waved at him in her rearview mirror as he stepped back into the elevator.

Then she broke down.

Her messy cry lasted a good five minutes. When she got it all out, she bent forward and reached into her glove compartment for some tissues.

As she straightened up, she heard a whisper of movement behind her. Her eyes flew to the rearview mirror and she met the steady gaze of a man in her backseat.

Chapter Two

Austin held his breath. He had to play this right or this emotionally overwrought woman just might go ballistic on him. And he'd deserve it.

He held up both hands. "I'm not here to hurt you. I'm a friend of Dr. Fazal's, and I think I know what happened to him."

One of her hands was gripping the steering wheel and the other was covering the center where the horn was located. If she drew attention to them, to him, it would be all over.

Her breath came out in short spurts and her gaze never left his in the mirror. "Do you have a gun on me?"

He could tell her he did and she'd probably do whatever he asked, but he didn't want to frighten her any more than he had—any more than she had been by to-night's events.

"I don't have a gun on you. You can lay on that horn and I'll hightail it out of your car, out of your life, but you may never know what happened to Hamid... And your own life may be in danger."

Her dark eyes, beautiful even with makeup smudged all around them, narrowed—not exactly the reaction he'd expected.

She blew her nose with the tissue and tossed it on the floor of the car. Turning slightly in the driver's seat, she asked, "If you know so much, how come you're not up there right now talking to the Boston PD?"

"For the same reason I didn't come and knock on your front door or give you a call. I'm trying to keep a low profile—for reasons I may not be able to tell you."

"Because you killed him?"

"I didn't kill him, and I won't harm you."

"How do I know that?"

"You're alive, aren't you?" He relaxed in the backseat, his hands on his knees in full view. "You already know I'm no threat to you. You sense it. In fact, you're a street-savvy woman, aren't you, Sophia Grant?"

She spun around to face him. "Who the hell are you? How do you know me? Dr. Fazal?"

He splayed his fingers in front of him. "I'm going to reach into my front pocket."

Nodding, she curled her hands into fists as if ready to take him on.

He slipped his military ID from his pocket and held it in front of her face. "That's me. I'm US military, and I'm on an assignment."

She squinted at the laminated card and shifted her eyes to compare his face to the picture on the ID.

He asked, "Can we go somewhere and talk? You might feel more comfortable in a public place."

"I might feel more comfortable if you sit in the front seat where I can see your hands."

He held up his hands again, pinching his ID between his fingers. "They're right here. I'd rather stay in the back for now. I don't want to be seen in your car in case…"

"In case someone's watching me, following me?" She

started the car's engine. "Why would someone be interested in me?"

Why *wouldn't* they be? Austin dragged his gaze from her luscious lips and met her eyes. "Because you worked with Dr. Fazal."

"It wasn't suicide. He didn't kill himself." Her chin jutted forward as if daring him to disagree with her.

"He may have killed himself, but only because he had no choice. The men after him would've killed him anyway— and probably after hours or days of torture."

She gasped and covered her mouth with one hand.

A twinge of guilt needled his belly. He'd gone too far. Just because she hadn't screamed and hit the horn or fainted didn't mean she had a hard shell impervious to pain.

"I'm sorry, and you're right. Dr. Fazal was not suicidal, but I would like a better idea of what was going on with him. Can you help me out?"

"I knew it." She smacked the steering wheel. "Those idiots were trying to tell me he killed himself when the office had obviously been searched."

"Searched?" His pulse sped up. "Was anything taken?"

"Just his computer as far as I could tell. The cops had me look around, but I was too rattled to see straight." She put the car in Reverse and backed out of the space. "I know a place in Cambridge, not too far from here— dark, not too crowded, but crowded enough so that we won't be noticed."

"Sounds good." He ducked down and lay across the backseat. "I'm going to stay down. I want you to check your mirrors when you drive out of the parking structure to make sure you're not being followed. Keep an eye out. Slow down and let cars pass you, take a few turns if you think someone's tailing you."

"You're not making me feel any better."

"You'll be safe—with me." The same couldn't be said for Dr. Fazal, and Austin felt the failure of showing up too late to protect him gnaw at his gut.

The tires squealed and the car bounced as she pulled out of the parking structure. Austin's forehead hit the back of the driver's seat. "Did you see someone?"

"All clear so far. Why?"

"You stepped on that gas like you had the devil himself on your tail."

"To get out of that parking structure, you gotta move or you'll be waiting there all night."

Apparently, every intersection she blew through had the same problem as the car sped up, lurched around corners and jerked to a stop every once in a while. If Fazal's killers didn't end him, Sophia's driving would.

"No headlights behind you?"

"Not for any length of time. Don't worry. I got this. I'm no stranger to losing a tail."

"Should that concern me?"

"It should make you happy. We're almost there."

Rubbing his forehead, Austin sat up and peered out the window. They'd already crossed Longfellow Bridge and were speeding into Cambridge.

A few minutes later, the car crawled along a street lined with bars and restaurants as Sophia searched for a parking space.

He tapped on the window. "There's a public lot with space."

"Are you kidding? I'm not paying twenty-four bucks to park my car."

"I'll spring for the parking. We could be driving around here all night looking for a place."

"Your call, but it's a rip-off." She made an illegal

U-turn in the middle of the street and swung into the lot, buzzing down her window.

He pulled a crumpled twenty and a five from his pocket and handed them to her.

The attendant met the car. "That's twenty-four dollars, please."

She gave him the money, and then pinched the one dollar bill he gave her between two fingers and held it over her shoulder. "Here you go."

When they got out of the car, Sophia crossed her arms, gripping her biceps and hunching her shoulders.

"You don't have a jacket? It's cold out here for just a long-sleeved shirt."

"I had a sweater." She slammed the car door and locked it. "It has Dr. Fazal's blood all over it."

"I'm sorry. Take my jacket." He shrugged out of his blue peacoat and draped it over her shoulders, his hands lingering for a few seconds.

She hugged the coat around her body and sniffed. "Thanks."

They joined the Friday night crowd on the sidewalk—students, professors, young professionals, a few tourists. They could fit in with this bunch, even though Sophia still wore a dazed expression on her pale face.

She led him to one of the many bars, crowded but not jammed, a duo at one end singing a folk song.

"We can probably still get a booth, but we'll have to order some bar food."

"That's okay." He tipped his chin toward a booth in the back of the long room that three people had just left. "There's one."

He followed her as she wended her way through the tables scattered along the perimeter of the bar. Her black hair gleamed under the low lights, and he had a sudden urge to reach out and smooth his fingers along the silky strands. He shoved his hands into the pockets of his jeans instead.

A waitress swooped in just as they reached the table. "I'll clear this up for you."

When the waitress finished clearing the glasses from the previous customers, Sophia slid onto the bench seat and he sat down across from her.

Hunching forward, she buried her chin in her hand and the small diamond on the side of her nose sparkled. "Tell me who you are and what the hell is going on."

"My name's Austin Foley, and I'm in the US Navy."

She blinked her lashes, still long and dark even though her mascara had run down her face. "How do you know Dr. Fazal?"

He massaged his temple. How could he explain things to her without compromising classified information?

Of course, the rescue of Dr. Fazal was no longer classified, and if anyone had a right to know about Dr. Fazal's past, Sophia did. Maybe she already knew. All their intel on Fazal and Sophia indicated that the two had grown close.

"What did Fazal tell you about his past before coming to the US?"

Sophia bit her bottom lip as the waitress approached the table. "Now, what can I get you?"

"I'll have a beer—whatever you have on tap."

"Club soda with lime for me."

The waitress left, and Sophia leaned toward him over the table. "I only know that his wife and two daughters died in a terrorist bombing in Islamabad. The US government resettled him here for safety, but then you know that already. You claim to know more than I do, so you'd better start spilling or I'm calling my new best friends at the Boston PD."

Austin squeezed his eyes shut and pinched the bridge of his nose. If he'd thought handling Sophia Grant would be easy, he'd been completely mistaken. She'd probably catch him out in a lie in about two seconds, too. Were there any girls back home like this? If so, he'd never run into one, and given the size of White Bluff, Wyoming, he'd run into all of the women.

"Okay." He ran a hand across the top of his head, his hair still short from active duty. "Dr. Fazal helped out the US military, helped us nail a wanted terrorist hiding in the area. His life wasn't worth much in Islamabad after that, so we hustled him out of Pakistan."

She nodded. "That doesn't surprise me. I figured there was more to his story."

Nothing seemed to surprise this surprising woman. "We settled him in Boston. You know he went to medical school here?"

"Yes." She drummed her fingers on the table. "Were you one of the guys who helped rescue him?"

"Uh-huh."

The waitress delivered their drinks and Austin held his up. "To Dr. Fazal."

Sophia clinked her glass with his. "To Dr. Fazal."

She took a sip of her drink and laced her fingers around the glass mug. "What were you doing here at the precise moment he got murdered?"

Austin ground his back teeth together and took a bigger swig of beer than he'd intended. He gulped it down. "He'd contacted us a few weeks back, said he was being watched, followed."

"So *that's* why he'd been agitated."

"Was he?"

"For the past several days—distracted, even curt with me, which was unusual."

"After his initial contact, we didn't hear from him again. I guess he thought we could help him, but I was too late." His hand curled into a fist on the table.

"D-do you think that's it? The people he betrayed in Pakistan wanted revenge?"

"That's what it looks like on the surface, but it's hard for me to swallow that they'd go to all this trouble to get to him. The main guy he betrayed is dead. Were his followers that loyal to track Fazal to the US and murder him here? That's taking a huge chance on their part, and how did they even get into the country if they're on a no-fly list?"

"You're asking me? I'm just a physical therapist in training. You're the—" she waved her hand at him "—navy guy. What is a US military man doing operating on domestic soil, anyway?"

"This is strictly under the radar."

"That's the reason for all the cloak-and-dagger stuff? You're lucky I didn't scream bloody murder and run back to tell the cops a man had broken into my car and had been lying in wait for me."

"Some of it's luck."

"Some?" She raised her dark brows as she took a drink from her glass.

He shrugged. "We had a little intel on you. I didn't figure you for the screaming type."

"That's creepy." She swallowed. "The government can just spy on anyone these days. Is that it?"

"I wouldn't call it spying."

"I would." She flipped her black hair over one shoulder. "So, what do you want from me? I can't give you any more information about Dr. Fazal than I gave the police."

"The Boston PD thinks he may have committed suicide. Now I just gave you this other info about Dr. Fazal. Does this change your view of what was going on with him?"

"He never said anything to me about it, but his killers were definitely searching for something in the office."

"That worries me, makes me think this is about more than revenge."

"What could they have been looking for? Dr. Fazal already gave up what he knew about the terrorist in Islamabad, right?"

"Maybe he had more information that he didn't even tell us." He grabbed a plastic menu from the end of the table. "Are you hungry? The waitress didn't make us order anything, but you probably haven't had dinner."

"I'm not hungry." She clapped a hand over her mouth. "My date."

"You had a date tonight?" Of course she did. An attractive, vibrant woman like Sophia Grant wouldn't be sitting at home alone on Friday night.

"I did. I was supposed to meet him downtown."

"Give him a call. Is there still time?"

"I don't have his phone number, and he doesn't have mine, thank goodness, or he would've been calling me."

"That's a weird date." He drew his brows together. At least this guy wasn't her fiancé or the love of her life if they didn't even have each other's phone numbers.

"It was a date on Spark."

"Spark?"

"Where've you been, Islamabad?" She tapped her cell phone. "It's a dating app."

"Is that safe?"

"Safer than this." She drew a circle in the air above their table.

"Got me there." He shoved the menu aside and finished his beer. "You'll let me know if anything unusual happens, won't you?"

"Yes, but shouldn't I tell the police, too?"

"Of course, but I'd appreciate it if you didn't mention our meeting. I'm not supposed to be here, not supposed to be investigating this."

"My lips are sealed." She dragged her fingertip across the seam of her mouth. "Where should I drop you off?"

"I'm at a hotel downtown, but since you're in the other direction I can catch the T back to the hotel—unless you want to head downtown to meet your Spark date."

"You know where I live?" She pushed her half-full glass away from her. "Forget the date. It was just our second. He probably figured I got cold feet."

"Does that happen a lot? I mean, with Spark dates."

"Quite common." She reached into her purse and pulled out a wallet.

"I'll get this. I can call it a business meeting."

"Ah, but you're not supposed to be here, remember?"

"Somebody somewhere has to reimburse me." He dropped a ten on the table. "I'll walk you to your car."

"I really don't mind dropping you off." She scooted from the booth, hugging his coat to her chest.

"That's okay, as long as you keep a lookout when you drive home, just like you did on the way over here."

She jerked her head up. "Do you think I might still be in danger?"

"Not if Dr. Fazal's killers found what they were looking for tonight."

"And if they didn't?"

"They might be at his house right now. Hopefully, the police got there first, but Fazal's killers will return. They might return to the office, too, if they got spooked the first time."

"They might've heard Norm—he's the nighttime janitor."

"Are you going back to the office next week?" He held the door of the bar open for her as she huddled inside his coat.

"Just to wrap up business. All of my patients were Dr. Fazal's patients. We worked together and he referred his patients to me after their surgery, so I could rehabilitate them. I'm not sure what's going to happen now, and I'm not sure what's going to happen to Ginny our receptionist and the two nurses who worked with him." A tear escaped from the corner of her eye and she dashed it away.

"You're going to miss him. He was a good man."

"The best."

Austin tipped his head toward the parking lot down the street. "I'll walk you to your car, and you can drop me at the nearest T station."

The attendant manning the parking lot had called it quits for the night and the entrance was chained off. The exit had spikes to make sure nobody sneaked in that way.

Austin put his hand on Sophia's back as they made their way through the cars.

Out of the corner of his eye, he sensed movement and his reflexes jumped into action. He spun around just in time to see the dull glint of a .45 in the moonlight.

Chapter Three

The mysterious stranger walking beside her shoved her to the ground. She thrust out her hands as she fell to her knees, her palms shredding against the asphalt.

Her instincts had failed her. The guy was turning on her, attacking her. She coiled her body into a crouch. She whipped her head to the side, ready to launch herself at his legs—but which legs were his?

Austin had one arm wrapped around another man as they staggered back and forth under a circle of light from the parking lot. Austin had his right arm thrust in the air at a weird angle, grasping the other man's wrist.

Sophia froze as her gaze focused on the gun clutched in the man's hand, pointing at the sky. How long would it be pointing upward?

As she scrambled toward the other side of the car, someone grunted. Gunfire ripped above her head. She flattened her body against the asphalt, the smell of oil invading her nose. The smell of gunpowder replaced it.

"Hey, hey!"

The male voice came from a distance but Sophia didn't dare lift her head.

A rough hand grabbed her arm, and Austin's harsh whisper grated close to her ear. "Are you okay?"

"Yes. What…?"

He practically yanked her to her feet. "Let's go. Now."

"But…"

He snatched the keys still clutched in her hand and herded her into the car from the driver's side, coming in right behind her. She crawled over the console as Austin made it clear he was taking the wheel. He started the car, and she turned her head toward the passenger window.

A dark figure limped away between the remaining cars as a cop came running up the sidewalk, shining his flashlight into the parking lot.

Without turning on the headlights to the car, Austin pulled out of the lot on the other side of the officer's probing flashlight. When he hit the street, he kept his speed slow and steady until he turned the corner. Then he accelerated until he reached the next major thoroughfare when he put on the lights and reduced his speed to the limit.

That's when Sophia realized she was breathing in short spurts. The whole attack had gone down in a manner of seconds and she still couldn't quite believe it had happened—except for her stinging palms…and the gun in the cup holder.

She rubbed her hands together, loosening bits of gravel into her lap. "What the hell just happened?"

"Are you absolutely sure you weren't followed when you left the medical building?"

If she hadn't fully absorbed the terror of the altercation in the parking lot before, it now hit her like a wall of water.

She gripped the edge of the seat, digging her fingernails into the nubbed fabric. "D-do you think that man had something to do with Dr. Fazal's murder?"

"Of course. Could you have been followed?"

"I don't think so." She pressed her fingertips to her temples. "I watched, just like you said."

He made a sharp right turn and her head bumped the glass of the window.

"Sorry." He pulled the car to a stop along a side street near the MIT campus and jumped out.

With her head spinning, she tumbled out of the car after him. He was already on the ground, scooting backward beneath the car, propelling himself with the heels of his boots—cowboy boots. What kind of navy guy wore cowboy boots?

"What are you doing?" She crossed her arms over her chest, hugging Austin's jacket around her body, noticing for the first time the fresh, masculine scent in its folds.

He swore and rolled out from beneath the car, clutching something in his fist. Hopping to his feet, he uncurled his hand. "They were tracking you already."

Her mouth dropped open as she stared at the black quarter-size device cupped in his palm. "Why? What do they want from me?"

"I don't know." He tipped his hand and the object fell to the pavement, where he crushed it beneath the heel of his boot. "I don't know what they wanted from Fazal. If it was just revenge they were after, they got that. They didn't have to search his office. And why come after you?"

"Come after?" She fell against the back door of the car.

"I'm sorry, Sophia. Let's get you home."

"Home?" She shuffled away from him. "If they already put a tracker on my car, won't they know where I live?"

"Not if they placed the bug at the office." He kicked the pieces of the tracking device with his toe, scattering them into the gutter.

"Was that man in the parking lot going to shoot me?"

"I don't think so." He cocked his head to one side and scuffed the bristle on his chin with the pad of his thumb. "He could've taken the shot from farther away. When I saw the gun out of the corner of my eye, the guy didn't have it raised and ready to shoot."

"I suppose that's something to be thankful for."

"He could've wanted info from you."

"But he wasn't expecting you—or at least wasn't expecting my date to be a trained…whatever you are." She waved her hand up and down his body.

"SEAL." He rubbed his hands on the thighs of his jeans. "I'm a navy SEAL."

She narrowed her eyes. "You're a long way from foreign soil where you usually do your thing, aren't you?"

"I thought I explained to you that's why I can't come in contact with the police. It's—" he shrugged "—unorthodox for us to operate stateside."

"Unorthodox or illegal?"

"Depends on who you're asking."

She jerked her thumb over her shoulder. "And that's why we sneaked away under the cover of darkness and extinguished our headlights back there when the cop showed up?"

"I don't want to have to explain anything. That's not my mission."

"This is a mission?"

"Did you think I was just dropping in on my old friend Dr. Fazal?"

Her nose stung with tears and she squeezed her eyes shut. "He was my friend...and so much more."

He dropped his hand where it lay like a weight on her shoulder. "Do you want me to take you home?"

"Will I be safe there?"

"I'm staying with you—for now."

She studied his strong, handsome face, and the question echoed in her head. *Will I be safe there?*

He blinked. "I'll keep watch over you."

Sighing, she hoisted herself off the car. "I suppose I don't have much choice. I have to go home at some point, might as well be now."

When they got back into the car, Austin turned to her. "You can call the Boston PD right now and let them know you feel threatened—that you think you're being followed. They might step up patrols around your house."

She chewed her bottom lip and traced the scratches on her palm. Have this navy SEAL, who'd already taken out a guy with a gun, watching over her or the Boston PD, who'd made her life a living hell when she was a teen—easy choice.

"Let's see how it goes before I call in the big guns."

Austin started the car. "Where to? I know you live in Jamaica Plain, but I don't know how to get there without a GPS."

"Back across the bridge. I'll be the GPS." She glanced over her shoulder. "Should I look out for a tail?"

"I think I solved the problem, but it's not a bad idea."

She called out directions as she shifted her attention between the side mirror and the mirror on the visor, watching for headlights and suspicious cars.

Her life growing up had hardly been rainbows and

unicorns, but it had just shifted into a strange kind of nightmare that didn't quite seem real. And the man next to her? The most unreal part of it all. He'd literally popped up in the backseat of her car, spouting crazy theories and scaring the spit out of her.

She slid a gaze at his profile. Pretty much everything that had happened tonight, except for Dr. Fazal's murder, had originated with this man.

Yes, she'd seen the stranger with the gun, but had never seen that gun pointed at her. Maybe he was a cop trying to rescue her from Austin. Of course, he had run away, too.

The tracking device on her car? That could've been anything. What did she know about tracking devices?

If Austin had never appeared in her rearview mirror, would she be home snug in her bed, oblivious of gun-wielding assailants and bugged cars? She scooted closer to the door and leaned her head against the cool glass of the window.

With or without Austin, she still couldn't escape the reality of Dr. Fazal's death. He'd seen so much in his life but had gotten to a place where he could appreciate the simple pleasures...and he'd been teaching her to do the same.

A sob escaped her lips and fogged the glass of the window.

Austin touched her knee. "Are you thinking about Dr. Fazal? He was a good man—honorable, courageous. We were both lucky to have known him."

The sincere tone of Austin's voice washed over her like a soothing balm, and a tear welled up in one eye. Only Dr. Fazal had been able to make her cry. Now if she let herself go, she'd never stop—and she already knew tears did nothing but signal your weakness to the world.

She clenched her teeth and dragged in a breath through her nose. Rubbing the condensation from the window with her fist, she said, "He was a great guy... and I'm going to have to find another job."

She could feel Austin's gaze boring into her, and then he removed his hand from her knee.

She tossed back her hair. Let him think she was a cold bitch. She'd opened herself to Dr. Fazal and he'd left her...just like everyone else had. Not that it was his fault. He never would've abandoned her.

"Next?"

"What?"

"Right or left?"

She jerked her head up. She hadn't even been checking the mirrors. She bolted up and grabbed the visor.

"It's okay. I've been watching."

"Left."

She trapped her cold hands between her knees and took a deep breath. "Why are you here? You were responsible for getting Dr. Fazal out of Pakistan and, what? You kept tabs on him?"

"Me personally? No." He cranked up the heat in the car. "US intelligence? Yes."

"CIA?"

"Sort of. There are intelligence organizations under the umbrella of the CIA that are deep undercover."

"You work for one of these organizations?"

"I'm a United States Navy SEAL."

"But one of these organizations contacted you, right?"

He nodded once.

She hunched forward, stretching her fingers out toward the warm air seeping from the vent. "Are you revealing too much? You're not going to have to kill me now, are you?"

He raised one eyebrow without cracking a smile at her clichéd joke. "You're in the middle of this. You deserve to know."

"Am I? In the middle of this?"

"Fazal's killers put a tracking device on your car and tried to pull a gun on you. What do you think?"

The warm air blowing from the vent couldn't melt the chill stealing across her body. She snuggled into Austin's jacket and the comforting scent from its folds. "I think I'm in the middle of it. These intelligence agencies must've known Dr. Fazal was in danger since you showed up at the precise time he was murdered."

Austin's hands tightened on the steering wheel. "I failed him."

"Had you been watching him?"

"I just got to Boston this morning. I read the file on the plane. I read about you, your job, your car, even your address."

Checking the mirrors again, she slumped in her seat. "So much for privacy."

Her paranoia about authority hadn't been misplaced all those years. They really *were* out to get her. Did Austin also know about her messed-up past?

He snorted. "There is no privacy."

"You knew all that, but you hadn't seen Dr. Fazal yet?"

"I showed up at the office building minutes after the first responders did. Then I located your car in the parking structure and waited for you."

"You were supposed to protect Dr. Fazal?"

"I was." His jaw formed a hard line.

"Those intelligence organizations don't sound very intelligent. They should've called you in sooner. You could've done something then."

She didn't know why she wanted to make this supremely confident man feel better. Maybe it was the clenched jaw showing that he was human after all. He clearly felt as if he'd failed Dr. Fazal—and she knew all too well what failure felt like.

"Maybe. Or maybe his killers made their move today because they knew we were on to them."

"Who are *they*? Who killed Dr. Fazal?" She tapped on the window. "Turn right."

"It depends on the motive. If it was revenge for working with us to capture the terrorist we'd been tracking, then we know it's that terrorist group, but if it's something else…" He shrugged.

"What else could it be?"

"You tell me. Why'd his killers search his office? Why'd they come after you?"

She turned to him, her mouth gaping open. "You expect me to know that?"

"You worked with him. You were close to him. He treated you like a daughter. We know that."

Her throat felt heavy and she cleared it. "He told me very little about his life before. He always emphasized looking forward."

"You said you noticed something different about him in the past few weeks. Was he nervous? Jumpy?"

"Yes." They'd had a dinner planned and he'd cancelled it. He never canceled plans with her because he knew how much stability meant to her.

"How so?"

"He was secretive. He took a few phone calls behind closed doors. He also saw some mysterious patient. He gave me his file, but he never included the person's information in the regular patient database."

"Is this your street?"

"The apartment building at the end of the block on the right."

"That behavior was unusual for him?"

"It was in retrospect. If he hadn't been murdered today, I probably wouldn't have thought much about it—except for the dinner."

"What dinner?" He pulled the car alongside the curb in front of her apartment building and left the engine running.

Did he expect her to hop out and go up to her apartment by herself while he left her car at the curb and loped off into the night? Hadn't he assured her he'd keep watch tonight? Of course, he owed her nothing.

She coughed into the sleeve of his jacket. "We had dinner at least once a month, and he canceled this month."

"He never canceled before?"

"Never. I mean, I did once or twice, but once Dr. Fazal made plans he kept them."

"If they'd just killed him, that would've been the end of it. But why the search?"

This time she knew it was a rhetorical question, as Austin stared out the window at nothing.

He reached for the ignition. "Should I park here or do you have a parking spot?"

She released a breath. He wasn't ditching her—yet. "If you go up ten feet, there's an entrance to our underground parking garage. I'll direct you to my spot."

They rolled into the garage and she pointed out her parking space, which she'd left what seemed like a lifetime ago but had only been that morning.

"I'll go up with you just to make sure everything's okay, and then I can check your security and monitor the front of your building and watch the elevators."

"A-all night?"

"Whatever it takes."

He said those three words with such conviction, she had a feeling Austin would always do whatever it took.

"Thanks." Was that enough? What did you say to someone who'd just saved your life? She hadn't even thanked him for that. "A-and thanks for saving me from the man with the gun back in Cambridge."

"Of course."

She slipped out of the car and he was beside her in a second. When they got into the elevator, she pushed the button for her floor. "I'm on the third floor."

As they passed the second floor, Austin pulled a gun from his waistband and crowded her to the back of the car. He raised his weapon and the door opened—on her empty floor.

She huffed out a breath, feeling dizzy with relief. "My place is on the left, smack in the middle of the floor."

She held out her hand for her key chain but he shook his head.

When they reached her door, he tucked her behind his body and dangled the keys from one finger. "Which one?"

She tapped her front door key and he inserted it into the deadbolt lock above the door handle and unlocked it. Then he opened the door, and stepped inside, leading with his gun.

"Wait outside the door for a minute."

She held her breath as he stepped inside, continuing to lead with his gun.

He disappeared inside and her heart skipped a beat. "Everything look okay?"

"Just a minute."

His voice sounded muffled, and a picture flashed in her head of Austin going through her closet and personal effects. Gripping the doorjamb, she leaned into her small living room. "Nothing looks out of place in the living room."

Austin emerged from the hallway, his gun still out but dangling at his side. "I wanted to make sure no one was hiding in the back."

"First time I've ever felt good about my small apartment."

"Nothing's out of place?" His eyes flicked over the sparse room, devoid of personal photos and treasured mementos.

She pulled back her shoulders and marched to the console that housed her TV and a few books and placed the cracked photo of her and Dr. Fazal, which had been stashed in her purse since she'd left the office, on a shelf.

"Everything looks fine in here. Nobody under the bed?"

"Or in the closets or hiding in the tub behind the shower curtain, but only you can determine if anything's messed up."

Again that quick glance around her sterile living room. Could she help it if she traveled light? She'd always had to pick up and go at the drop of a hat, so she kept her possessions at a minimum.

"I'll check the bedroom and bathroom—good thing there's only one of each."

Austin trailed her as she took a few steps down the short hallway and turned into her bathroom. A small row of bottles stood at attention on the right-hand side of the vanity, her electric toothbrush claiming the left. She tugged open the mirrored medicine chest that contained toiletries, no medicine. She didn't believe in drugs.

When she closed the cabinet, she met Austin's green eyes in the mirror. How had she missed those eyes before? Probably because this was the first time she'd seen him in full light. Even the bar in Cambridge had been dark.

"All good."

She pointed to the shower curtain dotted with blue seahorses. "You moved that, right?"

"I swept it aside and back again."

"Next room."

She kept her distance as Austin awkwardly backed out of the bathroom. His presence overwhelmed the small space—overwhelmed her.

He stood aside, flattened against the wall as she brushed past him on her way to the bedroom.

She walked into her room and surveyed the matching bed, nightstand and dresser, and a little smile curled her lips. She'd just bought the matching set two months ago—her very first matching furniture, her very first new furniture.

She passed by the bed and ran her fingertips along the green-patterned bedspread. Then she tripped to a stop as a wave of adrenaline washed through her body and a strangled cry twisted in her throat.

"What's wrong?" Austin placed his hand on the small of her back.

She turned toward him and had the strongest desire to throw herself against his solid chest. Instead she dragged in a long breath and whispered, "Someone was here."

Chapter Four

Austin's gaze dropped to Sophia's trembling bottom lip and he had the strongest desire to take her in his arms and make this all go away for her. But a woman like Sophia—prickly and independent—wouldn't appreciate the gesture. Would she?

"How do you know?" He flicked a lock of her black hair from her eye and she jerked back. He dropped his hand.

"It's the bed. Someone was on my bed."

His gaze skimmed the neatly made bed covered with a green floral bedspread and fluffy pillows stacked against the headboard. "How can you tell?"

"Look at the center of the bed." She tugged his sleeve. "There's an indentation. The pillows are flat...and the smell."

He lifted his nose to the air and sniffed the faint perfumed odor. He'd figured it had come from a candle or room freshener. It was that faint.

"What is that smell?"

"It's men's cologne. I hate men's cologne." She grabbed one of her decorative pillows and pressed it against her face. "And it's all over this pillow."

He took the pillow from her, dipping his head to the

pillowcase covering it. He noticed a spicier, slightly musky scent now and raised his eyebrows at Sophia. She'd make a great detective, but she was perceptive just about her own possessions. The occupant of this apartment could be a monk if he didn't know better. Everything had a place. Fazal's killers couldn't have picked a worse apartment to try to get away with a covert search.

"They were very careful. This guy—" he motioned to the bed " must've had a temporary lapse or maybe he just got tired after a full day of killing, stalking and searching."

Sophia sucked in a breath and grabbed his sleeve again. "What does this mean? Nobody followed us from Cambridge."

"They already knew where you lived, Sophia. Probably knew all about you, like we did."

"What are they looking for?" Her head cranked back and forth, taking in the bedroom.

"The same thing they were looking for in Fazal's office when they killed him."

"Why do they think I have it?" Her eyes widened even more. "Do you think Ginny, Morgan and Anna could be in danger, too?"

"The receptionist and the nurses? I don't think so. They didn't have the same kind of relationship as you did with Dr. Fazal."

She hunched her shoulders. "I don't know what they think I have or what I can tell them. Dr. Fazal wouldn't confide anything like that in me. Sh-should I just talk to them and tell them that?"

"No!" He took her by the shoulders, his thumbs pressing against the creamy skin above her sweater. "You don't want any contact with these people. Do you think they'll just question you and release you? They'll question you, all right, but it won't be pretty."

She clamped both hands over her mouth, her eyes glassy with unshed tears.

"I'm sorry." This time he did pull her against his chest, wrapping his arms around her. "But that's a really bad idea."

Her body stiffened, and he loosened his grip to allow her an escape. Sophia Grant would always need an escape. She surprised him by leaning into his body, although she kept her arms dangling at her sides.

"What should I do now? They obviously broke into my apartment without any great effort and without anyone seeing them."

"Right this minute?" He took her hands. "You're going to call the police and let them know what happened. The Boston PD has a criminal investigation open in the case of Dr. Fazal's murder, and you're going to let that play out."

"You don't think the cops will ever find his killers, do you?"

"No, but given who the victim was in this case, the FBI will be moving in shortly, anyway."

She broke away from him and swept her arm across the bed. "And what do I tell the cops? I noticed a wrinkle on my bedspread? You believed me because you know who we're dealing with. They'll just think I'm crazy—been there, done that with the cops."

"Your coworker and friend was just murdered today and you found the body. I think the officers will be understanding."

She rolled her eyes. "You don't know the cops like I do. And you won't be here to back me up, will you?"

"No, I can't be here, but you need to report this and get it on record—whether they believe you or not."

She backed away from him and fell across the bed, flapping her arms like she was making a snow angel. "This'll make it a little more believable."

"You could've just contaminated some evidence." He eyed the rumpled covers.

She peered at him through the strands of hair that had fallen across her face when she'd collapsed on the bed. "C'mon, Foley. You and I both know the guys who broke into my place didn't leave any evidence behind— just the smell of some cheap cologne."

His nostrils flared. Did the aftershave he used smell like cheap cologne? Good thing he hadn't shaved this morning.

"Then call the cops and I'll take a walk around the neighborhood. They're going to ask you if anything's missing. Is there? Computer?"

"I take my laptop with me to work, and it's still in the trunk of my car."

"Not a great idea to leave it there." He snapped his fingers. "Why don't you give me your keys so I can go down and get it? You can call the cops in the meantime, and while they're here I'll take a look at your computer—if that's okay."

Hoisting herself up to her elbows, she asked, "Look at my computer? What for?"

"To see if I can find out what Fazal's killers might be looking for. Maybe you do have something from Hamid and you just don't know it."

"I really don't want anyone going through my computer files."

"I understand." He held up his hands. Not that he didn't already know a lot about her life.

She studied his face as if reading him. Then she bounced up from the bed. "Okay. You can look through my computer, but stick to my emails and a folder on my desktop called Work. Anything Dr. Fazal sent me went into that folder."

"Got it." He followed her into the living room, where she swept her key chain from the table by the front door.

She dangled it in front of him. "I'm going to call the police right now. You don't have to come back up here."

"They might ask to see your keys." He tossed the key chain in the air. "Call them now, report the break-in and make it known you found Dr. Fazal's body today. They'll come out for that. I'll return your keys and hang around until the cops get here, so you don't have to be afraid."

"I won't be afraid. I have a nice little .22 tucked in my closet—not that I'm going to show it to the cops."

His brows shot up. "Did you check to see if it's still there? In fact, you'd better give this place the once-over again to see if anything's been taken. The police are going to ask you, and it'll seem off if you haven't bothered to check."

"I will. Go."

He grabbed the jacket she'd shrugged off earlier and headed back to her car. The trunk lights illuminated her laptop case and a canvas bag, so he grabbed both. When he got back to her apartment, she met him at the door.

"I called the police and they're sending two patrol officers over to take a report."

"Gun still there?"

"The gun and everything else—not that I have anything of value in here—but we both know these so-called thieves were not here to snatch some jewelry and a camera."

"I'll be watching from the twenty-four-hour fast-food place down the block. As soon as they leave, I'll be back." He dumped her keys into her outstretched palm.

As he turned, she grabbed a handful of his jacket. "Where was I between the time I left the crime scene and the time I walked into my apartment and realized someone had been in here?"

"Stay as close to the truth as possible. You stopped for a drink to settle your nerves, but you were nowhere near Cambridge. We don't want them putting you near the shot that was fired and start asking why you ran from the officer there."

"Glad to see I'm not the only one who lies to the police."

Slinging Sophia's laptop case over his shoulder, he made his way to the sidewalk in front of her building. He looked both ways. Did Fazal's killers realize that Sophia had a companion now—one who could take down a man with a gun? They might just have him pegged as a random boyfriend who knew a few moves.

He strode to the next apartment building and ducked behind a wall, away from the glow of the streetlamps. He transferred his weapon from his waistband to the pocket of his jacket and waited.

About fifteen minutes later, a patrol car rolled down the street and stopped in front of Sophia's apartment. Austin waited until the two officers disappeared into the building, and then he loped down the sidewalk toward the orange neon sign boasting all-night burgers.

Pushing through the glass doors, he did a quick survey of the room, his gaze sweeping past the old homeless guy in the corner warming his hands on a Styrofoam cup of coffee and a hipster couple sucking down a couple of milk shakes. He narrowed his eyes at a single man sitting at a table against the wall, clicking away on his laptop.

Must be here for the free Wi-Fi.

Austin approached the counter and nodded to the young woman welcoming him with a big smile and a jaunty hat. He had to give her credit for keeping up the enthusiasm at this time of night.

"Can I get a cup of coffee and an apple pie?"

"Is that for here or to go?" She tapped the computerized register.

"For here, ma'am."

He waited for his snack at the counter, and then took a seat across from the front door where he could keep an eye on it and the man on the laptop.

He pulled Sophia's computer from its case and centered it on the table next to his coffee and prefab pie. As the laptop powered up, he drummed his thumbs on the edge of it and held his breath. He'd forgotten to ask her about a password.

The monitor blinked to life and an array of folders appeared on a backdrop of wildflowers. He recognized the scene as a standard selection from the computer's templates—not that he ever expected Sophia Grant to have a personal photo as her computer's desktop background. Did she even own any personal photos?

He spotted the Work folder and double-clicked on it. The folder contained more folders, some with last names as titles and some with dates.

Only Sophia could tell him if these folders had anything unusual in them. Would Dr. Fazal have put any sensitive information on Sophia's computer if that data could endanger her life? Maybe he'd done so inadvertently.

The folders with the last names were obviously patient files. What had Sophia said about a mysterious patient? Fazal had given her the person's file but hadn't entered the information in their patient database, so maybe it was one of these.

She'd have to show him which one.

Yawning, he popped the lid off his coffee and took a sip. He broke off one corner of his pie to get the slightly burned coffee taste out of his mouth.

The couple with the shakes made a move and exited the restaurant with their heads together. The guy with the laptop followed the pair with his eyes before meeting Austin's gaze for a split second and then returning to his work. Probably idle curiosity—unless he was a private eye spying on them.

Austin took another bite of his warm apple pie, licked the cinnamon goo from his lips and brushed the sugar from his fingers. He closed the Work folder and clicked on the email icon.

Sophia's inbox opened, and a few new messages loaded—all from the same person, someone named Spark or Sparks. He hunched forward and then jerked back when he realized Spark was the online dating site she'd mentioned earlier.

His fingertips buzzed. He wanted to open one of those messages, but she'd realize he'd been snooping. He tracked down the list of messages and saw a few more from Spark—already opened. Didn't he have a right to snoop a little? He was trying to protect this woman.

He double-clicked on one of the messages and immediately felt a sinking sensation in the pit of his stomach as he read some guy's advertisement for himself. He closed the message.

He had no right to delve into Sophia's private business that had occurred before Fazal's murder. He took another bite of his pie. But he'd ask her to go through her new messages and look for anything unusual. She had to be careful now.

He entered Fazal's name in the search field of her inbox and went through those messages, but didn't see anything that raised any red flags. It would be better to do this whole computer exercise with Sophia by his side.

He checked the time in the corner of the computer display and closed out Sophia's mail. The cops had to be done by now. He stowed away the laptop and dumped his trash in the bin.

Calling out a thank-you to the bored fast-food workers, he pushed through the doors and into the cold Boston night air. He shoved his hands into his pockets, curling the fingers of his right hand around the handle of his gun.

When he saw that the patrol car had left, he picked up his pace until he was jogging, his boots scuffing on the sidewalk. He went up through the garage to take a quick look at Sophia's car. Arriving at her apartment door, he tapped once with his knuckle. She had a peephole and he expected her to use it.

She must've been waiting for him because the door swung open immediately. "Well, that was a big waste of time."

"Was it?" He swung the laptop case from his shoulder and put it on the coffee table in front of the sofa. "What did they have to say?"

"A whole lotta nothing."

She'd changed from her dark slacks and sweater into a pair of sweats and a Boston University sweatshirt. She'd pulled her dark hair into a ponytail and must've washed her face, as her dewy skin was devoid of makeup.

"Looks like they left a while ago. I'm sorry. I should've come back sooner." If he hadn't been prying into her Spark emails...

"They left about ten minutes ago and if they'd had their way, they would've left even sooner."

"Did they believe you?" He pointed to the kitchen. "Can I have some water? That coffee was pretty bad."

"I'll get it." In just a few steps, she reached the kitchen and poured him a glass of water from a dispenser in the fridge. As she handed him the glass, she said, "They didn't say they didn't believe me...but they didn't believe me."

"Even with that messed-up bed."

"I know, right? Imagine what they would've thought about that crease in the bedspread."

"But they knew about Dr. Fazal's murder?"

"That's basically why they came out. They thought I was just being jumpy, but they were okay. Stayed longer than they wanted to or had to." She dipped down and patted her laptop case. "How about you? Did you find anything?"

He felt a warm flush spread through his chest under her dark gaze. *She knew.*

"I think you're going to have to do the investigating. I don't know what those patient files are supposed to look like and if there's anything weird about them." He tapped his chin and as his scruff scratched his fingertips, now he wished he would've shaved after he got off the plane this morning. "I thought about the patient you'd mentioned before—the one Fazal didn't enter in the regular database."

"Yeah, his mysterious patient who didn't need any follow-up exercises."

"Do you remember his name?"

"Peter Patel."

"Patel?"

"Indian, right?"

"A very common Indian name."

"Like Smith or Jones would be in the US."

"Exactly."

"So, if an Indian man…"

"Or Pakistani."

"If he wanted a common name, he might choose Patel."

"The mystery patient could've been a friend of Dr. Fazal's."

"A friend he didn't want to acknowledge for some reason."

"A friend from the past, from Dr. Fazal's homeland, someone who knew what he'd done."

She twisted her ponytail around her hand and screwed up the side of her mouth. "Do you think Patel killed Dr. Fazal?"

"If Peter Patel, or whatever his name is, was Dr. Fazal's enemy, I doubt Fazal would've pretended he was a patient and protected his identity. I'm thinking he was a friend, someone who needed help."

"And that help may have gotten Dr. Fazal murdered—figures he'd think of someone else before himself." She rubbed her nose with the back of her hand.

Austin tipped his head toward the laptop. "Do you

want to take a look now or are you ready for bed? It's late."

"I'll look now." She sat on the floor in front of the coffee table and crossed her legs beneath her. "What are you going to be doing tonight while I'm...sleeping?"

"Keeping watch." He sank onto the couch across from Sophia, his knees banging against the coffee table.

"Outside all night?"

"If you don't mind, I thought I'd camp out on your couch. I'm a light sleeper. If anyone tried to break in, I'd know it."

She tapped her keyboard. "Do you think someone might try it?"

"Someone got in here before, and it doesn't seem as if he found what he wanted. He'll try again."

"Are you going to take up permanent residence on my couch?" She peered at him over the laptop lid.

"Sophia, you're going to have to get out of here. It's not safe."

"Are you kidding? Where will I go? How will I afford it?"

"I can take care of all of that. You're a possible source of information for this case—and it's a very important case. We'll keep you safe."

"I've heard that one before." She held up one finger. "Got him. Peter Patel, knee injury."

He hunched forward and she spun the computer to the side so he could see the monitor. An intake form filled the screen—name, address and other vitals.

"Can you print this out?"

"Done." She clicked the screen and a printer across the room buzzed to life. "Are you going to pay Mr. Patel a visit?"

"Since he won't be coming back to the office, yes."

"Can I come?"

"No." He tapped the screen. "Do you see anything out of the ordinary?"

"Other than the fact that this information wasn't entered into our patient database? No." She pushed up and crossed the room to grab the printouts. Then she slid them on the table in front of him. "Anything else you want me to check out?"

"Let's start with Patel."

She kneeled in front of the computer and her fingers flew across the keyboard. "My Spark date from tonight sent me an email. Said he understood if I changed my mind but asked if I wanted to try again."

"No." He grabbed Patel's paperwork and squinted at it as if it were the most fascinating data ever.

Her dark eyes narrowed. "That's rather intrusive considering you and I just met today."

"I don't think it's a good idea to date random strangers—especially now."

"I'd been chatting with this guy long before Dr. Fazal's murder, and we already had one date."

"Even if you weren't a target for terrorists, online dating isn't safe. You can't meet guys the old-fashioned way?"

Doubling over, she banged her head on the coffee table and snorted...or coughed...or maybe that was a laugh. Then she tipped her head back. "Old-fashioned way? You mean bars? I don't do bars, don't drink. Besides, online dating has become one of the most common and popular ways to meet people. Where have you been hiding?"

"Umm, a variety of places around the world—wherever I'm deployed."

"Oh, yeah. I forgot about that." She shut down her computer and snapped the cover shut. "Trust me. Online dating is the way to go."

"Seems kind of impersonal."

"You got that right." She formed her fingers into the shape of a gun and pointed at him. "I'm going to sleep. I'll get you a blanket and a pillow for the couch. Should I take my .22 to bed with me?"

"That's okay. I'll take care of the firepower."

"You don't trust me? I'm a pretty good shot."

"That's a handy skill to have, but I'll keep watch. You go to bed and think about where you want to move tomorrow."

She put her laptop away and disappeared into the hallway for a minute. She returned with a folded blanket and a pillow from her bed in her arms with a toothbrush in its original package on top.

She tossed the toothbrush to him. "Courtesy of my dentist."

"Floss, too? I'm a flosser."

Tipping her head to one side so that her ponytail swung over her shoulder, she said, "I figured you for a flosser. Top right drawer of my vanity."

"Thanks, Sophia."

She folded her arms, grabbing handfuls of her Boston U sweatshirt at her sides. "No, thank *you*. I really don't know what I would've done—or where I'd be now—if you hadn't appeared in the backseat of my car after..."

Choked up by emotion or embarrassed by it, she spun around and made a beeline for her bedroom, slamming the door behind her.

He grabbed the toothbrush and took it with him to the bathroom. He knew where she'd be about now—sitting under some hot light, probably tied up and getting interrogated by some very bad people. He would never allow that to happen to her.

After brushing his teeth he settled on the couch and flicked on the TV, his Glock beside him. Being on watch without his Win Mag always felt a little strange, but then everything about this assignment was strange.

He'd been too late to protect Dr. Hamid Fazal, but not too late to protect Sophia Grant. Now that he'd met the woman with the sad childhood and the hard shell, he'd do anything to keep her safe.

He'd never kept anything from his superiors before, but he just might want to conceal his crazy attraction to Sophia. Ariel, the woman he was supposed to be reporting to didn't need to know, even though he'd never allow his emotions to get the better of him.

That had happened only once.

Chapter Five

The next morning, Sophia tiptoed out of her bedroom into the living room, but she needn't have bothered. Austin, sitting on the edge of the couch, the pillow and folded blanket at one end, was clicking away on his cell phone. A flosser and an early riser.

She crossed her arms over the baggy T-shirt she wore to bed to match her equally baggy sweats. For the first time in about ever, she wished she had one of those filmy negligees to slink around in. Maybe she could actually get the man to notice when she walked into a room.

She cleared her throat. "Good morning."

He jerked his head up. "Whoa. Why are you sneaking around?"

"I thought you might be sleeping." She tugged on the hem of her T-shirt. "All quiet last night?"

"Yep." He returned to his phone.

"Coffee?" She strolled into the kitchen and grabbed the coffeepot. "Do you think the people after me know that you're here?"

He rose from the couch and stretched, his plain white T-shirt straining across an impressive set of muscles. "I think so, but whether or not they know who I am and why I'm here is a different story."

The water from the faucet had spilled over the top of the coffeepot and splashed over her hand while she'd been ogling Austin's physique. She shut off the faucet and tipped the excess water into the sink. "Would they have any reason to believe you'd be here?"

"Me, personally? No." He crossed his arms and leaned against her kitchen table, dwarfing it. "But they might suspect that US Intelligence is onto them, especially after the murder of Fazal. They know there's no way we'd let Fazal's death go unnoticed and uninvestigated."

"Was Dr. Fazal doing any work for the intelligence agencies? I mean currently?"

"Not that I know of, but then, I'm not privy to that kind of information. I protected the doctor once, and was called in on this assignment because he contacted an intelligence officer and because of the chatter."

"What kind of chatter?"

Austin put a finger to his lips. "Top secret. Do you just drink coffee for breakfast or do you actually have food in that kitchen?"

Holding up her hand, she ticked off each finger. "Bagels, cereal—the healthy kind—eggs."

"If it's okay with you, I'll toast a bagel. Cream cheese?"

"Just butter."

"I can work with that." He circled into the kitchen, immediately making the space feel even more small and cramped than it was.

She pressed her back against the counter, sliding her hands behind her. "Bagels in the breadbox, next to the toaster."

Her phone buzzed on the counter and she checked

the display. A knot tightened in her belly. "It's Morgan O'Reilly, one of Dr. Fazal's nurses."

"Aren't you going to answer it?"

"I—I'm not going to say anything about you."

"That's right."

She blew out a breath and answered the call. "Hi, Morgan."

The woman sniffled. "Oh, my God, Sophia. I can't believe it. Was it a robbery? Is that what the cops are calling it? They told me the office was trashed."

"It was, but I don't know if anything was missing. I expect the cops will want Ginny to do an inventory of the drugs."

"We didn't have that many drugs. I could think of a few offices that would have a lot more than us." Morgan blew her nose. "We're going in today, Anna and I. The cops told us we could come in after noon. Do you want to join us? You'd know as much as we would if something was missing."

"Yeah, yeah, if the cops said we could come in." She reached across the kitchen and nudged Austin.

"I think they want us to start picking up the pieces to see what's what."

"I'll definitely be there."

She glanced at Austin, who nodded as he dropped two halves of a bagel into her toaster.

She and Morgan comforted each other with a few more meaningless words, and then she ended the call. "We're all meeting at the office after twelve o'clock."

"Are the police going to be there? Is it still a crime scene?"

"I don't know. Since they gave us a specific time, maybe not." She turned toward the counter and poured the coffee into two mugs. "Were you planning on coming along?"

"I'll go with you, but I'm not going into the office. I don't want to explain myself to the Boston PD. Remember—" he pinched a bagel half between two fingers and tossed it onto a plate "—I'm not supposed to be here."

"Milk? Sugar?"

"Black."

She carried both mugs of coffee to the table and sat down. "Do you have a car?"

"It's at my hotel. I walked to the office."

"Your hotel is downtown?"

"Just a few blocks from Dr. Fazal's office." He sat across from her, putting the plate between them. "Do you want the other half?"

She picked up one half of the bagel and bit into it. The butter ran down her chin and she swiped it away with her fingers. "What's the plan?"

"I'm going to drop you off at the office where you can have a look around with the others. If you see anything out of the ordinary, take a picture for me." He tapped his chin. "More butter."

Her face warm, she jumped up from the table and ripped two pieces of paper towel from the rack. In her sweats and T-shirt with butter dripping off her chin, she must've presented an appealing picture. Not that she'd ever cared what kind of picture she presented before this hot navy SEAL had landed on her couch. Who knew she'd ever be attracted to a military guy, since she usually avoided authority figures like the plague.

When she returned to the table, she waved a paper towel in front of him and he snatched it from her.

She wiped her chin with the other. "Where are you going to be while I'm sifting through the office?"

"I'm going to pick up my laptop at the hotel before I drop you off." He plucked the white T-shirt from his chest with two fingers. "Shower and change, and then I'll find a nice Boston coffeehouse where I'm going to do a little research on Peter Patel."

"Then should we come back here?" Her gaze darted around her small apartment, which had been her first real home.

"Absolutely not. This place is compromised." He swallowed the last bit of his bagel and dragged the paper towel across his mouth. "You can stay at the hotel with me...for now."

She gulped a mouthful of coffee. "How long is this twenty-four-hour protection going to last? I have a life—sort of."

"Until we can figure out who murdered Dr. Fazal, why and what they want with you."

"Couldn't that take years?"

Austin's green eyes flickered. "It's not going to take years, and I know Dr. Fazal would want us to protect you so any life you have can be put on hold for your own safety."

"Maybe this is all some big mistake." She collected the plate and her coffee cup. "It could just be a robbery turned deadly."

"Could be, but I doubt it. Not after the chatter we heard involving Dr. Fazal, not given Fazal's background. I'm sorry, Sophia." He pushed back from the table and took the dishes from her hands, his fingers brushing hers. "Why don't you get ready, pack a bag, take what you'll need for a week or two."

"A week or two?" She raised her eyebrows.

"To be on the safe side."

He kept using that word—*safe*—but she didn't feel safe at all, not when her world had just been turned upside down for the umpteenth time in her life.

"Give me about half an hour, and help yourself to another bagel."

In her bedroom, she grabbed the new pair of jeans she had been planning to wear on her date last night and a red sweater. She slipped from her room to the bathroom and ran the water to warm it up. She dropped her sweats on the floor and then touched the edge of the toothbrush Austin had used last night.

There hadn't been many toothbrushes perched on the edge of the sink like this in her life. When she dated, she tended to keep the guys away from her apartment. It had taken her a long time to have a space just for herself after all the foster care living, and she didn't take it for granted.

Still—she dropped Austin's toothbrush next to hers in a cup—that one looked right.

She showered in a matter of minutes, keeping her hair on top of her head. She dressed in front of the mirror and shook out her hair, the black locks dancing loosely around her shoulders. She ran her hands through the strands, keeping the messy look. She didn't want Austin to think she'd tried too hard with her appearance.

She gathered her sweats and tucked them beneath one arm. Poking her head out of the bathroom door, she called out. "Just give me another fifteen minutes to pack up a few things."

"Take your time."

She sniffed the warm, buttery aroma in the air and

stepped into the living room, still clutching her dirty clothes. "Did you toast another bagel?"

He came out of the kitchen with a plate in one hand and waving a fork in the other. "I made some eggs, too. Sorry, I was starving. Do you want some?"

"No, thanks, and you don't have to apologize for eating." Her gaze tracked over his solid form. A bod like that needed more than a half a bagel to fuel it.

"I'll be done before you finish packing." His eyes widened and he pointed the fork at her. "You look… more relaxed. Are you feeling better?"

"Not much." She pressed a hand to her belly. "When I think about Dr. Fazal, I feel sick to my stomach."

"I know. I'm sorry." He dropped his gaze to the plate of steaming scrambled eggs. "I understand."

His low voice vibrated with emotion. He must've lost a few of his fellow SEALs in combat.

"But if we can do something to find his killers—" she hugged her clothes to her chest "—that will make me feel better. Justice is sweet."

"Justice is…justice." He stabbed a clump of eggs with his fork. "Start packing."

She accomplished the task in twenty minutes and when she came into the kitchen, Austin had washed and dried all the dishes.

"Wow, a navy SEAL and handy in the kitchen. Thanks."

He snapped his fingers. "Nothing to it. I grew up on a ranch with three brothers and two sisters, and we were all expected to do the chores—outside and inside."

"A ranch?" She nudged one of his cowboy boots planted firmly on her floor. "That explains these. Where's the ranch?"

"Wyoming."

"Never been there."

"You're a city girl, huh?"

She shrugged. "Never had a chance to be anything else."

"Ready?" He took the handle of her wheeled suitcase. "My hotel first, and then I'll drop you off at the office. We'll get you there by twelve fifteen."

"Hang on." She charged across the room and swept the framed photo of her and Dr. Fazal from the TV stand and stuffed it into the side compartment of her suitcase.

As they got to the door, she turned and took in her small apartment, her first place all to herself, her refuge.

"You'll be back."

The reality of her situation hit her again when Austin crouched beneath her car to search for bugs. He popped up, brushing the seat of his jeans. "Just want to make sure they weren't busy in the night."

"And were they?"

He spread his empty hands in front of her. "Not this time."

He slid into the driver's seat since he'd be dropping her off. It felt strange giving over so much control to someone so quickly, but she almost felt like her life depended on it—and maybe it did.

As they got closer to downtown, her stomach tightened into knots. Could she return to the place where someone had shot and killed Dr. Fazal?

Her phone buzzed and she peered at the screen. "I think it's the Boston PD."

"Answer it."

"Hello?"

"Ms. Grant? This is Detective Marvin."

"Yes, hello, detective."

"We're done collecting evidence in the office, and you're free to return."

"One of the nurses already told me. We're all meeting there after noon."

"Good. Let us know if you come across anything."

"We will."

"And, Ms. Grant?"

"Yes?"

"Dr. Fazal shot himself."

"No!" Her hand curled around her phone so tightly, the edges cut into her palm. "That's ridiculous. You saw the office."

Austin had put his hand on her thigh, his eyebrows raised to his hairline.

"I said he shot himself. I didn't say he committed suicide. We'll look at all possibilities."

"Nothing you say will make me believe Dr. Fazal killed himself after upending his own office."

Austin had sucked in a breath.

The detective ended the call and Sophia reported to Austin what he'd said. "Someone could've shot him and then placed the gun near his hand, right?"

"Yes. Without seeing the evidence report, it's hard to figure out what happened." He squeezed her leg. "It's like I said before, Sophia. Dr. Fazal would've taken his own life before he'd allow himself to be questioned and probably tortured."

"Before he'd give up what they wanted? Because we know they wanted more than his death. You said that yourself."

"I still believe it." He tapped the windshield. "I'm in the next block."

He wheeled her car into the circular front drive of a large chain hotel. "I'll check with the valet to see if we can leave the car here for thirty minutes."

Austin exited the car and cleared things with the valet before waving at her. Seemed as if the attendant had a hard time saying no to Austin, too.

Austin popped her trunk and the valet lifted her suitcase and laptop from inside. Austin pressed some money into the valet's hand and grabbed her suitcase.

They breezed past the reception desk and landed in front of the elevator. He punched the button and looked over his shoulder. "That's another good thing about having you stay here. You don't have to check in and leave a trail."

What was the other good thing? She let that question pass as she stepped into the elevator. "Leave a trail? You mean, like a credit card? I know enough not to use a credit card if someone's following me."

"Doesn't matter if you pay with cash. It's that interaction. Until we know who we're dealing with, we have to expect a high level of sophistication. They've already identified and bugged your car, located and broke into your apartment. These are no amateurs."

"And killed Dr. Fazal." She slumped against the wall of the elevator car.

"They're not going to get away with it." His jaw tightened and a glitter of anger sparked in his green eyes.

She could almost believe him, but people got away with stuff all the time. She'd had a couple of sets of foster parents who'd gotten away with plenty.

The car finally stopped on the fourteenth floor, and the doors whisked open. She pressed the button to hold the doors open as Austin wheeled her bag out of the elevator. She followed him halfway down the hallway, and he stopped in front of a room across from the ice maker.

He fished a card out of his pocket and held it up. "Home sweet home for the time being, although I've spent all of ten minutes here."

He slid the card home and pushed open the door, holding it open for her. When she crossed the threshold, her gaze skimmed across the king-size bed. Was this the other good thing about having her stay here?

He parked her suitcase in the corner and transferred her laptop from the top of the suitcase to a desk by the window. "That sofa folds out to a bed, by the way, and I'll be bunking there."

She shouldn't have expected anything less from this chivalrous cowboy, even though she'd never met anyone quite like him.

"It's your room and you're a lot bigger than I am. You keep the bed and I'll take the sofa bed."

"We'll figure it out later." He shrugged out of his jacket. "Right now I'm going to shower and change. We have an hour before you need to be at the office."

"We'll have plenty of time. The office isn't far from here." She stood at the window, pressing her forehead against the glass. Somewhere out there, Dr. Fazal's killers lurked, waiting for their chance to strike at her. Could she trust Austin to protect her?

Biting her bottom lip, she turned to watch him pulling clothes out of his suitcase. Right now she didn't have a choice.

He glanced up, folding his arms over a pair of jeans. "Are you okay? I won't be long. You can help yourself to the minibar, courtesy of the US government."

She rolled her eyes. "I've had enough from the government. I'm good."

He disappeared into the bathroom, and she plugged in her laptop and powered it up. She scrolled through her emails and tripped across another one from Tyler, the guy she'd stood up last night.

They'd been chatting back and forth for a few weeks and had met face-to-face over coffee. She at least owed him an explanation. She composed a quick email letting him know a friend had passed away unexpectedly and they could reschedule later if he was still interested.

She clicked Send and then buried her chin in the palm of her hand as she wedged her elbow on the desk. Was she still interested?

Everything about Austin Foley had overwhelmed her senses from the second he popped up in her back seat. Of course, Austin wasn't real. He'd appeared like a knight in shining armor just when she'd been plunged into darkness and despair—and he'd disappear just as suddenly once he learned what he was here to learn. She'd probably still be dealing with the darkness and despair once he'd vanished. Dr. Fazal was gone.

The bathroom door opened behind her, followed by a burst of citrus steam. She twisted around in her chair.

Austin peered at her from the folds of the white towel engulfing his head. "I left my shirt in here."

Lucky her. As he toweled his hair, she tried not to stare at the muscles that rippled across his bare chest and abs.

He tossed the towel onto the bed and crouched in front of his suitcase, pawing through the contents. "I'm glad I packed some long sleeves and flannels. It's still cold even though spring's right around the corner."

She took in his back and the way his broad shoulders narrowed to his waist in a perfect V. The man didn't have an ounce of fat on his body.

He twisted his head over one of those broad shoulders and heat crested over her face. She turned back to her laptop on the desk. "Yeah, cold for spring."

He whistled some tuneless melody and slammed the bathroom door several seconds later.

She covered her still-warm face with both of her hands. She needed to get a grip. Austin probably had a wife and children—he still looked young. Navy SEALs had families, didn't they? He would. He seemed like the God, country, family type all over. She'd already checked out his bare ring finger, but that didn't mean anything. He probably removed his wedding ring on assignment. Hell, he probably used his stellar hotness to gain cooperation from female witnesses like her.

She spun around when he returned to the room, his coppery brown hair damp and shiny, his face freshly shaved.

"How often do you do assignments like this?"

"Assignments like this?" He cocked his head. "What do you mean?"

"You know." She flapped her hands in the air. "Skullduggery and protecting unsuspecting witnesses and… investigating stuff."

"This is my first and most likely last time."

"Really?"

"Sophia, I'm in the US Navy. I'm supposed to be operating overseas on missions approved by the Department of Defense. I am absolutely not supposed to be conducting any type of surveillance or covert actions on home soil."

"So, why are you?"

"I was asked…ordered by higher-ranking personnel than my commanding officers. I thought I had made that clear. I report to some faceless woman—or at least I think she's a woman—named Ariel. I'm here because I'd been instrumental in spiriting Dr. Fazal out of Pakistan."

"If you got caught by the police, would these high-ranking personnel stand by you? Bail you out? Or would they hang you out to dry?"

"I'm not going to get caught by the police—or anyone else."

He'd just answered her question. He was on his own, and the same authority figures who'd ordered him stateside to protect Dr. Fazal would disown him in a second to protect their own backsides. He knew it…and didn't care.

She tapped her computer screen. "It's almost twelve o'clock. Are you ready?"

"Shoes." He swept up a pair of running shoes from the floor and sat on the edge of the bed to put them on.

"No lucky cowboy boots today?"

"Lucky?" He grinned in a kind of aw-shucks way, and an answering smile tugged at her lips.

"I don't know. We've been having pretty good luck with you wearing those boots."

"These might be lucky, too." He tied one shoe and stomped it on the carpet. "Might have to do some walking this afternoon."

"There's a coffee place about a half a block down from the office building."

"I noticed it before. That's where I'll be when you finish cleaning up the office."

It didn't take them long to get from the hotel to the

medical office building, and Sophia used her parking card to get into the lot. She directed Austin to a different level from where she usually parked just in case her stalkers were looking out for her car.

When they stopped at the elevator, Austin held out his hand. "Let me have your phone. I'll put my number in your contacts, but I'll be waiting for you at the coffee place, so just come on over when you're done."

He tapped his number into her phone and held it out to her when he finished.

She glanced at the new contact. "Supreme Dry Cleaners?"

"That's me." He raised his right hand. "Just in case someone ever gets hold of your phone."

A little shiver zipped across the back of her neck. This espionage stuff was getting too real for comfort. "Got it. See you in about an hour."

He pushed through the metal door to take the steps to the street level, and she stabbed the elevator button to call the car. As she watched the door slam behind Austin, her stomach flip-flopped just like it had last night when he'd left her before the cops arrived.

In less than twenty-four hours, Austin Foley had become a crutch for her, a security blanket, a required accessory...like a cell phone or a purse. She didn't like it.

When the elevator doors opened on the floor of the office, she closed her eyes and took a deep breath before stepping out. If the other residents on the floor had been rubbernecking into Dr. Fazal's office, they must've gotten their fill already because all the doors on the hallway were firmly closed. Of course, not many of the doctors worked on Saturday.

A crumpled ribbon of crime scene tape pooled on

the floor in front of the office, and she stepped over it as she entered the waiting room. She released a noisy breath as Ginny, in jeans and tennis shoes, jumped up from the floor.

"Oh, my God, Sophia. I can't believe this happened." Ginny wrapped her in a hug, rocking her back and forth. "I know how close you were to Dr. Fazal, and you had to find him. I'm so sorry. I'm so sorry for all of us."

Sophia patted Ginny's back. "I-it's terrible. Have you called all the patients?"

Ginny gave her a final squeeze before releasing her. "Don't worry about that. I called everyone who had appointments this week. I referred them all to Dr. Bishop, and I talked to him, as well. I'll take care of the rest of the patients later."

"Morgan and Anna?"

"Morgan's in the back and Anna's not in yet." She swept her arm across the waiting room. "I've been cleaning up the reception area. There wasn't much out of place in the waiting room, but then all we have are magazines and pamphlets up here. Still, they rifled through those, too. What in the world were they looking for among our magazine racks?"

"Obviously not drugs." Sophia pressed her lips together. She didn't want to give anything away about the motive for the killing, but some things were obvious.

"Maybe his killer was already drug-addled and just went crazy."

At least Ginny wasn't spouting the ridiculous suicide theory. "Have you seen the cops yet?"

"I was here when they finished gathering their evidence. You know Dr. Fazal's computer was stolen?"

"I told the police that last night."

"And all the drugs." Morgan poked her head out of the supply room. "So, maybe Ginny's theory is correct. Some junkies broke in here, grabbed the meds, maybe demanded more and when Dr. Fazal didn't give them up, they shot him."

"There was nothing to *give up*." Sophia squeezed the back of her neck. "What else could Dr. Fazal give them?"

Morgan shook her head. "I don't know. It looks like they searched through everything. I suppose you've seen your office since you were here last night. That must've been horrible."

"It was." Sophia brushed a hand across her eyes. "I'm going to see what's what in my office. If Anna doesn't show up, I'll help you with the rest when I'm done."

"I'm here." Anna stumbled into the waiting room with tears streaming down her face. "I can't believe this."

Ginny gave Anna a bear hug and the two women clung together for a few minutes, their tears mingling. Their unbridled emotion socked her in the gut. Sophia didn't even know how to break down like that, wouldn't even know how, and witnessing their pain and grief only made her shell grow harder.

She slipped away from the cryfest and stepped into her office. She maneuvered around the two chairs facing her desk and sank into the chair behind it. She powered on the computer and rested her fingers on the keyboard while she waited for it to come to life.

Why had Dr. Fazal's killers taken only his computer? They probably figured they'd be too conspicuous lugging a host of computers out of the office, although apparently nobody had seen them leave.

She went through her email and opened a few files, but she didn't know what she was looking for. Sighing, she dropped to her knees and gathered up the papers and file folders littering the floor.

They'd probably stolen the drugs to make it look like a typical crime, although they had to know the FBI would be keeping tabs on Dr. Fazal, or at least would be alerted in the event of his murder.

What did they want? What secrets had Hamid been keeping? What secrets had he been keeping from her?

She plopped back in the chair and spun it around to face her bookshelf. The books had been rifled through, too. So, had they been searching for something on paper? A computer file? From the looks of the office, they didn't know.

She ran her hands down the spines of the books to straighten them on the shelf. Then she leaned forward to retrieve a couple that had been left on the floor.

A bright pink sticky note beneath the desk caught her eye. She slid from the chair to the floor and reached for it. Still beneath the desk, she peered at the note, wrinkling her nose as she recognized Dr. Fazal's scratchy handwriting. She clambered back into the chair and held the note under the desk lamp.

As she deciphered the words, her heart slammed against her rib cage. Dr. Fazal had left her a clue.

Chapter Six

Austin flexed his fingers before attacking the keyboard. Entering *Peter Patel* in the search engine returned multiple pages and too many entries to count.

He tried narrowing it down by entering the data from the patient file but didn't get any hits.

Slumping in his chair, he stretched his legs out to the side and took a careful sip of coffee. It beat the stuff Sophia had brewed in that old coffeemaker of hers, but that concoction suited her—strong, bracing and no frills.

Would she keep up that strong front back at the office where she'd discovered Dr. Fazal's body? None of this could be easy for her, and yet she'd responded like a soldier.

How far would Fazal's killers go to contact Sophia, and what exactly did they want from her?

Someone like Sophia wouldn't go for any type of witness protection, but how could they keep her safe in Boston if these guys were determined to interrogate her...or worse? How could *he* keep her safe?

The key could be this guy, Patel. He sat up and grabbed his phone, and then hunched over the laptop to scroll to Patel's phone number from the file.

He tapped the number into his cell and listened to the

phone on the other end of the line ring and ring. Patel didn't even have voice mail? If this were a cell phone number, a recording would come on indicating the person hadn't set up voice mail.

He jotted down Patel's address on a napkin, and then entered it into the computer. The location in Brookline wasn't too far. If Patel wouldn't answer his phone, Austin would pay him a surprise visit.

He accessed his email and pored over the new pictures of his nephew his sister had sent. This baby made him an uncle six times, and he had fun with the role even though he knew his turn would have to wait. His family didn't even know he was stateside, and he couldn't tell them. There was a lot he couldn't tell his family.

The door to the coffeehouse flew open and he glanced up, his heart doing a flip-flop when he saw Sophia's pale face framed by her disheveled black hair.

He kicked out the chair across from him and she dropped into it, waving a pink square of paper in his face. "I found something."

"What is it?"

She smacked the sticky note on the table next to his laptop. "It *is* Patel, and Dr. Fazal was trying to warn me."

He peeled the note from the table and held it close to his face, his eyebrows colliding over his nose. "What the hell does this say?"

"Shh." She put her finger to her lips and looked to her right and then to her left. She leaned forward pointing at each word upside down as she read it out to him in a whisper.

"Leave. New. Patient. Files."

"Is that what that says?" He flicked the edge of the

note. "I'm underwhelmed. What does it mean and how is it a warning?"

She ripped the note from the table and pressed it to her heart. "He's telling me to leave the new patient files alone, and the new patient is?"

"Peter Patel."

"That's right. He's the only new patient who hasn't been entered in the database, so it would only apply to him. Also, this is not something I'd normally handle. It's Ginny's responsibility to enter patient files into the database."

"Where did you find this note? You hadn't seen it before…before his murder?"

"No. It wasn't there when I left my office that night. I found it beneath my desk, where it must've floated when my office was trashed."

"Is this—" his eyes dropped to the note still pressed against her breast "—a typical way for him to communicate with you? Sticky notes?"

"Not unheard of, but not something he'd do frequently. It would definitely get my attention, and don't you see? It's cryptic enough that nobody else would consider it important or out of the ordinary."

"Cryptic for you as well, but gets the job done. The only reason I can think of that he'd warn you off Patel is if he believed Patel would reach out to you."

She covered her mouth with the pink square. "Do you think that was Patel last night in Cambridge with the gun?"

"I don't know." He swirled the coffee in his cup. "If Patel came to see Dr. Fazal, maybe to warn him about something, and Fazal was protecting him by pretending he was a patient, I just can't see someone like that harming you. Dr. Fazal would never do that to you."

"But Patel might try to reach out to me, anyway?"

"If Dr. Fazal knew he was a dead man, he might want to warn you away from Patel just to keep you out of the loop. Patel could be a desperate man. Once he hears about Fazal's murder, he might turn to you instead. Maybe Fazal is warning you against that inevitability."

"He was thinking of me even at the end." She cupped the note between her two hands, almost as if in prayer.

"He was warning *you* away from Patel." He tapped the napkin with Patel's address. "Not me."

"Are you going to track him down?"

"Yes."

"I'm coming with you."

"That's exactly what Dr. Fazal didn't want."

"Well, he misjudged his enemies if he thought they'd leave me alone. I'm in this, whether or not that's what Dr. Fazal wanted."

"Not what he wanted."

"Do you think I'll be safer in that hotel room on my own or safer with you?"

He opened his mouth and then snapped it shut. Of course she'd be safer with him. He leveled a finger at her. "If you come along with me, you need to do exactly what I say. I know you think you're street smart and savvy, but this is a different world."

"You're lucky I am street smart and savvy because I recognized you as one of the good guys right away." She pushed his finger out of the way. "When do we go?"

"Let me wrap up a few things first. Were the police at the office when you were there cleaning up?"

"No, but Ginny, the receptionist, saw them when she got there. I gather they didn't have any news."

"What about the…uh, arrangements for Dr. Fazal?"

"The funeral?" She dropped the pink note in her purse. "Morgan told me some of his colleagues are organizing a memorial service, and they actually want me to say something. According to his religion, he needs to be buried as soon as the coroner releases his body—whenever that is. The memorial service can take place sooner."

He jerked his thumb at the counter. "Go get yourself a coffee while I finish."

"I prefer the stuff at the donut shop across the street."

His lips quirked as he suppressed a smile.

"What?"

"Nothing. If you want to run across the street, I'll probably be done by the time you get back."

"I'll wait here." With one finger, she dragged the napkin with Patel's address to her side of the table. "Brookline, huh?"

"Looks about five miles away on the directions."

"It's close." She held up her cell phone. "Do you want me to put it in my GPS?"

"Go ahead. Do you want to drive or navigate?"

"Since it's my car, I'll drive."

"I'll wear my seat belt."

She nudged his shoe with her foot. "Are you implying that I'm a lousy driver?"

"Not at all. I'm just all about safety."

The nudge turned into a kick. "Liar."

"There." He clicked Send on his request. "I just submitted Peter Patel's name to our database to see if we have anything on him."

"You don't think Peter Patel's a fake name?"

"I do, but it's worth a try. Maybe it's a fake name he's used before, so it might come up as an alias for the real person."

She tilted her head. "Is this what you do as a navy SEAL? Intelligence? Espionage?"

"Me?" He raised his eyebrows. "No, although I've had some training."

"Then, what do you do?"

"I'm a sniper."

Her dark eyes glittered as she narrowed them to slits. "You kill people from a safe distance?"

He pressed his lips into a thin line, and a muscle ticked in his jaw. "I save and protect people."

"I-is that how you protected Dr. Fazal?"

He nodded once and snapped his laptop closed. "You ready?"

"Just need to enter the address in my phone's GPS."

While she tapped her phone, he put away his laptop and tossed his cup. He didn't need to explain what he did to civilians like Sophia. He didn't imagine that she'd understand, and she shouldn't have to.

"All done." She squinted at her phone. "We should be there in seventeen minutes."

"With you driving, we could cut that down to ten."

"I'll be careful, but your concern seems pretty funny coming from a guy who takes bigger risks than traveling in a fast-moving car."

As he opened the door for her, he shook his finger. "A lot of soldiers come back from their tours and die in car accidents."

"You're right."

They walked back to the medical building parking structure and jogged up one flight of stairs to their level.

Austin pressed the car keys into her hand. "Here you go."

Clutching the key ring, she stepped back from the car. "Sh-should you check it out again?"

He pulled the bug detector from his jacket pocket and held it up. "I have something better, so I don't have to crawl beneath the car."

Pressing the button on the device, he waved it across the car's bumper, along the sides and over the hood. "All clear."

She clicked the key fob. "Wow, that's really some James Bond stuff right there."

"Naw." He stuffed the detector in his pocket. "Pretty basic, actually."

He dropped into the passenger seat beside her, and she handed him her cell phone. "Navigate, please."

As she pulled out of the parking lot, he glanced at the phone and directed her to turn right at the next lights.

On the drive to Brookline, she stayed just under the speed limit and her tires didn't squeal once.

"The address is another two blocks up on the right."

She slowed the car. "Nice neighborhood."

"It's coming up." He dropped his gaze to the phone. "Just about…"

"Are you kidding me? It's seven twenty-eight, isn't it?"

He jerked his head up and swore as they rolled past a house under construction. "Pull over. I suppose we should've expected this. A phone number with no voice mail and an address with no house."

She parked the car and Austin jumped out. Stuffing his hands into his pockets, he approached the half-finished house.

Sophia hovered at his elbow. "Doesn't look like anyone's living here, either."

A truck rumbled up behind them, and Austin stepped to the side to allow it to pull into the dirt driveway. A man exited the truck and clapped a hardhat on his head. "Can I help you folks?"

Austin cleared his throat. "New construction or a remodel?"

"New construction. A developer bought the property and razed it. You interested? We had a buyer, but he pulled out."

Sophia asked, "Was the buyer named Patel?"

"No, ma'am. Why? Someone you know?"

"A friend. He's looking, too."

The man fished a card from his front pocket. "If you're interested, here's the number for the sales office. The developer has a few other properties in Brookline."

"Thanks." Sophia took the card and Austin nodded at the man, who turned toward the bed of his truck.

When they got back into Sophia's car, they turned to each other at the same time.

Austin smacked his knee. "Fake name, fake address, fake phone number. How are we going to find this guy?"

"Dr. Fazal's memorial service. If he was a friend, he just might show up."

"If he wants to keep a low profile, he won't show up. He might be worried the same guys who took out Fazal are now gunning for him."

"What was between those two?" She gripped the steering wheel with both hands. "Patel shows up, Dr. Fazal starts acting nervous, pretends Patel's a patient, probably to talk to him in private and cover his tracks, and then Dr. Fazal winds up dead—murdered. Why did he have to come here and stir up trouble for Hamid?"

A sob caught in her throat, and her fingers curled around the steering wheel in a death grip.

Austin brushed his knuckles down her arm and covered one of her hands with his. "Hamid was never out of trouble, Sophia. Nobody had to stir it up for him. He must've been living life with one eye on the rearview mirror ever since we got him out of Pakistan."

"But he *was* happy. He wasn't afraid—until this Patel showed up."

He squeezed her hand. "You made him happy. He cared about you, and that gave him a reason to live and hope."

"I hope so."

"Do you need to go back to the office?"

"No. Ginny's doing the bulk of the work, notifying patients, getting their files together for the next doctor. They still need their treatment." She started the car and glanced over her left shoulder.

He placed his hand on the steering wheel. "Are you sure you don't want me to drive?"

"Why? Did I scare you on the way over?"

"Your driving was okay. My heart rate went up only once." And he didn't want to tell her that was when she'd puckered her lips to drink from her bottle of water. "You look tired and stressed."

"I am tired and stressed, but I think you just like being in control."

He shrugged and then rolled his shoulders. "I'm not gonna deny that."

"I'm good." She pulled away from the curb to prove it. "Back to the hotel?"

"Unless you have somewhere else to be?"

"I have nothing and no one right now—not even a job to go to."

"You have patients, too, right?"

"My patients are all Dr. Fazal's patients. They're not going to follow me anywhere. I'm still in training. I'll definitely have to look for another job, and with my background?" She gave a dry laugh that seemed to lodge in her throat. "That ain't gonna be easy."

He turned his head to watch the passing scenery—clumps of old snow on the side of the road and stark trees trying to form hard buds in the still crisp air. "All that stuff… It's in your past. You were practically a juvenile."

"Ah, practically, but not quite." She twisted her head around, her gaze doing a quick search of his face. "How much do you know about me?"

She focused her attention back on the road, and he studied her profile, her wide, generous mouth at odds with the hard glitter she let creep into her eyes all too often. What he knew about this woman only scratched the surface.

"Of course, we did a background check of the people closest to Dr. Fazal."

"That wouldn't be many, since he liked to keep to himself."

"I know that."

Sophia's phone buzzed between them on the console.

"Are you going to get that?"

"I may be a bad driver but I don't answer the phone when I'm behind the wheel."

His hand hovered over the phone. "Should I?"

"If it's important enough, the caller will leave a message."

Was she expecting a call from someone on that dating website? His youngest sister, who lived in LA met guys online, too. When he and his brothers had found out they'd hit the roof, but she just laughed at them. Said everyone met people like that, and it was perfectly safe. Nothing was perfectly safe. He glanced at Sophia. Especially when extremely lethal terrorists had you in their crosshairs.

When they edged into the semicircular drive in front of the hotel, he said, "It's going to be tough having two cars. Just leave it with the valet, and he'll park it."

"Valet? Are you kidding? That costs a fortune."

He rolled his eyes. "You have a thing about paying for parking, don't you?"

"It's expensive to park in Boston and spaces are at a premium."

"I'll pay for it—work-related expense."

"How long are you going to be on this job, anyway?"

"Should be hearing something about that soon."

She pulled in front of the hotel and jammed on the brakes. He jerked forward and back, his head hitting the headrest. "Wow."

"Is there a possibility that you'll be ordered to return to regular duty?"

"I was sent out here on a mission to protect Dr. Fazal—that failed."

"Okay, but…" She huffed out a breath. "Yeah, you're not supposed to be here, anyway."

She opened the car door for the valet standing at her window and snatched the ticket from him.

Austin didn't want to leave any more than Sophia

wanted him to, but his job description didn't include protecting anyone but Fazal—mission over.

Sophia charged ahead, and he took long strides to follow her. Her stiff back and squared shoulders screamed anger, but he already knew her anger masked fear or disappointment. Maybe he did know Sophia better than he thought he did.

He caught up with her. "Is this a race?"

"I just want to be alone, but I can't even go back to my own apartment, can I?" She punched the elevator button with the side of her fist.

He ran his hands down her arms and she practically vibrated beneath his touch. "We'll have you back home soon."

"Yeah, when you decide to ditch this place. Then I guess I'll be free to do what I want—including die."

The elevator doors opened and he bit down on his reply as a stream of people exited the car. Three other people entered the elevator after them, and Austin shifted toward the panel of buttons to make room.

He lowered his voice. "Did you check your call?"

"It's from Ginny, probably with some questions about the office. She left a voice mail. I'll listen to it when we get to the room."

When the elevator settled on his floor, they squeezed out of the car and walked silently to the room.

He opened the door for Sophia, and she took her phone out of her jacket pocket and wedged her shoulder against the window. She tapped her cell and listened, her eyes getting wider and wider with each second.

His pulse ratcheted up several notches. "What's wrong? What's she saying?"

"I'll let you listen." She tapped her phone and a woman's high-pitched, strained voice came over the line in a rush of words.

"Where'd you take off to so fast, Sophia? You left, Morgan left and Anna took off right after her. I was stuck doing the patient calls. Do you know how hard it was to repeat over and over that Dr. Fazal was dead?" A sob broke into her words and then she continued.

"Of course you do. You found him. And if that wasn't stressful enough, a man came by the office and he was looking for you. I mean, really looking for you. He said he was a friend of Dr. Fazal's and he did have a similar accent. He just wouldn't take no for an answer. Finally I told him to give me his number and I'd give it to you. So here it is, but you'd better call me back before you contact him."

She recited a phone number and ended the message with an urgent "Call me."

Sophia crossed her arms. "What do you think? Is that Patel or…maybe the guy from last night?"

"I'm not sure, but you're not calling him back on your phone. You don't want him to have your number." He dragged his own phone from his pocket. "We can use mine. It can't be traced, but you'd better call Ginny first and get all the details. Is she usually…excitable?"

"She can be, but I've never heard her like that before. It could just be the added stress of contacting the patients this morning. I'll call her now."

"Speaker, please."

Sophia placed the call. It rang four times, and then a man answered.

"Hello?"

"Hello?" Sophia's eyes jumped to Austin's face. "Who's this?"

"This is Officer Kelso with the Boston PD. Are you calling Ginny Faraday?"

Austin's heart thudded in his chest, and he held his breath.

Sophia lowered herself to the edge of the chair. "Yes. Why are you answering her phone? Where's Ginny?"

"I'm sorry, ma'am. Ms. Faraday was just involved in an accident, a hit-and-run."

Sophia gasped, and Austin took two steps and crouched beside her.

"I-is she okay?"

"I'm sorry, ma'am. Ms. Faraday was fatally injured."

Chapter Seven

The man on the other end of the line kept asking questions, but Sophia had slipped into a fog. Ginny had just called her. How had this happened?

Austin took the phone from her slack fingers. "Officer Kelso, my friend is in shock. Can you tell us what happened?"

"From witness accounts, Ms. Faraday stepped off the curb and a car careened around the corner and hit her. The car took off."

Sophia hugged herself and rocked forward. An accident. It was just an accident.

"Is your friend related to Ms. Faraday?"

"No, a coworker."

"Does she know a relative we can contact? This just happened. Ms. Faraday is—is still at the scene."

Sophia closed her eyes and covered her mouth with both hands. Death and loss. When did it ever end?

Austin poked her arm. "Next of kin for Ginny?"

Her eyes flew open. "Kara Germanski. She's Ginny's sister. I'm sure her number's in Ginny's phone."

Austin relayed the information to the cop and then ended the call. He placed her phone on the table and remained on the floor by her side.

Twisting her head toward him, she whispered, "Unbelievable. How can someone just run over a human being and leave her in the street?"

"Sophia."

"No." She covered her ears.

"Ginny was murdered."

She doubled over and touched her forehead to her knees. "Why? Why would he hurt her? She took his number, gave it to me."

"We don't know that the man she spoke to was the one driving the car or even if they were working together. Maybe the number you have is Peter Patel's. Maybe someone saw her talking to Patel and took care of business."

He put a hand on her bouncing knee. "We need to go back to the office and retrace her steps. I need to get hold of that accident report to see if there were any witnesses who said anything about the car or the driver."

She poked at the phone with her fingertip, scooting it away from her. "Should I call him now?"

"No. Let's go to the office first. Are you going to tell the nurses?"

"Oh, my God. I can't handle that right now. Anna is going to fall apart." She ran her hands across her face to make sure *she* wasn't falling apart. "Do you think the police are going to connect Ginny's death to Dr. Fazal's?"

"Any good detective would. They'll investigate it."

"Should we go back now?"

"I need to make a few phone calls first. Do you want something from the minibar or the vending machines?"

"Is that a hint to get me out of the room?"

"Or I can leave."

She pushed up from the chair and swept past him. "I'll get a soda from the machine. Do you want something?"

"Anything with caffeine. Do you need some money?"

"I got it." When she stepped into the hallway and the door slammed behind her, she leaned against the wall. She couldn't believe this was happening.

She thought she'd left the violence and ugliness behind her when she'd finally gotten away from the south side. Hadn't everyone always told her if she finished school, got a degree and found a good job trouble would stop following her? She'd done all of that, and it looked like trouble had found her, anyway. It always would.

She launched herself off the wall and crossed the hall to the room with the ice and vending machines.

She braced her hands against the buzzing machine, hanging her head between her arms. If Austin was in there getting orders to abandon this mission and return overseas where he belonged, she'd be in real trouble.

Did the US government care about that? Care about her? She puffed out a breath. Who was she kidding? When had any government entity ever cared about what happened to her? Child Protective Services had failed her at every turn.

Austin cared. She hadn't been imagining that, but he'd disappear in a flash if his superiors ordered him to scrap the mission.

She fed a dollar bill into the machine and selected a diet soda for herself. Then she put another bill in and punched the button for a soda for Austin. She couldn't blame him if he had to follow orders.

Maybe she could ask the sniper for some shooting pointers before he left. She needed the practice.

When she returned to the room, she held out a can to

Austin, stretched out on the bed, his arms crossed behind his head. "Caffeinated, as you requested."

He curled his hand around the can, his fingers pressing against hers so that they were both holding on to the can. His eyes met hers across the space between them. "Good news."

"They caught Dr. Fazal's killers, Ginny's killers and I'm completely out of danger."

His lips twisted. "Why'd you do that? Now my news isn't going to make an impression."

"Try me." She pulled her hand away from his and popped the tab on her own can.

"After I told my commanding officer everything that was going down out here, he checked with Ariel, who authorized me to stay at least until I can identify Peter Patel."

"That is good news." Taking a sip from her can, she turned away from him so that he couldn't see just how much that news meant to her. She had to play it cool because soon he would leave—even if it wasn't today.

"I'm ready, even though it doesn't look like it." Austin swung his legs off the side of the bed. "Do you want to walk over or drive?"

"Might as well walk. I could use the fresh air to clear my head."

"Me, too." He held up his can. "We can drink and walk at the same time."

She slipped her jacket from the back of the chair. "Do you think the cops will still be at the scene? Ginny won't still be there, will she?"

He glanced at the alarm clock by the side of the bed. "It's a fatality. An accident-investigation team will be at the scene for hours…and Ginny's body will be, too. Do you want to give it another few hours?"

"It'll be getting dark in a few hours." She stuffed her arms into the sleeves of her jacket. "Besides, you want to talk to the cops, right?"

"They're not going to talk to me until I get some sort of approval from the FBI. Since the FBI doesn't want to acknowledge I'm here looking into Fazal, that's not going to happen, but I can look at the accident scene myself."

With their sodas in hand, they stepped outside the hotel and into a cool, sharp breeze. Sophia flipped up the collar of her jacket while glancing over her shoulder.

"Are you okay?"

"I'm just wondering who's watching and following." She hunched her shoulders. "Someone must've been watching Ginny. The man who approached her, whether that's Patel or not, must've known the other two had left."

"Oh, they're out there." He gulped down the rest of his drink and crushed the can in one hand. "I'm just wondering if they know you have a bodyguard."

"Is that what you are?" She lifted one eyebrow, liking the sound of his job description.

"The man who approached you in Cambridge might just think I got lucky in disarming him."

"Lucky? Yeah, I can't see your average accountant or engineer taking down a guy with a gun like that."

"Of course, they might be wondering why we took off when the officer arrived on the scene and why you never reported the incident."

"The first they do know, but how would they know whether or not I reported the incident? We could've taken off because we didn't realize the man approaching us was a cop."

"True, but don't be so sure they don't know what's going on with the Boston PD."

She choked on her soda and it fizzed in her nose. "Really? They would have access to that information?"

"Online information is out there for the taking—as long as you know how to access it."

"That's a scary thought."

"Don't you periodically get emails from stores or government agencies telling you that your personal information has been compromised? It's the same thing—hackers hacking."

"Nothing's safe, is it?"

He tugged on her purse strap. "You're safe—with me."

She stretched her lips into a smile. The way she'd felt when she discovered that Austin might be leaving proved that she wasn't safe with him at all. How had she grown so dependent on him when she hadn't even known him two days ago? She'd never been this dependent on anyone before—except Dr. Fazal.

They spotted the accident scene a block away. Emergency vehicles formed a barrier around the corner. Sophia swallowed when she saw the coroner's van.

Her steps dragged, and Austin touched her shoulder. "Do you want to wait in the coffeehouse, or better yet, the donut shop?"

"No."

Austin's hand dropped to the small of her back and he kept it there as they drew closer to the scene, and she had no intention of shrugging it off.

They hung out on the fringes of the crowd still clustered around the corner. Sophia couldn't see Ginny's body and didn't want to.

Austin turned to the man next to him. "What happened?"

"Hit-and-run. Car hit a pedestrian, and he died."

The guy in front of the stranger cranked his head over his shoulder. "She. It was a woman."

Austin whistled. "Anyone see it happen? Anyone get a look at the car?"

The shorter man in front answered again. "Not that I heard."

Austin took her arm and put his lips close to her ear. "Let's retrace her steps."

Leading the way, Austin led her through a clutch of people that had formed behind them, and they walked through the front door of the office building.

"Did Ginny drive?"

"She took the T in." She jerked her thumb over her shoulder. "I'm sure she was on her way to the T stop one block up."

They took the elevator up to the office, and she unlocked the door. Ginny and the others had done a good job of cleaning up.

She stood in the middle of the waiting room and turned around. "This room wasn't that messed up—nothing to search, but I noticed the magazines had been rifled."

"So, they could've been looking for something flat, a piece of paper or a disk of some sort." Austin thumbed through a celebrity magazine and then stuffed it back in the rack.

She pulled open the door to the back office and gestured to her right. "This was Ginny's domain, the reception area. They trashed this."

"She didn't say on the phone where the man approached her looking for you, did she? In the office or outside?"

"No, but I'm pretty sure she would've kept the office door locked once the other two left. She'd been making patient calls."

"So, he knocked or waylaid her when she left the office." He tipped his head toward the back of the room. "Do you want to show me your office and how Dr. Fazal's body was positioned?"

She squeezed past him and stepped into her office. "This is my space. I found the pink sticky note under my desk, here."

He got on his hands and knees and peered beneath her desk. "If it became unstuck when the intruders started searching in here, it probably floated to the floor and they never saw it."

"Even if they did see it?" She shook her head. "It wouldn't have meant anything to them. That's why Dr. Fazal wrote it that way. He didn't want me talking to Patel…and I'm going to do just that."

"Dr. Fazal had no way of knowing I'd be here to help you."

"I think he would've approved. I know he held the guys who rescued him in high regard. I just never knew it was the SEALs."

"*He* was the hero. He sacrificed everything—his home, his safety—to help us bring down a very dangerous man."

She blinked. "Do you want to see where I found him?"

"Yes."

She led him to the doctor's office, which Ginny and Anna had put back together. Sophia laced her fingers in front of her, twisting them into knots as she moved around the desk. They'd never get rid of that blood on the carpet.

"There. He was lying on his back, the gun next to his hand."

Austin crouched down and looked beneath the desk. "Did it look like he was down before the room was tossed? I mean, did you notice papers on top of him or beneath him? The cops would note that, but probably didn't tell you."

"I think the search went on after his death. I just had that impression. The picture was beneath his leg, but that was the only thing I noticed. It was as if he grabbed it or swept it from the desk when he fell."

"That framed picture of the two of you? The one with the broken glass?"

"Yes, the officer allowed me to take it with me that night."

Tapping his chin, Austin rose to his feet and took a turn around the room. "You said he kept a gun in his drawer?"

"Yes, but I don't know if it was the one in his hand. Maybe he went for it and had just enough time to shoot himself. I know he wouldn't have killed himself without a good reason—a noble reason."

"He ruined their plans. They expected to get information from him and he made sure they'd never get it."

"But they obviously didn't find it if they came after me and then…Ginny."

"They killed Ginny. I don't think the man in Cambridge went after you with the same intention." He pointed at her. "They think you know something or that Dr. Fazal gave you something."

"I don't and he didn't." She wrung her hands. "Can't I just tell them...?"

"No! That won't work. Do you think they'll believe you? They might believe you after a few hours or a few days of..." He ran a hand through his short hair.

She didn't want him to finish that sentence. She didn't want to imagine what they'd do to her if they captured her. The thought of it had been enough to make Dr. Fazal put a gun to his head and pull the trigger.

She rubbed the scar on the inside of her left forearm. She wouldn't be able to endure it.

Austin looked around the room and peppered her with more questions, but none of the questions or her answers brought them any closer to figuring out what Dr. Fazal had been hiding from his killers—if anything.

"Okay, let's follow Ginny's probable path down to the street and see if we can discover anything."

"Do you think she's still down there? It's getting dark." Sophia pressed her palm against the windowpane. The office faced a different direction from the front entrance.

"Most likely. It can take hours for an accident investigation to wrap up in the case of a fatality." She watched his reflection in the window as he approached her from behind.

He looked almost unreal, like an apparition she'd conjured from her imagination. Then he touched her shoulder blade and she knew he was real...and he was the only thing standing between her and utter devastation and collapse.

"Are you ready?"

Her eyes met his in the glass and she nodded.

They exited the office, and as she locked the door behind her, the elevator opened on the floor. A vacuum cleaner poked its nose out of the door followed by Norm.

"Hey, Norm. Did you hear about what happened to Ginny?"

"I did hear, Sophia." He shook his head. "Crazy Boston drivers, and he didn't even stop."

Austin pressed the elevator button with his knuckle to hold it open. "You didn't happen to see anything, did you?"

"No. I haven't left the building since I came on duty a few hours ago. I just heard the sirens and a few people in the office were talking about it. Damn shame." He shook his head. "She must've been still upset about her argument up here. She probably wasn't paying any attention."

Sophia's heart jumped. "Argument? On this floor?"

"She was talking to a man in the hallway." Norm rolled the vacuum a few feet forward. "Right here."

"What did he look like?" Austin had let the elevator go and was focused on Norm like a laser.

Norm ducked his head. "Dark skin, dark hair, medium height. He had an accent, kind of like Dr. Fazal's. I figured it was a friend of Dr. Fazal's."

"Had you ever seen him here before?"

Norm licked his lips and glanced at Sophia.

"This is Detective French, Norm. He was looking into the accident."

"Oh, okay. I never seen him here before, but he sounded like the doctor. I thought maybe he was upset about, you know…the murder."

Sophia put her hand on Austin's arm. His intensity

was going to send Norm running for the stairwell. She asked, "Did you overhear any part of the argument?"

"Naw, they were quiet. Just sort of whispering back and forth, but I could tell they were having a disagreement about something."

"You don't think this man could've been the one driving the car that hit Ginny, do you?"

Norm's eyebrows jumped. "I thought that was an accident. Someone hit Ginny on purpose?"

"We don't know that for sure." Austin crossed his arms. "So, how about it? Could the man talking to Ginny have had enough time to go down to the street, get in a car and drive around to the front before Ginny got to the corner?"

"No. No way." He leaned on the vacuum cleaner handle. "He got in the elevator with her. They went down together. So, unless she took some big detour when she got to the sidewalk, he probably left her right before she crossed the street and got hit. He could've even witnessed it."

"Okay, Norm. Thanks."

"Thank you. I appreciate it." Austin shook Norm's hand.

"Do you have a card or something? The detective who was here for Dr. Fazal gave me his card in case I remembered anything else."

Austin made a show of patting his front pocket. "Fresh out. Ms. Grant knows how to reach me."

Norm turned and trundled down the hallway, pushing his vacuum cleaner in front of him and muttering. "I sure hope the hit-and-run was just an accident. 'Cause if it wasn't, there's something hinky going on with this building and that office."

Austin called the elevator again, and when they stepped inside, they looked at each other.

Wedging his shoulder against the mirrored wall, Austin said, "The man arguing with Ginny was Patel, but is he working with someone else who ran down Ginny? Of course, why run her down if she'd given Patel your info? Patel would've had to signal someone that he'd come up short. It all happened too fast."

"In which case, the guy in the car who hit Ginny is not working with Patel." She held out her phone, tilting it back and forth. "And now I have Patel's number."

"Are you ready to call him?"

"What should I say?"

"Tell him who you are, and ask him what he wants. Don't let on that you already know about him. Play dumb."

"That's not going to be very hard to do since I have no idea what he wants." The elevator opened onto the lobby floor and she stepped out first, still clutching her phone. "Now?"

"Let's get back to the hotel so we can have some privacy. I'm going to be listening to every word on Speaker, and my phone has the ability to record the conversation, too."

Sophia pushed through the lobby door first and stepped onto the sidewalk, glancing to her left. The emergency vehicles were still there, although not as many, and the crowd had thinned. As dusk had settled, the accident investigators had lit up the area with bright white lights, giving the scene the quality of a movie set. She wished it were just a movie, not her reality... not Ginny's.

Hunching her shoulders, she huddled into her jacket.

As they drew up beside the accident scene, Sophia noticed the coroner's van, no longer blocked by the fire engine, and beside it a gurney draped with a white sheet.

A gust of wind whipped down the street and lifted a corner of the sheet at the top of the gurney. For a moment, Ginny's red hair streamed freely in the breeze.

Sophia gulped back a scream and stumbled heavily against Austin's body.

He caught her around the waist and pulled her close, steadying her against his solid frame. "It's okay. You're going to be okay."

Was she? Or had her violent past caught up with her and wrapped its icy fingers around her throat again?

Chapter Eight

Through some miracle he made it back to the hotel without having to sweep up Sophia in his arms and carry her for five blocks—not that he would've minded.

She must've gotten a glimpse of Ginny on the stretcher. He should've taken her out of the building a different way. She hadn't said one word to him during their walk back. She'd allowed him to keep hold of her and guide her as they walked.

He had to get her out of Boston, away from this investigation. If the men who'd killed Fazal thought she had something they wanted, they'd never let her escape.

When they got to the room, Sophia collapsed into the chair by the window.

"Do you want something? Water? I think there are some tea bags by the coffeemaker."

Without answering, she closed her eyes. When a few minutes passed, he thought she'd fallen asleep. Then she wriggled upright in the chair, and her eyelids flew open.

"I have to call Patel now."

"Patel can wait. You need food."

"I'm not hungry." She brushed her hair back from her face and gathered it in a ponytail in one hand. "I need to contact Patel and ask him what the hell he's doing here and why he brought this misery down on Dr. Fazal. I need to ask him what he said to upset Ginny and if he got her killed. I need to demand answers, and I'm gonna get them."

"Hang on." He held up one hand as he marveled at her quick turnaround. What resources had she just mustered to come out of her shock and fear over Ginny's death? "You don't have to do anything right now until you feel better."

"Oh, I'm fine." Her glittering dark eyes kindled with sparks of anger. "Dr. Fazal and Ginny are dead. There's nothing I can do for them now except get justice—and that justice starts with Patel."

He scratched his chin. He knew exactly how she felt. Hell, he'd lived it after his brother died.

"Are you ready to do this? Ready to keep your temper?" He squared his shoulders and looked deep into her fathomless eyes. "Because if you're not, you can blow the whole thing sky-high. You want answers from Patel, you're going to have to come in with a measured approach. Can you do that?"

She took a deep breath and released it slowly, rolling her shoulders. "I can do it."

He removed his phone from the charger and handed it to her. "Then do it."

"Do I have to do anything special to record the conversation?" She eyed the phone cupped in her hand.

"It's all set up to record and it's already on Speaker. All you have to do is enter the number Ginny gave you."

She swept her thumb across her phone's display and then tapped a number into his phone. The phone rang three times.

"Hello?" a man answered in accented English.

"Hello? Is this Mr. Patel?"

"Who is this?"

"This is Sophia Grant. My coworker Ginny Faraday gave me your number."

"Is she dead?"

Sophia's eyes flew to Austin's face, and he nodded.

"Sh-she is. It was a hit-and-run accident. How did you know that?"

"It happened right after I spoke to her." He cleared his throat. "Do you know who I am?"

She raised her brows at him and he mouthed *Dr. Fazal* and *patient*.

"I do recognize your name from Dr. Fazal's patient files. Y-you know what happened to him, don't you?"

Patel let out a sigh. "That's why I'm calling you, Ms. Grant. May I call you Sophia? I feel like I know you from Hamid's letters."

"His letters? I thought you were his patient."

"Sophia, your life is in danger."

"Because of Dr. Fazal's murder? Was Ginny's death an accident?"

"No. I'm sorry. It's all my fault. I should've never come here."

"Are you going to tell me why Dr. Fazal and Ginny were murdered? Why I'm in danger?"

"Not over the telephone. Are you on a cell phone?"

"Yes, but…" She put a hand over her mouth. "But I have complete privacy."

He choked out something between a laugh and a sob. "There is no privacy with these people."

"What people? Who are they?"

"Meet me tonight."

"Tonight?"

Austin nodded. He'd be with her every step of the way.

"Ten o'clock. I'll be wearing a baseball cap you Americans like so much, a Boston Red Sox cap and a red scarf."

Austin glanced at the clock. They had four hours to kill.

"Ten o'clock. Where?"

"Hamid's favorite place in Boston…and come alone."

Patel ended the call, leaving her with her mouth hanging open.

"Cryptic but not very practical." He scratched the stubble on his chin, as his stomach growled.

Sophia placed his phone on the table and traced its edges with the tip of her finger. "I know exactly where he means."

"Dr. Fazal's favorite place in Boston? A restaurant? A park?" God, he hoped it was a restaurant.

"The Old North Church." She scooted forward in her seat, her eyes shining. "That was also Patel's way of assuring me he was Dr. Fazal's friend. A friend would know that about him."

"Wouldn't the church be closed at ten o'clock at night?"

"I don't imagine he means inside the church."

"Which is a shame because it would be a lot easier to keep watch in an enclosed area."

"He told me to come alone." She sucked in her bottom lip, her eyebrows forming a V over her nose.

He swept his phone from the table and saved the recording of the conversation. "You can't think I'm going to let you go meet him by yourself."

"If he sees you, he might take off."

"He's not gonna see me." He pocketed his phone. "Is

there someplace outside the church where you think he's going to be, or are you supposed to wander aimlessly around the perimeter looking for a Red Sox fan?"

"Across from the church's main entrance there's a small square. There are also a few benches beneath some trees before you get to the square. He could be there. Unless there's an event at the church tonight, there won't be many tourists mingling around."

"We're going to check it out before the meeting—on our way to get something to eat. I'm starving. I can sort out a plan to watch you to make sure nobody tries to disrupt your conversation with Patel. You might try to ask him his real name while you're at it."

"Should I tell him about you?"

"See how the conversation goes. If he has information, we need to know about it. He might be relieved to turn it over to us, and we can offer protection."

"Your protection didn't help Dr. Fazal."

His jaw tightened as he turned away from her. He didn't need any reminders of his failure. He could manage that on his own.

SOPHIA JUMPED OUT of the chair and it tipped over and hit the floor. She reached Austin's stiff back in two steps and reached out for his shoulder. He flinched when she squeezed it.

"I'm so sorry, Austin. I didn't mean to imply that it was your failure. You did everything you could, and you almost reached Dr. Fazal in time. I-if your commanding officers had sent you in sooner, I know you would've saved him— because you saved me."

He did a half turn, and her hand was pressed just above his thudding heart. She had the strongest desire to cup his hard jaw in her palm and ease the pain that flashed from his eyes.

He really had cared about Dr. Fazal, and he felt his loss almost as keenly as she did.

His thick, stubby lashes fell over his eyes as if to protect his private thoughts from her. "Okay, yeah. I know you didn't mean it that way."

She gave his chest a pat before stepping back. She usually liked keeping her distance from people, even men she was dating, but something about Austin Foley lured her in. It couldn't be because they had anything in common, because it sounded like he'd come from a wholesome background of family, fresh air and farm animals, and she'd come from...dysfunction, grime and animals of a different kind.

"Let's eat. You said you were starving, and now that I have my meeting with Patel, I've recovered my appetite. We can walk to the church from here."

"Maybe to do our initial surveillance followed by dinner, but when we go back for the meeting we have to drive."

"Why is that?"

"Because I'm not carrying a sniper rifle case along the Freedom Trail."

"Sniper rifle?"

"I'm going to cover you, Sophia, the best way I know how. If anyone gets near you...they're gone."

"What if they have the same idea and take me out before you even know they're in the area?"

"They're not going to take you out. They need you. They want to question you. They didn't need Ginny."

She puffed up her cheeks and blew out a breath. How could Austin get away with shooting someone on a Boston street corner? This would have to be covered up at a high level, but then it had taken high-level personnel to authorize a navy SEAL to operate stateside.

She had a feeling she didn't want to know any more.

"We can eat at Faneuil Hall—lots of choices there. We can walk or take the T from the church."

"I'll let you lead the way. Just as long as we're back at the hotel by nine o'clock, so I can get ready. Right now I'm going to shave and brush my teeth, unless you want to freshen up first." He stopped at the entrance to the bathroom.

"You go ahead. I'm going to make some phone calls to Anna and Morgan. Someone has to tell them about Ginny."

As Austin closed the bathroom door, she grabbed the framed picture of her and Dr. Fazal that she'd taken from the floor of his office and traced the crack on the glass that ran through his body. "I know you didn't want me to contact Patel, but Austin's here now—and he's going to make everything okay."

SOPHIA PUSHED AWAY her plate with her half-eaten meal and dug her elbows into the table. "Do you think you'll be able to see what's going on from the top of that building at night?"

"My scope has night vision." Austin aimed his fork at her plate. "Are you going to finish that fish?"

"Help yourself. I can't eat another bite."

"If you don't want to do this, you don't have to meet Patel. I'll meet him. If he clams up, I'll take him in. He's involved in whatever got Dr. Fazal killed, and our intelligence agencies have every right to question him."

"That doesn't mean he's going to talk to you." She

took a sip of water. "He wants to talk to me. I'm sure he'll be more open with me, and then if you want to pick him up later, you can do so."

"Oh, I'm sure the FBI is going to want to pick him up later." He sawed off the edge of the salmon and popped it in his mouth. "You sure you don't want to eat the rest of this? You hardly touched your food."

"I'm too nervous to eat." Her gaze swept from his empty plate to her own, which he was in the process of emptying. "I guess nerves don't affect your appetite."

"I'm not nervous."

"You do this all the time?"

"In the middle of an American city? Uh, no." He signaled to the waitress. "Do you want dessert?"

"I'll have a bite of whatever you're having." She twisted the napkin in her lap. "So, this is a new experience for you, too, but you're not anxious about it."

"It's a job. It has to be done. I'm the one who has to do it."

He smiled at the approaching waitress as if they'd just been talking about the weather. "Can we get the caramel apple pie—and two forks?"

"Coming right up."

Five minutes later she watched Austin dig into that pie as if he wasn't going to be watching the Old North Church through the scope of a rifle.

Shoving the plate toward her, he said, "Try it."

She picked up her fork and then reached forward to dab a spot of caramel from his chin with the tip of her finger.

His eyes darkened for a moment to a murky, unfathomable green. She plunged her fork into a glob of ice cream.

"Make sure you get the apples, caramel and nuts."

The gooey sweetness exploded in her mouth and she closed her eyes and rolled her lips inward. "That's yummy. Can we just sit here, finish this delectable dessert and forget about Patel?"

"You can." He rested the tines of his fork on the edge of the plate. "I already told you, Sophia. I'll take care of this. The FBI will get info out of Patel—one way or the other."

"He wants to talk to me. If he'd wanted to bring US intelligence into this, he would've called you. I'm sure Dr. Fazal had you guys on speed dial."

"If he had, he didn't use it after making contact with Patel. Maybe if he'd called us first, we... I could've moved in sooner."

"There must be some reason he didn't after that first call, and I'm going to find out why tonight." She stuffed another piece of pie in her mouth before she could chicken out—besides, she had a navy SEAL sniper watching her back.

Austin paid the check, and if they weren't on their way to a meeting that could result in someone's death, this would've been a pretty damn good date—better than the Spark dates she'd been on.

When they hit the sidewalk, Austin stretched and said, "Let's take the T back to the hotel."

Yeah, because he had to get his rifle ready to shoot someone.

The short ride on the T brought them back to the hotel faster than she expected, faster than she wanted.

They got to the room, and Austin pulled a case that looked more secure than Fort Knox from the closet.

"If you didn't want to heighten the suspicions of the

hotel staff—" she rapped her knuckles on the hard case "—I think you failed."

"I don't care if their suspicions are heightened. I just don't want them getting inside."

"What if they just hauled away the whole thing?"

"Impossible. It has a GPS tracker on it. They can give it a try though." He stuffed a black cap into his pocket. "Do you want to run through the plan once more?"

"We're going to park in the structure down the block, and then split up at the building on the corner. You're going to find your way to the roof of the building, and I'm going to keep walking toward the church. I'll come up from the right-hand side, and if I don't see Patel, with his baseball cap and scarf, I'll pace a few times in front of the church."

"What's the signal if you see anyone but Patel approaching you?"

"One if by land and two if by sea?"

"Funny. Tell me."

"I'm going to raise my scarf over my head, like this." She grabbed her scarf on either side and pulled it up toward her head.

"That's right."

"And you're going to take out the interloper."

"Take him out as in kill him? No. Let's just say I'll make him think twice before approaching you."

"Where were you during my formative years?"

"If I'd have known you and known you needed protection? I would've delivered."

He'd made the pronouncement with a half smile on his face, but she believed him.

"Are you the eldest of the three brothers and two sisters?"

He nodded as he hoisted the case from the bed.

"You must've protected them, too—scared the stuffing out of your sisters' boyfriends and put the bullies in place who were picking on your brothers."

Her words had wiped the smile from his face, casting a shadow over his features. He shrugged. "I never cared who my sisters dated."

She'd said something wrong but didn't know what. She was supposed to be the complicated one. "Okay, then. Let's do this."

She picked up the framed photo again, and this time a piece of glass fell out and hit the carpet. "I'm going to get a new frame for this."

"Where was that taken?" Austin leaned over her shoulder.

"It was at a conference in Chicago, where I won an award. H-he was so proud of me. Nobody has ever been proud of me like that, and I doubt ever will again."

He took the frame from her hands and placed it on the credenza. "Don't sell yourself short, Sophia. You're about to do something pretty amazing right now."

"I just hope Peter Patel has some answers."

As they walked through the hotel, only a few people gave Austin's case a second glance. Probably thought he was the trombone player for the Boston Pops.

When they got to his rental car in the hotel parking lot, Austin did a thorough search of the vehicle. They drove to the church in silence.

Sophia couldn't stop her leg from bouncing, so she settled for closing her eyes and taking deep breaths. She didn't want to meet Patel only to faint at his feet.

Austin found parking on the first floor of the structure and retrieved his weapon from the trunk of the car.

"Remember, if anything happens, you take off running back to the car—unless you're being followed. Then you run toward the street and the most populated area you can find."

"Got it." She saluted, but she felt like throwing up.

He must've seen the look before because he cupped her face with one hand. "I'll be watching you. I'll keep you safe."

"I know." She'd never been surer of anything in her life.

He held her hand as they left the structure and as they strolled down the sidewalk just like any other couple on a date.

Then he gave her fingers a squeeze and slipped into the building where he'd be watching her from the roof.

Loosening her scarf around her neck, she followed the red line on the sidewalk that marked the Freedom Trail, traversed by millions of tourists every year.

The white walls of the Old North Church gleamed in the darkness and she focused on the beacon of light the church represented. Nothing would happen to her here, not at Dr. Fazal's favorite place in all of Boston.

He'd loved the story of Paul Revere and his midnight ride. He respected rebels. He'd been one himself.

A couple walked toward her and veered left toward the square. Sophia let out a sigh and then sucked it back in when she saw a lone figure in a baseball cap sitting on a bench under the trees across from the church's entrance. Was his scarf red?

The lights around the church didn't extend that far, so she squinted into the darkness. Should she call out? He hadn't seemed to notice her—hadn't made a move.

Sophia glanced over her shoulder. Several feet behind her, two women walked up to the gate surrounding the church and peered through the bars. Then they wandered toward the street.

Sophia straightened her spine and marched toward Patel, who hadn't yet lifted his head. Did he want her to identify herself?

"Mr. Patel?" She slowed her steps.

He didn't budge.

She swiped her tongue across her dry lips. "Mr. Patel?"

She got within five feet of the bench when the smell hit her full force—the same odor from Dr. Fazal's office, the same odor from that nightmarish afternoon when she was four years old.

She gagged and stumbled forward, falling to her knees in front of Patel.

Then she noticed it—blood dripping from his neck, soaking his red scarf, pooling beneath the bench.

So. Much. Blood.

Chapter Nine

Austin's pulse flickered in his throat. What was she doing?

Through his scope, he saw Sophia crouch in front of the figure on the bench. Were they talking? The man, Patel, still had his head down, his chin practically resting on his chest.

Sophia now blocked his view of Patel's body, but it looked like she'd taken his hand in hers. What the hell was going on?

He did a quick sweep of the surrounding area. The couple who'd strolled into the quad was still sitting there, their backs to Sophia and Patel. After the two women who'd peeked in at the church, nobody else had come along.

He brought Sophia and Patel back into focus. She cranked her head over her shoulder. His heart skipped a beat and he sucked in a breath.

Something had gone wrong.

His muscles tensed as he got ready to push off the wall. Then another figure came into his sights. A man had come around the corner, moving at a brisk clip, his hand in his pocket, his focus on Sophia.

Austin got the man in his crosshairs, and then he adjusted his aim downward and fired off a shot. The cement post in front of the man exploded.

The stranger jumped back, his head twisting from side to side.

Austin muttered under his breath, "You're not getting anywhere near her, you SOB."

He squeezed the trigger again and another cement post shattered into pieces. One of them must've hit the guy, because he jerked like a puppet and grabbed his leg.

Sophia lurched to her feet and Austin silently yelled at her to run. She must've heard him.

As the man stumbled back and the couple in the square jumped to their feet, Sophia took off. Patel remained on the bench, and Austin could now see a dark stain spreading across his front.

The stranger had taken one step toward Sophia's retreating figure and then thought better of it. He spun around and limped off in the other direction.

Austin could no longer see Sophia and just hoped to hell she was heading back to the car in the lot. He kept watch for several more seconds.

The couple had approached Patel. They both sprang back at the same instant. The man got on his cell phone, and there was nothing more Austin could do.

He pushed away from his station, slinging the case over his shoulder, where it banged against his hip as he ran toward the staircase. He broke down his rifle at full speed while he negotiated the steps.

By the time he reached the bottom of the building, his rifle was in pieces. He leaned against the door to the street and stashed the parts back in the case. Then he pushed out onto the sidewalk and strode toward the parking structure.

He found himself chanting Sophia's name like some magical incantation—as if that would be enough to make her appear beside the car. The sirens in the distance quickened his pace.

His bullets were untraceable, and if Patel had been shot, there would be no match between his bullets and the ones that had killed Patel. Who knew what the cops would make of it?

Had the couple in the square noticed Sophia? Would they be able to provide some kind of description of her to the Boston PD? It didn't matter. The FBI could get her out of anything at this point—if they wanted to.

With his breath coming hard and fast, he turned into the parking structure. He zeroed in on his rental and his gut knotted. No Sophia.

He pressed the key fob and the car's lights flashed once. A head poked out from the post beside the car and relief swept through his body.

He called out to Sophia, "Hop in."

He opened the trunk and hoisted his weapon inside. When he slid into the driver's seat, he reached across the console and took Sophia's face in both of his hands and landed a hard kiss on her mouth.

"God, I'm glad to see you."

"Same." She snapped her seat belt, which suddenly hit him as ridiculous after what she'd just been through.

He laughed, and she scowled at him.

"What happened to that man you shot at? You missed him."

"I missed him on purpose. There are just so many dead bodies we can leave on the streets of Boston. Besides, I didn't see a weapon on him. I'm not authorized to commit murder." He threw the car in Reverse and the tires squealed on the polished cement as he wheeled out of the structure. "He took off in the other direction from you. I guess he didn't want to take his chances on where the next bullet would land."

"I didn't even notice him coming up on me until you took the shot."

"What happened to Patel? I didn't see that he was dead until you'd moved away from him."

"Someone slit his throat." She squeezed her eyes shut as if trying to erase the image from her vision.

"I'm sorry you had to see that." He checked his rear-view mirror as he pulled up to the intersection. An ambulance flew past him. "They probably followed him or were able to track him. Even if they hacked into his phone, they wouldn't know Dr. Fazal's favorite place in Boston."

She hugged herself, and he wished it were his arms wrapped around her body.

She tipped her head to the side, resting against the window. "I guess the one silver lining to this is that Dr. Fazal's killers aren't out to kill me."

"Yet."

Her body twitched and he clamped down on his bottom lip. He didn't want to blacken the one bright spot she'd been holding on to, but he did want her to face reality and get rid of the crazy idea that if she opened up to these guys they'd believe that she didn't know anything about Patel and Fazal and let her go about her business.

They'd never allow that.

"One thing they do know now..."

"What's that?" He glanced at her profile.

"If they believed I was with some random boyfriend the other night in Cambridge who'd gotten lucky and disarmed a man with a gun, those crazy shots from no-where just disabused them of that notion."

"You're right." He lifted his shoulders. "And that's not a bad thing."

"Will it make them give up?"

"Probably not, but it might make them more desper-ate and that might make them more careless, and that's not a bad thing either."

They returned to the hotel and he hauled his weapon case from the trunk. Fewer people were milling around the hotel now than when they'd left, and nobody gave his strange case a second glance.

When they got to the room, he locked the rifle up again and stored it upright in the back of the closet. He grabbed two bottles of water from the minifridge and tossed one to Sophia, who'd stretched out on the bed and kicked off her boots.

He dragged a chair to the foot of the bed and slumped in it, facing her. "I wonder how they got around Patel to…to kill him."

"I don't know. I wonder how long he'd been on that bench before I arrived."

"I guess all we really know is that they followed him and didn't want him communicating any information to you. Also, the fact that they killed him indicates to me that they didn't need any info from him…or they'd al-ready gotten it."

She dragged a pillow into her lap and punched it. "I was hoping we'd get some answers tonight."

"We don't even know who Patel is—was. That, at least, would have helped."

Gasping, she rolled off the bed and lunged for her purse. "We can find out."

He eyed the phone she had pinched between two fingers. "Did you take his picture?"

"God, no, but this is even better." She dangled the phone in the air. "I got his fingerprints."

"What?"

"When I realized he was dead and that he wouldn't be telling me anything about why he came into Dr. Fazal's life, I got so frustrated. Crazy angry at him. I took out my phone and curled his hand around it."

"*That's* what you were doing." He smacked his forehead with the heel of his hand. "I thought you were holding his hand or something. I couldn't figure out what was going on. How in the hell did you have the presence of mind to do that?"

"Presence of mind? I felt like I was losing my mind. I didn't even remember I'd done it until you talked about not knowing his identity."

"You did do it, and I think that's amazing. I'm impressed." He shook out a napkin from the coffee area and placed it on the table by the window. "Put it here."

"Can you lift the prints from the phone?"

"Me personally? No, but the local FBI office can do it for me. I'll contact them tomorrow, and we can find out who Patel is and his connection to Dr. Fazal." Austin circled his finger over the phone. "Where are his prints?"

"I pressed the pads of his fingertips against the screen at the top. I've just handled the phone by the edges and haven't touched it since I brought it out just now. Will that work?"

"Not only will it work, it's brilliant. Really quick thinking on your part."

"Like I said, it was more like I was on autopilot." She coughed. "As you've probably figured out from researching my background, I've had a lot of contact with the police over the years."

"I don't know as much about you as you seem to think, but from what I do know, if you had a lot of contact with law enforcement it wasn't your fault."

She wedged her hands on her hips and tilted her head. "You don't strike me as the type of person who would make excuses for someone's bad behavior."

Usually he wasn't, but his impression of Sophia had done a one-eighty since he'd met her and spent some time with her.

"Some excuses carry more weight than others." Shoving his hands into his pockets, he braced a shoulder against the window. "Do you remember much…about your father's death?"

She blinked, and her face tightened.

For a minute he thought she was going to tell him to go to hell, and maybe he deserved that for prying. Had anyone but the therapists ever asked her about that afternoon when she was four years old?

"Interesting that you should ask that now." She caught a strand of her dark hair and twisted it around one finger. "When I smelled the blood pooling around Patel, and before, when I smelled it in Dr. Fazal's office, it reminded me of that day more than anything."

"I've heard smell is one of the strongest triggers for memory, so that makes sense."

"Yeah, except for most people it's the smell of apple pie and Mom's old perfume that tweak those memories." She flipped her hair over her shoulder. "I was in the bedroom when my parents started arguing."

"Was your father abusive? I know your mother didn't get off on self-defense because, well…"

"Yeah, she's still in prison." Sophia dropped onto the bed and fell backward. She continued as she stared at the ceiling. "My father wasn't abusive, unless you call it abuse when a drug pusher yells at his wife for using his product."

His hands curled into fists. Her father *was* abusive—abusive for creating that kind of world for a child. "Is that what they were arguing about?"

"Yes, but this time he miscalculated. My mom was already high…and desperate for more. When he denied her and called her a junkie, it was the last straw. She grabbed his gun, which he kept handy for drug deals, and shot him twice. Then she had all the crank she wanted. I'm sure she would've OD'd if a neighbor in the apartment next door hadn't called 911 when she heard the gunshots."

"Is that when you came out of the bedroom?"

"He was lying on the kitchen floor. My mother didn't even try to keep me away from him. The first cops on the scene told me I had blood on my dirty bare feet." Sophia spoke in a monotone, as if she were recounting the plot of a TV show and not her life.

He joined her on the bed, sitting on the edge. "God, I don't even know what to say. How you got to the point in your life where you are now after a beginning like that is a testament to your fortitude and spirit."

She rolled her eyes to the side, catching him with her gaze. "I had a lot of speed bumps on the way—running away from foster homes, fights, shoplifting—but not drugs, never drugs."

"Do you ever see your mother?"

"She's only about twenty-five miles away in Framingham."

"That means you do see her?"

"Once in a while. She's clean, remorseful, got her GED and found God."

"Sounds like progress." He toed off his running shoes and stacked a few pillows against the headboard. "Is she getting out anytime soon?"

"She got twenty-five to life. She's coming up for parole soon."

"Will you be there for her?"

"Was she there for me?"

"No." He eased back against the pillows. "I'm not implying you should let her into your life. Just asking."

She slid from the bed and grabbed the remote. "Do you think there's anything on the nightly news about Patel's murder?"

"It's past eleven. If the local news had the story, we probably missed it."

Sophia clicked on the TV anyway, probably to get away from his probing questions.

The Boston-area news had already switched from hard news stories to the warm and fuzzy human-interest ones—and there was nothing warm or fuzzy about a man getting his throat sliced on a bench across from the Old North Church.

Austin yawned. "I'm going to wrap it up. Once I get the go-ahead to bring your phone in for dusting, I'll take it to the office, and if the FBI can't find a match in the national database, the prints can be sent to Interpol—thanks to you."

"Do you think they'll give me a medal?"

"I think I can arrange for that." He winked at her.

"Actually, all I want is to be safe in my own apartment again."

"I think I can arrange for that, too."

She placed the remote next to the TV and started pulling cushions from the sofa bed. "Do you think the Boston PD will be able to identify Patel from his fingerprints?"

"Not if he's a foreigner. If they can't ID him, they'll send his prints to the FBI, anyway. We'll just get the information faster this way. Like I said before, my operation is not going through the normal channels."

"But you think the FBI will take the prints from the phone, anyway?"

"Someone there will receive special orders to do so."

"I always figured there was a conspiracy between law enforcement agencies that went completely over the general public's head. In a way, I feel vindicated."

"The general public probably doesn't want to know what's going on." He jumped up to help her pull out the sofa bed. "I don't know why you're getting this bed ready. This is mine."

"This is your room and you're quite a bit bigger than I am, so you should get that comfy king-size bed."

"Shucks, ma'am. That wouldn't be the chivalrous thing to do."

"Hey, if you insist. You don't have to twist my arm." She turned from the sofa bed and opened her suitcase, emerging with a bag dangling from her fingertips. "Can I have the bathroom first, too?"

"Of course. I'll get my bed ready."

"I'm kinda liking this chivalry thing." She swept past him and clicked the bathroom door behind her.

Clenching his jaw, he pulled out the couch and smoothed his hands across the sheets. If she could read his real thoughts on the matter, she'd rethink everything about him.

Because he wanted nothing more than to lay Sophia across that king-size bed and explore every inch of her body—with his tongue.

What would she think about his chivalry then?

Chapter Ten

The following morning, Sophia emerged from a sound sleep, one twitching muscle and one thought at a time. With her body fully stretched out and her mind fully aware of last night's horrific events, she lifted her head to peer at Austin splayed out on the sofa bed.

A tickle of guilt played out across the back of her neck as she eyed Austin on his stomach, his leg hanging off the side of the bed, his arm flung over his head and the sheets tangled about his body as if he'd been wrestling with them all night. He probably had.

She scooched up to a sitting position, her eyes gradually becoming accustomed to the gloom of the room. With the sheets shrugged from his broad shoulders and twisted around his waist, he looked like a Greek god who'd fallen to Earth for a nap between battles.

On her hands and knees, she crawled to the end of the bed to get a better look, and got an eyeful of his smooth, bare back, strong enough to carry the weight of the world's safety—or at least her own.

He cleared his throat and thrashed his legs, the sheet bunching and scooting farther down his back.

She released a small sigh when she saw the edge of his black briefs. Not that she was hoping for a glimpse of his bare backside, but it would've considerably brightened her morning after a bad night in a series of bad nights.

Her gaze traveled from his buttocks, teasingly concealed by the sheet, over his smooth back and across those muscled shoulders until it collided with a pair of green eyes. She couldn't see their greenness in the dim light, but she knew the color by now. She'd gotten lost in that color a few times.

The heat surged in her cheeks, but he wouldn't be able to see the blush any more than she could see the color of his eyes. "Oh, are you awake? I—I thought I heard your phone go off."

"My phone's over there." He rolled onto his back and flung his arm out to the side. "Are you okay?"

"I'm fine. Why?"

"Isn't it early?"

She twisted around to see the glowing numbers of the alarm clock. "It's seven twenty. Is that early?"

"I guess not." He rubbed his eyes. "It's so dark in here."

"Those drapes do a pretty good job of shutting out the light, and I think we're facing west."

Closing his eyes, he made a halfhearted kick at the sheets wound around his legs. "Seems earlier."

"I'm sorry. You didn't have a very good night's sleep, did you? Bed's too small for you."

"That's not why. I can sleep in any condition, and have. This sofa bed is heaven compared to some of the mattresses I've endured—and some of the rock ledges that have doubled as mattresses."

She held her breath waiting for him to explain why he'd had a restless night. Could it have been because she was in the bed two feet away from him? No. A man like him? A woman like her? Just no.

"Did you sleep well?"

"I was exhausted. I don't think I slept so much as passed out." She jerked her thumb over her shoulder. "Do you want the shower first since I had first dibs last night?"

"You go ahead." His legs finally free of the sheets, he stretched and all the muscles in his body rippled. "I'm going to make a few phone calls and see where we can take your cell to get those prints."

She peeled her tongue from the roof of her dry mouth. She really wanted to hang around to see him in his briefs, but she didn't want to be too obvious, so she crawled out of the bed and shuffled to her suitcase.

As she crouched beside her bag, she tugged at the hem of her T-shirt. She really needed to buy herself some new pajamas.

She dug through her clean clothes and pulled out a pair of black leggings and an oversize sweater. At least it had a wide neckline that exposed one shoulder, so she wouldn't be completely lacking in sex appeal.

She hugged a camisole to her chest and shook her head. Sex appeal wasn't required for submitting the fingerprints of a dead man. Had she lost all perspective?

A soft noise behind her caught her attention and she cranked her head over her shoulder. Her eyes widened and her pulse throbbed as she took in the sight of Austin strolling to the window in nothing but his black briefs. Right now, this was the only perspective she wanted.

Before he could catch her checking him out again, she staggered to her feet, her clothes bunched in her arms, and scurried to the bathroom.

Once in the shower, she got a grip and returned to reality. She and Austin were in a bubble right now—a bubble of fear and uncertainty. Other than Dr. Fazal, she'd never had a protective male figure in her life. She had to separate her emotional connection and dependence on Austin from the real reason he was acting as her guardian.

He had a job to do, and once the CIA or whoever was pulling his strings had decided he'd done as much as they needed, they'd yank him off the case and send him back overseas.

She had to prepare for that eventuality and stop having ridiculous thoughts about him—and his body. She still had Tyler Cannon, her Spark date, waiting for her, and maybe a few more connections to check out once she was able to use her phone again.

She finished her shower with her feet on the ground and her head out of the clouds. After towel drying her hair and pulling her black camisole over her head, she tucked her sweater under her arm. Forget the sex appeal.

She marched back into the room, her glance sweeping past Austin, entering a text in his phone. At least he'd had the decency to cover all those flexing muscles with a white T-shirt and his jeans from last night.

He looked up from his phone. "Wow, I bet you look good in that red color."

"This?" She held up the sweater she'd been ready to dump back into her suitcase. "Yeah, I like red."

She stuffed her arms into the sweater and yanked it over her head. It was a just a sweater, not a shimmering cocktail dress.

"I made contact." He held up his phone. "The CIA's sending me to a guy, Melvin, in the Massachusetts Department of Justice. He'll lift the prints and send them to the FBI first for a check against the national database. If there's no match there, he has a connection to Interpol and we can see if we can get a fingerprint database from Pakistan."

"That sounds like a long shot. Does Pakistan even have a database with fingerprints?"

"I don't have a clue. That's not our area."

"What are the police going to find when they search for Patel's identity?"

"I don't know. Maybe he'll have fake ID. What I do know is that I've already contacted the agency that's running the show out here and indicated that I need to get into Patel's homicide file."

"They can do that?"

"They have computer guys—and one amazing woman—who can hack into anything."

"Who is *they*, Austin? Who's calling the shots for you other than the navy?"

"I can't tell you that, Sophia."

"Would anyone, including me, even know this organization?"

"No." He slid open the closet door and pulled some clothes from a few hangers. "We'll get going as soon as I'm done."

"Take your time." She parked herself in front of the full-length mirror on the closet door and ran her hands through her damp hair.

She caught his eye in the mirror. "What?"

"You *do* look good in that color."

He slammed the bathroom door, and she smiled at her reflection in the mirror—a big, silly grin that spelled trouble.

WITH HER CELL phone back in her possession and clutched in her hand, Sophia took the seat across from Austin in a small breakfast café across the street from the Commons. "Do you really think Melvin will have an answer on those prints at the end of the day?"

"It's a rush order, and Melvin seems like a competent guy." Austin shook open the plastic menu. "He'll get to the national database, anyway. It's going to take longer for Interpol to get back to him—even with the CIA pressuring them."

She turned her coffee cup upright and smiled at the waiter. When he'd filled her cup and Austin's, Sophia continued. "The CIA knows about your assignment, but you're not reporting primarily to them, are you? The CIA is not calling the shots here."

"Why are you so interested?" He peered at her over the top of his menu, wiggling his eyebrows up and down.

"It fascinates me—the dark, twisting corridors of power."

"You make it sound…nefarious. It's all done to protect people like you—" he tipped his menu toward the other tables "—and the people in this restaurant, and the people waiting for their tours to begin in Boston Commons."

She rolled her eyes. "If you say so."

He hunched forward, opened his mouth and then must've thought better of it. "I think I'm going to have the pancakes. You?"

"I'm not a breakfast person." She cradled her coffee cup with two hands. "Maybe some toast."

As they gave their order to the waiter, Austin's phone vibrated on the table. He ignored it until their waiter left, and then he grabbed it.

"Not the fingerprints yet."

He shook his head. "Almost better. The initial police report on Patel's murder."

"Are they still calling him Peter Patel?"

"They are." He swept his fingertip across his phone's display. "Which means he must've been carrying fake ID."

"Have they made any connection between him and Dr. Fazal?"

"Not that I can see, but when we get back to the hotel I'll bring the report up on my laptop." He placed the phone beside his coffee cup and tapped the screen twice. "I got what I wanted right now though."

"What's that?"

"The hotel where he was staying."

"Have the police been there yet?"

"I'm sure they have, but it doesn't mean I can't check it out."

"We. *We* can check it out. I'm not sitting around in that hotel waiting for you. Besides…" She dropped her lashes and ran the tip of her finger along the rim of her cup. "I—I just feel safer when I'm with you."

When she looked at him through her lowered lashes, she caught her breath. His raised eyebrows told her he wasn't buying her "poor pitiful me" act.

"You'd be perfectly safe in that hotel room, especially since you're packing your own heat. You want to come along because you want to be in on the action—you want to be proactive in getting justice for Dr. Fazal. I get it."

The waiter arrived with a stack of blueberry pancakes for Austin and some rye toast for her. "Anything else I can get you?"

They both declined, and Austin dumped a pile of whipped butter on top of his pancakes.

"You don't have to use tricks with me, Sophia. You don't have to pretend to be someone you're not—because I like you, as is."

She watched him dig into his pancakes through narrowed eyes. He didn't want to take care of the soft, helpless woman? She'd rarely been soft or helpless in her life, but she could've given it a try—for Austin.

Back at the hotel an hour later, Austin brought up the police report on Patel's homicide on his laptop and scrolled through it. Patel had died, bled out, probably moments before Sophia discovered him. Thank God Patel's killer hadn't ambushed Sophia before Austin had him in his crosshairs.

There were no akas listed in Patel's file, so as far as the Boston PD was concerned, the murder victim was Peter Patel, a visitor to Boston from California and staying at the Cambridge Arms Hotel—even his room number was listed in the report. Money and credit cards had been lifted from Patel's wallet to make it look like a robbery. Of course, the cops had to be thinking, what street criminal would slit a man's throat to get cash and credit cards?

"What did you find out? Where was he staying?" Sophia sat on the bed beside him, crossing her legs beneath her.

His gaze glanced across her creamy shoulder where her sweater dropped off and then meandered to her dark eyes, sparkling with interest and intelligence. He preferred this engaged presence to the scared female persona she felt she had to employ to convince him to take her with him when he went to Patel's hotel room. Did she really believe he wanted a damsel in distress? Did he? Had he?

If he examined the truth head-on, most of the women he'd dated back home had been softer, more domesticated, more interested in a diamond on their left hand than one piercing the side of their nose.

"Hotel?" She cocked her head and her inky hair fanned across her exposed shoulder.

"The Cambridge Arms. Know it?"

"Nope. Sounds like one of those places thrown up to accommodate the parents of all those college students." She tugged on her earlobe. "The cops think this is a robbery?"

"Uh–huh. His killer even stole money and credit cards from his wallet."

"Oh, and just decided to slice him from ear to ear after they got their eighty bucks?"

"I'm sure that's under their consideration."

"When do we head over to the Cambridge Arms and what are we going to find? The cops have probably already been there, right?"

"I'm sure they have. They probably even removed some items from the room if they thought something had particular significance."

"Will we find anything left that could help us?"

"We might. I'm not going to pass up the chance to find out."

Her cell phone buzzed and she leaned forward to snatch it from the bedside table. Her fingers played across the display as she made a slight turn away from him.

Austin ground his back teeth, and he tapped his keyboard a little harder than he had to. When he'd had possession of her cell, he couldn't help noticing a few more messages rolling in from that dating app. Was that what she was doing now? Answering her so-called dates?

He sniffed. Was that the kind of guy she wanted? Someone who spent time trolling for women online instead of meeting them face-to-face?

He rubbed his hand across his mouth. And how exactly was that any of his business?

She cupped her phone in her palm. "When are we going to Cambridge?"

"As soon as I finish going through this report."

"You don't think we should wait until nighttime?"

"Less conspicuous during the day, and we don't have to worry about turning on any lights in his room—in case someone's watching."

Dragging her bottom lip between her teeth, she tossed her phone from hand to hand. "Do you think his killers know where he was staying?"

"They went through his pockets to take money from his wallet, so they saw his hotel key. They know."

"So, they might be there?"

"Which is another reason why we're going in the daylight. They know the police have been or will be in Cambridge. They'll wait until they think it's safe."

"What if the police catch us?"

"You forget." He thumped his chest once. "Even though I'm supposed to be under law enforcement's radar, if worse comes to worse and they make me, I have an out."

"It would cause some kind of…incident though, wouldn't it? A US Navy SEAL involved in an operation in the homeland."

"It would be a problem—but I don't intend to get caught."

"Oh, I won't get caught either." She flicked back her dark hair. "I got away with plenty back in the day."

"I'll bet you still do."

A pretty pink tinged her cheeks, and then she rolled off the bed. "I'll let you finish so we can get going. Something to drink from the vending machine?"

"I still have a water in the fridge."

"I need…something."

She banged out of the room, and Austin eased back against the stack of pillows. Despite the electricity between them, Sophia wasn't comfortable with flirtation—and he needed to stop flirting with her and stop thinking about what she was and was not comfortable with. He needed to protect her against Fazal's killers and that was it.

After the identification of Patel, he could be out of here and on the first plane back to Somalia. He and his team of snipers still had plenty of unfinished business with a nasty terrorist with the code name Vlad.

By the time Sophia had returned to the room, he'd gone through the rest of the police file and was stuffing his feet into his running shoes. "Did you get lost on the way to the soda machine across the hall?"

"I decided to take a quick look around the hotel. There's an indoor pool and Jacuzzi on the first floor."

"Yeah, this would be a great spot…if I was on vacation." He grabbed his jacket. "Are you ready?"

"Do you have a plan?"

He winked at her. "I always have a plan."

Except for a plan to deal with his attraction to a

woman he'd just met and might have to leave just as quickly.

The drive over the bridge and into Cambridge didn't take long, and Sophia seemed preoccupied with her own thoughts. She'd been through a helluva few days. Before this craziness she probably thought she'd seen her lifetime quota of dead bodies after her mother killed her father.

She'd needed to catch a break, and she'd gotten that break when Dr. Hamid Fazal came into her life. After losing his own wife and daughters, Fazal had probably taken Sophia under his wing without hesitation. Sophia would've trusted someone like Fazal immediately, given their shared losses.

Did she trust him? Most women did, but Sophia wasn't most women.

He spotted the Cambridge Arms and then circled the block. "I don't want to park in the hotel lot. We might need to be guests, anyway, and I don't want to draw attention."

"You'll never find a parking place on the street, but there's a public lot around the corner."

"I know how much you object to paying for parking, so I'll get it. All my expenses are reimbursable."

"The navy's going to be wondering why you shelled out so much for parking."

He rolled his eyes and made a U-turn into a public lot.

As they walked across the street, Sophia asked, "What's the plan?"

"I'm sure most of the hotel employees are aware that one of their guests was murdered. Even if they aren't, the police most likely left instructions to keep Patel's room off-limits."

"That's not very encouraging."

"But—" he held up his index finger "—most hotels have a master card key that opens all the rooms, and we're going to snag one of those."

"*You're* going to snag one of those." She poked his arm. "I promised Dr. Fazal my life of crime was over."

"Don't worry."

Getting the master proved easier than he expected, and he didn't even have to plan the disturbance down the hall that took the hotel maid's attention away from her cart. With the card in his jacket pocket, he led Sophia to the stairwell and up two flights to Patel's room.

The maids had already finished or hadn't started on this floor yet, which made their break-in easier. With his gloves still on, he slid the key home and pushed open the door, giving Sophia a nudge in ahead of him.

He caught the door before it slammed and eased it closed as he scanned the room. He flipped the inside lock. "Cops already did a number in here."

Sophia had pulled on her own gloves and circled the room, hands on her hips. "Where do we start and what are we looking for?"

"Any personal effects—pictures, postcards, letters. Examine every piece of paper you come across for names, addresses and places."

"Would the cops have already taken that stuff?"

"I'm sure they did. It is a murder investigation, and they need to contact the next of kin."

"Wherever they are."

"Probably Pakistan."

Sophia blew out a breath and rolled her shoulders. "Okay, I'll start with his suitcases."

Austin strode to the nightstand and opened the drawers, looking for papers and anything jotted down on the hotel menu or flyers. He even thumbed through the Bible.

"Nothing but clothes in here." Sophia flipped down the cover of one suitcase. "I'll check the side pockets."

He moved to the bathroom, hoping to find a leftover prescription bottle.

Sophia called from the other room, "Patel sure read a lot of different newspapers."

"Anything written on them?" He poked his head out of the bathroom when he heard a clicking noise at the hotel door. Never breaking contact with Sophia's wide eyes, he held a finger to his lips.

He crept from the bathroom and flattened himself against the wall behind the door. It opened slowly and then halted against the inside lock he'd flipped into place earlier.

Someone on the other side of that door sucked in a sharp breath.

Austin glanced at Sophia, who was still crouched on the floor next to Patel's suitcase, an armful of newspapers clutched to her chest.

Sidling along the wall, Austin made his way to Sophia and then grabbed her arm, pulling her to her feet. He pointed at the sliding glass door that led to a small balcony.

She shook her head and breathed into his ear, "We're three floors up."

She didn't have to tell him that, but whoever was outside that door wasn't leaving until they did, and soon there might be someone stationed outside, as well.

He took two steps toward the door and tugged at it. It opened on a whisper. When Sophia joined him on the balcony, he closed the door behind them and peered over the railing around the edge.

Turning toward him, Sophia grabbed his jacket. "I can't do this."

"Sure you can." He chucked her under the chin. "There's a balcony beneath this one. If we hang off the edge, we can reach it by swinging our legs and jumping onto it. We should be able to drop to those bushes below from the second floor."

"I—I'm afraid of heights. I can't."

He cupped her face in his hands. "You do it, or we have some kind of gun battle with the people trying to get into this room. I'll go first, and I'll catch you. Do you trust me?"

If she didn't want to do it, he'd go to battle for her, but he hoped she trusted him enough to take a chance.

Could she take a chance on him?

Chapter Eleven

Sophia swallowed. Her gaze drifted past Austin's shoulder to the hotel door, which had closed—for now. Who was on the other side? If it were the cops, they would've said something.

She focused on Austin's face, strong, confident. Did she trust him? More than anything else in her life right now.

She released a breath. "Tell me what to do."

Smoothing his gloved thumbs across her cheeks, he said, "You got this, but we're gonna have to hurry."

To make his point, Austin gave her a little shove from behind toward the railing that separated her from thirty feet to sudden death.

"Watch me."

Gripping the top of the railing he flung his body over the ledge. Sophia watched him slide his hands to the bottom rung of the railing and swing like he was competing in a gymnastics event.

She'd always been really, really bad at gymnastics.

When Austin disappeared below her, she clutched her suddenly tight throat. His voice floated up from beneath her. "Your turn. Hoist yourself over and scoot your hands as far down as you can."

Licking her lips, she glanced over her shoulder into the room. Had the door opened again?

She curled her hands around the railing and swung one leg over. She perched there like a giant awkward bird for a few seconds before rolling her body into oblivion. She squeaked once as her legs dangled in midair.

Austin's hand stroked her ankle. "Ready to swing?"

She began to work her shoulder muscles to propel her hips forward. She kicked her legs to increase her momentum just like when she was a kid on the swing set in the run-down park that was her refuge. She closed her eyes and swung harder. If she ever needed to escape, this was it.

"You're doing great. I'm going to tell you when to release and you're just going to let go."

Let go? Right.

But when Austin gave his command, she released. His strong arms wrapped around her legs and yanked her into the balcony below.

Her body flew into his and he stumbled back, taking her with him.

They landed with a thump and a crash into the metal chair stationed on the balcony.

Her eyes flew open and she looked into his face, meeting his slightly amused green gaze.

"That wasn't so hard, was it?"

With her body stretched out on top of his, their faces inches away from each other's, she'd never felt better. She rested her head against his shoulder. "That was crazy. Now you're telling me we need to jump off this balcony two stories high into those bushes down there?"

"We're in luck." He tipped his head back. "The guests in this room left their slider unlocked."

Raising her head, she squinted through the window. "They're not in there, are they?"

"I'm pretty sure they would've come running out here if they were." He shifted beneath her and grunted. "Are we going to stay out here all afternoon, or would you like to get going?"

She wouldn't mind lying on top of him for the rest of the day, but they had a killer or killers waiting for them.

She rolled off his body and onto her knees. "We'd better hurry before the people in this room come back."

Austin scrambled to his feet and pulled open the door, poking his head inside the room. "I think our luck is holding. Doesn't look like anyone's staying here."

She squeezed past him into the room, taking a deep breath of his masculine scent. She'd never forget it. If the tinny smell of blood would always remind her of her father's death, this woodsy scent would always bring Austin back into her thoughts.

They crossed the room and Austin tucked her behind him when they got to the door. "Hang on."

He peeked out the peephole and then eased open the door. "Let's head for the stairwell. I have my gun ready in my pocket. If I tell you to duck…duck."

"You got me this far. I'll be the best damned soldier you ever encountered."

He squeezed the back of her neck. "You already are."

When the fresh air hit her face and whipped her hair into tangles, Sophia almost collapsed from the relief.

Sensing her frailty, Austin took her arm and hustled her down the sidewalk. "Let's keep moving. We're almost to the car."

He wasted no time once they were buckled in throwing the car into gear and peeling out of the parking lot.

He smacked the steering wheel with the heel of his hand. "All that risk for nothing. The police left nothing behind—if Patel even left any clues in the room."

"I did take these." Sophia tugged at the zipper on her jacket and pulled out a bunch of newspapers.

"What the hell? How did you manage that?"

"I had just found them when someone tried the door. You'd told me to check for writing, but I didn't have time so I just zipped them up in my jacket. I thought I might lose them when I was swinging from the side of the hotel, but the bottom hem of my jacket is fitted and they stayed put. They may've even helped break my fall when I landed on top of you."

"For you, maybe."

"Did I hurt you?"

"You couldn't hurt me if you tried, but I did get nailed with the chair leg."

Could the same be said for her? Not that he would ever hurt her on purpose, but this flirtatious game he was playing with her could only end badly.

"Now that I have the newspapers, let me take a look to see if he wrote anything on them." She smoothed out the papers on her lap and flipped over each page, her gaze scanning the black-and-white print.

"There's nothing out of the ordinary here." She tucked the first paper under the other two and skimmed through the next one, and then the next. She slumped in the seat and sighed. "Nothing."

"Let's get some lunch." He drummed his thumbs on the steering wheel. "I'm driving in the opposite direction of Boston. Anywhere you want to go?"

"How can you think about food after the day we just had?"

"Look at it this way—you never know when you're going to need energy to jump out of windows and swing from balconies." He patted his flat belly. "I need sustenance."

"I hope that's the last jump I take from a window for a while." She looked out the window and studied the road signs. "Lexington. It's less than an hour away."

"Lead the way."

She gave him directions to a small lunch place with some booths for privacy. She didn't know what Austin's next move was going to be and maybe he didn't either, but they needed some time to figure it out—unless his shadowy superiors had already figured it out for him.

He parked the car down the street from the restaurant and ducked his head to read the street sign out the window. "We're near the Lexington Battle Green."

"Haven't you ever played tourist here before?"

"A long time ago. When I was in middle school our class took a trip here. I've been back a few times, but never did the full round of tourist stops."

"I guess it's not going to happen this time either." She grabbed the newspapers and got out of the car, slamming the door behind her.

They found a booth in the corner of the restaurant, and she ordered lemonade and a turkey wrap while Austin got a beer and a burger.

When the waitress delivered the mug, she tapped the side of it. "Aren't you technically on duty or something?"

"No clue. Do you think I've done something like this particular mission before? Sleuthing is a little out of my comfort zone." He took a sip of beer through the thick foam. "Does it bother you when people drink around you?"

"Not as long as they maintain control. I hate drunks."

"I promise I'll control myself." He raised his glass. "Let's have a look at those papers again."

She picked them up from the seat next to her and plopped them on the table. "I did notice one thing about the newspapers."

"What?" He turned the first paper around to face him.

"They're not current papers. All three are from different dates in the past couple of months."

"That's significant." He shoved his beer away and positioned the two other newspapers on either side of the first one, lining them up. His head swung from side to side as if watching a slow-moving tennis match. He flipped over the first page of the paper on his right, and then smacked the table.

"Did you see something?"

"All three of these papers—" he tapped each one with his finger "—have the same story."

"They do?" Leaning on her elbows, she hunched forward. "I guess I wasn't looking for that. What's the story?"

"They're stories about a symposium here in Boston on terrorism, or rather preventing it."

"That makes too much sense."

The waiter returned with a plate in each hand. "The burger?"

"Right here." Austin slid the papers to the side and tapped the table in front of him.

When the waiter left, Austin put his condiments on his burger and took a big bite.

"You're unbelievable." She reached across the table and snatched one of the papers. Her gaze tripped across an article on the lower right-hand side of the page, and she read aloud. "'Leading terrorism experts and advocates for at-risk youth are meeting to discuss methods for reducing the risks of home-grown terrorism.'"

Austin held up his finger as he took another bite of his burger. He wiped his mouth, gulped some beer and then smacked his lips. "Sustenance—now I can think."

"What do you think? Sounds pretty harmless to me." She trailed her finger along the lines of the rest of the article. "Sounds like a brainstorming session on keeping disaffected youth from being attracted to terrorist organizations. Hey, I'm familiar with one of the sponsors—Boston's Kids. I did some volunteer work with that group. They do good work, nothing sinister there."

"When is the symposium?"

"This week, just a few days from now." She picked up her turkey wrap. "What was Patel's interest and why did he think Dr. Fazal would be interested?"

"Since I don't know who Patel is—yet—I can't tell you. Fazal is connected because he fingered a terrorist for us—a big fish. Maybe Patel was trying to warn Fazal about something, a warning that the guys who killed both of them don't want out there."

"About this symposium?"

"Is there a list of attendees in that article?"

"Nope." She started to reach for the next paper, and he stopped her.

"Eat." He took his own advice as another fry disappeared into his mouth, and then he grabbed the newspaper. "This article discusses security for the event, nothing about the guest list."

"And the last one?"

He slid the paper in front of him with one finger. "Bingo—a list of attendees, or at least some of them."

"Why does that matter?"

"One or more of these members might be a target."

"Do you recognize any of them?"

"A few names. One of these guys wrote a book we had to read. He knows his stuff."

"Is that what you think this is about? Do you think someone at the symposium or the whole symposium is at risk?"

"That's what it looks like to me. Why would Patel be carting these papers around with him? The information that he gave Fazal or that his killers *think* he gave Fazal must involve this symposium."

"But still nothing concrete."

"We know more than we did an hour ago, and I have something more to report, which justifies my continued assignment."

"Why do you think Patel brought this intel to Dr. Fazal instead of contacting US intelligence?"

"Maybe Fazal was the only way he knew how to reach us."

"Then why didn't Dr. Fazal report it? Patel had been hanging around for almost a week before Fazal's murder. Nothing, right?"

"There are big chunks of the story we don't know. I'm hoping those fingerprints can give us Patel's identity, and I'm going to be reporting this latest information about the symposium. Maybe we already know something about it."

She held up her wrap. "I think you're on to something with this sustenance thing. I feel better already, and I'm not even half done."

"Finish up." He dipped the end of one fry into a puddle of ketchup. "Sustenance also includes some fresh air and a clear mind. We're going to take a stroll into Minute Man National Park and delve into a different war from the one we're fighting now—because make no mistake about it, Peter Patel launched us into battle without firing a shot."

WHEN THEY GOT back to the hotel, Sophia slipped away to the hotel shop to look for a frame but found some new pajamas instead. She needed them, anyway.

Austin spent the rest of the afternoon working, and she tried to keep busy with patient files. But she'd had enough.

She put away her laptop and bounced on the edge of the bed, watching Austin hunched over his laptop. "Did you submit the symposium presenter names, too?"

"Symposium, presenters, location, security measures. The FBI may already be working with the Boston PD on this, but I have no insight into what they're doing."

"I couldn't find a frame in the hotel shops. Do you think I'll have some time tomorrow to go out and buy a new frame for my picture?"

He glanced up. "You're not a prisoner, Sophia."

"You mean, I can walk out of this hotel any time I want and do whatever I please?"

"Not exactly." He paused, his fingers poised over the keyboard of the laptop. "Is there someplace special you want to go—other than picture-frame shopping?"

"Other than picking up where my life left off?"

Tipping the chair onto its back legs, he folded his hands behind his neck. "You can't go back to work yet, can you?"

"I have no patients, really. All of mine were Dr. Fazal's. They'll be seeing another doctor now and if they want to continue to see me as their physical therapist, we'll have to work through their new doctors."

"You're anxious to get back to your social life, your... friends. I can understand that, but you need to be careful who you contact right now. Fazal's killers could be watching people, you know."

"Oh, God, that would be awful. It's bad enough they got to Ginny." She glanced at her phone, where another message from Tyler had come through. She'd already explained about the death of her close friend. He could wait a few days. She'd even given him her cell phone number so he didn't have to keep messaging her through the Spark app.

She skimmed her fingertip over his message. She and Tyler had seemed to hit it off over coffee. Maybe once all the craziness subsided, they could reconnect. She stole a glance at Austin, back on his laptop.

Would Tyler measure up to Austin? Would any man? What other man could compete with someone who protected you from terrorists out to kidnap you? Austin would be a hard act to follow, but if she ever hoped to get into a relationship in the real world, outside of the fantasy one she was currently inhabiting with a larger-than-life navy SEAL, she'd have to get back out there and date—and Tyler would be her first.

She responded to his message that she'd be attending a memorial service for her friend on Tuesday and she had several loose ends at work to tie up, but they could reschedule their date later.

He replied immediately with a thumbs-up emoji, and she wrinkled her nose. She could never imagine that tough guy in the chair over there ever using an emoji.

Clearing her throat, she tucked one edge of her phone

beneath her thigh. "Do you ever use emojis when you text? You know, those little…"

"I know what emojis are. I use them all the time when I text my nieces and nephews—even my sisters." He stopped typing and raised his eyebrows. "Why do you want to know?"

Her shoulders rose and fell. "Just wondering."

"Why do I feel like I just failed a test?" A little horn trumpeted from his laptop, and he glanced down. "Email from Ariel."

A knot tightened in her stomach. Every time Austin's superiors communicated with him brought the threat that they could be yanking him off the assignment—yanking him out of her life. She licked her lips. "What's it about? I mean, if you can tell me."

"Yes." He pumped a fist in the air. "There's a match for the fingerprints. Peter Patel is actually Waheed Jilani from the same province in Pakistan as Dr. Fazal, near Peshawar. He must've been friends with Hamid back home."

"Do they have any idea what he was doing here or why he contacted Dr. Fazal?"

"No, but the area where they're from? It's a hotbed of terrorist activity, so maybe he heard something about a plot involving the symposium in Boston." He dragged a hand through his hair and mumbled, "Oh, my God."

"What?" She launched herself from the bed and crowded in next to him to see the laptop.

He snapped the lid shut. "Waheed Jilani's eldest son was just murdered—today."

Chapter Twelve

Austin gripped the edge of the laptop. God, he hoped Sophia hadn't seen that picture of Jilani's son. What the hell had the man done to warrant that outrage?

What information could he possibly have?

Sophia doubled over and then sank to the floor at his feet. "What is going on? What did Patel have?"

"Jilani. I don't know, but it has to be something important."

"And these guys, these—" she waved her hand at his computer "—killers think I have it or know it?"

"It must be something concrete because they wouldn't know one way or the other if Jilani told Fazal anything and if Fazal told you. It has to be an object, something they're looking for and can't find—even after tossing Fazal's office."

"And my apartment."

"If we could find it, we'd remove the threat. Game over."

"God, I want this game to be over." She drew her knees to her chest and folded her arms on top of them.

He placed his hand on top of her head, the soft strands of her hair like velvet beneath his fingertips. "We're getting closer. We know Patel's true identity, and we know the information has something to do with the symposium. I've passed the information along, and at least the FBI can up the security levels surrounding the event, although…"

"There has to be more, right? It can't just be a threat to the event."

"That's what I was thinking. A simple threat is too easy. Jilani could've told Fazal or even reported it to the Boston PD." He flipped up the lid of his laptop and logged out so that there was no chance Sophia would see that picture of Jilani's son. "I'm thinking the reason he didn't go straight to US intelligence with his information is because of the threat to his family."

"It didn't work, anyway." She'd rested her forehead against her folded arms, and now her head shot up. "We have to find whatever it is he gave Dr. Fazal. We owe it to him, we owe it to Dr. Fazal and now we owe it to Jilani's family."

Austin stretched his legs in front of him and slumped in his chair. "Are you going to try to get into the justice business?"

"If that's what you want to call it. People should have to pay for ruining other people's lives."

"Do you think your mother paid enough for ruining yours?"

"Locked away for almost twenty-five years? I suppose so. Who knows? Maybe her crime saved both of us. If she and my father had kept on like they were, she would've OD'd anyway and maybe I'd be dead, too. Foster care wasn't fun and games, but at least I'm alive."

"That's one way of looking at it." He nudged her hip with the toe of his shoe. "Are you hungry?"

"Not at all, but you don't have to tell me you are."

"I've been eyeing that room-service menu and a bottle of ibuprofen."

"Sore from your tumble on the balcony?" She rolled her shoulders. "I'm feeling it, too."

He stood up and stepped over her, reaching for the menu. "Would you like something to drink with your ibuprofen?"

"There's already hot tea in the room and a soda machine across the hall. I'm good."

"You're more than good."

"Excuse me?" She lifted one eyebrow.

"I've put you through hell since the moment I got here, and you've hit every curveball out of the park. Not sure how this would've gone down if you'd been someone different."

If Sophia had been a different woman, he'd probably be back on duty right now. Would he have fought so hard to stay on this assignment if Dr. Fazal's coworker hadn't been a black-haired stunner with hard eyes and tremulous lips?

Those lips quirked into a crooked smile.

"Something funny about that?"

"Kind of." She rose from the floor and stretched her taut body, which did a number on his blood pressure.

"You don't do well with compliments, do you?"

"It's just that I spent so much of my youth wishing I was someone else, and here you are telling me I'm just who I need to be."

"I'm sure you heard that from Hamid, as well."

"Yeah, I met him about twenty years too late. He's the father I should've had, and he's the friend I should've had for a lifetime." She touched the cracked frame.

"Do you want to buy a new frame for the picture tomorrow morning before the memorial?"

"Will we have time?"

"So far, I have nothing planned. You?"

She balanced a fist on one hip. "Is that a joke?"

"I thought maybe you needed to go back into the office, deal with more paperwork, patient referrals?"

"I do, eventually. Ginny did all the heavy lifting, calling the patients."

He picked up the phone's receiver. "I'm going to order something from room service. Are you sure you don't want something?"

"I'll make myself some hot tea later. All the excitement and the late lunch made me tired."

He pressed the button for room service and closed his eyes while the phone rang. If he was lucky, Sophia would fall asleep and he could try to forget his attraction to her for a few hours. If he was *really* lucky, she'd stay away and he could continue to drink in the way her hair kept slipping over one shoulder and the grace of her lithe body as she moved about the room.

For one amazing minute today, he'd had that body stretched out on top of his own. With her lips inches from his mouth, he hadn't even noticed the sharp pain stabbing him between the shoulder blades when he'd hit the leg of the chair on the balcony. He sure felt it now.

He ordered himself a steak, a twice-baked potato and some asparagus.

"Do you mind if I hit the shower before my food gets here? I'm going to aim that shower spray between my shoulder blades for a little relief."

"You can always go down to the hot tub."

"As inviting as that sounds right now, I don't want to wander around the hotel—just in case. When you went out earlier, I had second thoughts."

"God, I hope they haven't followed us here. I sort of felt safe in this hotel."

"We are. They obviously know now that you're with

someone who's not just a Spark date, but nobody has gotten a look at me yet. They don't know who I am, and my rental car isn't on their radar."

"My car is."

"That's why we leave it in the hotel parking lot. That's why you don't get in touch with any of your friends right now." He traced the edge of the plastic room service menu. "Maybe that's why you shouldn't attend Dr. Fazal's memorial."

She dropped the tea bag she'd been unwrapping. "Are you crazy? That's not an option."

"He'd understand. He'd understand more than anyone why you couldn't be there."

"No, no and no." She snatched up the tea bag and started twirling it around her finger. "He's family. You can do your sniper thing again to protect me, but I have to be there. I'm speaking"

"Okay. I'll think of something. Right now I'm going to take a shower. If room service shows up while I'm in the bathroom, don't open the door. Come and get me."

"There you go again. I thought we were safe here."

"You can never be too careful. You should know that by now."

"Go take your shower. I'll make my tea and watch some TV."

He grabbed a pair of sweats and a T-shirt on the way to the bathroom. He couldn't exactly lounge around in his briefs.

Once in the shower, he cranked on the faucet and turned his back to the hot water. The hotel had an adjustable showerhead, and he reached up and turned it to a pulsing spray. He rolled his shoulders under the onslaught of the water, and started soaping up his body.

He was supposed to be relaxing in here, but thoughts of Sophia kept seeping into his brain, making him hard.

He dropped his sudsy washcloth and didn't bother picking it up. Instead he rinsed off with much cooler water to temper his heated thoughts.

He turned off the water and snapped a towel from the rack just outside the shower curtain. As he dried off, Sophia tapped on the door.

"Room service."

"Already?"

"You've been in there for a while. If you'd been in the tub, I would've been worried about drowning."

He cursed under his breath, dropped the towel and swept up his sweats from the back of the toilet. He dragged them on and swung open the door of the bathroom.

"Is he still there?"

"I told him to hold on." Her gaze skimmed across his bare chest and it felt it like her fingers trickling across his flesh.

He shivered. He pressed his eye to the peephole and opened the door, blocking the entrance to the room. "I'll take it in, thanks. Check?"

The room service waiter pulled a sheet of paper from the front pocket of his white coat. "Here you go, sir."

Austin signed the meal to the room and added a hefty tip for keeping the guy waiting. Then the waiter loaded up the covered dishes onto a tray and placed it in Austin's arms. He backed up into the room, kicking the door closed.

Sophia cleared off a space on the table by the window. "That looks like enough food to feed an army—or rather a team of navy SEALs."

He snorted as he placed the tray on the table. "This? Not even close."

"While you're chowing down, I'm going to take a shower, too. Swinging from a balcony is almost as strenuous as an entire workout at the gym."

He plucked a lid from one of the dishes and waved it at her. He didn't even want to think about her in the same shower where he'd just been, naked, soaping up... thinking about her. Best just to eat his meal, pretend to work and conk out on the sofa bed.

SHE TURNED HER back on Austin and crouched beside her suitcase. As she dug through the bag, her fingers found the silky nightshirt she'd bought in the clothing store downstairs earlier that day.

Pressing the pretty but serviceable item to her chest, she sidled into the bathroom. She didn't want to come on as full-fledged sex bomb, but he might appreciate seeing her in something other than an old T-shirt, or she might appreciate him seeing her, or she might...

She slammed the bathroom door. She didn't know what she wanted. No, that wasn't true either—she wanted Austin Foley—lock, stock and rippling muscles.

She showered quickly and slipped into her new nightgown, its silky folds caressing her bare skin, heightening her sensitivity—everywhere. After washing her face, she let down her hair and brushed it out until it had a glossy sheen.

She squared her shoulders and marched back into the bedroom, hoping to find Austin snoozing on the sofa bed and making her decision for her.

He glanced up from his plate and his eyes widened. Then he coughed and took a gulp of water from his bottle.

Suddenly self-conscious, she scurried to her suitcase and dropped her clothes on top of the mess inside. Austin hadn't even put a shirt on. He wasn't going to make this easy at all—unless he grabbed her and planted a kiss on her mouth.

Austin Foley, Wyoming cowboy, navy SEAL and all-around good guy would never do that. Making a move on a woman without politely asking first had to be against his moral cowboy code or something—especially after knowing her for a grand total of three days.

If she wanted something with Austin before he took off and disappeared from her life completely, she'd have to take the initiative—and risk rejection. Hell, it wasn't as if she hadn't encountered rejection a few...or a hundred times in her life.

"How's the steak?"

"Perfect. Do you want a bite? Of steak?"

"No, thanks."

He held up a spear of asparagus, dripping butter. "Asparagus? There's so much butter on it, it doesn't even taste healthy."

She sauntered toward him, fully aware of her nipples peaking and chafing against the material of her night-shirt—and not giving a damn.

Austin's eyes never left hers as she drew closer. When she landed in front of him, she dipped, bending her knees slightly, mouth open.

He swallowed, his Adam's apple bobbing in his throat as he placed the tip of the asparagus on her tongue.

The buttery taste flooded her mouth, and she took a bite. Raising her eyes to the ceiling, she said, "Very good, and you're right. That didn't taste like a healthy veggie at all."

He popped the stem of the asparagus in his mouth and then ran the pad of his thumb just below her bottom lip. "Butter."

"Can't take me anywhere."

"Do you want any more?"

She allowed her gaze to drop to his bare chest and wander to his flat abs. "Not…now."

He stacked his dishes on the tray with a clatter, breaking the tension between them. Who knew asparagus could be sexy?

"I'm done." He shoved the tray to the other side of the table and stretched his arms over his head. A spasm of pain shifted across his features.

"Are you okay?"

"Still sore where that damned chair poked me in the back."

"That's my fault for landing on you."

"Better me than two stories below."

"Do you need any more ibuprofen?"

"Already took my allotment. I'll down another couple in a few hours."

"That's not helping you now." She backed up to the bed and patted the mattress. It was now or never. "You know in addition to being a physical therapist, I'm also a trained masseuse."

"Really?" He rolled his shoulders. "That must come in handy."

"It comes in handy when I jump on top of people and knock them backward into chairs. I'll give you a free session, relax your muscles and relieve some of that pain for you."

She held her breath. What if he turned her down? Would he view this as some kind of desperate attempt to keep him in Boston, keep him in her life?

His lids fell over his eyes as if in slow motion. "Sure."

She scooted off the bed. "I don't have any massage oil, so the hotel lotion will have to do. It's all in the hands, anyway."

"I'm sure it is." He stretched out on the bed and she hurried into the bathroom.

She grabbed the little bottle of lotion from the vanity and stopped in front of the mirror to assess the stranger in front of her. Flushed cheeks and bright eyes indicated a level of excitement she hadn't felt in years. How crazy for these incredible highs coming along with the depths of despair over losing Dr. Fazal and then Ginny. Maybe hooking up with Austin was just her way of climbing out of the pit of darkness.

Whatever the reason, she had a perfect male specimen waiting for her in the other room.

She returned to the bed with the lotion pinned between her arm and body, rubbing her hands together. "I'm going to warm up my hands so I don't shock you."

He rolled his head to the side, his green eyes glittering. "Nothing you could do would shock me."

The lotion slipped from her hold and bounced on the carpet. She ducked down, allowing her hair to fall over her hot face. Where had those gentlemanly manners gone?

She popped up, lotion in hand. "Just relax. I'm going to start with your scalp, without the lotion."

"Head on the pillow or off?"

"Let's get rid of the pillow, so you're lying flat."

He shoved the pillow to the side. "I'm all yours."

A girl could wish.

Curling her legs beneath her, she settled on the bed next to his right hip. She cracked her knuckles and rose to her knees. She dug her fingertips into his thick, short hair until they met his scalp. Then she pressed the pads of her fingers against the points behind his ears and down to the base of his skull.

He released a long breath. "That feels surprisingly good."

"You haven't had a head massage before? Even haircuts usually involve a massage when you get your hair washed."

"When I get a haircut, the navy barber doesn't exactly massage my scalp."

"Well, he should start." She finished with his head and moved down to his neck, pinching into the hard, corded muscles. "Lot of tension right here."

"Yeah, well, that's an occupational hazard. I have to hold my head in the same position for long stretches of time when I'm on a mission."

She drove her thumbs into either side of his neck, and he sucked in a breath.

"Sorry. With this much tension, there's gonna be some pain."

"Hurts so much, it feels good."

"If you say so, tough guy."

Her hands slipped to his broad shoulders, spanning the slabs of muscle beneath his smooth skin. She squeezed a puddle of lotion into her palm and rubbed her hands together. Her hands slid across his shoulders, and he seemed to melt beneath her touch, as his eyelashes fluttered and his eyes closed.

He tensed up as she worked toward his shoulder blades. "You're getting close to my injury."

"I can see it. A bruise is forming where the chair leg gouged you." She dabbled her fingertips over the red spot. "I'll work around it, and as your muscles get loose, that'll relieve some of your pain in that area."

"Go for it. I trust you."

Avoiding the bruised area of his back, she massaged his warm skin. His back formed a perfect V, tapering down to his narrow waist. The waistband of his sweats began just above the curve of his buttocks.

How far did she dare go? While he seemed to be enjoying the massage, he still hadn't made a move. In her book, this massage screamed, "Take me." Did he still have doubts that she wanted him?

Maybe he'd take the massage and reject her.

Her knuckles kneaded the area on either side of his spine on the small of his back. As she skimmed the band of his sweats, he seemed to stop breathing.

"Are you going farther?"

"D-do you want me to?"

"Oh, yeah, but not if this was supposed to be some therapeutic massage." He cranked his head around and pinned her with a gaze from beneath heavy lids. "You wanna stop, you stop, and I'll go bang my head against the wall."

A smile crept to her lips. "I don't want you sustaining any more injuries. I need you—to get me through this mess."

"Is that the only reason you need me?"

She didn't want to answer that question, didn't want to think about the variety of ways she needed Austin, so she peeled back his sweats.

His muscled backside curved into a perfect crescent, and her fingertips tingled as she ran them across his skin. He shivered beneath her touch.

She drove the heels of her hands against his tight glutes and along the sides of his hips while he moaned softly and buried his head in the crook of his arm.

After several minutes, he said in a muffled voice, "I can honestly say that's the first time I've ever had my backside massaged."

"Does it feel good? Do you like it?"

"Do you want me to show you how much I like it?"

Before she could answer, he rolled onto his back, dragging his sweats down over his hips. His erection rose from his body, hard and hot.

She lodged her tongue in the corner of her mouth. "Looks like you enjoyed that—a lot."

"I think I need a massage here, too."

"This is going to cost you extra." She cupped one hand between his legs and closed the other around his erection, running it up and down his shaft.

Tipping back his head, he made a low sound deep in his throat. He thrust his hips forward, and she pumped him harder until he grabbed her wrist.

He growled, his voice rough around the edges. "I can do a type of massage, too."

"Really?" She widened her eyes and batted her eyelashes as heat surged through her body.

"With my tongue." He sat up suddenly and grabbed the hem of her nightshirt, yanking it over her head.

The cold air made goose bumps rush across her chest, and her nipples hardened and ached beneath Austin's hungry gaze. He encircled her waist with his hands and flipped her onto her back. He loomed above her and slid her underwear down over her thighs. With one finger, he dragged them down her legs and flicked them off her feet.

She drew her knees to her chest, but he planted one hand on each knee and spread her legs apart.

"This is your idea of a massage?"

"Oh, yeah." He crawled between her open legs, burying his head between her thighs.

The ends of his hair tickled her tummy and she stifled a giggle.

He peered up at her. "Are you laughing at my attempts at therapeutic massage?"

"I…" Her words ended in a gasp as Austin drove his tongue into her core.

He played her, bringing her to the edge of passion and then teasing her by slowing down, drawing back, leaving her gasping for more. She dug her fingers into his scalp and urged him on. Her muscles tensed as he spun her higher and higher until she was almost afraid of the inevitable crash.

His lips sucked at her flesh, pulling her into his mouth. The tingling at her toes raced up her legs and pooled between her thighs. She arched her back, offering even more of herself to Austin's talented tongue.

When he grabbed her derriere with both hands, she lost it. Her orgasm clawed through her and she opened her mouth to scream, but she couldn't muster the breath to make a sound. Something between a squeal and a whimper eked past her lips as her hips bucked wildly.

Over and over the waves of passion ripped through her body, and she thrashed her head from side to side as colored light flashed behind her eyes, which were squeezed tightly closed.

Austin, his head no longer between her thighs, pinched her nipples, extending her orgasm with shots of pleasure. As she began to descend from her high, he kissed her mouth and she wriggled beneath him, sighing against his lips.

But if she thought this was some kind of calm respite after the storm, Austin soon dispelled that notion as he drove into her.

He whispered in her ear. "Sorry, but I'm too damned hard to wait."

She felt the truth of his statement filling her up, plunging into her deeply, making her whole. Wrapping her legs around his hips, she squeezed him, holding him against her body and going along for the ride.

He stimulated her sensitive points and her passion rose again, but she'd have to wait for another orgasm because his exploded inside her.

His low growl morphed into a full-fledged howl as he threw his head back. He lifted his body, bracing his hands on either side of her shoulders as he continued to spend himself.

She ran her fingertip from his chin down his glistening chest to his hard abs and ended where their bodies connected.

His gaze pinned her with a look so hot, she almost felt the steam rising from the bed. Even though he'd already reached his climax, he continued moving against her.

"Your turn again."

Even if she hadn't been close, the smoldering way he looked at her and the unselfish way he continued to pleasure her sent her over the edge.

Her second orgasm moved through her like hot lava, and she melted beneath him. He thrust into her a few more times before lowering himself on top of her and nuzzling her neck.

"It feels so good inside you, better than I even imagined—and I imagined a lot."

"Was I too obvious with the massage ploy?" She smoothed his hair back from his forehead with the palm of her hand.

He pressed a kiss against the pulse throbbing in her throat. "I was just waiting for a sign from you. I didn't want to take advantage of the situation."

"I knew you'd be too chivalrous to make a move."

"Enough of chivalry. I'm not done with you yet, woman." He wrapped his hands around her waist, and, still inside her, did a one-eighty so that he was flat on his back and she sat astride him.

With his fingertips, he tickled the tattoo of a rose she had imprinted above her hip bone. "At least it's not some guy's name."

She snorted. "That would indicate something more permanent than I'm willing to give."

A shadow crossed his handsome face, and she almost bit her tongue. Why'd she have to bring up her personal issues at a time like this, with a man like this?

He puffed out a breath, and then cupped her breasts in his palms, dragging his thumbs across her already aching nipples. "I knew these would fit perfectly in my hands."

"A lot of our parts fit perfectly." She folded her body forward and kissed his chin.

He jerked beneath her, his thumbs jabbing into her soft flesh.

"Ouch. What did I do?"

"Sophia, we're being watched."

Chapter Thirteen

Austin kept his gaze pinned to the glint of light on the door adjoining the connecting room. It had to be a camera.

Sophia had drawn back sharply, her knees digging into his sides, her face a mask of fear and confusion. "What are you talking about?"

He put his finger to his lips and pulled the sheet around her shoulders. Could they hear them, too? He had to assume they could.

He whispered. "Just follow my lead. Try to act naturally."

He scooted out from beneath her, rolling from the bed. He grabbed his sweats from the floor and held them in front of his crotch, although it didn't much matter at this point since whoever was watching had pretty much seen everything he had to offer. "What am I talking about? You wore me out. Let's take a shower—together this time."

"Austin?"

He turned his back to the camera lodged in the door and gave Sophia a hard stare from narrowed eyes. "You're insatiable. Shower first."

She swallowed. "Okay."

She started to slide from the bed, clutching the sheets around her, and he gave a quick shake of his head. She dropped the sheet, her body still shimmering from their lovemaking, and joined him by the side of the bed. They'd already seen everything she had to offer, too, and the thought prompted a white-hot anger to thump through his veins.

He still had to make sure that what had caught his attention was, in fact, a camera, but he didn't want to signal that he knew it was there.

Taking her by the hand, he led her to the bathroom, shielding her naked body with his as much as he could. He swung open the bathroom door and nudged her inside. Then he turned on the shower full blast.

He took her by the shoulders. "I think there's a mini-camera in the door adjoining our room to the one next to ours."

Sophia covered her mouth with both hands. "What? How?"

"I don't know, but we have to get out of here."

"Do you think they're in the next room right now?"

"Not unless the senior citizens in there have gone to the dark side. I saw them earlier with family and grand-kids—no way. Somehow the guys on your tail got access to the room long enough to plant a minicamera in the adjoining door. They don't have to be present, and even if I destroy it, which I will, they've been receiving their video and maybe audio on a computer somewhere."

A red stain blotched her cheeks, and she put one arm across her breasts.

"I'm sorry, Sophia."

"Oh, God." She shook her head. "What they saw us

doing just now isn't important, but how'd they track us to this hotel?"

"It's not the cars. I checked those thoroughly. Nobody followed us. It can't be my phone, which is untraceable and untrackable. It has to be your cell phone."

"They're tracking my cell phone?"

"They must've been able to ping it somehow and track it down, although that must've happened recently or they would've made a move on us before this."

"I don't understand."

"There's not much more to understand at this point. We're getting out of here and you're leaving your phone...and your car."

"Where will we go? I have to attend Dr. Fazal's memorial. I told you that."

"We'll go to another hotel. I have a second set of fake identity papers, so if they got my name from this hotel, I can check in as someone else. I think we'll be okay, as long as you leave your phone here."

"I feel sick to my stomach, but I'm ready to leave now."

He pushed the hair from her face and kissed her temple. "We can't leave right now. We have to pretend we don't know the camera's there, and I don't want them to see us packing up and leaving in the middle of the night."

Her face blanched and her bottom lip trembled. "I can't, Austin. I can't spend the night in that bed with them watching me, watching us."

"Sure you can." He tugged on her soft earlobe. "I'll be right beside you. We'll pretend we're going to sleep after a lusty night of sex."

"What if they come for us at night? What if they break into the room?"

"They're not going to break into the room. That's why they set up the camera next door. I have a weapon with me, and I'll make sure they see it."

A vertical crease formed between her brows. "How are we going to disguise the fact that we're leaving? They'll see you remove the camera."

"I'm going to remove the camera from the other side. They might think it's just a malfunction."

"How will get into that room?"

"They did it, didn't they?" He pulled her close and rubbed her back, one hand resting on the curve of her backside. "I'll take care of this, Sophia. You did a great job out there—and I don't mean the sex, although that was pretty fantastic, too. You kept your cool. We'll get through this."

"What now?"

"Quick shower and off to bed."

They climbed into the tub together and rinsed off while he cursed the circumstances and the wasted opportunity of having Sophia in the shower with him.

After they patted dry and brushed their teeth, he handed her a dry towel. "You can wrap up in this if it makes you feel more comfortable. I don't think that would be unusual."

"Neither do I." She snatched the towel from him and wound it around her body.

He scooped in a deep breath and pushed open the bathroom door. He said in a loud voice, "I'm going to get my weapon. You crawl into bed and find a movie."

As Sophia walked jerkily toward the bed, Austin crouched beside his bag and removed his gun. With the weapon dangling from his hand, he strolled back to the bed, where Sophia was huddled under the covers, the remote control in her hand.

He turned off the bedside lamp and slid between the sheets next to her, glancing toward the adjoining door. The tiny camera winked back at him. He placed his weapon on the nightstand.

"Did you find anything to watch?"

She pointed at the TV with the remote. "Have you seen this one before?"

"No. Leave it on."

Sophia dropped the remote in her lap. She'd pulled the sheets up to her throat and was sitting bolt upright, her arms at her sides—a perfectly natural way to watch TV next to a man you'd just banged.

He turned up the volume and punched the pillows behind him. Sliding an arm behind her waist, he said, "Scooch down here with me."

She turned a pair of round eyes on him and crossed her hands over her chest like a virgin on her wedding night, and he knew damned well she wasn't a virgin and this was no wedding night.

He lowered his voice. "You look ridiculous sitting like that."

She huffed out a breath and slid down. He draped his arm across her shoulders and pulled her close until her head was resting on his shoulder.

"That's better." He kissed the top of her head. "Try to sleep. I got this."

She snuggled her naked body closer to him, skin to skin, flinging one arm across his midsection and hooking her leg over his thigh. His libido stirred, along with a couple of choice body parts as he gritted his teeth. He should've left her in that virgin pose.

He had the strongest urge to take her again, right here, right now—and he didn't give a damn who was watching.

THE FOLLOWING MORNING, they went about their business in the most natural way they could muster. Sophia was a trooper.

When they heard their neighbors open their door, they sprang into action and met them at the elevator.

Sophia smiled at the older couple. "Busy day today?"

"Lexington and Concord, and Walden Pond on the way back." The woman held up a dog-eared map. "Do you know that Thoreau really wasn't roughing it at Walden Pond?"

"No, I didn't know that."

The woman's husband rolled his eyes. "Irene, nobody's interested in Thoreau."

"I know you're not." His wife tapped him with the map while she winked at Sophia.

They parted ways in the lobby, and Austin steered Sophia to the hotel restaurant. As soon as they took a seat at a table, he tapped his phone and put it beside his coffee cup. He'd set up his laptop to monitor any disturbances in the room and then transfer that data to his cell phone.

When the food arrived it could've been sandpaper, since all of his senses were on high alert, and he shoveled eggs in his mouth with one eye on his phone and the other on the entrance to the restaurant.

Fazal's killers knew they were here, and they'd use any opportunity they could to grab Sophia—because that was their current goal. They wanted to know what she knew, even if she didn't know she knew it. Thank God he didn't have to explain that one to her. She got it.

She got everything.

Sophia nibbled on the edge of her bagel. "Are we just going to hang around all day and wait for housekeeping to show up on our floor?"

"Yep."

"Being in that room creeps me out. I can't wait to leave."

"You and me both. How do you think I liked it, walking around that room naked, knowing some guy's checking out my junk?"

Sophia choked and sprayed orange juice into his plate of eggs. "*That's* what you were thinking about?"

"Believe me, that's what any guy's gonna be thinking about."

"At least you've got junk worth checking out."

"Thanks. That just made the situation ten times more disturbing." He gave her a grin. He liked making her laugh.

When they finished breakfast, they took their coffee into the lobby, where Austin could watch the floors above and the progression of the housekeeping carts.

About an hour later, he nudged Sophia's arm. She'd picked up a paperback in the gift shop and now nodded over it.

She rubbed her eyes. "Is it time?"

"The cart's on our floor."

"I hope you know what you're doing."

"It won't take long, and the guys watching us won't figure it out for a while, giving us a head start."

They got off the elevator on their floor and waited in the room with the ice and vending machines. When the housekeeping cart stopped in front of the room next to theirs and the maid opened the door, they slipped into the hallway.

He took Sophia's arm and pressed her shoulders against the wall outside the room. Ducking his head, he brushed his lips against her ear. "Stay here and keep watch. This won't take long."

He curled his fingers around the knife in his pocket and entered the room. With the maid in the bathroom, running water in the sink, he strode toward the door that led to his own room.

He ran his hand over the smooth wood until he felt a protrusion and circled it with his fingertip. Damn, they were good. These were no amateurs.

He stuck the point of the knife under one edge of the camera and worked it free. Pinching the small device between two fingers, he covered the lens side of the camera—the side that had been pointing into his room, recording him and Sophia in bed.

He placed it on the carpet and ground the heel of his boot against it. "Show over, assholes."

He left the mangled device on the floor for the maid to vacuum it up.

"Excuse me? I didn't think anyone was in here." The maid stood in the doorway of the bathroom with some towels in her arms and a perplexed expression on her face.

Austin pocketed his knife and withdrew his card key. He held it up. "Forgot something."

He breezed past her and out the door, squeezing past the cart. "Done. Let's get out of here."

He opened the door of their own room and flipped around the do-not-disturb sign on the handle. "How fast can you pack?"

"A matter of minutes. I've had lots of practice what with moving from one foster home to another."

"Good." He closed down his laptop and retrieved his rifle case from the closet.

Within thirty minutes, they'd packed their stuff, checked out of the hotel and were sitting in his rental. "My handlers almost booked me in a hotel near the harbor. I'd say that's a good second choice."

"That's closer to the Kennedy Library, the location of the symposium."

He entered the hotel name in the car's GPS. "I wish we had more information about what's going down there. Blind security can only do so much."

"I've been thinking about that."

"Me, too—a lot." He pulled out of the hotel's parking structure and tapped Start on the GPS.

"Boston's Kids is one of the symposium's hosts."

"You mentioned you knew about that group."

"I used to volunteer for that group. If Rick Stansfield is still the director, I might have an in."

"An in?" He hit the brakes harder than he'd planned and the car lurched at the red light.

"One of the articles mentioned a fund-raising party prior to the meetings. I think I can get us an invitation."

This time he slammed the brakes. "You're kidding, right?"

"I'm not." She tucked her hair behind one ear. "Of course, I no longer have my cell phone, but I can get Rick's number and give him a call."

"If there's going to be some kind of attack at that event, you need to be as far away from it as possible."

"Not if I can help prevent it. Do you know how devastating it would be for those organizations if there was some kind of terrorist attack at a symposium they're hosting?"

"I get it." He took her hand and toyed with her fingers. "But do you realize how devastated I'd be if something happened to you at that symposium?"

"You said it yourself. Security will be tight, and I've got the best security of all." She brought his hand to her lips and kissed his knuckles.

"I don't know if I could ever get clearance for something like this."

"I don't need clearance from the US government to attend a party hosted by an organization I've worked with in the past and for which I have an invitation."

"You may not need the go-ahead, but the security agencies overseeing this little exercise of mine are just about ready to throw in the towel on you after I told them you're insisting on attending Dr. Fazal's memorial tomorrow."

"Even better. Let them give up on me, which will free me up even further to do what I want."

"You may not have anyone to report to, but I still do."

"Then tell them you'll be attending the event as backup security. It'll be easier for you to get your weapon through, and believe me, I'd feel a whole lot better about being there if you're armed."

"I can try to do that. Call your friend when we get to the new hotel."

Once they checked in and got to the room, Austin tossed his phone onto the bed. "Knock yourself out."

"I'm going to find him on my laptop first. Since I can't get his cell phone number from my phone, I'll have to call the organization instead."

She clicked away on her keyboard while he stretched

out on the bed. Had she noticed he hadn't requested two double beds in the room? He'd barely gotten started with her last night before he discovered they were making an unintentional sex tape. Was it wrong for him to wish he could see that video? It just might get him through some long nights ahead once he'd left her.

And he'd have to leave her.

Chapter Fourteen

Sophia glanced at Austin sprawled on the bed as she brought up the website for Boston's Kids. The crease between his eyebrows concerned her. Did he think they wouldn't be able to pull it off, or did he think they wouldn't be allowed to?

She didn't know much about the military, but she did know a soldier had to follow orders. If his superiors wouldn't allow him near the gala for the symposium, Austin had to know she'd go, anyway. Was that what had him worried?

"Rick is still here." The cursor hovered over his contact information. "Can I call him from your phone?"

"Sure." He nudged the phone to the edge of the bed with his foot, and she leaned back in her chair to grab it. She entered Rick's number at the foundation and got a receptionist. They must be doing well.

"Can I speak to Rick Stansfield, please? Tell him it's Sophia Grant."

"One moment, Ms. Grant. I'll see if he's in."

She held up the phone to Austin and pushed the button on the side for the speaker, and he muted the TV.

A few seconds later, Rick's voice boomed over the phone. He never faked the hearty tone he used with the kids. Rick was the real deal. "How's my favorite volunteer? We sure miss you over here."

"I miss you guys, too. I've been busy with school."

"And the work continues. Good for you. Are you calling to join our ranks again?"

"Actually, I saw something in the paper about a symposium you're jointly sponsoring to discuss at-risk youth, and was wondering if I could buy a ticket to the gala to show my support."

"This symposium's a little different from what we usually do, since the focus is turning young people away from extremist organizations, but because of our work with kids and street gangs, we figured we'd have something to offer."

"Oh, I think you do."

"The gala is invitation only, and the tickets are a thousand apiece. I can send you an invite, but I can't waive or reduce the ticket price—even for you."

She raised her brows at Austin and he nodded.

"I'm not asking you to. If you can take care of the invitations, I'll handle the ticket price—and I need two."

"I can have two tickets waiting for you at the office tomorrow, although unfortunately, I won't be in to see you."

"That's fine. Give me the details, and I'll come by tomorrow to pick them up."

Rick gave her the name of the contact person at the office and the payment methods. "I look forward to seeing you at the gala, Sophia, and I hope you can come back to volunteer for what you're really good at—talking some sense into these girls."

"I will, Rick. Thanks." She ended the call and lobbed

the phone back at Austin. "Can you clear that with someone?"

"I'll try." He reached for the phone and made his own
call as he rolled off the bed and headed for the bathroom.

No listening in on speakerphone for her. As he started
talking he slammed the bathroom door behind him. No
listening at all.

She paced near the door a few times and heard Austin's voice, low but urgent. She gave up and fell across
the bed, turning up the TV. He'd tell her what he thought
she should know. He hadn't been wrong yet.

When he came out of the bathroom, she jerked her
head toward him. "Well?"

"Memorial first. You'll be attending on your own."

A shiver snaked down her spine. The US spy agencies really were washing their hands of her.

"But—" he held up his index finger "—there will be
personnel there on the perimeter, taking pictures and
running ID's. You just won't know who or where they
are, and I'll be there, just not with you."

She blew out a breath. "That's a relief. Where will
you be?"

"I'm not going to tell you exactly because I don't want
you looking for me, but I'll be watching the crowd—and
you. I don't have to tell you not to talk to any strangers,
right? A limo will take you there—one with very dark
tinted windows—and pick you up right at the curb. We
lucked out that the memorial is at a park, which gives
us good access. While you're giving your speech, if you
hear anything unusual—popping noises, blasts—hit the
deck."

"Got it. And the gala?"

"We're both attending, unless something happens

at the memorial. That one was harder to sell. If there's going to be an attack there, the agency isn't sure how your presence is going to change that or help. *I'm* not sure."

"I was close to Dr. Fazal. That's why you picked me out in the first place, isn't it? I didn't ask for this. You hid out in my car and ambushed me." She held up her hands. "I'm not saying it didn't work out, as I probably would've been kidnapped that night if you hadn't."

"Maybe it *will* be over at the memorial." He rubbed his chin. "For the gala, additional security will be there, and they'll pass me through with my weapon."

"Not the big huge one that hangs over your shoulder?"

"Not that one."

"Good, because that one won't go at all with your tux."

"Tux?"

"The event is formal."

He smacked his head. "Great. If I wasn't going to have enough headaches at that party, wearing a tux just sealed the deal."

"Speaking of clothes, any chance I can return to my place to pick up a dress? I didn't think I needed to pack anything formal while I was on the run."

"Buy a new dress tomorrow when I'm out renting my tux…if nothing happens at the memorial first."

She craned her neck to peer around him at the alarm clock on the nightstand. "We probably have enough time to go out now before anything closes, so we don't have to rush tomorrow."

"You up for it?"

"This has actually been a calm day compared to all the other days since you dropped into my life."

"Sorry about that."

"Don't be sorry." She launched out of the chair. "I'm kind of an adrenaline junkie, always have been. I'm not going to wilt under pressure."

"I noticed." He planted his feet on the floor. "Do you want to look up a few places on your laptop?"

"There's a mall nearby. I'm sure you can rent a tux there, and I'm pretty sure there are a couple of major department stores where I can find a long dress for the gala. It's not going to be haute couture but I don't wear haute couture, anyway."

"And I wouldn't know haute couture if it came up and bit my backside."

Her gaze dropped to that backside as Austin bent over his suitcase. "I'm going to put on a white T-shirt, and then I'll be ready to go."

He yanked off his long-sleeved T-shirt and pulled the white one over his head. Then he buttoned a denim shirt over it. His eyes met hers. "What?"

"How many hours a day do you work out to get a body like that?"

He threw his head back and laughed. "It's part of my job. We have to be in peak physical condition for what we do."

"You are."

"Thanks... I think."

"Oh, believe me. I'm paying you a compliment."

"I'll take it." He snatched his jacket from the hook by the door and checked the pocket.

Must be checking for his gun. The guy never let his guard down—but she wasn't complaining. She just didn't know how she was going to do without her personal bodyguard when this was all over.

It took them less than fifteen minutes to get to the shopping center. As they crossed a bridge from the parking structure to the mall, she said, "I almost feel safer in a big public place like this than hiding out in a hotel room."

"We should be safe here. They're not going to expect us to be out shopping."

"Maybe I can find a new frame for my picture while we're here. I think it's just a standard five by seven."

"I'd suggest splitting up to save time, but I don't want to leave you on your own—even in a place like this."

"Let's get your tux first. Hopefully, they can get your measurements and have something ready for you by the day after tomorrow, the morning of the event. If we get my dress first, we'll have to lug it around."

"Sold."

Austin went with basic black with a black silk vest. He also rented a pair of shoes, and when the measuring was done, he told the clerk he'd pick up everything in two days.

He brushed his hands together as they walked out. "Your turn."

"Wait." She pointed ahead at a stationery and gift shop. "I can probably find a frame in there."

It took her less than ten minutes to find a frame to fit the picture of her and Dr. Fazal. If only a life could be replaced as easily.

"How are we doing on time?"

"We're fine. Most of the stores close at nine o'clock. You don't have to rush."

"It's just a dress for one night, but I'd better buy something I can wear a few more times."

"I'm buying the dress for you."

"Is that going to be a business expense, too?"

"Of course."

She didn't believe him for a minute, but she'd settle up their debts later—her debts. How did you repay a man for saving your life, for keeping you safe?

They entered the store through the women's shoe department, and Sophia snapped her fingers. "I'm going to have to get some shoes, too. Is that in the US government's spy budget?"

"It's the line item right below bullets."

When they got to the racks of long, sparkly dresses, Austin ran his fingers across one row and whistled. "Fancy."

"I'm not crazy about ribbons, bows and sequins, just something simple."

"Something red. You look good in red."

"All of a sudden you've become a fashion consultant?"

"As they say, I just know what I like. And I like you in red." He pulled her close and touched her ear with his lips. "And nothing at all."

Her cheeks burned probably as red as one of those dresses he wanted her to buy. The brightly lit department store gave his intimate comment an erotic edge, which was heightened by the devilish glint in his green eyes, as if he could undress her here and now.

She punched his arm. "Behave yourself."

She staggered into the dressing room under the weight of several dresses and hung them up on one side of the mirror. She smoothed her hands over her face as she looked at her reflection. Usually she steered clear of bossy men—and Austin was definitely of the bossy variety.

She didn't mind it in him though. Must be because he listened to her, really listened to her, about the important stuff. She didn't even want to know what he'd said to his superiors to convince them to allow the two of them to attend the symposium gala.

Of course, those spy agencies he reported to didn't have any control over her actions, but if they'd refused to allow him to attend to protect her, maybe she would've had to give up the whole idea. Or maybe not.

She wanted an end to this madness, even if it meant an end to her relationship—or whatever she had—with Austin.

She grabbed the first red dress and undid the side zipper, stepping into it. She pulled up the strapless bodice, wriggled her hips into the rest of it and zipped it up.

Smoothing the silky material over her thighs, she adjusted the slit in the skirt to open down one leg. She stood on her tiptoes and turned from side to side. A little more body conscious than she was accustomed to wearing, but it deserved a vote.

She swept out of the dressing room, exposing a little leg and fluffing her hair behind her head. "What do you think, dahling?"

The way Austin's jaw dropped gave her a thrill. "That's it. That's the one. You look like an old-time movie siren."

She tripped and folded her arms across her décolletage. "I-is it too much?"

"Not from where I'm sitting. Let's buy it."

She left the rest of the dresses untested on the rack and Austin peeled off several bills to pay for the dress. Then he paid for a pair of heels, and her internal calculator racked up the expenses.

As they rode down the escalator, he put his hand on her back. "Do you need something for tomorrow, too?"

"The memorial? I have that covered." She hugged the plastic bag containing the frame and rested her chin on the edge of it. Dr. Fazal's death punched her in the gut all over again.

The drama surrounding his murder had been keeping her real feelings at bay. She was so busy escaping from bad guys and chasing down clues, she hadn't properly mourned Dr. Fazal—and buying a red-hot dress with a red-hot navy SEAL didn't feel proper at all.

Austin squeezed her shoulder as he steered her into the parking garage. "Are you okay?"

"I feel...guilty."

"Because you forgot your worries and pain for an hour and enjoyed yourself shopping for a pretty dress?"

"Days after Dr. Fazal's murder—and Ginny's—I'm planning to go to a party. It just seems wrong."

He popped open the trunk of the rental car and laid her dress across the carpet. Then he slammed the trunk and wedged his hip against it while he crossed his arms.

"You're not going to a party. You're putting yourself in danger by attending some function that could very well be the target of a terrorist attack. You're doing it on the off chance that you can identify someone there who might've been in contact with Dr. Fazal. You're doing it for Hamid and Ginny. You're doing it to find some measure of justice for them." He pushed off the trunk. "And you needed a dress to do it."

He opened the passenger door for her and she slipped inside the car.

When Austin got in next to her and started the car, she put her hand over his. "That was a vehement defense of plans you didn't agree with the first time around. If that's how you presented it to your commanding officers, it makes sense they relented."

He blew out a breath and gripped the steering wheel with both hands. "Let's just say I know what it's like to want justice for someone, retribution, even."

"I figured you did. One of your comrades in arms?"

"My brother, my blood brother."

"What happened?" She pressed her fingertips to her chin.

"He was a marine, deployed in Afghanistan. He was killed by a roadside IED, which was planted by a terrorist group that specifically targeted American military."

"I'm sorry, Austin." Her fingers curled around his hand. So, he'd lost a member of his perfect family. "Is that why you became a SEAL, to avenge your brother's death?"

"Tucker was younger than me. He followed me into the service."

"You wanted revenge against this one specific terrorist organization? How'd you manage that? There are so many of them now."

"It wasn't just the group I wanted. You're right. These organizations form and break apart and then morph into something else, but for me there's always one constant." His jaw tightened and a muscle ticked in the corner.

"Which is?"

"Vlad."

"Vlad? Sounds Russian."

"We don't know what he is, but he uses a Russian sniper rifle. Vlad has been around for a while. He was a sniper in Afghanistan. He moved on from that to form and lead various groups, and we don't even know where his loyalties lie. He seems intent on destabilizing the region and may have even gone global."

"I take it you didn't stop him?"

"I tried. Man, did I try, and almost faced a court martial for it. I defied orders once to go after him." Austin held his thumb and forefinger together. "I was this close."

"Then you came to your senses."

"It was that or destroy my career. I didn't think Tucker would want that." He shook his head while he started the car. "I don't get why they wouldn't let me go after him when I had the chance. Several SEALs died trying to take him down, and a sniper from our team was captured. We thought he was dead, but he escaped about two months ago. I have a score to settle with Vlad."

"Maybe that's why your superiors didn't allow you to track him down—too personal."

"Talk about personal. I can't help thinking this whole situation with Dr. Fazal has Vlad's stamp all over it."

"Really? This is something he'd be involved in?"

"He might be involved in it because I'm involved in it."

"Does he know who you are?"

"He knows my entire sniper team, and we know him."

"Does Vlad have a name?"

"I'm sure he does, but we don't know what it is. It's impossible to get any intel on him. He's guarded and protected."

"Which brings us back to where we started—what information did Patel-slash-Jilani give to Dr. Fazal about the symposium, and where is it?"

"Two very good questions, but it feels as if I haven't eaten for a very long time and I need to answer the growling in my stomach before I can tackle those other questions. Do you mind if we pick up some fast food and bring it back to the room?"

"Whatever you want. I'm not hungry."

"Yeah, but I'm going to force you to eat something anyway. You cannot live on bagels alone."

By the time they got back to their new hotel room with a couple of bags of food, Sophia actually had an appetite and wolfed down her chicken sandwich and fries.

She bunched up her paper bag and shot it into the wastebasket. "I'm going to take a shower since I was too creeped out to take one this morning with that camera watching my every move."

"I've got an idea." He swept the rest of the trash from the table where it joined her bag. "Remember how we had to pretend showering together last night so we could talk and get away from the watching eye of the camera?"

"I remember." Butterfly wings beat in her belly.

"Remember how hard it was to just stand there in that tub, letting the water run over our bodies, keeping our hands to ourselves?"

She arched one eyebrow at him. "I remember how hard it was."

He laughed. "Now you're talkin'. We don't have to pretend tonight. I'd like to soap you up and do all the things to you I couldn't do last night."

She crooked her finger at him. "Let's shower."

And for the rest of the night, she forgot about everything except the man who'd become such a big part of her life in such a short period of time.

She even forgot she'd have to say goodbye to him.

Chapter Fifteen

The following morning, Sophia got ready for the memorial. On her way to the door, she picked up the bag with the frame. "I forgot to swap out the broken frame for the new one. I guess I'll do it when we get back."

"You need to watch out for those shards of glass." Austin held out her jacket. "At least it's not raining today."

"Are you going to follow me right over?" She grabbed her jacket and threw it over one arm.

"I told you, I'll be right behind you. The limo's going to drop you off at the curb. Stay with the other mourners as you walk down the path to the gazebo. Security will be in place to watch you—including me."

"I'll be sitting with Morgan and Anna."

"I know you'll be meeting some strangers, friends and colleagues of Fazal's, but don't go off with anyone you don't know."

"You said that before."

"I'm saying it again."

They stepped into the hallway, and he stuck beside her all the way to the front, where he hustled her into the limo. He leaned inside and kissed her hard on the mouth.

"Be careful." Then he said a few words to the driver, who must've been CIA or FBI.

When the limo pulled away from the hotel, she stretched out across the leather seat. She would be enjoying this if she weren't on her way to say her final farewell to her good friend and mentor.

He'd tried to keep her out of this, but her close relationship with him had made that impossible. For that reason, his killers believed she had access to the information Jilani had given him—but she didn't, did she?

She'd racked her brain trying to recall their last conversation and if there were any hints in his words. Unless there were hidden clues in his description of the patient who'd broken his hand in a fight, she couldn't think of anything unusual about their chat.

The park was near Walden Pond, where apparently Thoreau hadn't roughed it as much as he'd let on. That was a detail Dr. Fazal would've relished. He'd loved the area and its history.

As the car slowed, the driver got on the speaker. "Ma'am, please wait in the car until I get the door for you. I'll let you out when I see other people heading for the gazebo."

"Thanks."

A few minutes later the car stopped, and a few more minutes after that, the driver swung open her door and helped her out as if she were a ninety-year-old dowager. She felt about ninety years old right now.

As a clutch of people surged into the park from the sidewalk, the driver gave her a nudge. "I'll be right here when the service ends. Look at my face. I'll be driving, nobody else."

As she studied his fresh, earnest face, a feather of fear brushed across her flesh. This was real.

She nodded and joined the group, waving at two of the doctors from their floor.

Chairs had been set up in the gazebo, and Sophia spotted Morgan, who waved. Sophia climbed the two steps and sat in the chair Morgan had been saving with her purse.

Morgan dabbed her eyes with a tissue. "I can't believe this is happening. Ginny's funeral is next week. The cops won't tell me anything. I'm walking around looking over my shoulder every few seconds."

"I know what you mean." Sophia flicked her fingers in the air at Anna, who had a lost look on her face.

When she joined them, Anna spent several minutes crying on their shoulders. Wiping her nose, she plopped into the chair on the other side of Morgan. "Have the police told either of you anything about Ginny? That's just too much of a coincidence to me, even though I keep hearing Dr. Fazal shot himself."

Morgan whispered, "If he did, it's because someone made him. He'd never commit suicide."

Sophia scanned the crowd, but didn't dare look for Austin. He'd probably be up high somewhere, looking at the world through his crosshairs. The thought gave her a warm feeling.

Her gaze moved past the people standing on the outskirts of the crowd, and she did a double-take at a familiar face. Her eyes widened as Tyler Cannon raised his hand.

Her Spark date had figured out where she'd be? She waved back, a crease forming between her eyebrows. On their coffee date, she'd told Tyler all about Dr. Fazal, so he must've put two and two together when she mentioned her friend's death. Of course Dr. Fazal's murder had made the news.

Was he just paying his respects or did he hope to talk with her? She'd talk with him, but a date was out of the question—especially after the night she'd spent with Austin. She didn't know if she'd ever be able to date another man as long as she lived.

Austin had made love to her last night differently from the night before. That time had been slow and tender. The man could do it all.

As Dr. Fazal's imam began to speak, the crowd hushed. Soon he turned over the mic to Dr. Pritchard, one of Dr. Fazal's colleagues, and soon enough it was her turn.

Sophia pulled the crumpled piece of paper from her purse and approached the podium at one end of the gazebo. With her voice shaking only a little, she was able to relate to everyone how much Dr. Fazal had meant to her, how much he'd cared about his patients. She touched briefly on the reason why he'd relocated to the United States and remarked upon his bravery.

This crowd had no idea how brave.

When she finished and took her seat, the imam completed the service with some prayers and an invitation to partake of some food and drink on the other side of the gazebo.

The memorial ended and that was it. He was gone.

Sophia covered her face with both hands and sobbed as Morgan patted her back. "I'm so sorry, Sophia. Do you want to grab a bite to eat?"

"You two go. I'll join you in a minute." She dug in her purse for a tissue and wiped the mascara from beneath her eyes. Why'd she bother putting on makeup? She'd known the service would end in tears.

"Sophia? I hope you don't mind that I showed up."

She looked up into Tyler's dark eyes. "I—I'm just surprised to see you here."

"I don't want to intrude on your grief, but I felt like I almost knew Dr. Fazal from your description of him. I wasn't sure if you'd be alone, and I just thought—" he spread his hands "—you might need some company. No pressure. No date. Just a friend."

"That's so kind of you, and I apologize for skipping out on our date." She mustered a weak smile.

"I have to admit, I was crushed and felt a little foolish sitting in that bar waiting for you, especially after our first and only date. I thought we'd hit it off."

"I thought so, too."

He took her hand. "Of course, when I figured out what happened, I felt really stupid."

"How could you know? I would've assumed that you'd stood me up, too."

"Do you want to get something to eat?" He jerked his head over his shoulder. "I was back there when they were bringing the food—looks good."

"I…" She swiveled her head around. The gazebo had cleared out, but she could see people gathering on the other side. "Maybe just a bite. I really have to leave. I'm sorry. In a week or so, I'll text you. Things are crazy right now."

Crazy in that since her Spark date with Tyler, she'd fallen head over heels for a navy SEAL with a very big gun.

"Yeah, crazy." He slipped his other hand from his pocket and rested it on her thigh.

A second later, she felt a sharp pinprick on her leg. "Ouch. I think you…"

She glanced at Tyler's face, but she couldn't focus. She blinked her eyes as his features blurred into a puddle. "Whaassappening?"

Her tongue felt too thick for her mouth, and she struggled to remain upright as her bones became cooked spaghetti.

Tyler lifted her in his arms and whispered, "Sorry, Sophia. You're coming with me."

AUSTIN ADJUSTED HIS SCOPE, sweeping it across the people gathering for the food set out on the picnic tables, and then tracking back to Sophia still sitting in the gazebo. He spit into the dirt below his perch in the tree. The guys out front had been taking pictures of the mourners as they arrived and checking license plates. No guests had raised any red flags…yet.

At least Sophia had finished her speech without incident, although he hadn't been able to hear it. Now she just needed to get out of the park and head for the limo, and he'd be able to breathe.

Her friend, the nurse, got up, leaving Sophia with her face in her hands. From his lookout, he muttered, "Go with her, Sophia."

Instead a man approached her and Austin's senses clicked into high gear. He took a deep breath when he saw Sophia's reaction to him. She obviously knew him. Was that a smile?

The guy took her hand, and Austin's feelings went a few notches beyond protectiveness. She wasn't pulling away from him either. He could be anyone. Sophia hadn't talked much about her friends, but he figured she didn't have a boyfriend since she was on that dating app…and she'd slept with him twice.

Austin's heart slammed against his rib cage. Sophia's *friend* had her in his arms. She was slumped against him.

Austin did a quick survey of the grounds. The FBI guys were all out front watching people, but none of them was watching Sophia. The rest of the mourners were on the other side of the gazebo, stuffing their faces. Nobody could see Sophia—except him.

He tracked back to the gazebo, where the man had swept Sophia up in his arms. He climbed over the low railing around the gazebo with Sophia flung over his shoulder like a rag doll. He was heading toward the copse of trees—right toward his hiding place—a gun dangling at his side. Austin's trigger finger twitched.

The agents wouldn't be able to get to her fast enough if he called them in now, and he had no idea where this guy's getaway car was or how many people were waiting to receive Sophia.

He had to act now, and he had to shoot to kill. He wouldn't risk Sophia's life trying to bring this man in. He wouldn't talk, anyway.

A deep calm settled over him. He took aim. He fired.

The man stumbled and pitched backward, Sophia still in his arms. He hit the ground, and Sophia fell on top of him. With the silencer, nobody had heard the shot; nobody had noticed a thing.

As Austin jumped from the tree, his weapon slung over his back, he called in the agents from the front. He took off full speed toward the fallen man and Sophia.

When he reached them, the ground beneath the man's head was already soaked with blood, but he nudged the gun away from his hand, anyway. Sophia had rolled from his body and lay beside him, her own head inches from the dark stain in the dirt.

He gathered her in his arms as two FBI agents came charging across the park. Austin kicked dirt at the dead man. "He drugged her. He was taking her away and had a gun on her. Get rid of him and call that limo to the other side of the park, so I can take her out of here."

The agents got on their phones immediately, and Austin moved through the trees with his gun on his back and Sophia against his chest.

As the winding road through the park came into view, Austin spotted the limo creeping at a slow pace. He emerged from the trees and waved it down. Before it even stopped, Austin had the door open.

He placed Sophia across the seat, tossed his gun on the floor and pulled the door closed, banging on the divider screen. The limo lurched forward and sped through the park.

Austin grabbed a bottle of water from the minifridge and leaned over Sophia, pulling up one eyelid. She'd been drugged, but her breathing was regular and her skin tone normal.

Scooping an arm behind her neck he hoisted her up to a sitting position. "Sophia! Sophia, wake up."

He cracked open the bottle of water and held it to her lips, tipping some liquid into her mouth. "Drink this."

She sputtered and her lashes fluttered.

"That's right. I'm going to pour some more of this down your throat."

He tapped the bottle, releasing more water into her mouth.

She coughed and most of the water ran down her neck, but he'd gotten a response out of her.

"Keep going." He dumped some water into his palm and splashed her face.

She bolted upright and clawed at him, knocking the bottle from his hands.

"That's it. Fight your way out of this." He retrieved the bottle and sprinkled more water in her face.

"Austin?" she choked.

"That's right, babe. I'm here. You're safe." He held the bottle to her mouth again. "Drink. Can you drink some water?"

She parted her lips and this time when he poured the liquid into her mouth, she gulped it down. He opened another bottle and gave her more.

She rubbed her face, smearing her eye makeup down her wet cheeks. "What happened? Where'd he go?"

"He drugged you. I don't know how."

She rubbed her thigh.

"He tried to take you away, but I saw him. I took care of him. He's gone."

Slumping against the seat, she closed her eyes.

Austin grabbed her shoulders and shook her gently. "Don't leave me. God, don't ever leave me again."

Chapter Sixteen

Sophia froze as Austin's fingers pinched into her flesh and his ragged words settled against her heart. He didn't mean what he'd said. She'd just given him a scare, and she didn't have to put him on the spot and let on that she'd heard his impassioned pleas.

She licked her dry lips. "More water?"

"Got it."

She wet her lips from the bottle he held for her. "What happened to him? Where is he?"

"He's dead."

She choked on the water. "Dead? Didn't the FBI want to capture and hold any suspects to get further intel?"

"I didn't have a choice."

"Did he have a weapon? I don't remember seeing a weapon, but I don't remember much after he stabbed a needle into my thigh."

"Is that how he drugged you? I didn't see him do anything to you, but he had a gun. Who was he? Why were you talking to him? I told you not to talk to any strangers."

"He wasn't a stranger." She plucked at her black slacks where Tyler had injected the needle. "That was Tyler Cannon—the guy I'd met on Spark."

"My God. They were already targeting you before they killed Dr. Fazal. Cannon, or whoever he is, was probably going to kidnap you on the night of your date, the night they murdered Fazal. He didn't figure you'd learn about Fazal's murder until the following day—and by then they would've had you tied to a chair and under a bright light."

She winced. Austin didn't even try to sugarcoat things for her anymore. She should feel flattered.

"We should get you to an emergency room to flush that drug out of your system."

She held up a bottle of water. "I'm flushing it out. We go to the hospital and they'll ask a million questions and the doctor will be required to call the police. Low profile, remember?"

"I don't want to you suffer any ill effects."

"I'm fine, feeling better by the minute." She took another swig of water. "Speaking of the police, what's going to happen to Tyler's body back there?"

"The FBI will cover it up. Those agents will remove the body, get someone in authority at the FBI to claim national security and whisk him away to identify him."

"He obviously wasn't on their radar, or they would've ID'd him when he walked into the memorial service."

He cocked his head at her. "You *are* recovering fast."

"My wonderful Spark date probably didn't want to give me a heavy dose of whatever he was dispensing, since his bosses would be anxious to question me."

"You got that right. You slipped through their fingers again."

"With a little help from my personal navy SEAL sniper."

"Listen." He captured a loose strand of her hair and twirled it around his finger. "We're attending that gala tomorrow night, and then you're done. If nothing happens there, I'm going to turn over everything I have on this to the agency in charge and then you're finished."

She widened her eyes. "We may be finished, but what if they're not? What if they still want to come after me?"

"I'm convinced whatever they're planning will happen at this symposium. Maybe we already have the information Jilani passed on to Dr. Fazal—and it's the fact that the symposium is the target. If we foil this attack, it should be over."

"Should be. How are you going to know for sure? The minute you leave and I go back to my new normal, they could strike."

He massaged his temples. "Let's think about that when the symposium ends. I'll let the real spies handle that."

She closed her eyes and leaned her head against the seat. He was going to turn her over to strangers. He might not ever want to leave her, but he was going to give a try.

"Are you okay?" He touched her knee. "I can have the FBI send a doctor to the hotel to check you out."

"I'm just tired."

He left his hand on her knee. "That's how they tracked you to the hotel—through Tyler Cannon and your phone."

"They knew I used Spark, too. I was such an easy mark…before you came on the scene." And she'd be one again when he left.

"Let's get through tomorrow night in one piece, and then we can think about the future."

The future? Did she even have one without Austin Foley by her side?

THE REST OF the afternoon and the evening after the memorial passed in a blur. She had more of the drug in her system than she'd thought, and Austin called in a doctor.

He'd assured her that the drug posed no danger and encouraged her to sleep it off. She didn't need any convincing, but it felt like a wasted night—having Austin with her and snoozing the time away when it was so precious.

She woke up the day of the symposium gala and fundraiser refreshed if anxious. After the fiasco yesterday at the memorial, she didn't trust the FBI to keep her safe.

But Austin would be there—and she trusted him with her life, if not her heart.

He tapped his laptop when she came out of the bathroom after showering and dressing. "I'm sending in my report."

"Has the FBI or the CIA identified Tyler Cannon yet?"

"He's Tyler Cannon, grew up in Minneapolis, attended MIT and was working as an engineer."

"And what? Was a terrorist on the side?"

"It would appear so. He did take two trips to Pakistan in the past four years. He could've been radicalized and groomed for when they needed him—and they needed him to get to you."

"That's crazy."

"That's what this symposium is targeting, isn't it?"

"It sounds like there's a lot of work to be done." She spun her own laptop around on the table to face her. "I'm going to delete my profile on Spark right now."

"Great idea."

When she was done with that, she opened her emails for the first time in a few days. Morgan and Anna had forwarded some patient communications to her, and an orthopedic surgeon had contacted her about assisting in his office.

She drummed her fingertips on the table next to her laptop as she formulated a response in her head. It looked like she might have a job on the other side, but when would she safely get to that other side?

What if nothing happened tonight? No bomb, no active shooter, no indication that anything was over? Would Austin leave, anyway? Would the FBI leave her to fend for herself?

She and Austin worked side by side in awkward silence, as if neither one of them wanted to face what came next. All they could do was stay focused on the gala tonight.

They had a late lunch in the hotel restaurant, and Austin decided to keep it light, telling her stories about his family and the ranch. She could almost picture it—the happy family life she'd never had.

"I have an idea." He toyed with the half-eaten fries on his plate. "If we have any reason to believe this isn't over tonight, can you take some time off?"

"I guess. I don't really have anything to take time off from since I'm already taking a break from school, although it looks like I might have an offer from another doctor's office."

"Can you delay that? I mean, if your life is in danger, getting another job is not going to do you any good."

"I suppose I'd have to. What do you have in mind?"

"My family's ranch in Wyoming."

She dropped her fork. "Are you serious?"

"Yep. My father's there. One of my brothers is there. They'd look after you…in my place. Nobody would find you at the ranch."

"I—I'm…" She pressed the water glass against her hot cheek. "Clearly speechless."

"Look, I know you're not much of a country girl, and you'd probably be bored out of your mind, but you'd be safe."

Safe and still a part of his life. Could she do it? Only if she knew he meant something more than just a duty to protect her. Maybe he wanted his family's opinion before he pursued anything with her.

"Think about it." He stuffed some fries into his mouth and checked his phone.

She'd ruined that moment. Why couldn't she jump up and down and accept his invitation with a big smile on her face? That's how she really felt.

He slipped his phone into his front pocket. "After I see you back to the room, I'm going to pick up the tux. Then I need some shut-eye before the big event."

"I don't. I feel as if I've slept for two days straight. I suppose you don't want me going outside."

"Negative. I'm sorry."

"That's okay. I've had enough excitement in the past few days to tide me over for about the next twenty years of my life."

Austin dropped her off at the hotel room, and she got back on her laptop to finish going through emails. She also took a peek at Austin's hometown, White Bluff, Wyoming. Fresh air, clean water, hunting, fishing, rodeos—basically, a world away from her own.

She heard Austin at the door, and she closed out the website and snapped her laptop shut. Leaning against the door, she peered through the peephole and opened it.

He held up his tux, wrapped in plastic. "All ready, and the jacket's roomy enough to accommodate my gun."

"Well, that's a relief."

"Everything okay here?"

"As far as I can tell."

He hung up the tux in the closet. "You know that whole Wyoming thing? Dumb idea. The FBI can probably find you a safe place, a big city where you can melt into the crowd—more your style."

"I don't know."

"It's all right." He stretched and yawned. "I'm going to hit the sack. If you want to watch TV, go ahead. I can sleep through anything."

He seemed determined not to let her speak, so she sealed her lips. Out on his own, away from this room, away from her, he'd probably realized how unrealistic it was for the two of them to make any plans.

This terrorist plot had thrown them together, they'd experienced a chemical attraction to each other and had some hot sex. That didn't make a future.

He pulled off his boots and collapsed on his stomach, fully clothed.

Her hesitation about Wyoming obviously hadn't troubled him much since his heavy breathing into the pillow told her he'd fallen asleep in a matter of minutes.

His about-face didn't stop her from sneaking another peek at White Bluff. He probably had dogs there, and she had a soft spot for dogs. Ruffy, a mixed-breed mutt, had been the only member of any foster family she'd ever missed.

A few hours later, she took a quick shower and changed into the red dress. As she took the new shoes from the bag, she pulled out the frame, still wrapped in plastic.

It was about time she replaced that cracked frame with a new one. Dr. Fazal deserved that.

She unwrapped the frame and placed it on the credenza next to the photo of her and Dr. Fazal. She turned the broken frame over on its face and pulled the backing from the slots.

As she yanked it free, something flipped into the air and fell on the floor. She bent over and saw a small, square, black object beneath the credenza and picked it up between two fingers.

A wash of adrenaline cascaded through her system, and she spun around toward the bed. "Austin!"

He stirred, pulling the pillow over his head.

"Austin, wake up." She bounced on the bed next to him and nudged his shoulder.

"What? Is it time to go?"

"I found it. I think I found what Jilani gave Dr. Fazal and what their killers have been looking for."

Austin's eyes clicked open and he sat up. "What is it?"

She cradled the object in the palm of her hand and held it out. "It's a minidisc. I found it in the back of the broken frame. He must've hidden it there, and then when he died in his office, he swept it off the table, maybe so they wouldn't notice it. There would be no reason for Dr. Fazal to put a disc in the frame like that. He didn't even use minidiscs. Can your laptop read it?"

"Damn right it can." He took her face in his hands and kissed her forehead. "You're a genius."

"If I'd replaced the frame earlier, we would've found it then."

"We found it now." He scrambled from the bed, wide awake now, and powered up his laptop. "There's a drive for minidiscs on the side."

She handed it to him with trembling fingers. He inserted the disc and released a breath. "Pictures."

He double-clicked on the first image, and a picture of two men popped up. Sophia didn't recognize either one of them but Austin jerked.

"Do you know them?"

"I don't know the man on the right, but the guy on left? Oh, yeah. I know him. That's Vlad."

Sophia narrowed her eyes at the man in the picture with the dark beard, dark sunglasses and a black and white kaffiyeh wrapped around his head. "I thought you didn't know who Vlad was."

"We don't have a name or background on him, but we've seen pictures, and this—" he stabbed a finger at the screen "—is Vlad."

Austin clicked through the rest of the photos, which showed the two men obviously discussing something and Vlad handing off something to the other man, a thin, dark-haired man with an intense stare.

"These pictures are what got Dr. Fazal killed? Jilani? Ginny? Why? What's so important about a known terrorist talking to some guy?"

"Because the guy he's talking to is not a known terrorist. At least I've never seen him before." He opened an email.

"What are you doing?"

"I'm going to send these photos to the FBI, the CIA and the other agencies involved to see if they can identify him—exactly what Fazal's killers didn't want."

"I still want to go to the gala."

"Oh, we're going, all right." He sent the email and pushed out of the chair. "I'm going to get ready in record time."

Fifteen minutes later, Austin was adjusting his bow tie in the mirror with a stubble on his chin and bed head. Didn't matter. He looked just as handsome as if he'd spent hours prepping.

He checked his laptop and shook his head. "Nothing yet, but I'll keep my phone close and my gun closer."

The same limo driver from the memorial was waiting for them at the curb, and he opened the door for them after exchanging a few words with Austin.

Austin slid in next to her and touched the minifridge with the toe of his rented shoe. "I'd offer you some champagne, but we both need to keep our wits sharp tonight."

"And I don't drink."

"My mom would love that about you. She thinks my dad, brothers and I drink too much beer when we get together. She'd think you were a good influence."

"With the crappy background and the mom in prison?"

"Looking at where you are today? She'd like you even more." He took her hand. "I forgot to tell you, you look beautiful. I'm a lousy date."

"That gun strapped over your shoulder makes you the perfect date for this evening."

He squeezed her hand. "We're almost through this, Sophia. Now that the intelligence agencies have those pictures, there's no reason for these guys to pursue you. And they'll make it clear they have the photos when they start to track down the man with Vlad. Vlad and his cohorts are going to realize immediately the photos have been leaked."

"I don't understand why Dr. Fazal or even Jilani didn't hand over the photos to the CIA right away. Do you think Jilani took the pictures?"

"I think he took them before he realized what he had. Vlad's terrorist cell may have threatened Jilani's family if he turned them over to authorities. He didn't know what to do and went to Dr. Fazal, since he already knew Hamid had connections in the intelligence community."

"But they got Jilani's son, anyway."

"They found out he had the pictures and had communicated with Fazal."

The driver buzzed down the partition. "We're about a block away. I'm going to line up with the other limos."

"Thanks, Kyle."

"What are we going to do once we're inside?"

"Watch. If you see anything suspicious or anyone suspicious, let me know. I'll alert the security personnel already in place, and we get out of there."

"Got it."

The limo crawled forward, and Kyle got out and opened the door for them.

Austin took her arm, his body vibrating with tension as they walked up the steps to the library.

They swept into the ballroom, and it seemed like a world removed from what they'd been dealing with all week. How could it all culminate here?

"Sophia, you made it." Rick strode toward her, hand outstretched.

She clasped his hand and made a half turn toward Austin, but he'd melted away into the crowd. "It's so good to see you."

"And you." He hooked his arm with hers. "I'd like to introduce you to a few of the symposium panelists, people striving to make a real difference, like you did."

She snatched a crab puff from a passing tray. Her nerves had prevented her from eating much all day, and now she felt weak and light-headed. Austin was right about staying well nourished.

She popped the puff into her mouth just as Rick led her to a group of three people.

"Sophia, this is Sylvia Fuentes and Paul…"

But she couldn't hear the names over the roaring in her ears as she met the dark gaze of the man in the pictures with Vlad.

Chapter Seventeen

Sophia had recognized him. She knew.

He knew, too.

Austin group-texted the agents stationed around the room, but cautioned them from making any sudden or obvious moves. The man whose photo had been taken with Vlad was with Rick Stansfield, Sophia's friend. He hadn't come through the front door, hadn't come through security.

They didn't know what he had on him or what he had planned.

He hoisted the .300 Win Mag, which had been waiting for him in the balcony above the room, on his shoulder, and for the first time wished he was looking at his quarry face-to-face instead of through a scope. He wanted to be by Sophia's side.

The group text lit up. No ID had been made on the man yet, but for this function he was Paul Alnasseri, executive director of Reach Out for Redirect, an organization committed to mentoring disenfranchised youth. One of the agents had gotten hold of a program for the symposium.

Austin's heart skipped a beat as Alnasseri put his

hand on Sophia's back and they broke away from the group.

He licked his dry lips, and his trigger finger itched. If Alnasseri had a bomb, he might very well have a kill switch—a button rigged up to set off the bomb even as he went down. He couldn't risk that. He wouldn't risk that.

Three agents began to move in a circle around Alnasseri and Sophia. Austin's shoulders tensed.

All they knew about him was that he had met with Vlad, a whole network of his associates had killed to keep that information from getting leaked and he was at the symposium under false pretenses and probably a false name. For the FBI, that wouldn't be enough to take him down, no questions asked.

But he wouldn't have a problem doing it. Not if it meant saving dozens of lives; not if it meant saving Sophia's life.

Alnasseri's head slowly cranked from side to side. He knew he'd been made. Even in tuxedos, the FBI agents looked like FBI agents.

A shout echoed from below and Austin watched with a clenched jaw as Alnasseri pressed a gun against Sophia's temple.

Alnasseri's voice rose. "Stay back. It's over."

Some of the people on the opposite side of the room weren't even aware of the drama, but a ripple of awareness zigzagged through the people near Alnas-seri and Sophia, and some of them started backing up. A few screamed. Several dropped to the floor.

If he set off a bomb now, there would be massive carnage. If Austin shot him dead, Alnasseri might have enough time to squeeze the trigger and kill Sophia—and there might be massive carnage, anyway.

Alnasseri started ranting and threatening, and when he mentioned the word *bomb*, chaos erupted.

Austin tightened his finger on the trigger. He had to take the shot. Sophia had to know that.

In a split second, she disappeared from his view and Austin fired. Alnasseri fell to the floor, the gun dropping from his hand.

A stampede of people headed for the exit doors, and Austin held his breath, bracing for the explosion.

None came.

Epilogue

Sophia took a deep breath of the fresh air that carried a hint of sweetness from the multicolored flowers scattering down the side of the hill, announcing spring in Wyoming. Jenny, Austin's mother, had called them Indian paintbrush, and they did resemble an impressionist's watercolor canvas. She could get used to this.

A crunch of a cowboy boot on the dirt behind her brought a smile to her lips, and the arms that wrapped around her from behind widened that smile.

Austin kissed the side of her neck. "I heard you were naming the cows. Don't do it."

She turned in his arms and cupped his stubbled jaw with one hand. "I'll stop when Maisie has her puppies and I can adopt one of my own."

"You're not going to bring the pup back to Boston and your apartment, are you?" He turned his head to kiss her palm.

"Your nephew, Kip, told me I could leave him here, and I can visit when I came back...if I'm coming back."

"What do you think?" He traced her lips with the pad of his finger. "My family loves you—almost as much as I do."

"I can't believe how they just opened their home to me, a perfect stranger."

"They're like that, and when I told them what you'd

been through and what a huge help you'd been to me, it was a no-brainer for them."

"Did you tell them about Vlad? That the man responsible for Tucker's death was involved in this latest scheme?"

"I don't talk about that with them. They don't need to know the details, especially since I believe Vlad had set his sights on Dr. Fazal, anyway, because of his connection to me. Jilani handing off those photos to Fazal just gave Vlad the excuse to come at him."

"Paul Alnasseri was the perfect mole. They must've been grooming him from a very young age, and he'd completely stayed off the intelligence community's radar."

"Until the wrong guy was in the wrong place at the wrong time—to our benefit. Even Jilani probably didn't know what he had until he brought the disc to Dr. Fazal in Boston and saw the symposium lineup."

"Do you think that's when he changed his mind and asked Dr. Fazal to keep the information quiet?"

"Yes, because Vlad's associates threatened his family."

"Poor Dr. Fazal was out of it, away from the madness, and Jilani had to implicate him."

"Like I said, Sophia, I think Vlad was going to hit Fazal sooner or later."

"I'm just happy Alnasseri died before he could activate his bomb."

"And I'm happy you had the presence of mind to duck down in the chaos."

"Because I knew you had him in your crosshairs and you'd be taking the shot—whether I was standing there or not. And you have to go back to it all." She dropped her hands to clutch his jacket. "I'm going to be worried every minute of every day."

"You're going to be busy with your new job, finishing

school and coming out to Wyoming to visit your puppy. There are so many ways for us to communicate, you'll probably get sick of seeing my face and hearing my voice."

"Never, Austin Foley." She stood on her tiptoes and kissed his chin.

"And when I'm done with this tour, you'll be waiting for me?"

"Where else would I be?"

"No more Spark dates?"

"Too shallow and meaningless."

"You used to thrive on shallow and meaningless."

She shoved the tips of her fingers in his back pockets. "That's before I met you."

"You take me, you get the whole bunch." He jerked his thumb over his shoulder at his family's sprawling ranch house.

"I'm counting on that." She squinted at the house. "Your nephew's waving his arms and shouting something. Shh."

Austin cocked his head. "It's the puppies. Maisie's having her pups."

"Let's go." She grabbed his hand and tugged.

"This means you're going to stop naming those cows, right?"

"Of course—except for Sydney and Clyde and Hopper and…"

He scooped her up and tossed her over his shoulder. "City girl."

* * * * *

Don't miss ALPHA BRAVO SEAL, the next book in Carol Ericson's RED, WHITE AND BUILT series, on sale next month wherever Mills & Boon Intrigue books are sold!

MILLS & BOON®

INTRIGUE
Romantic Suspense

A SEDUCTIVE COMBINATION OF DANGER AND DESIRE

A sneak peek at next month's titles...

In stores from 6th April 2017:

- **Lucas** – Delores Fossen *and*
  Sheikh's Rescue – Ryshia Kennie
- **Quick-Draw Cowboy** – Joanna Wayne *and*
  Alpha Bravo SEAL – Carol Ericson
- **Firewolf** – Jenna Kernan *and*
  Necessary Action – Julie Miller

Romantic Suspense

- **Pregnant by the Colton Cowboy** – Lara Lacombe
- **Cavanaugh on Call** – Marie Ferrarella

Just can't wait?
Buy our books online before they hit the shops!
www.millsandboon.co.uk

Also available as eBooks.